So Not Yonkers

A Novel

by Patricia Vaccarino

Modus Operandi Books

Modus Operandi Books • New York

Published 2023 by Modus Operandi Books
www.modusoperandibooks.com

ISBN: 978-1-7365462-3-9
Library of Congress Control Number: 2023902846
Printed in the U.S.

ACKNOWLEDGEMENTS

Larry Frumkies
April 15,1950 – December 22, 2020

William "Bill" Powers
November 19, 1948 – October 20, 2021

You are forever in our hearts

MY OWL

His one eye is a jewel
seeing through a prism
transcending time. Distance. Light.
And the motion of the night
to reach two halves of the same leaf.
I see the ghost of this pale
leaf sitting beside my owl.
He hears a chorale of birds
unseen in the copse of trees.
Peace. War. Blood.
Wooden limbs.
Arteries. Skin. Veins.
Flesh and bones.
His one eye is blind.
The other sees too much.
Is my owl dead or alive?
I will never forget him.

—Concetta *"Cookie"* Colangelo, 1973

"You can take the girl out of Yonkers, but you can't take Yonkers out of the girl."

—*Anonymous*

December 1972 to December 1973

Praise for Patricia Vaccarino's So Not Yonkers

So Not Yonkers offers watercolor word portraits of a small city in decline, as seen through the eyes of a wiser-than-her-years protagonist, combined with the grit of a Martin Scorsese mobster movie.

—Manny Frishberg, Journalist, Author, City of Emeralds

Reminiscent of the work of Joseph Conrad, the novel **So Not Yonkers** by Patricia Vaccarino is engaging from the first page. Ms. Vaccarino's work resounds as a beautiful film rather than a typical novel. I can hear the music.

—Joel Diamond, former Yonkers resident, award-winning Musician, Composer

Cookie Colangelo has a controversial relationship with freedom. What characterizes "Cookie" as a young adult is exactly what she does not know. Her inexperience in life is counterbalanced by her audacity. Very few books serve us this level of rich historic authenticity of the 1970s, thus making it a true American novel of Salinger-like unyielding spirit.

—Milan Heger, Artist

Vaccarino is great at painting a sensory-filled picture complete with sights of the dubious subway and racetrack, the rancid smells of the Hudson River during the hot August summer, the yummy tastes of pizza and lasagna, the feel of the scratchy school uniform designed to torture the wearers, and the sounds of a tragic pedestrian hit and run accident.

—Therese Frare, former Yonkers resident and award-winning photographer

Somehow through Vaccarino's talent for detail and imagery, she managed to capture the essence of Yonkers in 1973 in a way that made me feel I was back there interacting with the characters in her book I could have easily known.

—Jeffrey Gurian, former Yonkers resident, Comedy Guru, Author, Radio Personality

The story could only have taken place in Yonkers, where there existed social and political corruption, seen and unseen racial tensions, open gangster activity, ever-increasing economic inequality, a wavering sense of moral direction, an acceleration of American greed, coupled with a fiercely independent nature of the underdog. Yes, it is all there, cleverly gathered in the rawhide saddlebag of this "Don't mess with me" teenage girl.

—Ed Murphy, former Yonkers Resident, Music Promoter Notodden, Norway

"Cookie," born Concetta Colangelo, so wise beyond her years, is already a streetwise grifter on the make at 16. She's the antithesis of J.D. Salinger's naive same-age Holden Caulfield a quarter century earlier. Vaccarino offers twice the weight of Salinger's novel and packs far more richness. Cookie's capers circa 1973 stay ahead of the law amid a backdrop of the seediness and debauchery of denizens of the downtown punk new wave scene of Max's Kansas City, among Manhattan locales. Cookie's relationships with colorful personalities like the flamboyant drag queen Gwendolyn are for the ages and they live in this must-read book.

—**Larry Jaffee, Author, Record Store Day: The Most Improbable Comeback of the 21st Century**

Growing up "Down the End" gave us a certain dánacht to navigate our day to day meanderings, and for some, to look beyond. In the end, Cookie went in search of sunsets, like some others of us did, and I believe she is still on that ride...

—**Tim Phelps, former Yonkers resident, Chef-Instructor/Educator**

A fast moving novel full of surprises, **So Not Yonkers** is a character study as seen through the eyes, heart, and mind of Cookie Colangelo. Race and class division play out in Cookie's world. Cookie's lucid voice comes through her journal entries. She experiences the multiple aspects of love, friendship, denial, loyalty, jealousy, sexual attraction and repulsion, heartbreak, fear, family strife, mental illness, the mob, and the dual power dynamics of having and not having money.

—**Dean Landsman, Author, Digital Strategist**

Cookie Colangelo careens through a gritty world with a passion for living and exploring beyond her working-class heritage. Hold on to your seat as the pages fly, and you find yourself surrounded by characters that make Yonkers come alive.

—**Nick Licata, author of Becoming A Citizen Activist and Student Power, Democracy and Revolution in the Sixties.**

Cookie is a writer of sorts, keeping a fairly precise diary which is not only a form of expression but mirrors her personality as well. The book is a mix of feelings, historical facts about Yonkers (the town that the author herself, left behind) and a good dose of truth about the human condition, including the education of a young girl who matured successfully in what was a not-so-friendly environment. The references to places like the smell of the famous Stella D'Oro bakery in the Bronx, and the mention of streets, parks and certain stores and shops in Yonkers, gives the book an authenticity that couldn't have been obtained through research alone.

—**William Lulow, Photographer**

Preface

Sixteen-year-old Yonkers girl Concetta *Cookie* Colangelo wrote eighteen journal entries in 1973 that document her theft of several hundred thousand dollars. After stealing the money, she doesn't know what to do with it. It's not like she could deposit it in a bank.

She stole the money from her father's office, but no one seems to care that the money is gone, not even her father.

From Max's Kansas City to the Upper East Side celebrity haunt Elaine's, Cookie does her best to use her newfound wealth to become *So Not Yonkers*. There are many casualties along the way. The two friends she had long held close to her heart had drifted away like clouds racing in an unsettled sky.

And her two new friends who have been born into wealth are using her for her money. Long on culture and breeding, but short on cash, Farley Stewart and Isabella María Fernanda Donovan are freeloaders. Isabella María Fernanda Donovan *Izzy* has the hots for Cookie, or for that matter, she has the hots for anyone. Cookie's relationship with the artist Farley Stewart *Stewie* gives her cursory knowledge of the art world, but she pays an awful price.

So Not Yonkers takes us on a dark journey encountering racism, sexual harassment, homophobia, violence, death, lost love and lost friendship. Zelda the Gypsy, a Drag Queen named Gwendolyn, a giant oak acorn, and a painting by the great abstract expressionist artist Clyfford Still help Cookie Colangelo find redemption.

On the day that Cookie leaves Yonkers, she resolves to write new pages between her eighteen journal entries:

"Someday...Hell if I know when... I'll write new pages in between the old pages in my journal. I'll write about more than my feelings. I'll tell you what was really going on. I'll fill in the blanks. My palimpsest of extremely bad writing. Someday I might use commas. I don't know. I hate commas. Don't you?"

This is her story...

Saturday December 16th 1972

Most people don't get that Yonkers is not located upstate New York. New Yorkers will have you believing that Yonkers is in the sticks and its people are all a bunch of foul-mouthed hicks. New Yorkers have made the whole world think and say nasty things about Yonkers. For as long as I can remember and I do remember everything... Yonkers would not agree to be the sixth borough of New York City. They've given Yonkers a bad name. They treat Yonkers like a naughty little girl who has wet her pants too many times.

Let me tell you something. I know.

They've given Yonkers a bad name cause they can't make Yonkersites pay taxes straight to hell to New York City. Cause it's always about money.

I'm here to set the record straight.

My name is Cookie Colangelo and I know that most New Yorkers are always bullshitting. They're always trying to make you think that everything about New York City is bigger and better than anywhere else. They put up with all kinds of filth! They put up with all kinds of misery and abuse but think that's okay cause it's still New York City with a golden halo wrapped around the collective crown of its tall ugly buildings. Let me tell you something: All that concrete and steel is built on the backs of working people.

Girls like me.

New York City ain't no prize in a box of Cracker Jacks. I hate to badmouth the greatest city in the world. But somebody's got to tell the truth and it might as well be me. What New Yorkers say that is so spectacularly not true is when they say: "if you make it here you can make it anywhere." That is a big fat lie. There are lots of losers out there and most of them live in New York City. No offense or nothing. Most people are scraping by and making bets at the Yonkers Raceway cause their lives depend on it. It's a numbers game. It's always about the money. It always was and it will always be that way.

Okay. You see. I'm done reading what I have written here in my journal for today cause what I've written is forever. I have no intention of adding a single comma. I hate commas because they slow the flow of my words to the point of nightmarish exhaustion. I always sign my name in cursive. Scrawling the leaking tip of my green fountain pen across the bottom half of the lined page in a black & white notebook is so fun that it takes my breath away! I love my own fancy penmanship! My signature is bold with small hooks of curls and cones swirling to form letter C-shapes.

Concetta "Cookie" Colangelo.

The Cs are swell.

Alright. I find it impossible to pen a string of perfect sentences in the back seat of a car. I'm gonna put the cap back on my fountain pen and stick my notebook in my brown rawhide saddlebag that I keep slung across my chest. I will not dare to put my bag on the ground. It's bad luck. Even putting my bag on the floor of Johnny's expensive new car is not a good thing to do. That's bad luck too. I know these things. I know mostly everything. I'm real smart that way. I bet you've already guessed that. Goodbye for now.

One

Johnny kept an eye on Cookie from his rear-view mirror. His face was red and shiny. The guy looked overheated. It was hard for Cookie to think of her father as anything but a guy— that's what he was, a hot Italian guy. For once he was not complaining about his lot in life and being down on his luck. He gave Cookie a small secret smile.

No one else in the car saw Johnny smile, not her mother or her sister. Kitty was feeling good and not having a spell. Donny's blanket of blonde corkscrew curls fell way below her shoulders as though she expected her hair to be yanked and rolled into a knot on the top of her head.

Johnny had come home early on Saturday afternoon to take his family out to dinner. The trip was an excuse to show off his new Casablanca Yellow Cadillac. He turned the dial of his new radio, cranked it high and sang along to a show tune being sung by Tony Bennett. He kept rhythm, rapping his fingers on his steering wheel, catching the beat of the snare drum he was playing in his head.

They sped south on Broadway through Getty Square. *Ghetto Square.*

The sun had already left the sky. It was a brief moment when all was right in the world, so fleeting and so rare that Cookie wanted to draw her arms close to hug her heart.

But she knew if she did, the moment would go away sooner than it was supposed to. Good times never lasted for long.

She leaned into the extra wide seat and sighed, contemplating the luxury of Johnny's car. Its new car smell began to give her a headache. She was glad Johnny had bought himself a nice car but now he hid his keys. She was trapped in the city of hills, relying on the kindness of friends and strange people for rides.

Johnny found a place to park on the heel of the hill on Herriot Street around the corner from Louie's Italian Restaurant. The temperature sank below freezing. The dark sky churned with an unbroken bank of swollen clouds. Weather forecasts predicted snow and freezing rain.

Louie's brick storefront, painted red and yellow, had windows on both sides of a single glass door that pushed open to the street. You had to be careful when you were trying to go in that someone wouldn't come barreling out and accidentally knock you over. A plastic Italian flag, the kind you peel and stick on glass, was pasted inside of one window. The other window held a lit neon sign in red scrawling script: *spaghetti and meatballs*.

Johnny held open the door, motioning with his other arm to rush them into the restaurant. He tugged a sprig of Donny's curls and patted Kitty's round bubble of a bottom. He gave Cookie the same sheepish smile again, deferring to her as though she was in charge. Smirking at Johnny, she stormed into the restaurant.

The place was a joint, one of the best Italian restaurants in Yonkers, where everyone came to eat the Ziti Siciliano, Louie's Baked Lasagna, or the Shrimp Scampi. Of Louie's three signature dishes, everyone had their favorite. The aroma of fresh garlic simmering in olive oil made her stomach rumble, and she immediately craved lasagna.

Five booths flanked the left wall. Worn green leatherette seats nicked with small rips and slits exposed patches of yellow cushion foam. The long banquette on the right sat ten people. Upholstered in faded rose brocade, the booth sat everyone side by side, so they could look into the restaurant, without having to face one another. Most tables were covered with white linen. Except for two old people seated at one table, the place was empty.

Donny brushed up against Kitty, giving her mother a shock caused by static electricity. Kitty recoiled at the jolt, then she started to giggle, enjoying a cheap thrill and hoping for another.

Flashing a goofy smile, Donny took her mother by the hand as if she was a fluffy seeing-eye dog bounding over the worn red carpet. She guided her mother to the long banquette set for ten. Kitty could hardly keep up with Donny and laughed in a breathy, sexy sort of way. Both girls knew their mother liked to sit at the far end of the booth so she could see who was coming and going—an old Sicilian trick to avoid getting whacked. The funny thing about Kitty wanting to sit facing the door had nothing to do with being Sicilian. She was Irish and crazy.

Johnny was the Sicilian. Ever since he had gone to see *The Godfather* at Loew's Theater, he thought it was his responsibility to act like a true Sicilian. He saw the movie five times.

Cookie moved into the cushy banquette and slid next to her mother, patting her hand to make sure she stayed calm.

Kitty smiled. "You put your lipstick on real nice, Honey."

Johnny squeezed into the banquette next to Kitty, squirming noisily in his seat, trying to make himself comfortable. The four of them sat lined up in the banquette like cars on a train. Not being able to look at each from other across the table was probably a good thing.

The waitress shot over to their table, balancing a basket of bread and a stainless steel pitcher of water. "I love your car, Johnny. It's gorgeous. I bet it cost you a pretty penny!" She stuck a cigarette in between her two coral-painted lips and slapped menus onto the table. She set a paper kiddie placemat and a box of crayons in front of Donny so she could color in the black & white outlines of clowns, balloons and circus animals.

Donny glared at her and crumpled the placemat into a wad.

Cookie smirked. "Can't you see that she's too old for that kind of kid stuff?"

"Cookie," Johnny crooned. "Be nice. Come on." He winked at her in a way that meant they were both on the same side, and that was a lie too.

Johnny flirted with the waitress and called her Shir, even though her name tag said Sharlene.

"Anybody else joining you, Johnny?"

"Just my sister, maybe. You know Ro-Ro, don't you, Shir?"

"Sure do." Sharlene's voice was husky. "Nice lady." Smoke poured from her nose and mouth while she stubbed out her cigarette in the round black ashtray on the table. Johnny lit a Tareyton, tossing his match into the ashtray, a companion to her smoldering butt.

"I'd love to take a ride in your car, Johnny."

"Just let me know when, Shir. I'm around. You know my number." He winked.

"I'll bring you some more water and an extra place setting."

Both Cookie and Johnny watched the back of the waitress's legs. Cookie saw a run in her flesh-colored stocking. Johnny saw something else and grunted. "Madone."

"Two extra place settings, please," Cookie called out. "One for my sister who's not a little kid no more!"

Donny's blue eyes slanted as sharp as the blade of a knife. She gave Cookie a nod and a thumbs-up. Cookie nodded back. They were aligned against a common enemy.

No one touched the plastic-coated aqua menus that were

the same color as 1950s kitchen appliances. If you were from Yonkers, you knew what you wanted before you walked into the restaurant.

Johnny called to Sharlene, "We're ready to order, Hon." He looked around the table. "You're ready, right?"

The waitress rushed to the table and filled Johnny's water glass, not looking at anyone else. Condensation coated the bottom half of the dull stainless steel water pitcher. Water and ice cubes clinked into Johnny's glass. "I usually don't work Saturdays. They called me in because the weather's going to be bad and I can walk home." This time, she winked.

Johnny stared at the waitress's white bib that spread across the front of her black uniform and smiled. "You're looking damn good, Shir. I swear you never age a day. What's the perfume you're wearing?" He gave Kitty a nudge. "You should find out what she's wearing and get some. I like that color lipstick she's got on too."

Kitty giggled as if Johnny was flirting with her and not the waitress. "Oh, Johnny, don't be that way. She'll get the wrong idea and next thing you know everybody will be saying you're banging her when I'm not looking."

"So, who's looking? Me look?"

He turned to Sharlene and winked again. "Four lasagnas and the dinner salads with the shredded parmesan cheese on top. Give me a small strip steak on the side. Make it rare. I want rare. Got that? Rare. We'll take some antipasto and..." He handed the menus to Sharlene. "Find out what they want to drink. Won't you, Hon?"

He nodded toward Cookie. "Give her something that will make her shut up and listen to me for a change."

"Coke," Cookie said. "Just bring us a pitcher of coke."

"I'll take a scotch on the rocks. J&B. Light on the ice. We're celebrating tonight. Aren't we, Cookie?" Johnny gave his daughter that sick grin again! Cookie felt like punching him in the face.

"What's the occasion?"

"Cookie's got her first real job. I'm talking about the kind of job where they take taxes out of your paycheck."

"I've given up drug dealing." Cookie lit a Marlboro and blew smoke to the ceiling. "Now I've got to pay taxes like all of the other dumb schmucks in Yonkers."

"Nice," Sharlene said. "Congratulations. I'll give you a free spumoni if you want."

As soon as the waitress was out of earshot, Kitty pulled out a compact of Revlon pressed powder and examined her face in the small mirror. "Look, Johnny, I'm getting those red spots again."

"I don't see nothing."

"The doctor can't get rid of them. I don't know what to do." Kitty snapped her compact shut and looked frantic. "What am I going to do if my whole face turns into a giant red scab? I'll look like a lobster!"

Donny kicked Cookie's foot under the table. "She doesn't have any spots," she whispered.

"You imagine things." Johnny shook his head, muttering, "There's nothing wrong with her face. Do you see something wrong with her face? Tell me I'm not seeing something!"

It wasn't often that the Colangelos went out to eat in a restaurant—that was usually reserved for special occasions: funerals, weddings, graduations. Cookie remembered Johnny taking them here when she graduated from the eighth grade, but the memory was dim and best left forgotten.

Now here they were acting like they were a big happy family.

Sharlene came back to the table and made a big point of ignoring Cookie, Donny and Kitty, only looking at Johnny, nodding sympathetically. Everyone seemed to know he was the victim of a crazy wife and two nasty daughters. She set down a platter of Louie's House Antipasto and another basket of warm bread. Smoked eggplant, marinated mushrooms and peppers, kalamata olives, prosciutto, and thick slices of provolone cheese covered the plate.

Cookie stubbed out her cigarette and reached for a chunk of bread, scooping up smoked eggplant. Small glass flasks of red wine vinegar and olive oil sat on the table next to a small uncovered bowl of grated parmesan cheese. Louie's was known for rolling out their own dough to make pasta and bread. Everything was fresh and made to order, except for the lasagna that sat pre-baked on long metal sheets.

Donny showed her Etch-A-Sketch pad to Cookie, so she could see what she had written. *Big fucking asshole!*

Then she lifted the plastic page to instantly erase her words.

Johnny flinched at the sound of the crisp tear. "You gotta play with that thing while I'm talking to you! I don't get it. This one wants to erase everything she writes, and you..."

Johnny turned his attention to Cookie. "You're always writing in that goddamn notebook, writing girl stuff that no one wants to read, but that's not going to do nothing for you! Nothing!"

"Cookie has a way with words." Kitty smiled at her husband flirtatiously. She wore dazzling red lipstick that matched her low-cut cashmere sweater. "Leave her alone, Johnny."

"Don't interfere with none of this, Kitty. You don't know what you're talking about. She's not going to get a nice guy to support her by writing about her feelings all the time. It's bad enough that she's got so many feelings in the first place!"

Sharlene came back with the drinks. She set Johnny's scotch in front of him but before he could take a sip, Cookie snatched his rock glass and took a slug, grimacing at the bitter oak aftertaste that stung her tongue.

Johnny pretended not to notice. He leaned his head to the side, staring at Donny, squinting as though he was seeing things. For a moment he looked flabbergasted, then stunned.

He swung all the way around in his cushiony seat. "Will you look at the kid? She's got breasts. Jesus Christ, do you see that? She's growing breasts already!"

Donny did not show the slightest sign of embarrassment. She kept her head down, busily drawing on her Etch-A-Sketch.

"The kid's got breasts for Chrissakes! How old is she? How old is she now? It must be all the hormones in the milk and the meat sent here by the red Chinese!"

Donny held up the Etch-A-Sketch for Johnny to see. Big breasts flashed across the page like balloons. He turned red and looked away. He reached for his drink, but it was gone.

"Thought she put my drink here."

"Here's to you!" Cookie held up his rock glass and took a swig. "A girl's gotta do what she's gotta do!"

"You got that straight!" Sharlene kicked open a stand in front of the long table where she set her serving tray. Stainless steel covers kept the food warm on the plates. Even though you couldn't see the food, everyone was getting lasagna and salad, except for Johnny, who got the extra steak. Sharlene clanged the metal covers as she uncovered the plates.

"Jesus Christ, Kitty, you shouldn't let Donny walk around like that! When are you going to get the kid a brassiere?"

"Oh, Johnny, don't be like that," Kitty demurred.

Ro-Ro flung open the door and burst into the restaurant like she was riding in on a tank. Even though Ro-Ro was tiny, she was thick, muscular, with a big head and no neck. She was also loud, gushing, giving Johnny a hug. "Look at you, Johnny. I saw the new car outside. A Cadillac. You've gotta be proud of yourself."

Cookie figured she had taken the bus. Ro-Ro could not drive. Many women didn't drive and made their husbands chauffeur them around town. It was a Yonkers thing.

Johnny's scotch was mostly gone. Cookie pushed the glass in front of him. "That Cadillac must of cost you a lot of money. How'd you get the money to pay for the car?"

"What are you, a wise guy?"

"You can bullshit everybody, Johnny but you can't bullshit me! I'm your daughter. A chip off the old block."

Johnny looked proud of himself. "The meatballs are a killer, Ro. So's the lasagna."

"The meatballs are a killer, Hon." Donny mimicked Johnny's baritone voice. "So's the lasagna, Hon!!"

"Sit, eat, relax," he told Ro-Ro. "Just ignore them." He nodded toward where the girls sat and winked at his sister.

"Shir," he called. "Bring me another plate of lasagna, would you, Hon?"

"No! I want the scungilli, hot with the peppers!" Ro-Ro shoveled two fat slices of prosciutto wrapped around provolone into her mouth. Her other hand clutched her purse. "I'm in the mood for the scungilli! Not the salad. I want the scungilli hot and spicy-hot over pasta."

The blood drained from Johnny's face. He looked like he was going to get sick. "I don't know how you can eat that stuff. I've got an allergy to shellfish. I got sick on the seafood in Japan before I shipped out to Korea to fight them red Chinese."

Ro-Ro stuck her fork into Donny's lasagna and took a bite. "Mmm, that's good…thanks for giving me a taste."

Donny pulled her plate to the side, away from Ro-Ro.

Delving into lasagna requires skill. Eight layers of thin sheets of pasta are carefully placed, one on top of the other. In between each layer there is culinary beauty alternating among feather- light ricotta, savory sausage patties, and mozzarella that melds all of the layers together. Baked in delicate but rich red sauce, its glorious top is completely covered with pure *mozzarelle'*, the kind that only melts the moment it enters your mouth.

Lasagna makes people focused, even noisemakers—the people who talk too much and say nothing. Only the clatter of forks could be heard. White napkins began to bleed the stain of red sauce.

Do you eat each layer, peeling away the top to the bottom or do you fork into messy chunks that capture eight perfect layers? Perfection is cutting deep into its heart to create four distinct squares. Cookie savored every bite, biting off one forkful at a time, never taking on more than she could chew.

Sharlene brought Ro-Ro her plate of spicy-hot steaming scungilli over a thick ropey pasta, Bigoli. Johnny couldn't stomach it. "I don't know why you got to order that stuff, especially when I invite you to dinner. You know I'm allergic."

He got up from the table, making a fuss about going into the kitchen to say hello to Louie. Even from the dining room, Cookie could hear her father talking in the kitchen about his new car. Cookie completely took over his scotch and drank all that remained.

Ro-Ro shoveled food into her mouth, talking and chewing between bites. "Johnny's seafood allergy is all in his head," she said. "He believes in junk science and thinks it's real or something."

A sinister smile crossed Donny's face. "Where've you been? Long time, no see." She placed her hands on her budding breasts. "Look, I've got boobies now."

"Do you hear the way she's talking to me? I can't believe you would say such a thing."

Both girls knew Ro-Ro had been missing from the family scene for years, long enough to constitute abandonment. Ever since the day Kitty ate an apple and placed the apple core inside of Ro-Ro's pocketbook, Ro-Ro had nothing to do with them.

Everyone knew the apple core story was true.

Ro-Ro kept one hand flat across her purse on her lap. It did not go unnoticed. Donny nudged Cookie. Both girls leaned in on either side of their mother. Kitty sat quietly, staring into space, drifting in her private world, seeking comfort in a myriad of color that framed the outer edge of her gilded reality. She was far away from Ro-Ro, the last car on the train. Cookie nudged her mother to make sure she was still of this world. Kitty's eyes gleamed with mischief, a touch of crazy pride.

Ro-Ro shoved scungilli and bigoli into her mouth. Nothing was more disgusting than listening to Ro-Ro's slurping sounds. When she finished her own food, she scavenged the remaining antipasto. She reached for the plate where Cookie had left a morsel of lasagna and sausage. "You're not going to eat that? I'll take it."

In between bites, she asked, "Still palling around with the colored boy?"

Cookie lit a Marlboro and blew smoke downstream in her direction. "He's black, not a colored boy. Where do you get that shit? Herman Lynch is my best friend."

"What about that older guy you were dating, the kooky Vietnam Vet guy with the long blonde hair?"

Cookie had not come to terms with Stanley being gone. She told herself she felt nothing at all. She wanted to be anywhere but here, perhaps in a cemetery or at a small empty church— any dark place where she could grieve for the missing in action, the lonely, the wounded, and the dead.

"You really are a bitch." Donny folded her arms across her chest.

Ro-Ro cleared her throat. "Excuse me? Concetta, are you going to let your little sister talk that way? Aren't you going to set an example and correct her?"

Cookie crumpled her napkin next to her plate. "She's right. You are a bitch."

"You were always fresh. The both of you. The freshest girls I know of! Poor Johnny's gotta put up with the likes of you!"

"Talking about me?" Johnny returned to their table with the stride of a big man who owned the restaurant. "I can't ever seem to please you, all you broads. Get them spumoni and the ice cream cake, then get me the goddamn check, Shir, unless you gotta add your two cents too! I'm expecting nothing like that if you want me to leave you a good tip."

Cookie turned around in her seat, looked out the window, jutted out her chin, and nodded like a wise guy. "Come on, Johnny, how'd you get a car like that?"

His voice boomed from the corner of the restaurant. He wanted to impress Cookie. He was always seeking her approval. "Do you want to know how I got the new car? She wants to know how I got the Cadillac? Jesus, can you believe this?"

Johnny looked around the booth, but no one was listening. "I'm the smartest guy in the whole world. The smartest Italian guy, no less, and that's like saying a lot."

"Come on, Johnny, I'm your daughter, I know you're full'a shit. So, tell me, how did you get a car like that?"

"I've got connections. In here," he said, tapping his finger against his temple. "Everything's in my head." He nodded knowingly to make his point.

"Cookie starts her new job next week," he told Ro-Ro. "I got her the job at the drugstore because I know people, the same way I got the Cadillac. I know people," he said, turning to Cookie. "And they know me. They know me and they owe me. How's that for telling it like it is?"

He reached for Cookie, giving her cheek a quick affectionate stroke. "Now that you're sixteen, I'm not paying for you no more. You're on your own, kid. You got a good job at the drugstore. Now you can make some money for yourself before you find some guy and settle down, then you don't have to work no more unless your husband wants you to. But what kind of guy wants his wife to work? Over my dead body. See your mother here. Think I'd let her work?!"

Two

Cookie refused to get into Johnny's Cadillac. She would go anywhere to get away from Johnny and his notions about what she ought to do with her life. Brumal clusters of clouds threatened a big storm. The buses were running slow to nonexistent. Bright lights, wreathes and kitschy Santa Clauses dotted most storefronts. The snow began with the pinprick-sized lethal flakes that always turn to ice. Only one bus stopped, bleating diesel exhaust that rose like steam in the frigid air. She heard the steady scrape of windshield wipers sticking on ice. Even though it was the wrong bus, she thought of taking a ride just to stay warm.

And then it began snowing harder.

She could not see the sky, nor could she see the Hudson River. She knew what lurked beneath the surface on this cold night—angry dark clouds casting suspicion on anything that could be good, noble or true. Once she started walking home, she knew there was no turning back.

Blinded by snow welting her eyes, she did not know where she was going, and even if she had known, she would not be able to see very well. The snow fell in tornado-like whorls, covering everything, leaving no boundary between the sidewalk and the road. Cheery Christmas lights glittered like uncommon red and green jewels against the shining-white mounds of new fallen snow.

The night had grown as quiet as death. She was on the outer edge of the projects, close to where her two best friends Reenie and Herman lived. She put her head down to protect herself from the wind and braced herself for a climb up Palisade Avenue.

The storm grew worse, approaching white-out conditions. Cookie knew she could stumble upon something awful without ever having had the chance to see it coming.

She walked along New Main Street, where open entrances to back street alleys acted as a crude map, guiding her out of Getty Square. The narrow alleys offered her respite from the wind and the snow, but not from the cold. Now she could see. She moved as fast as she could to generate heat. She craved a Marlboro but was too cold to stop moving long enough to light one.

The alleys ran along the backs of buildings that provided the wide berths of eaves hanging over the ground. The eaves acted as buffers to ward off the increasing velocity of the snow. A small car had stopped in the alley. Plumes of smoke as long as jet trails fanned through the snow. She immediately felt warmth from the car's motor, which was racing. And yet the car's lights were off. A slim gash of red above the car's wheels was the only area not covered with snow.

Yellow light drifted into the alley from an open door. Wind swilled icy white froth inside the entrance over the sawdust that lay on the ground. Garbage cans heaped with snow formed a hedge against the brick wall. A spare sign above the open door told Cookie she had arrived at the back entrance to Trunz Butcher Shop. She remembered going there as a kid. The butcher shop's owner had a long loop of a moustache and spoke with a heavy Hungarian accent. He liked to give kids slices of bologna for free.

The image of the butcher blew away with as much force as the cyclonic snow. A different kind of love was happening, and she could not believe what she was seeing. What she had stumbled upon took her breath away.

The guy stood in the entrance, leaning over a girl who was pressed to the ground in a half squat position, or maybe she was kneeling. Cookie couldn't tell for sure. His hands gripped her breasts for support. Then he freed his hands to yank her by the hair, pulling her head back, then jerking her head forward, tossing her as if she was a rag doll, until he was finished with her. The girl's muffled sobs incensed him further. He smacked her face. Then he moved her head down to his crotch. He kept his hand on the back of her head. Soon her sobs were stifled and replaced with heaving and a guttural breath.

It was just the beginning…that is if she was any good, Cookie surmised to herself. She had experienced enough in her short lifetime to know who was good and who was merely performing a social obligation.

This girl was clearly being coerced against her will. Cookie's eyes were fixed on them and froze into a stare. She didn't want to watch, yet she was reminded of what she had not even thought about since Stanley de Falco had left Yonkers.

And she knew what was happening here was not the same thing she had experienced with Stanley.

From the corner of his eye, the guy saw Cookie and turned his head in her direction. He gave her a certain kind of look. At first Cookie thought it was anger, a warning of what he would say or do if she didn't run as fast as her legs would take her. Instead, he smiled. It was then she realized his look was one of indiscriminate want. He would have taken Cookie, the girl, anyone. She was not sure who he was or the girl. Not that it mattered. She got the hell out of there.

She heard the girl crying, his yelling and the sound of slaps. His voice grew more heated and agitated. His yelling took on the same ugly tone as a racial slur or commonly held epithet. *Bitch in heat. Gutter Slut.* Foul language. Dirty words. She didn't know exactly what he was saying, but knew it was not borne of love or affection. Even from a distance, their shouts pummeled through dense snow, permeating the quiet night with hatred. A wild annihilating fight had started and the girl had no chance of winning.

Even though she wore woolen gloves, Cookie's fingers were numb. She wished she had worn mittens so she could rub her fingers together for warmth. She plunged her hand deep into her coat pocket, feeling for Johnny's keys. He might hide the keys to his Cadillac, but she had long ago made a copy of the keys to his office. She was going to the building where Herman and Reenie lived—that was the plan—and if they weren't home, she'd let herself into Johnny's office and stay there for the night.

The wind picked up and carried the snow in blanketed gusts that rose in the air, settling nowhere until accumulating in chaotic drifts against the utility poles and stumps of trees, some living, some dead, all lashed with thick white coats of snow. Snow banked against the doorways of stores, all shut now. Everyone knew this storm was coming and the shop owners had closed early.

Then she saw the small red car, trying to get up the hill next to Schlobohm. *Slow-bomb.* The projects. Skidding, briefly turning sideways, the car spun around before straightening to take the hill again. The car was most definitely red—that much she could see under the monstrous snow falling away from its roof and hood. The car continued its approach in fits of starts and stops, with its tires spinning, and the sound of its clutch grinding gears in its impossible attempt to climb the hill through the mounting icy snow.

The car did not drive or stall but crept forward with the stodgy force of a broken sled, driving through one red light, then another. The passenger door suddenly opened. A girl fell out of the car, landing in a nearby snowbank. Whether she was pushed or she threw herself out of the car did not matter. Using her arms, the girl drew herself to her knees and attempted to stand.

The car spun around, a chaotic whirligig, heading back down the hill. Cookie heard the car throttle down to first gear and watched it crunching snow down the hill. If the driver of the sports car worried about skidding out of control on the ice, it didn't show.

The car didn't have very far to get down the hill and soon came to the flat plane of New Main Street, pulled to the side of the road and parked, but no one got out of the car.

"Will someone please help me," the girl cried out.

Cookie didn't recognize her until a strong gust of wind blew back her long straight black hair, mostly covered now in snow. Her features were contorted in a primitive mask-like scream. Frozen, unable to talk, she barely uttered a whisper.

"Reenie," Cookie called.

She had never seen Reenie Ruggerio look so frightened. The stiff bob of her head barely yielded a nod, to let Cookie know that she could see her. Tears wet her cheeks. Her face had puffed up and her right eye looked as though it had been stitched shut. Slivers of blood pooled in the cracked corners of her mouth.

"Reenie, you've been hurt."

Cookie could see that she had been crying. "What's going on?"

She tried to touch Reenie's face but the girl stumbled backwards. She put up her hands to protect her face, too tender to touch.

"I don't know what's happening," Reenie cried. "He threw me out of the car!"

Cookie walked up to her and faced her. Reenie was swollen and bruised, but in the cold night air it was hard to tell how badly she had been hurt. She scooped up a handful of snow and pressed it to Reenie's cheek. "Does that feel better?"

Reenie nodded. She wouldn't make eye contact with Cookie.

Cookie looked to the sky as if she wanted to join the storm, and get out of here, away from Reenie and the trouble she had brought onto herself.

"What the hell are you doing with a guy like that?!"

Reenie was shivering, cold to the core of her bones. Cookie was afraid to hug her. She looked brittle, as if she was sure to break.

"Who was that?"

"My boyfriend."

"That's the guy you've been going out with?"

"He's got a nice car."

"So?"

"It's an Alpha Romeo."

"You're lucky there was snow on the ground when he shoved you out of the car!"

"But I love him," Reenie whimpered. "He never used to act this way."

Cookie did eventually hug Reenie that night and the girl clung onto her for dear life. They walked on Walsh Road toward the apartment that Reenie shared with her grandmother and her junkie brother Billy Dee. Reenie refused to talk about what had happened. Vast silence stood between them, more silent than the snow, a deafening quiet that smothered all signs of life.

Wending around the narrow alley that ran behind Schlobohm, Slow-bomb, a few black guys in the hood were sharing a bottle. She also saw a six-pack of Ballantine Beer in red and gold holiday wrap, set on the ground in the snow. Standing in front of a fire, the guys had doubled down on their hoodies. They had built a fire in a garbage can to keep themselves warm. Cold beer, hands warmed by fire, the street was their lifeline and there was no way to keep them from hanging out in the cold night, even in the face of a storm.

A blizzard is what it was turning out to be in Cookie's estimation. She held onto Reenie, offering protection, and Reenie clung to her. Two sets of eyes not seeing were better than one. The two girls propelled themselves against the fierce wind and trudged on.

Cookie couldn't shake the image of Reenie's bruised face. She had astonished herself by watching the scene in the alley. She had her own experiences with sex that were too private to share. No one else could touch the place where she held Stanley. Okay, she had heard the ringing pop of squeaking bedsprings, when her parents got it on in their bedroom. She had seen bodies flying in the back seats of cars and kids locked in heated embrace as they disappeared into the woods at Untermyer Park. She had witnessed kids making out in parking lots and on street corners, but this was different. This was violent. Until now, she had never witnessed a violent sexual encounter. Cookie thought she had established her own guidelines for what love ought to be, as crazy as that sounds, and she knew what Reenie was calling love was not.

Thursday December 28th 1972

The weather in Yonkers is as changeable as a teenage girl's heart. I know cause there isn't anything sweet about being sixteen. Sweet sixteen. Never been kissed? I'm sweet sixteen and I couldn't declare that I have never been kissed. Man! I have been kissed! Oh Man!

It's all starting to come to me now. I remember seeing Stanley the way he looked at me the last night before he left for California. I close my eyes. I imagine him basking in the sun on the beach in Malibu. He is leaning back on his elbows with his legs fully extended. His long blonde hair hangs loose down his back. A fine trace of sand clings to his ankles and the soles of his feet and the narrow band of skin around his waist in the exact places where I kissed him.

I kissed him about a million times. And I'd do it all over again.

It's been eight weeks since he's been gone. I have not heard from him. He had not promised me anything. I did not expect him to write. But then again? I was sure he would.

Stanley has taken a couple of trips around the world. He has more education than a regular Yonkers guy. He has probably gotten himself a good job by now. Three thousand miles. La La Land. A warm climate. Why would he bother writing to me? I just thought he would.

I hate what's happening to Reenie and I don't know how to stop it. I have no instructions for living or dying. I only know love means different things to different people—the way I love Stanley (even though he's gone) and the way Reenie loves that guy (even though he's kicking her to the curb like a dirty dog) are just not the same. One is real and the other feels like a dream. I won't say which one is real and which one is the dream cause I don't know.

My school uniform skirt is the kind of wool that's scratchy

and leaves red marks inside of my thighs. Red welts. White skin. My skin is too white. That is what the Italian girls say. Their words hurt me more than the uniform itching the soft parts inside of my legs. It is good to feel something. I want to feel anything and not feel dead for one more day.

Johnny won't let me drive his new car. I'm stuck having to walk everywhere. Grudgingly. Trudging. (Pssst I like to rhyme.) I'm on my way to Getty Square. Ghetto Square.

Can you believe that Johnny wants a cut of my crummy little paycheck to pay for my room and board? It's like he wants to teach me a lesson about money or something. Like I don't know about money. I know all about money and I know that I ain't got none.

Ain't! The word ain't makes me laugh. I know the word ain't is wrong. I like to use it anyway. Ain't that a pisser?

I'm only happy when I'm writing my words in my black & white notebook and remembering Stanley de Falco and not remembering that when he left Yonkers that he left me too.

I'm only sixteen and already a working stiff. I'd rather be dead. Again. I wish I could die. I wish I could die sixteen times in a row and light a candle and call that my sixteenth birthday. I love you! Stanley!! Even though you've clearly forgotten about me!!!

-ccc

Three

The pale winter sun clung behind clouds that were full, round and imposing, and the color of orange wood smoke. Brisk wind whipped up a clot of bad air, an oily stew of sewage, old rubber tires, and dead fish from the Hudson River. The last big winter storm had come and gone. Mounds of black-crusted snow rose in stiff peaks against curbs and sewer portals. Only patches of dirty snow remained on the ground. Damp in the low forties and overcast, there were no signs of freezing temperatures, but that could change any moment.

H.L. Green Co. and W.T. Grant Co. sat side by side on the flat plane of Palisade Avenue in Getty Square. Known as *Greens* and *Grants*, the two department stores presided over *Ghetto Square* with the commanding presence of slum lords. Pretending to be competitors, even when everyone knew they were not. Greens and Grants were god-awful twin bullies, fixing prices for the same close-out sales. Selling the same stuff, clothing, record albums, furniture, kitchen utensils, pots and pans, and small pets: canaries, parakeets, turtles, toads and goldfish, the differences between the two stores were small. Yet everyone favored one over the other.

Both Greens and Grants had their own in-store Santas. Across the street from Greens and Grants, Woolworths, once known as the *Five and Ten*, had two Santas—not a nice thing to do to little kids still believing there was only one real Santa Claus. But it did not matter. Yonkers kids knew the truth from an early age. Santa was fake, made up by big business to screw working people out of their hard-earned money—yet, Santa brought them gifts; it was the first time and the last time, actually the only time in their lives that Yonkers kids got something for nothing.

Santas might have been everywhere in Getty Square, but there was only one Zelda. Greens beat Grants hands down because of Zelda. The mysterious gypsy was staked out like a gun moll in the front entrance of Greens next to a red-and-white striped popcorn machine.

Cookie saw Zelda as soon as she walked into Greens. Feeling down, she couldn't resist a visit with the gypsy. She needed all of the luck she could get, even if it was spewed out from this kitschy arcade coin-op machine. She pushed a fake slug instead of a quarter into Zelda's coin slot, opening Zelda's eyes, lighting her crystal ball. The gypsy mannequin shot out a fortune.

Soon you will meet a new friend. Cookie stuffed the little slip of paper into the pocket of her navy peacoat. She looked at Zelda to get sweet affirmation, but the fake gypsy had shut her eyes, and would need another coin to again come to life.

Outside on the street, she eyed Woolworths as if it had been ousted from her life for good. She didn't go there anymore. Woolworths wasn't known much for anything except banana splits and ice cream sundaes. The cool thing about Woolworths was its gaggle of white balloons tied around the cash register. The balloons were filled with small sheets of paper that had different prices written on them. You had to pop a balloon to find out the price you'd have to pay for a banana split or an ice cream sundae. If you were lucky, you could get a sundae for a nickel.

Greens was famous for its root beer floats, French fries, and grilled cheese sandwiches pumped out of an old fashioned in-store restaurant called the Maple Room. Grants had wickedly delicious hot dogs served up on thick toasted buns, better than city dogs, better than kosher, better than any other hot dogs in the entire world.

Greens had the larger collection of Simplicity and Butterick sewing patterns, but Grants had the best selection of curtains, lingerie and double-A and triple-A cup training bras for nubile girls.

Imagine training breasts to grow! Girls who wore training bras were forever doomed to be flat chested.

Girls with big breasts and big bucks bought expensive satin bras edged with lace at Mimi's on the corner of North Broadway and Main Street.

No Yonkers girl had breasts as swell as the pair owned by Toni Ferlinghetti. The Queen Bee of Italian Girls stood in front of Grants display window, smoking a cigarette. She had the audacity to smoke right outside of Grants like she owned the block, and in many ways she did. Leaning against the storefront glass, Toni eyed Cookie with a familiar brand of contempt. They had a long history of hating one another, but for some strange reason they never strayed too far apart.

Toni had taken to teasing her hair into a big black bush and wearing gobs of makeup. Her heavily hooded eyes screamed with shimmering blue eyeshadow, thick stripes of black eyeliner, and eyelashes so excessively crusted with mascara that they had achieved the texture of centipedes. Her pearlized lip gloss was as nude as her legs. Black corduroy mini-skirt. Four-inch platform shoes. Tight ribbed, short-sleeved black sweater capped with a natty silk scarf in a blue-black-white geometric print. She was all legs and hair. No one dressed that way in the dead of winter except Toni Ferlinghetti. Despite her scant skirt and skimpy shirt, she did not appear to be cold.

Cackling the edge of an "Hello," through her grey plume

of smoke, she gave Cookie the once over that was neither kind nor polite.

Cookie dished her a look that could kill. "Aren't you cold dressed like that? Or I should say not dressed?"

"Ha-Ha." Rolling her eyes was a dead giveaway that she was not amused. "What are you doing? Looking for trouble? Still sweet on that Stanley guy? That kooky Vietnam Vet baby killer!?"

Cookie gave her the finger and kept walking. She wanted nothing to do with the likes of Toni Ferlinghetti.

"I've got a job at Grants." Toni stuck out her tongue at Cookie while she pointed to the storefront window. "I'm working right in there at the makeup counter, selling makeup. I get a ten percent discount on everything I buy and free samples."

"Looks like you used up all your samples in one day," Cookie shot back. She felt even worse about her job at Rite Aid. Working at Grants was a step up.

"Ta-da..." Toni snapped her fingers. "You're too white. Let me know if you want any makeup. You sure could use some color!"

As Cookie turned the corner onto Main Street, the Christmas decorations looked tired enough to be stuffed back into a cardboard box and not have to hang around until New Year's Day. The glass wax stenciling on the windows of Rite Aid Drugstore on Main Street twirled the images of trees, misshapen angels and spaghetti-shaped strands of fake snowflakes.

Her pay at Rite Aid was $1.75 an hour. She thought she would have gotten used to it by now, but every day was bleak. In her estimation, it would take thirty-six months of saving every penny she earned to buy a car, even a beater. And she was never going to have enough money to go to college.

It took effort for her to yank open the heavy glass doors of the drugstore. She skulked inside, keeping her head down.

She did not bother to look to see who else was working the shift. She would rather sell her body on the streets than work in this drugstore.

She wasn't thinking as she slid into the back office. She had to move fast, get in and get out. She scrambled to find her timecard, but it was never in the same place where she had last left it. The store manager Artie Jelinek always scrutinized her timecard, treating her like a thief, but it was all a put-on, a way for him to get close enough to her to cop a feel. She found her thick yellow timecard in the last slot by the door and punched it into a white metal time clock that read 3:01.

She opened the large black metal locker where the work uniforms were kept in a bin and pulled out an oversized navy smock. She moved faster now, snapping the smock's buttons over her school blouse and skirt, panting a bit. She had to get in and out of the back room before she was accosted by Artie. He was as sore to look at as he was quick to grab, but she was quicker and usually managed to get away.

Four cash register stations were ringing all at once in the front of the storefront window. Cookie's usual station was occupied by Philomena Sukla. With her blue tinted aviator glasses and her tight brown *fro*, Philomena looked like a pilot at the helm of an aircraft. She pressed the cash register keys in precise staccato snaps. She was the fastest cashier among the bunch of girls. Accurate too. Her drawer was always even. Once it came up a penny short and she cried. Artie had just given her a raise. She was paid $1.85 an hour, ten cents more an hour than any other girl.

While Cookie waited to get her cash drawer from Artie, she stayed busy, patrolling the aisles, scanning for empty spaces on the shelves. Facing-out cans of shaving cream, she pulled forward stray cans hidden in the back toward the front to make the shelf look full. When she was a kid, she'd hoard Johnny's shaving cream so she could use it as a tool for mischief, lathering houses and trees on Halloween. She imagined mounds of shaving cream frothing up as if it was being mixed in a bowl, shooting cloud shapes into the sky. She had a thing for clouds, thinking she could read meaning in their shapes as if they were tea leaves. She managed to see clouds everywhere except in the sky. The December sky was as grey and bitter as her Grandpa Jack's old pipe tobacco. By the time she finished her shift at Rite Aid, the sky would turn to soot.

She heard many voices in the store coming from all directions. This place of narrow aisles, chrome, metal and glass was always busy, except late at night when most of the lights were turned off. A dim fluorescent light illuminated the storefront window after hours. The voices grew louder, a peal of a girl's laughter, and a guy's.

She swung around the corner into the shampoo and hairspray aisle. Artie's hand slid around Carole Zukowski's waist. As soon as he saw Cookie, his other arm swung out. He clutched Cookie as though he owned her. She squirmed hard to get away from him. Carole grimaced but put up with him. Any way you look at it, both girls were getting mauled. Cookie wriggled her entire body, a mass of arms and legs until his clutch eased, but she did not get completely away.

Breathing hard, she stared at Artie, more embarrassed for herself than for him. Artie grinned at her. He was showing off, even though he did not have an audience. She realized the collar of her schoolgirl blouse had bunched up from under the top of her smock. Artie's fingers nestled below her breast, probing to find an opening underneath the cup of her bra and wedged inside. His fingers pinched her flesh, his sure mark on her that was meant to last longer than his actual touch, a firebrand in her memory. He was in and out of her bra quickly, depositing a rough squeeze on her breast, under the smock, on the outside of her blouse. His hand slid out of her smock and his arm dropped to his side. Then he was gone as though the whole thing had never happened.

Four

Tony Amendolito did not need an introduction. He was not the new friend Zelda the Gypsy had predicted. Tony worked for a security company that had been hired by Rite Aid to ensure that employees were not stealing money. Pulling a small black and red switchblade from his pocket, he flicked it open, then shut, nonchalantly opening and shutting the blade as if what he was doing was nothing, except staying in rhythm with the ring from the cash register.

Tony liked to play tough guy. He was a company man, traveling from store to store, giving employees lie detector tests. He came around often and with no warning. No one ever knew who was next to get the test.

Cookie's heart skipped at the sight of Tony Amendolito, and not because he wasn't too bad to look at. He was short, built like a bull. His black hair puffed up in soft waves inches below his ears. The way he looked had nothing to do with the small blip in her chest. He reminded her of Reenie's boyfriend, the guy who had kicked her out of the car that snowy night.

And Cookie did feel nervous. Tight throat, sweaty palms, she experienced all of the symptoms that should have told her she was scared of taking a lie detector test. It wasn't that she had anything to hide. She didn't like anyone thinking that she had done something wrong. It was the same feeling she had when Fangs the evil nun pulled her out of line and savagely beat her over nothing.

She had to tell herself, she wasn't afraid. Cookie Colangelo didn't take no guff from nobody.

Carole Zukowski pressed her lips together, suppressing a smile. "I already took the test."

Artie gave Carol an appreciative squeeze. "And you passed with flying colors, Honey."

Cookie wondered what Artie would do when he stuck his tongue into Carole Zukowski's mouth. The girl was pretty, but she didn't have any teeth—not due to drug addiction but neglect. Her family didn't have money and couldn't afford trips to the dentist. Or maybe she was cursed with bad teeth. Plenty of people don't take care of their teeth, but they don't end up losing them. It's sad to see a teenage girl who had lost all of her teeth. Her dentures slipped so often that she had developed a slight lisp.

Artie had not lost sight of Cookie. He reeled her back in by the sleeve of her smock. "You're next," he told her.

Tony Amendolito's menacing nod meant "I don't want no trouble. Let's go."

Arty pulled Cookie close to him. "Oh, come on, Honey, it won't be that bad, sooner or later, we've all got to do it, even me. It's company policy. They just want to know everybody's on the up and up. I've taken the lie detector twice already. The company says we have to do it."

She could feel Artie's flabby waist bearing down on her arm. His gold-rimmed wire spectacles slid to the edge of his small beaked nose. His breath tickled her ear and smelled sour but minty, as if the effect of his mouthwash had worn off.

"It won't be that bad," he whispered. "I'll make it up to you. Promise," he said, squeezing her waist.

She stole away from his clutch and followed Tony Amendolito.

Staying close on Tony's heels, Cookie would rather be anywhere else in the world, even on a death march to get her head whacked off by a guillotine.

As they descended into the cellar, Cookie stepped over boxes piled high on both sides of the steps. Overstock. Rite Aid was a busy store, thronging with customers. The stock boys couldn't work fast enough to empty the boxes and get the merchandise on the shelves. Cookie held her hands out against the walls to keep herself from tripping down the narrow steps.

"I just wanna tell you that I've gotta girlfriend," Tony called to her.

And what does that have to do with anything? Cookie wondered. Rude, crude and dumb, he was a Yonkers guy who believed he was God's gift to women.

At the bottom of the steps, Tony set his bag on the ground. He was carrying a black suitcase, larger than a regular brief-case but not quite the kind of bag anyone would take to the office or away on vacation.

"Just so you know, I've got a girlfriend."

"So? Like I should care?" She felt so cold, alone. She hugged her arms around her chest. The temperature in the basement dipped low, not quite freezing, but cold enough to lodge into her bones. Her body core temperature was rapidly plummeting. She felt her life force draining away and she began to shiver.

"All the girls like me and it's been that way my whole life."

He pointed to a metal folding chair in between two small tables, all pushed against white concrete wall. Newspapers and boxes were piled everywhere. More overstock. The cramped cellar smelled of cardboard and Tony's manly cologne, an astringent aftershave.

Tony worked fast. Snapping open his briefcase, he pulled

out a black cushion with wires and plopped it on the seat of the metal folding chair.

"Sit there," he told her.

He pulled up two side tables, pressing her arms on top. "Keep your arms flat."

"My girlfriend's not gonna like this," he said, taking two thick black bands full of wires and sensors, lifting them over her head, positioning one band below her breasts and the other above her breastbone. Two of his fingers lingered a few seconds under the curve of her right breast. Cookie winced. His fingers probed a tad closer to the bottom of her breast.

"I don't tell my girlfriend all the things I got to do in my job and all the pretty girls I get to meet."

"But it's a job, you see." He abandoned her breast and wrapped a cuff around her arm, cinching it tight like a noose.

Yelling, "Come on, relax your fingers," he pressed two of her fingers into small pocket cuffs, protruding with skinny wires.

All wired up, Cookie drifted, telling herself she was in the realm of the unfamiliar. The entire side of Tony's suitcase was a monitor with graphs, charts, columns, and squiggly lines, resembling something she had once seen on a science program—a seismograph measuring earthquakes.

Tony asked her warm-up questions. *Do you have a mother? A father? Where do you go to school? Do you have a boyfriend?*

Cookie turned her head to the side and clenched her jaw to stop her teeth from chattering. She refused to answer any of his questions, especially when he asked, "Are you a virgin?"

Tony's wide forehead furrowed into tracks of bands of bulging knots. He looked confused because he did not get her to respond. He yelled, "It's not working like it's supposed to!" He yanked the bands around her chest. "It feels tight enough."

Feeling like she was suffocating, Cookie intentionally held her breath, bracing herself for him to cop a longer feel. His fingers dropped as though his meandering touch was accidental.

"I'm sorry. Jesus! I said to relax!"

He leaned over and glanced at the edge of her skirt, riding high up her bare thighs. Prodding her feet, he pressed her toes to make them lay flat on the floor.

"I told you not to cross your legs!"

"I didn't."

"Shut up. I mean, be quiet unless I ask you a question. I ask the questions around here."

Cookie closed her eyes and refused to open them until this whole thing was over.

"Ever steal anything?"

"Johnny got me the job at the Rite Aid. I don't even know how my father knows the store manager. You know Artie, right?"

"Uh-huh." Tony nodded.

"Jobs are hard to come by in Getty Square. There are always more kids needing to work than there are jobs."

"Didn't I tell you, no talking!"

Cookie went on. "Johnny constantly surprises me because he always ends up knowing so many people."

"I told you to shut up!"

"Artie is much younger than Johnny and a creep. Say what you want about Johnny Colangelo. My father's a jerk, but he does not try to cop a feel from a teenage girl and act like he's doing nothing wrong."

"I know your father! So what! What has that got to do with anything? You're confusing me!"

She had his attention now and knew he would lay off. She had grown too cold to talk. Her body trembled more from fear than the cold temperature of the basement. She shook her head but remained silent. She knew mentioning Johnny had put the skids on Tony's assault. Tony muttered to himself, a stream of guttural he-man invectives and profanities. Cheap background noise. The only thing she could make out from his rant was that her body temperature had dropped too low for her to complete the lie detector test. She would have to take it again, some other day.

Sunday January 14th 1973

Clouds did not take shape or visibly move. And that is too bad cause I own the clouds. Dim and dirty is the best way to describe Broadway and 242nd Street. Disgusting too.

I don't know why I'm feeling bad. Something is wrong and I can't figure it out. The world around me is not the way I want it to be and I can't do anything to make it change. I'm only sixteen and I shouldn't be feeling like this.

The IRT subway line runs on the west side of the Bronx and Manhattan. From 242nd Street to South Ferry that is where it runs. At one time the city had planned to add another terminal station north of 242nd Street. Nobody wanted the rich Riverdale kids who went to school at Horace Mann to have to walk four blocks.

But it never happened. There was also a rumor that the city planned to run the subway line all the way to Getty Square. But that never happened. A lot of things that are supposed to happen here never happen.

It's because of money. That is what I think. It's always about the money.

The subway station at 242nd Street has always been known as the end of the line and it is the end of the line. Believe me.

You see I go from one end of the line to the other end of the line. I better tell you why now just in case I don't make it to the end of my story. *Ha-Ha.* The North End is called Down the End cause that was once the last stop for the Yonkers Trolley. The terminal station at 242nd Street is the last stop for the Broadway IRT line cause it goes from the South Ferry that's all the way at the very bottom of Manhattan. Then it goes north up to the Bronx.

You might wonder why they don't call the South Ferry station the end of the line. They don't call anything in Manhattan the end of the line. Too many rich people live there.

The end of the line is for working people. You see. Me. Cookie Colangelo. I'm stuck going from one end of the line to the other.

242nd Street is a strange place. I did see people passing by—all men greeting me with confrontational stares. They make clicking noises and bold comments. I had long grown used to their unwanted (comeons or is it come ons?) and paid them no mind. They're always trying to pick me up!

A man came around to my side and worked hard to get my attention. He was close enough for me to hear the sound of his breathing. A small tingle of paranoia crept up my back. He stared at me while I pulled a pack of Marlboros from my pocket. He wore quilted navy coveralls. He's got on the kind of clothes worn by men who work with their hands. There are a lot of men like this. Dark men. Italian. Greek. Hispanic. Black. All of them are one and the same to me. Dark. Men.

Except this guy wore a stocking cap covering the top of his long black hair. His rough hand nudged me from behind. He prodded me to show that he was offering me a light. He actually touched me and I don't like that! His sudden move took my breath away. I wasn't accustomed to being man-handled unless it is my boss who is always trying to cop a feel. Or Tony Amendolito who was going to cop another feel until I found a way to stop him.

I saw the stocking cap man's crude expression while he held a match to light my Marlboro. He leered at me with his wide open mouth showing red gums. I didn't want anything from him. My hands were stiff from the cold. I dropped the cigarette to the ground and left it there.

He gave me an angry look. I thought he was warning me of what he would say or do if I didn't run away fast. "You're too young to be so ugly!" That is what he told me. The way he said it was so convincing. "Ugly!" He hissed at me. His eyes looked black. I remember that. It got me feeling so bad that I wondered if I was ugly.

-CCC

Five

Cookie waited in the Bronx to meet her very best friend in the world. She planned to meet Herman Lynch at the subway station on Broadway and 242nd Street. She stood at the foot of the steps leading up to the platform of the subway station. The elevated terminal rose in the air about thirty feet. Her eyes traveled upward, far beyond the terminal. The pale January sun could not be seen in the cold grey sky. A gothic scrolled street sign revealed its proximity to Van Cortlandt Park and hinted of the station's past, dating back to another century.

The station had been there seemingly forever. The wooden platform was the same type of well worn wood as the boardwalk in Atlantic City.

Back in 1973, the IRT subway line ran on the west side of the Bronx and Manhattan from 242nd Street to South Ferry. Today the route is the same, but the subway is called the Number 1 Train.

A small oval clock behind the glass storefront of a taxicab station read four o'clock. She heard the roar of the train overhead, gratingly skimming along the tracks into the station. A straight shot of steep steps descending from the station to the street level looked like one day someone would stumble or trip and take a hard fall. The station didn't have heat. There was no reason to climb the rickety steps to the top of the platform. Cookie kept her hands in the pockets of her navy peacoat, shuffling to stay warm, moving her feet but not really walking anywhere. She had not dressed warm enough to stand outside in the cold for very long.

Small staggered squalls of people drifted down the steps from the station but there was no sign of Herman. She figured Herman would be on the next train. Dented cars passing on Broadway spattered dust into the light wind. Spans of concrete loomed overhead. She thought she saw the landscape of the moon in the craters and potholes on the road. Car tires popped along the holes and ruts of broken pavement. There was no one here she wanted to see or meet. The man who had been bothering her earlier had gone away. She didn't have to look to know that he was no longer there. She could just feel that he was gone. It gave her a hard won chance to write about him in her black & white notebook.

Herman Lynch might have been the only person in the world she could count on, except for his grandmother Mabel Kerry, and Reenie Ruggerio. Cookie knew she needed to get another job. She would rather end her life than continue to work at Rite Aid. She lived in dread of having to shuck off Arnie Jelinek's creeping paws. She refused to take the lie detector test again. She hadn't done anything wrong. It was just the principle of the thing. She had never stolen anything.

Soon, though, she would steal more money than she could have ever imagined.

She heard the outbound train departing from the station in an ear-splitting squeal. The subway was noisy, so she did not hear the commotion to the south on 240th Street. Two squad cars and a Medic stopped abruptly by the steel subway stanchions. A small crowd of onlookers crept close to the scene. She did not expect to see the strange convulsive movement of a man sprawled on the pavement. She thought she saw blood but could not be sure and closed her eyes for a moment of silent prayer.

One of her relatives from long ago had died on the subway track. Grandmother Delia told the story of young Tommy Murphy who had too much drink one night and fell into the tracks on 238th Street in front of an oncoming subway. His body was smashed from limb to limb, broken pelvis, bloodied and bruised, but his face remained intact—that's how they knew it was him. Dead at twenty-two.

"Poor working stiff lad," Grandmother Delia had moaned. "Had Tommy Murphy been pushed into the tracks, instead of suffering from a nasty fall, there was no way of telling!"

Cookie desperately wanted Herman to show soon! She wanted to explain to Herman how she felt about Stanley leaving Yonkers. None of this prattle about Tommy Murphy that rocked around in her head! She wanted to talk about Stanley! A part of her believed he would never leave her. Another part knew he was gone for good. She felt that his leaving was not self-contained. He did not simply leave Yonkers. He had robbed light from her life. She wanted to tell Herman all of these things. She knew he would understand.

Herman had not been on the subway that had arrived at 4:00 p.m. Enough time had elapsed for everyone to have exited the train. Herman Lynch had never let her down. Then her thoughts took a darker turn. What if he had gotten off the train at 238th Street by mistake and someone had hurt him? As much as the black & white hate each other, they needed each other so they had a good reason to feel bad and feeling bad is good among those who live on the outskirts of the big city. New York men. The natives. The kind of men who mutter similar obscenities while they lose money together on the same bet at the Yonkers Raceway.

This section of the Bronx was mostly populated by dark men, Italian, Greek, Hispanic and Black, who called each other names. *Honky. Nigger.* Yes, they do call each other these names! These are the common names they hold high and affectionately toward each other. They are pet names. When they become angry, they yell the same pet names in a different tone of voice.

Now that she thought about it, they were all rather unkind.

Someone was hurt on the street and it could be Herman Lynch. She was always worrying about Herman not only because he was black but because he was different. He was different enough for black people in his own neighborhood to hate him.

The crowd began to thin. The dark cars were leaving, along with the police vehicles and the unmarked cars that had stalled to stare. Only a lone medic remained behind. Cookie wondered if this is how the place looked the night Tommy Murphy was killed on the subway track. She felt herself drifting in the cold air and felt weak enough to lean against the timber banister by the bottom of the steps. She did not know whether she should stay or leave and closed her eyes, again in prayer but to a different sort of god, a god of her own design and making. Her prayer would make Herman arrive any minute on the next train. She knew he wouldn't be late.

It happened so quickly that she did not see the hands coming from behind to cover her eyes. She did scream, not the blood curdling shrills heard in horror movies. Instead, it was a single startled wail, "No!"

"Cookie, what's with you?"

Herman's brown eyes flickered with confusion. "You know I always do that, Cookie girl."

"It's always been our thing," he told the young blonde beside him. Cookie couldn't tell if the blonde was a guy or a girl. Not that it mattered. The blonde was beautiful, elegant, as surreal as the first glimpse of seeing beauty in repose, a recollection after waking up from a vivid dream, the kind of dream she wanted to hold onto, and never let go if only she could remember the dream in its entirety.

Her heart was pumping hard at the sight of it all—the beautiful blonde with Herman Lynch. Herman looked warm in his overly large Pendleton wool-quilted coat. Plaids and checks in three shades of brown with a solid slate blue complemented his smooth brown skin. His Hush Puppies took on the same brown, the darkest brown tone, that existed in the configuration of his plaid coat. A soft blue cashmere scarf wound cowl-like around his neck. Herman Lynch had become a mighty fine dresser.

"Come on, Cookie, I want you to meet my friend."

Her eyes found his pretty blonde friend carrying a plush black coat that was draped over two arms, with sleeves rolled up, exposing bare white skin.

"This is Henry Kagan." Herman beamed his familiar grin. A delicate scar hid every trace of the harelip that once stalled his smile and had cut it into two.

"Cookie Colangelo."

Henry Kagan stood toe-to-toe with Herman but was his opposite in every other way. Henry was svelte and fine boned with porcelain skin so translucent that pale blue veins dappled shoots of sapling shapes along his forearms and the backs of his hands. He held out his hand to her. His fingers were long and slender. She was afraid if she took the hand that he held out to her, she would disappear.

And maybe that would be a good thing. She immediately felt as though she should be on guard. She did not know this Henry Kagan with his high cheekbones and light brown lashes that looked impossibly dark next to his luminous white skin. He was blonde, so blonde, fine whitish hair cradled his beautifully sculpted head like a knitted cap. The only attribute that was not in perfect harmony with all the rest of him was his ears, overly large and pointy, with a slightly elfin quality.

And they were off and moving. The three of them. The

fluidity in which they moved told Cookie that Henry Kagan was also a dancer. She felt clumsy and slightly out of step in between them. Herman lit a cigarette, took a drag and immediately shared it with Henry. Moving in tandem, mirroring their arm and leg movements, jumping over ruts on the sidewalk and turning in between crushed tin cans and fast food wrappers, they patterned a pas de deux of street dance. Herman's brown skin juxtaposed with Henry's unearthly shade of pale became a study to behold, a composition of dark and light, night and day blending into a threshold Cookie would have to cross.

Cookie felt jealous that Herman had never offered her a drag from his cigarette. That too, had always been their thing. Every so often, from under the fringe of his long blonde bangs, Henry looked at Cookie and gave her a shy smile, letting her know that he did not find her to be an obstacle to his newfound bond with Herman.

Things were changing so fast that she could not keep up. She had sought out Herman to confide in him and to receive his comfort. Talking to him from her heart was not possible. She felt like an outcast, the third wheel cycling outside of Herman and Henry who moved together as though they were one.

"Herman," she cried out, "I need to talk to you!!"

"Are you okay?"

"No, I'm not okay."

"What is it?"

Cookie shook her head but did not speak. She wanted to tell Herman so many things, but she was too shocked to see that he was not alone and could not summon the words to express the things that had been troubling her. At one time it had been the two of them, sometimes the three of them when Reenie Ruggerio was around. All of these other people had been coming between them. She had been with Stanley until he left for California. Reenie was with some older white guy who was psycho and drove a hot car. And now Herman was *so not alone.*

Henry's eyes danced between Cookie and Herman to determine the depth of their affection for one another. A thin smile emphasized the natural curl of his mouth. He gazed at Herman, slowly blinking his lashes as if he was letting Herman know that he was okay, okay with Cookie, okay with everything.

But it wasn't okay for Cookie. Herman had Henry! What a couple! Tongue in groove. Inseparable. Complete unto themselves. They had walked north, blocks away from the subway station into uncharted territory, the domain of buses, trucks and cars, still in the Bronx, but almost into Yonkers.

They stopped walking by the bus station on Broadway across the street from a bakery that looked like a dive, a hole in the wall, but had some of the best cakes in the city—known for *made from scratch* carrot cakes slathered with dreamy cream cheese frosting. The entrance to the old two-story red brick building had a flimsy aluminum screen door. A large orange awning that arched over the top of the building said *Lloyd's Carrot Cake.* The cartoony picture of a carrot running like the road runner (from the cartoon) ran across the orange awning.

"You have to get to taste those cakes," Herman told Henry.

Henry lit a cigarette and eyed Herman. "Too bad they're closed."

"It's Sunday." Cookie lit her own cigarette. "Thank God, it's Sunday cause I don't have to work."

Herman and Henry had not stopped moving, a small fact that did not go unnoticed by Cookie.

"Why do you have to work?" Henry asked her.

"Are you serious?" Cookie damn near blew smoke into his face.

Herman could tell that she had a big mad coming on.

"Cookie," he said, almost imploring her, shaking his head. "Henry's not from Yonkers."

"I'm so not Yonkers." Henry smiled.

"I got that." Cookie spewed a long plume of smoke and smiled for Herman's sake. She blew smoke rings upward toward the cold grey sky.

"Lloyd's got other cakes too, chocolate, red velvet, coconut cakes."

"The list goes on." Herman nodded and smiled. "German Chocolate Cake is my favorite."

"I'll remember that." Henry smiled.

Herman shot up from the ground and spun into a double pirouette.

Henry nodded approvingly. "Hold your arm out here," he demonstrated, "but not too far back," pulling Herman's elongated arm slightly behind his torso. "That will give you greater momentum to control your turn."

"Henry's been dancing since he was eight."

Henry's nod was modest. "I don't have Herman's energy. Herman is a natural. A star. What Herman doesn't have in training is more than compensated by his sheer athleticism and talent."

"Sheer athleticism and talent," Cookie said snidely. "I dare say! Do people really talk that way?!"

Herman looked bewildered. "Come on, Cookie, don't be like that!"

Cookie thought for sure Henry would stay behind in the Bronx. He looked like a rich kid from Riverdale. And he was clueless! Imagine asking her why she had to work! After the bus came, he would be gone and it would be the two of them. Then she could talk to Herman. She was so captivated by Henry's ethereal beauty that she had not dwelled on his black cashmere coat, which he put on, nattily leaving one button undone under his collar.

Dirty water clogging the curb was the final resting place for fallen leaves. The dank air was thick with unidentifiable fumes, some sort of putrid waste, maybe offal from the nearby butcher shop, and the awful stench of overflowing sewers. Even though it was Riverdale, it was still the Bronx. Mounds of garbage bags spilled over the sides of garbage cans strewn across Broadway. But Henry was so beautiful he looked like a pale flower growing in between the cracks of the broken sidewalk.

When the bus came, Henry hopped on with them and paid Herman's fare and his own. They sat across from one another in the back of the bus. Cookie perched herself on the back seat, sharing it with no one until Herman and Henry moved in synchrony as if both had the same thought to join her. She sat in the middle between them. Herman tilted his body to the side and leaned forward so he could see both of their faces. The way Henry and Herman looked at one another told her all she needed to know. Henry Kagan was more than Herman's friend. He was his lover. They were deeply in love. She felt so happy for him, yet, at the same time, she felt so terribly alone.

Six

Cookie was easily within walking distance to Reenie's apartment, but it was in the same building where Herman lived, and it was clear to Cookie that she was not wanted there. Herman had taken Henry home to meet his grandmother, Mrs. Mabel Kerry, but it did not go unnoticed to Cookie that she had not been invited to have dinner with them. She thought they would all move in the same direction, but Herman and Henry formed a tight knot and gave her a quick kiss-off. Brusquely moving in tandem away from her, she was left standing alone on New Main Street in Getty Square.

She knew she should have spoken up and said something to Herman. She knew he would not have wanted to hurt her on purpose. Tongue-tied, confused, she was too stunned to do anything other than to sulk. She considered the possibility that her annoying behavior had caused them to leave her.

The Carnegie Library was closed on Sunday. So was Rite Aid Drugstore. Otherwise, she could have tried to work an extra shift. Fat chance of that! It was hard enough working there, every day after school and most Saturdays. She did not want to admit it to herself, but the two friends she had long held close to her heart had drifted away like clouds racing in an unsettled sky.

She rounded the corner by the Yonkers Savings & Loan Building where her father had an office. She peered into the front glass store front of Happy House and smiled when she saw the lights were on. She pulled open the glass door and was welcomed by warm air that bore the scent of old wood and lemon oil.

Giorgio DeSutter had changed a bit since she had seen him last. His hair had grown increasingly wispy, a pale flutter of grey, like feathers belonging to a pigeon.

"Concetta." He flashed a too quick smile. The way he said "*Con-chetta*" was as if she was an abandoned infant that needed to be left on a hillside to die. He did not seem very happy to see her.

"I was just closing shop. What brings you here? It's been awhile hasn't it?"

"I have to give you credit, Mr. DeSutter, you really know how to make a girl feel welcome."

"I'm sorry. It hasn't been a good day for me. Hardly anyone came by today. As a matter of fact, aside from you, only one other person came here today. A looky-loo no less."

He looked at her with mild disdain, but she knew he didn't mean it. He had been born with a naturally dour expression. He had gotten rid of his pencil-thin moustache, which had given his face a gamine look—too innocent to be held accountable for his arrogance. Now he no longer had the moustache to prevent him from looking condescending, a complete snob. Despite the loss of hair on his face and head, his skin tinged with pink powder gave him a youthful appearance, younger than when she last saw him.

"What brings you here, Concetta? Hmm? I can always tell when you have something on your mind."

She wanted to cry out, *I'm lonely and don't know what to*

do with myself, but it was not possible for her to gush with such raw feeling.

Her attention roamed the gallery in search of where a cool glow was coming from. Crenellated bands of light splashed on an alabaster plinth and two small pink marble pillars, nestled in a far corner, all stark, bare, as if there was nothing in the store to show. She walked toward the window. Festoons of grey mist sprinted diagonally across the sky. The sun had gone down, and that did not bode well for Cookie or Mr. DeSutter. They both knew he needed to close the store and go home.

She walked carefully along the polished floor in between a black onyx counter and a wood-paneled glass display case that had once swelled with magnificent glass objects but now lay barren and dark. She stood there and stared at the display case, obviously unlit and lacking miniature glass animals, its usual menagerie of color. Its emptiness struck her as more than sad. It was a bad omen looming on the horizon. If only she could read clouds the way some mystics can read tarot cards.

When she didn't say anything to him, he began making assumptions as to why she was there.

"Still mooning over the blonde Adonis, eh? Concetta, by the time you're forty, you will have had so many men at your beck and call that you will have grown weary from all of the attention. You look younger than your chronological age, but the day will come when you will make these men wish they had noticed you sooner."

Then he stopped and looked at her. "How many times do I have to tell you that?"

Cookie didn't know what he was talking about. He had said the same thing so often that it had become meaningless. Aside from being annoying, he was wrong. And she resented him for the arrogance resonating in his voice.

"Well, just don't stand there! Say something!"

She crossed her arms and walked toward the back of the gallery in its inner sanctum, where a vertical window box framed in silver held a collection of obsidian disks in different shapes and sizes. She counted seventeen of them. Each stone, regardless of its unique design, was uniformly unblemished, smooth and polished to a high sheen. She wanted to touch one, but the glass of the display case stood in her way.

"Black clouds," she mused. "Your stones remind me of clouds before a big storm."

He hovered over her, emitting small pants and huffs to show his impatience. "You're being overly dramatic as usual!"

Cookie knew his bluster was all for show. Giorgio DeSutter was caring, the most sensitive person she had ever known, but she also knew that he wanted to close the store and go home.

"Have you been listening to anything that I've said?" His tone was imperious, but his eyes revealed some kindness.

"For you to be quiet is more disturbing than all of the nasty gum cracking and popping that you used to do! At least you cut that out, or I hope to God that you did for your sake!"

Cookie pointed to a round table of gilt-coated wrought iron legs, topped with thick opaque glass. Hundreds of Steuben glass animals, an entire menagerie, eager and animated, destined to climb into an imaginary Ark, once sat on the thick glass surface, catching flashes of amber from the afternoon sun. But now the animals were gone.

He seemed to know what she was thinking. "We've returned the entire shipment and will not be getting any more in."

"And the *Roogee* music boxes?" she asked.

"*Reuge*," he corrected her.

"Where are they?"

"Gone."

Cookie felt tears well in her eyes but she wasn't the crying kind of girl, a crybaby.

Giorgio DeSutter had always been careful not to get physically too close to her, or to anyone. He was adept at maintaining polite distance. It was uncharacteristic for him to touch Cookie on her shoulder as he did now.

"Are you okay?"

"I think so. Things are changing, that's all. Herman has a new friend."

"Henry?"

"So, you've met him?"

"Yes. Henry has a beautiful soul, not to mention his physical attributes, which are quite pleasing to the eye, or at least to my eye. He's also quite a talented dancer."

Cookie studied Giorgio's face and embraced his loneliness, so distinct and full, not of sadness but a surety of wanting to be alone and remote from everyone else in the world. She had always known his aching loneliness was there. It was an unspoken understanding between them.

"Henry has nothing to do with his feelings for you. Believe me, I know. Herman thinks the world of you."

"I need a new job," Cookie blurted. "I can't work at that place no more."

"Anymore." Giorgio corrected her.

"You can give me a job. I could sweep the floors and keep the shelves tidy. I can come in every day after school. You don't even have to show me what needs to be dusted. I'll take the garbage out. Anything you say. I even know how to operate a cash register."

She eyed the ornate antique cash register that sat alone atop a podium as if it was meant to be unobtrusive among glass *objets d'art*. "That old thing is a piece of cake to operate."

"I can't help you, Cookie."

"And I will be very, very careful. Everything is beautiful and glass, or mostly everything...."

He did not look so young now. The lines in his forehead deepened as he frowned, shaking his head. Stubborn resistance to Cookie, of giving her what she wanted—a job, dramatically altered his countenance. A sudden flash of darkness in his eyes made his face appear stiff and bitter.

"I'm sorry, Cookie. You're not listening to me. I really can't help you."

"Don't you understand what I'm saying? I'm at the end of my rope. I can't go back to that drugstore! Ever again!"

"I'm sorry. I fear having to tell you what I'm about to say for my own sake as well as yours." He took a long, thoughtful pause and looked upward to the soft yellow dome lights in the vaulted ceiling.

"Happy House is not doing well. Fortunately, I still teach music part-time at Gorton High School. Happy House will probably close by the summer, perhaps earlier in the Spring. The neighborhood has changed. The people who live here cannot afford expensive glass objects. They can barely feed their children. And the people who used to come here... They've stopped. They're afraid."

"Afraid of what?"

"The complexion of the neighborhood has changed," he whispered. "Of course, their fears are completely unfounded."

He tilted his head forward and gave her a perfunctory smile. "I will keep you in mind and ask around."

"If the store closes, how will I find you?"

"Ask Herman. He knows how to find me at school."

He moved impatiently toward the door. Like so many business establishments in Yonkers, there was only one door, one way in and one way out.

"Now I do have to close."

He scurried her along, almost pushing her out. "It's late."

She remembered the owl he had given her and thought mentioning it to him might soften his haste to get rid of her.

"I don't think I've ever thanked you enough for the glass owl. It meant a lot to me."

"The owl with the damaged eye? Yes, I know. It was throwaway to Happy House, but it was a treasure to you."

"You're not being very nice to me today. And I need someone to be nice to me."

He held the door open, letting in a waft of icy-damp air. "You once told me that you were going to leave Yonkers one day..."

His words rang flat but authoritative and true. "That's what you ought to be thinking of—how to get out of here."

And with that, she was dismissed.

Cookie had a way of building a hard veneer around her troubled heart. She began doubting herself, wondering if she was the same Cookie Colangelo who had once been as tough as a gangster and as carefree as a hippie, or the *soigné* siren of the night, heartfelt and in love with Stanley de Falco. She found herself feeling as though she had been bruised and bloodied, the same as Reenie Ruggerio. When Mr. DeSutter bid her farewell, she felt like a singularly flawed child who had no hope. She had no choice but to go to the hillside alone to die.

Wednesday February 14th 1973

I think about love a lot. No one else comes to mind except for Stanley. It's been cold and colder still without him. I imagine him on the beach in Malibu and it makes me feel warm. I can see clouds over his head. The clouds I see are soft puffs like pillows too magnificent to ever join together in a solid bank that will eventually darken the sky.

There were so many twists and turns between me and Stanley—enough to make me dizzy. The wind blew clouds big and billowy. Then small. Then big again. There were too many shapes of clouds to count. I try but I can't capture my feelings for him by writing. I can feel what is left. I feel the aftermath. I remember what I felt standing close to him and not even touching. I remember the way he moved his hips when he walked and when he leaned over the jukebox at the Midget Bar and when he stood over me. (Pssst I'm still not using commas cause I hate them.)

Let me tell you what he did to me. It was fun. (I can't write it here because Donny snoops on me and tells Johnny everything I do just to get me in trouble.)

Herman's gone all the time. He's dancing in the city. And he has Henry. Reenie Ruggerio is in a bad way. She is in big trouble. She is in the kind of trouble a teenage girl should not find herself in. (I can't write about it. Not right now.) She's still with the same psycho white guy and it's weird considering she used to only like black guys. I'm worried about her. I haven't seen her since the night that guy pushed her out of his car. Her grandmother's been sick. Her brother Billy Dee is strung out on smack. I worry that he's going to O.D.

Reenie needed two hundred dollars. I borrowed the money from Arky Lovato cause I don't know no one else whooz got that much cash. Arky is always good for having a wad of dough lying around.

I'm going to see Reenie later today. (I can't explain what's going on. I don't want to think about it.)

I have a new friend. Her name is Isabella María Fernanda Donovan. What an awful mouthful of a name! It's as awkward to pronounce as my full name: Concetta Mary Bernadette Colangelo. Why do you think I go by Cookie? I told her kids in Yonkers don't have names like Isabella María Fernanda Donovan. I dubbed her as Izzy and she puts up with that. She even seems to like being called Izzy. She has hair longer than any other girl I know and a Spanish accent. She lives in Riverdale with her Hispanic mother and Irish father. She tells me I need to learn how to talk right so people will not know that I'm from Yonkers. Whatever that means!

Izzy is doing bad in school. She's doing almost as bad as me. Sister Mary Eau Claire says neither of us are going to be able to graduate from high school—that would really suck cause I want to go to college.

Izzy wants me to get over this Stanley guy.

The worst time to be without Stanley is on a day like today cause it's Valentine's Day. I love Stanley too much to ever make my dreams match with my everyday life. The same clouds that I see right now could float over his head tomorrow and maybe he'll know that they are from me—that I sent them there like a lit-up postcard that says I love you.

It's been freezing outside and inside of my heart. The day will come when I will never think of Stanley again. (I'm starting to tell myself not to think of him. To tell myself stop. Stop.)

I have to go to work at my crappy job and you know what that means? I have to steer clear of my boss! What kind of way is that to work? What kind of way is that to live? Izzy tells me to get rid of my Yonkers talk. She says if I get rid of the Yonkers talk I will get a good job and have a good life. She said nothing about husbands. I like that.

-CCC

Seven

Reenie threw up sunburst-colored chunks in the scraggly red-leaf hedges bordering the parking lot. She used the back of her sleeve to wipe vomit from her mouth. Arky and Cookie stayed in the jeep. It was difficult explaining to Arky why they had to be at an unmarked building at seven in the morning. For once, Arky Lovato didn't say anything too stupid and he agreed to return in a few hours to drive them home. The heat in Arky's jeep was turned on high. Arky had not showered for the occasion and he stank.

Cookie wondered why he could not smell himself. She thought most humans knew when they smelled bad. It was entirely possible that Arky, who often went for days without taking a shower, had grown accustomed to his own stench. Despite his poor hygiene he was always good for a free ride and a honking laugh.

Only no one was laughing on this morning.

Arky did not know what was about to happen and if he had, he might have not had much of an opinion. His fingers slashed the cold morning air with nicotine-stained fingers. "It's so good to be back together again, but it's kind of early, don't you think?"

Arky cranked the volume on the radio that was tuned into Roberta Flack's "Killing me Softly." He flicked the dial to the morning news. *Today is February 14th, 1973. It's been eighteen days since the Vietnam peace agreement was signed. Navy Commander Brian D. Woods of San Diego has come home. Woods, a Naval aviator, was shot down in September 1968. After spending 1,609 days in captivity, Commander Woods is the first American prisoner of war to return home after the cease fire.*

Cookie heard the news about Vietnam, but she did not dwell on it. Stanley de Falco was in Malibu, far away from getting shot in the ass in the rice paddies of the Mekong Delta.

Arky handed her a wad of twenty dollar bills. Cookie didn't need to count it. Her days as small-time drug dealer and working as a cashier at Rite Aid had given her the experience to identify two hundred dollars by how it felt in her hand.

Cookie took the money, fled from the stink of the jeep, and joined Reenie in the parking lot.

The three-story red brick building was well over a hundred years old. The ground floor level was constructed entirely of granite blocks. Yonkers had always been famous for its abundance of granite. The roughhewn grey stone architecture had long ago dominated the older parts of the city. Facing east, the foundation of the building took on a speckled sparkle in the early morning sun. The old age of the building was in direct contrast to the clinic that it housed, which was new.

Reenie had been instructed not to eat a thing. Cookie took a seat next to her in the waiting room. The clinic was located on Hamilton Avenue in South Yonkers, right around the corner from the Professional Hospital on Ludlow Street. Cookie's one hand latched onto the red-painted metal pole banister while her other hand clutched Reenie's arm as they climbed two flights of concrete steps. Once they entered the old building, they descended a different flight of steps that led to the basement. Cookie felt as though she was descending into a dungeon. Whatever she wanted to call this place mattered little. Today was a day when death would triumph over life and life would triumph over a most certain death.

The clinic was so new that the reception room lacked a cushy couch or armchairs. The girls sat on two tan folding metal armchairs, the kind sported in old high school gymnasiums that are put up before or taken down after every game. The only other furniture consisted of a circular plywood table covered with leaflets and an end table with a lamp. Under the end table, a built-in cubby stored telephone directories. If Cookie didn't know better, she'd think this place went out of its way to make people feel uncomfortable. She felt the dingy walls closing in on her, closed her eyes and saw stars surrounding the lit imprint of dull images, like clouds. She felt bad for Reenie. She was quiet, hardly making her usual wisecracks. Cookie knew her friend was hurting and didn't know what to do about it.

A nurse came to where the two girls sat. Brisk and efficient, the nurse was fortyish, stout and wore a white uniform; she carried a clipboard and acted more like an office manager than a healing sort of person. Cookie handed her two hundred dollars. The nurse took the money and slowly counted the wad, mostly ten dollar bills, a few twenties and fives, and a whole bunch of ones. She wrote a receipt and ripped it out of a small notepad. Handing the receipt to Cookie, she said to Reenie, "I need to ask you a few questions."

"Can my friend come with me?" Reenie asked.

The nurse nodded and led both girls to a room as small as a closet in an old row house with fading yellow walls and two folding chairs. The nurse stood over Reenie and wrapped a cuff around the girl's arm. No one spoke while the nurse pumped the blood pressure cuff to tighten the band. The nurse pulled out a stethoscope, listened quietly, then released the cuff in a whoosh of air.

"We offer deep sedation or general anesthesia," the nurse

said, scanning her clipboard chart. "It says here that you've opted to be awake."

"I want to be awake."

"And you're sure that you want to go through with the procedure?"

Reenie nodded. "I can barely take care of myself."

"No one is pressuring you?" She cast a passing glance toward Cookie.

Reenie shook her head. "I knew from the moment I didn't get my period what I wanted to do."

The nurse handed her a form to sign. "Make sure you read everything."

Both girls scanned the page. They saw the words. Anesthesia. Complications. Infection. Recovery. Birth control. But little of what they read registered in their minds. They didn't talk about it. Neither girl had questions.

"I don't think of it as a baby. I found out so early," Reenie said.

The nurse walked Reenie through the release form. "Have you considered using a form of birth control? After today?"

Reenie nodded. "I guess I'll go on the pill." She signed the form and handed it to the nurse.

The nurse instructed Reenie to follow her. Cookie remained in her seat. "I better wait here."

"Please come," Reenie implored. "Is that okay?"

The nurse nodded. She did not smile or frown. She teetered on the brink of sincerity or warmth, neither of which came.

The small operating room contained a steel-grey counter and a single cot. The scent of a heavy duty cleaner, the kind used to wash walls and floors after someone has thrown up, permeated the space. Cookie fancied herself watching clouds that she could not see but only imagined. The room was cloying, reeking of astringent, full-strength antiseptic, threatening to slowly take her sins away, and to take away her breath along with it.

Lord have mercy, she felt like saying, just like the *Blind Owl* Alan Wilson, *Lord have mercy on my wicked son.* Daughter too. Girls are wicked too, Cookie thought. What did the Blind Owl know? He was dead. And she wouldn't have said *Lord have mercy* anyway because it was too corny to say it in real life and it only worked if you were singing the blues like the Blind Owl.

The doctor entered the room and barely looked at Reenie. Never once touching her, instead he focused on the chart.

"Regina Maria Ruggerio?"

"Reenie."

"We're going to give you a light sedative," he said, patting Reenie's cot. Her legs stretched in front of her body. The nurse started an IV, explaining Reenie would receive ibuprofen, lorazepam, and lidocaine.

"Drugs." Reenie smiled.

"You'll feel a little groggy," the nurse said. "That's why it's good to have your friend here... to help you home when it's over." She handed Reenie a hospital gown and a white sheet, explaining to leave the back of the gown open and to drape the sheet over her lap.

"Right." Reenie looked like she was about to throw up again and placed her hands over her mouth.

The nurse handed her a paper bag. "When was the last time you ate anything?"

Reenie shook her head. "I had pizza last night."

Cookie sat on a small stool in the corner. She tried to look away. "You're not alone, Reenie. Don't worry, I'm here with you."

"We're all, all of us, alone," Reenie said.

"Stop talking like me, Reenie. That's my job! Besides, you're not good at being deep and profound."

"Neither are you," Reenie shot back.

"You'll have to wait forty-five minutes before we'll start the procedure." The nurse left and closed the door with a curt metal click.

Reenie stripped off her faded jeans and got into a hospital gown that had white ties, like the shoelaces on sneakers, meant to be tied in the back. Cookie tried to tie the gown for Reenie, but she shied away from Cookie, scrunching the flimsy fabric behind her back. "I can do it myself."

Cookie had never seen a hospital gown and could not remember ever having been in a regular hospital. She had been to the nuthouse to visit her mother. This place felt the same except it was makeshift and very new—the first legal abortion clinic in the city of Yonkers. There had been other places where a girl could go, but you had to know someone. The law permitting legal abortion had just been passed by the Supreme Court. *Roe v. Wade.* Abortion clinics sprouted in the Bronx, Yonkers and Tarrytown, and every teen girl knew where they were located.

Reenie offered an occasional wisecrack. "Do I really have to put my feet up in those things? Looks like torture to me. Do you see those stirrups, Cookie?"

Cookie turned away from Reenie. She felt awkward about the situation and did not know what to say. She had never been one for making small talk anyway.

She wished she had a window to look out to find the sky, an uncommon cloud or two, floating toward a place beyond here. A queasiness came to her stomach when she thought of Stanley, knowing she had not been careful, any more than Reenie had been. Cookie was lucky. Reenie was not.

What would Stanley have done if Cookie had gotten pregnant?

There is no way she could have a baby. Marriage was not a possibility. Having a baby and giving it away to an orphanage run by nuns like Fangs was a sentence worse than death. She would rather be the arbiter of an unborn child's death than to deliver a baby to a lifelong sentence of madness, pain and despair. Pity too.

Everyone pitied the child who was unfairly victimized.

Looking away. Shunning the child. Pretending it did not exist. No one came to the rescue of an unwanted child. Every baby that comes into the world has unlimited potential, a veritable blank slate to receive new ideas and great grace from well meaning, God-fearing people. *Give me a fucking break!*

Cookie loved to take a joy ride with her own half-baked ideas.

Learning about birth control was by word-of-mouth. Most guys wore condoms. They complained they couldn't feel anything but did it because it was a lot better than getting a girl knocked up. Cookie didn't know anyone who was on the pill. She knew girls who watched their monthly flow and the consistency of their secretions on the crotch of their panties. Increasing wetness meant fertility. Drops as rubbery as hard snot meant the egg had dropped and disintegrated. The ovulation cycle was as mysterious as a fertility goddess if you believe in such things. The rhythm method was the only form of birth control sanctified by the Catholic Church. The church certainly did not suggest girls should check their panties! Instead, they told girls to keep an eye on the calendar to count neat moieties of ten days, from period, ovulation to a dry-safe spell. One size fits all. As if every girl in the world shared the same cycle of fertility and death.

Or they'd warn you not to have sex at all.

Forget about the little tongues of fire simmering inside, in the deep, like a hot furnace in the core of a volcano about to explode into a bed of burning embers.

Girls do want to have sex!

Girls were the givers of life and the givers of death. Cookie wanted to live above the underworld, rising to the level of clouds, floating along until eventually even the clouds deceived her.

"The drugs they gave me are not nearly as good as your ludes," Reenie said.

"I'm not surprised. I used to have the best ludes," Cookie said wistfully. "I'd rather deal drugs than work at Rite Aid."

"Then why don't you?"

Cookie shrugged. "I'm trying to play by the rules. You know....the good girl. I'm trying to be a good girl."

"Good luck with that."

"I know who I am." Cookie shrugged. But deep down inside, she knew only partially of who she was. Grasping for who she wanted to be was lonely and very confusing, as though she had to try on things for size to see if they fit. Most things did not last, whispering by with the futility of insignificant clouds in the sky. She remembered the tiny tendrils of roots, fibrous cords, covered with green moss, a blanket spreading across the ground, the natural bed she and Stanley had made. The scent of the air was rich with hummus from the earth and the fallen leaves. She remembered his scent too, as open as the earth, as fragrant and as full of musk as every tree in the woods.

"I knew I was pregnant the moment I didn't get my period," Reenie said. Her legs extended, sprawling the full length of the cot. She stared up toward the ceiling as if she was examining the stars in a night sky. "I never thought this would happen to me."

Reenie did not look like she was enjoying herself the night she was pushed out of the car. She might have been raped. For some weird reason, rape happened all of the time. Rape had been happening since the beginning of time, but nobody called it that.

The nurse returned, checked the IV bag and took Reenie's blood pressure again. She cranked a lever on the cot until it took the shape of a reclining armchair. She guided Reenie to lift her legs into the stirrups and placed her feet into metal footrests. Cookie heard the clink of metal. Twice.

"The doctor will be here shortly," the nurse said.

Cookie stared at the machinery next to Reenie's cot. A canister was attached to a long thin tube and a pump and a clear plastic tank. When the doctor returned, Cookie turned her head away from the machinery. From the corner of her eye, she saw the doctor insert a long thin needle in between Reenie's open legs, where it disappeared and stayed hidden even after Reenie said, "Ouch."

Cookie felt the stab too, a single pierce of sharp pain. She felt funny down there, down deep inside, in the same place where she had given Stanley a welcome mat to slide in and out of her small door. She cringed when she heard Reenie let out a moan. She did not need to look to know what was happening. The machinery turned on in a slow hum, then began to pick up speed, whirring like a Kenmore vacuum cleaner. The machine grew louder, purring in a rhythmic surge of mechanical energy, along with the discharge of fluid. A slight drag on its motor. Slowing. Reenie didn't say anything. Her breathing remained steady. She never cried out. Not once.

Cookie heard the machine shut off and listened to the sound of battening latches and switches. She saw shadows rebounding from the wall. The doctor and nurse had shifted away from the cot. As quickly as it had begun, it was over. The doctor left. The nurse placed the long tube and hose back into its holding sack. The clear plastic tank was no longer empty but full of watery red-colored liquid. Cookie looked up at Reenie. Her head had flopped to the side of the cot. She looked exhausted.

Cookie approached her cot with small tentative steps.

"Are you okay?"

"Truthfully, it was incredibly painful. I felt so much dragging and tugging." She looked at Cookie through cold eyes. "But it was much quicker than I thought it would be."

Cookie swallowed some. She was too tough to summon tears or to tear off the thick callous hide protecting her skin, her flesh and bones, and her heart. The hardest part was imagining what Reenie felt—having something soft and mushy inside that didn't belong there. Her innards were suctioned as if she was a sewer line constructed of galvanized pipe, full of the roots of overgrown trees, an invasive species. They were not the same trees she had relished that day with Stanley in the woods.

"She'll have to wait for about an hour, then she can go," the nurse said. She helped Reenie pull her legs out of the stirrups, then lowered her cot to a prone position. "I'll be back with some juice and crackers."

"How do you feel?"

"I have cramps."

"Bad? How bad?" Cookie wanted to know. "Now I'm starting to feel like I have cramps too."

"It's like my period but not as bad."

"What are you going to do about the guy?" Cookie lit a Marlboro and took a long drag. She threw the match dead center into the drain of the metal sink. When she went to hand the cigarette to Reenie, she noticed her hand was shaky. She told herself it was because she hadn't eaten anything.

Reenie brushed away the cigarette. "No. Not now."

"The guy? What are you going to do about the guy?"

"I don't know."

Cookie stroked the side of Reenie's face. A breakout of tiny pimples, hardly noticeable, dotted her forehead and upper cheeks. Her skin felt cool, too damp to touch for long.

Cookie rummaged in her rawhide saddlebag and pulled out a small yellow box of Whitman Sampler Chocolates. "Happy Valentine's Day."

"Some valentine." Reenie used her thumb to flick open the cardboard box. "Only four?"

"Do I look like I have oodles of money?"

"I don't feel like eating just yet. Want one?"

Cookie shook her head. "The chocolates are for you."

Reenie pulled her legs to the side of the slim cot as if she sought a fetal position of her own. Blood scattered small red flecks in the middle of the sheet. It was Reenie who had been on the table, spread apart like a sacrificial lamb, but it was

Cookie who had endured the ordeal for her. Cookie descended into the darkest regions of the earth and went to hell and back. Giver of life. Giver of death. She thought of dark clouds wearing black diamond fingers, getting blown by the wind and turning into the torrential rain of death and despair, falling hard; the rain was never going to stop.

Girls get pregnant; boys do not; yet they both have fun, and that's so unfair!

Cookie knew she had much in common with Reenie Ruggerio. She, too, had played Russian Roulette within the realm of the ubiquitous baby making machine that followed her everywhere and whenever she thought about kissing a guy, any guy, not only Stanley de Falco. No one wants to have their innards plunged like a clogged toilet about to overflow. Hell! No one wants to talk about it, or think about it, or know about it. Death had come but Reenie's life was spared. *Lord have mercy*. Reenie was wicked; Cookie was wicked, but at least it was over.

Eight

Zelda the Gypsy was right. Cookie had met a new friend! Isabella María Fernanda Donovan, who Cookie had nicknamed Izzy, was new to her school, an unproven but interesting attractive nuisance in Cookie's life. She did not expect that she would form a bond with Izzy on the same day as Reenie's ordeal. Cookie left Reenie after lunch hour, returning to school and timing her arrival so she would spend less than ten minutes in history class.

Miss Palmer did not acknowledge Cookie's late entrance into class. She wore her dark silver hair unfashionably short in a style that was frequently termed as a military buzz cut. Izzy sat in the next to last seat of the last row. Sitting in the penultimate seat was not nearly as bad as sitting in the very last seat in a row full of dummies. It was the equivalent of being stuck in a town stockade. Permanently imprisoned in the last seat meant Cookie was the dumbest girl in the class, but it was a wild ruse. Snickering snidely to herself, she knew she was smarter than everyone else in the room, maybe the world.

Miss Palmer arranged seat assignments by grade. The solid A students sat in the first row, viciously sparring with one another to get the first seat. Most of the students who sat in the middle three rows could care less about their seat assignments and were most accepting of their mediocrity. Seat assignments were always in a state of flux, subject to the latest test scores.

Being last in the class offered some distinction. It's a hell of a lot better than being ambivalent about perpetually floundering in the middle. There is tremendous freedom when you're at the bottom and can't sink much lower. Cookie immediately thought of Janis Joplin's song "Me and Bobby McGee." *Freedom's just another word for nothing left to lose.* Isn't that the story of life?

Despite her poor grades, Izzy had a beautiful speaking voice and was often asked to narrate the lines of Ophelia and Hamlet in English class. In history class, though, she had nothing at all going for herself. History required the rote memorization of spectacularly unnecessary facts about American government.

Cookie yearned to touch Izzy's hair. Unlike her own mass of cowlick fronds, Izzy's hair was straight, shiny and long. Izzy always kept her head tilted down, which could have been a gesture of humility or respect, or maybe keeping her nose pressed to her book gave her the appearance that she was studying. And what a nose Izzy had. From the side, her nose was ever so slightly turned up, a true retroussé nose, as the girl had described to Cookie in a lilting French accent on more than one occasion.

Cookie tried to get Izzy to turn around and peer into her face, but she would not budge, shirking one shoulder with mild annoyance. Cookie secretly suspected the girl had completely zoned-out to rid herself of the excruciating drone of Miss Palmer's lesson about the U.S. Constitution.

What good was it to be free in America when you have a boss like Artie Jelinek always trying to cop a feel?

If Izzy knew that sitting last in the row defined her as an

object of ridicule and subject to suspicion, she never said so. No one had anything to do with her, except Cookie, who had a soft spot in her heart for underdogs.

She tugged on a swath of Izzy's hair and gave her a good poke in the shoulder that would elicit a response. Izzy took the cue, stood up from her desk and nodded. Both girls turned to each other, grinned and walked out the side door of the classroom. Miss Palmer did not acknowledge their departure.

Cookie was surprised to see she had a welcoming committee. Behind Izzy stood Sister Mary Eau Claire. Izzy beamed a wide chiclet-toothed smile, but Sister Mary's usual good natured countenance had pinched into a scowl.

The nun beckoned with her hand. "Come with me."

Whisking down the hall, the two girls were on either side of the nun, trying to avoid looking at one another so they would not smirk and bring more trouble upon themselves.

Sister Mary did not corral them into a private space, nor did she mince words. "You must have some idea of how badly the both of you are doing in school!"

Cookie examined her fingernails, thinking she could use a good trim or take a chance on wearing the most flamboyant shade of nail polish ever created by Brucci—Vamp Red, the same color as the blood stains left on Reenie's cot at the clinic.

"I don't think you understand the gravity of the situation! You must know if you continue on this present course, you will not be able to graduate from high school! Am I making myself clear?"

Cookie nodded as though she understood, but she did wonder why the nun was so upset. Cookie had always managed to pull it together at the last minute. She fancied herself as being as wily as a fox crawling under barbed wire into a chicken coop.

The nun practically shoved them toward the front door of the school, and it was so rude, so unlike the Sister Mary Eau Claire that Cookie had grown to love. The nun turned her gaze to the sky and cursed, "Damn," which was unthinkable. Cookie knew something else was troubling her.

"It's supposed to rain, which means the roof will leak! I can't take much more of the leaking roof! One day it will cave in and kill all of us!"

Immediately after the last painful minutes of Sister Mary's tirade, Izzy latched onto Cookie and would not let go.

"I'm sorry," Cookie mumbled. "I will try harder. Promise. So, help me...."

Izzy trailed Cookie down the steps of Blessed Sacrament Academy, known commonly as BSA, and colloquially as the Bull Shit Academy, the Catholic, all-girls school where they both had the misfortune to find themselves.

On Park Avenue, Cookie could feel Izzy deliberately keeping pace with her. It was clear to Cookie that she was being stalked by Izzy but paid her no mind. She wondered why she ventured into the public domain at all. People, new and foreign and strange, astonished her into a state of complete fascination, where she was reduced to becoming a creature with insatiable and compulsive curiosity.

This was not the case with Izzy, however, who would be the dumbest girl in history class if it had not been for Cookie. The thought of talking to Izzy gave her a headache and made her feign boredom. She fixed her blank stare off into the dull grey distance toward the Hudson River, when she was really gazing at nothing.

Cookie did not want a new friend.

She looked to the sky to find solace in three fat white puffs of cotton that were unattached to one another. Clouds mystified her as much as they held meaning. Cookie and Izzy walked in the same direction, against the wind from the river. She was trying to tell herself to stop. She had resolved not to trouble Stanley's mother over her own heartache. But she knew she was losing control and wanted to break the promise she had made to herself.

She came to the Café Trento on Ashburton Avenue, where Stanley's mother worked, and hesitated before going into the bakery. She told herself *Stop*. She had to let go of Stanley. He was gone. There was no way Bertha wanted to hear her moping on and on about her son who probably didn't tell her what he was doing, or not doing!

The sky was sliding by in parade of snails that appeared as conch-shaped clouds, oddly reminiscent of a plate of hot scungilli, disappearing under one big cloud after another. A cauldron of light grey mist drifted to the west in a pattern of unusual air currents. Cookie felt chilled, then only seconds later a hot spot in the sun made her feel warm enough to take off her jacket.

Restivo's Florist brimmed with customers, some wearing heavy overcoats, others sporting red sweaters or red short-sleeve shirts in honor of Valentine's Day. They swung in and out of the florist through the same door, one door like so many other doors in Yonkers: Louie's Italian Restaurant, Greens, Grants and Happy House. Only here, people leaving the florist carried bouquets of roses, carnations and small plants staked with small red plastic hearts.

An Alpha Romeo convertible streaked into the alley between Café Trento and the florist. Cookie was intrigued with the car, red and shiny, gleaming with Italian racing precision. Cookie immediately saw who was in the passenger seat.

Toni Ferlinghetti gave Cookie a smidgen of a smile, barely moving her lips and a shy wave, before turning away. She acted as though she did not know Cookie. Cookie tapped on the window to say hello, prompting Toni to roll down the window. "Toni? It's me, Cookie! Long time, no see! What are you doing in that car?"

A guy burst out of the car, yelling, "Hey, don't touch the car! You put prints on the car and you're gonna get hurt."

Cookie shrank away from the car, but she took note of the guy. Tony Amendolito. The Rite Aid lie detector guy. He scanned Cookie's body as if he had committed every inch of it to memory and had already taken her by force. But he did not acknowledge that he knew her.

Enraged, his forehead throbbed in rippling rows, and he shook his fist at her. "You don't put no fingerprints on my car, got that! You hear me?"

Suddenly she put it all together. Tony Amendolito was the same guy who had been with Reenie Ruggerio that December night in the snow. He had thrown Reenie out of the car. Cookie stood still, stunned, remembering what Reenie said had happened that night.

Izzy gave Cookie a furtive glance and spoke under her breath. "I can't believe he treated you like that! He's so rude and uncouth."

Cookie kept losing track of Izzy, forgetting that she was there, but Izzy had never left Cookie's side. The girl had appeared in her life like a sudden apparition who had been put on this earth by none other than Zelda the Gypsy.

Giving Cookie a shy smile, Izzy lowered her eyelids as if she was attempting to be modest. "You've got to get away from these Yonkers guys." Then she tucked a loose strand of Cookie's hair behind her ear and whispered. "I'll take you to the city where there are lots of young men who would never treat a girl this way, but you've got to stop talking like you're low class. You live next to the biggest city in the world!"

Cookie nodded and looked into Izzy's eyes as though she understood. She was not even mildly interested in having Izzy as a friend but found the girl both endearing and very attractive. She meant to be polite, not unkind, and speculated that if Izzy was her new friend, it didn't mean she could throw Reenie to the wind as though she was a castoff. Reenie acted tough, but deep down inside she had a big heart. No one deserved to be mistreated, the way Tony Amendolito had treated her. Besides, Reenie didn't have anyone else, except Cookie.

In the alley between the bakery and the florist, a young dark boy about nine began beating a garbage can with a baseball bat. He wore a white cotton muscle shirt, exposing his sinewy tendons. No jacket in the cold—that meant something. He banged maniacally on the can without mercy. He was obviously upset. His primitive notion of anger, revenge, extermination, the Italian vendetta, was exposed for all the world to see as he clanged a wooden bat against a metal can. The sound of his hatred continued to thunder as both girls watched Tony leave the florist carrying a small wrist corsage in a plastic box.

"Stay away from the car! Got that?" He gave Cookie a dirty look before he got back into his car.

Toni Ferlinghetti had never bothered to roll down the window, but she could hear her. "Shut up, already," Toni yelled at him. "You're always mouthing off and it's gonna get you killed someday."

"Toni and Tony," Cookie said. "Who would believe such a thing could happen!"

Izzy locked arms with Cookie and led her down Ashburton Avenue. "I know how you feel about Stanley. I am waiting for Antonio. And he is so gorgeous! She closed her eyes in dreamy state. "I am betrothed to him, but he is far away, across the sea, in Barcelona," she emphasized.

She pronounced the c in Barcelona as a th, as if she had a lisp.

The girl blathered on. "My mother grew up in Puerto Rico, but she also has relatives in Europe. We have relatives everywhere. All over the world," she said, grandly sweeping her arm through the air.

Izzy's eyes were large and brown, yet widely set apart, inquisitive, as if she had been meaning to look into Cookie's soul. "Everyone knows your heart has been broken, Miss Cookie."

Cookie felt her face flush, but she wasn't about to gush with grief, not to this Izzy creature or to anybody.

She thought of Reenie. She had undergone an abortion acting as though it was nothing. She knew Reenie well enough to know she was hurting inside but didn't know how to express her feelings. Cookie felt cold and very alone, afraid for Reenie, afraid for herself. She could have easily been in Reenie's place.

Izzy tugged Cookie's sleeve. "I've been noticing you and I want to be friends with you."

She lunged for Cookie and embraced her. Cookie had no compelling reason to stop her. Their schoolgirl torsos came together in folds of soft wool and crisp cotton shirts; the tips of their toes were almost touching. Cookie felt something sharp stab her chest. Izzy wore a necklace that had a gold charm of the Sacred Heart of Jesus. The reddish gold heart was shaped like a Valentine's Day candy box and encircled with an aura of light. A tiny diamond chip winked at her. The heart itself bled small beads of gold blood. Then Izzy confronted Cookie with a silly, if not impertinent, question. "Will you be my Valentine?"

Saturday March 17th 1973

Johnny used to march in the St. Patrick's Day Parade with the Yonkers Military Band. I remember seeing him in the parade when I was a little kid. He played a big drum that sparkled in the sun.

He'd be wearing a Kelly green uniform. Bright yellow-gold braid ran down the sides of his trousers and across the shoulder of his suit jacket. His shoes were spanking white. I don't know how he kept those shoes so white. Mud from the dirty street splattered all over his shoes. I think he had white shoe polish to get rid of the black marks. A big yellow-gold plume sticking up from his Kelly green top hat looked like a tassel on a fancy curtain. His hat had a white chin strap—I never saw nothing like that before. It's not like that hat was going to fall off his big head.

I'd stand at the bottom of Herriot Street with Grandmother Delia. He'd always find me in the crowd and give me a big grin. He couldn't wave to me with those darn drum sticks in his hands. Think about how'd that look—some guy waving big sticks in the air!

I don't know what kind of drum he played. I don't know anything about music. I do like the way music sounds. I can't sing or dance or play any musical instrument. Johnny did his best to get me to play. Guitar. Flute. Piano. Organ. Nothing took.

Johnny got exhausted and gave up on me.

Don't you give up on me too!

I'm only writing this cause I want you to understand who I am. Maybe then I'll know too.

There are rumors floating around—saying that the parade is going to stop passing through South Yonkers. The people who have moved into South Yonkers are different. And the people who march in the parade are scared of the new people who've moved in. The new people all look like Herman and Mrs. Kerry or Izzy. And you know what that means? They're black or Puerto Rican.

They don't want no black people around the parade route cause they'll be standing on the street and be up to no good—that's what most white people say. And nobody's not ever going to let black people be in the parade.

Johnny once said to me that "Blacks & Whites don't mix. Not around here! This is Yonkers!" Whatever that means! Cause Johnny has lots of musician friends who are black! But he doesn't see it like that! He says that "They're not black. They're musicians!"

Johnny played those drum sticks every night and on the weekend in jazz clubs in Harlem. He'd be jamming with real musicians. Most of them were black. He loved his music so much. He loved his music more than me or Donny or Kitty. Then something happened to Johnny. He stopped playing music. I don't know why. He just stopped.

He got exhausted and gave up on himself.

What was I writing about? *Oh. The parade.*

No one's going to the parade this year. Not Reenie. Not Herman. Not Mrs. Kerry. Not even Grandmother Delia. Nobody I know is going. I've got to work that day anyway. The haunting wail of the bagpipes will mourn for me now cause I am one of the dead. I am a working stiff who's never gonna get out Yonkers. I wish I could get the hell out of Yonkers! But I don't have no money!

Things have gotten bad at work. Tony Amendolito hasn't come back to give me a lie detector test. Every time I see Artie Jelinek—I-I get away from him—fast. He won't give me a cash register cause I haven't taken a lie detector test. I always get away from him before he can cop a feel. I have a feeling that something really bad is going to happen today cause it's St. Patrick's Day. And you know what that means? Everyone's going to be outside. Acting crazy. Acting wild. Drinking too much. The luck of the Irish doesn't mean nothing. I mean anything. The luck of the Irish will only get you so far.

-ccc

Nine

Arky's dented relic of a jeep idled on Palisade Avenue alongside of Cookie, where she waited for the bus in front of Morsemere Market. She cursed her lime green cotton jacket that she wore to celebrate St. Patrick's Day. It was the only green coat she owned. The temperature had dipped from high to low. The rain set her hair in frizzy ringlets that crept down to her shoulders. She felt herself shivering. She certainly wasn't scared of Arky Lovato, but Toni Ferlinghetti, who rolled down the jeep's window, was a monster.

Wearing a thick green headband festooned with green ribbons and dangling plastic shamrocks, Toni gave Cookie a look that said, you're dead.

The jeep threw out a low throaty noise as if it needed a new muffler. Snake-shaped smoke plumed from the jeep's tail pipe, dispersing nasty-smelling fumes into the air. Arky beeped his muffled horn, rolled down the window and called to Cookie.

She couldn't understand what he was saying. He had graduated from pot and hash, mushrooms and acid, and downers and ludes. Whatever he was on, made him talk as slow as a wooly-headed cotton picker from Arkansas. If he said more than two words, he coughed as though he had a touch of postnasal drip.

Cookie knew why he had come looking for her. He wanted his money.

Toni Ferlinghetti did the talking. "What's this I hear about you owing Arky two hundred dollars?"

Cookie gave her the finger. "It's none of your business."

"I'm making it my business." Toni turned her attention to Arky. "And wipe the stupid look off your face!"

Toni was never good one-on-one. The threat of intimacy caused her to get ornery—that was her key attribute as the reigning Queen Bee of Italian Girls. She cracked her gum nonchalantly, spacing her string of pops far apart as if she was taking gum chewing to a higher form of art.

"Get in," Toni told Cookie.

"I've got to go to work."

"We'll take you." The back door behind Toni creaked open in a nasty crunch of rusty metal. She had a menacing look in her dark eyes, a feral gaze that was a sure sign of trouble. "I said to get in."

Against her better judgment, Cookie hopped into the back of the jeep. She didn't have to go with them, but it was better than standing around in the rain, waiting for a bus. She was relieved to find out that Arky didn't smell bad. He always took better care of himself when Toni was around. Cookie rummaged in her saddlebag and pulled out her pack of Marlboros. Before she could strike a match, Toni turned around in her seat and lit her cigarette with a lighter.

"What I want to know is why you borrowed two hundred dollars from Arky?"

"It's none of your business."

"Like I said, I'm making it my business."

"Yeah," Arky said. "I was supposed to have my money back by now."

She felt her stomach tighten but had no trouble speaking the plain truth. "I'm working as hard as I can. I'll have it for you next week. I promise."

He turned around to look at Cookie. "Promise?"

"Will you keep your eyes on the road and drive," Toni shrieked. "You're gonna get us killed!"

The jeep was a wreck that couldn't go fast enough to get into a deadly crash. Cookie stared out the back window and tried to find the sky, but it was lost in grey mist—the worst kind of cold rain, fog drizzling from fallen clouds. Angels going to hell and back; the sky felt that way to her. Even though she couldn't see the sky, she knew what it looked like because it belonged to her.

She was sorry she had borrowed money from Arky, but it was the only way to get cash fast. Reenie couldn't sit around and wait. And she had no money. Her boyfriend, who turned out to be Tony Amendolito, had told her if she didn't get rid of it, he'd beat it out of her.

Cookie stared at Toni, wondering how she had gotten involved with Tony Amendolito, but there was no way in hell she was going to ask her.

"We're getting too old to be acting this way." Cookie's tone was philosophical. "I guess, we're all growing up, whether we want to or not." She didn't think they were listening.

"Cookie, for once I agree with you." Toni lit a cigarette and took a drag. She turned around, and surprisingly, gave Cookie an agreeable smile that was almost charming. "I can't believe I just said that. Who'd think I'd ever agree with you. But when you're right, you're right. We are getting old."

Toni looked fragile, almost sincere in the harsh grey light of the afternoon. "Cookie," she said affectionately, "I am getting old and if I don't get engaged soon, I'm going to be all washed up."

"You're only sixteen."

"Seventeen. I turned seventeen." Toni fidgeted with her

cigarette and fluffed her hair as if that one nervous tick would never prevent her from becoming a starlet manqué and somebody's muse.

"It's never going to stop, is it? You think you're going to marry your way to freedom, but things don't work out that way."

"What are you talking about?"

"I don't need to spell it out for you, do I?"

"I was never good at spelling," Arky said. "That's why I didn't finish high school."

"Who asked you?"

Cookie leaned against the front seat and talked toward the back of Toni's head. "You've got to make your own way in life. You can't rely on a guy or getting married. No one does that anymore. It's 1973 for god sakes! You won't even learn to drive!"

"Don't try to second guess me." Toni turned around and glared at her. "I know what I'm doing."

Cookie shrank back into her seat. Toni Ferlinghetti knew she had a powerful effect on people. She was abusive on purpose. It was her way of thwarting the slightest suggestion of veiled criticism that might come her way in the normal but negative discourse of dealing with the world at large and so close to New York City.

Cookie was immediately overwhelmed with disgust for their lives that were so small and insignificant that they could dismiss reality in its most base form as fantasy or a cruel illusion. But here she was, she was there with them too. Wasn't she? Whatever phase of life you're in, you're always defined by the company you keep. Cookie had no idea why she was with the two of them in a broken-down jeep, as if it was indeed a privilege and an honor.

She needed air. She needed to breathe. She tried to roll down the window, but it was broken and would not budge an inch.

"You know what, Cookie? You've always been a big know-it-all, but for your information, I've got a boyfriend, a serious boyfriend."

"When's the big date?"

"It's coming, I can tell you that. I'll let you know."

Cookie laughed. "Is he rich?"

"Well for your information, he drives a red Alpha Romeo and has a good job."

"Tony Amendolito?"

"How do you know who my boyfriend is?! What are you nuts! You're talking about my boyfriend! My frigging boyfriend!" Toni's face turned fierce. "I'll fight you!" She pointed her cigarette as if it was knife, about to poke Cookie's eyes out. "See this little finger?! I'm willing to lose it in a fight to kill you! I'll fight you to the death and stomp on your face!"

Cookie threw her head back and put her hands up to protect her face. "I don't want your boyfriend. I was just being polite. Believe me, if he's into you, he's not my type."

"And what type is that? That darkie with the deformed lip or the Vietnam vet psycho baby killer?"

The more Cookie thought about it, the reality of Toni and Tony as a hot item would mean he would leave Reenie alone. The jeep trawled down Palisade Avenue toward Getty Square as if it were a seaworthy fishing vessel waiting for a big catch. Rows of eight-story, soot-stained brick buildings sat behind concrete barricades and chain link fences. The Schlobohm projects cordoned off people as if they were untouchables under siege in a war zone. Nobody was proud of Schlobohm, and referred to it as Slow Bomb, yet everyone in Yonkers knew someone who, at one time or another, had lived there.

"That's where you're gonna end up!" Toni gazed out the window toward the projects and flicked her burning butt into the street. "Rolling in the gutter with the ghetto trash, that's where you belong! With the animals. They're just animals! Such filth! Filthy animals! They're disgusting! They disgust me!"

Cookie imagined a cloud or two, then more, shaped like rocks; stones, some heavy, some light, multi-colored, jagged and sharp; clouds were like rocks and stones, and they were after her heart. She saw archipelagos of clouds razoring through white crested mountains in the sky. The fog had settled and hovered in the air, dissolving into mist, a fine rain.

Up ahead, orange parking cones blocked the road, where a sign read: *Street closed.* The jeep lurched to a stop.

"Looks like we're at the end of the road," Arky said.

"It's to keep the animals out of the parade. Disgusting! They fucking disgust me!"

"The road's closed for the parade," Cookie told them. "Just let me off here." She squirmed in her seat and moved toward the door. "I'll walk into the square or catch a bus."

Toni's face grew dark, harsher than before. "You're the one who started the trouble. Remember? If you don't give Arky his money back, then I'm going to stick my boyfriend on you, and he'll hurt you! Got that?!"

Arky pulled to the side of the road to let Cookie out. She dashed into the street, where she pressed her back close to the jeep to be safe from other cars, but traffic was nonexistent. Everything was closed off for the parade.

Toni rolled down her window, but not to say goodbye. "You know what's worse than death? It's when you owe somebody money and you're not paying it back!"

Cookie looked at Arky. He shrugged and threw his hands up as if he had absolved himself of the situation. "You never treat me like I'm a person. You treat me like I'm invisible, but let me tell you, I'm nobody's patsy."

"Yeah!" Toni smiled. "You see, he's sticking up for himself for a change!" She slapped him on the arm to show her approval. "You're doing great!"

"What have you done to him?" She had never heard Arky talk that way before. "You stay out of it," she told Toni. "This is between me and Arky! I'm working extra hours to make more money!"

Toni's shamrocks shook on her headband, yet her words were measured. "If I were you, I'd watch my back!"

"I'm tired of the violence. The hatred. I don't want to be here no more." Cookie kicked the jeep's rear bumper, causing it to dislodge. One side of the bumper scraped the ground in a metal heap that would drag along the road if it wasn't fixed. The bumper had been held together by black duct tape. She pressed the tape on the bumper to hold it back in place, but it kept falling off, hitting the ground. She had not meant to cause Arky harm. He had always been her friend, but money changes things.

Ten

Jumbo bottles of mint green Scope were the color of Johnny's military band uniform, the same Kelly green and metallic gold combination, so Irish, and common to the colors worn by the sports teams of Sacred Heart High School. Cookie pulled the bottles from the back of the shelf to the front, where they could be seen. The whole point was to make the shelves appear to be full of product, inventory, stuff.

She peered to the side occasionally, never turning all the way around in case Arty Jelinek was slinking down the aisle, intent on putting his hands down her pants. What a groovy place to work!

First came the mouthwash, then toothpaste, tubes of Compound W to thwart off warts, Anbesol to kill mouth pain, and toothbrushes glowing in neon orange, green and pink.

Without being assigned a cash register, she did not have a purpose. The hours passed slowly. Black storm clouds oozing from a turbulent sky at night can never be seen in their entirety. The outer edges of clouds at night could only be felt, of that she was certain, and also of knowing that a strange terror awaited her. If he touched her again, she was going to scream.

She saw a box of Breck Shampoo on the floor of the aisle and fancied herself in an ad as a Breck Girl, except her hair was the color of a scruffy street sparrow, a distinct disadvantage. Most Breck Girls were blonde with pretty hair.

The large box of Breck Shampoo was in the wrong aisle and heavy. She pushed it along the floor with her foot, into the next aisle that had hair products. Shampoo with names like Pert, Agree, and Lemon Up stared at her. The scent of Herbal Essence Shampoo tricked her into remembering what Stanley's hair used to smell like—it was silly to think that shampoo told the story of their brief lives together.

It was taking too long to push the box with her feet, so she braced herself to pick it up, and did just that, heaving it forward. The momentum swept her away and forced her into the next aisle, where she startled two young black girls. Cookie dropped the box.

The two girls had not seen her until it was too late. One had paisley pedal pushers, the other sported flouncy stovepipe pants. Both wore oversized, long-sleeve sweatshirts, big and loose for good reason. The one in pedal pushers had snatched a jar of Ultra Sheen Extra Dry Hair Conditioner and stuck it in the waist band of her pants. Caught, red-handed, then and there. The girls stared at her, hardly breathing, not moving.

"What have you got in your pants?" Cookie had seen her do it and now she was going to shake her down. "Put that back!"

The girl in pedal pushers jumped over the box of Breck Shampoo, scoring a high jump over the hurdle. The other girl wasn't nearly as athletic in her stovepipe pants and tripped over the box. Cookie was right behind them. As they reached the front of the store, Cookie had gained on them and grabbed their sweatshirts. The girls felt lighter than air and didn't put up much of a fight or protest. The smooth polished skin of their brown faces glowed—they were young, maybe eleven or twelve, same age as Donny.

"Whatever you've taken, put it back!"

Confusion erupted behind the cash registers. No one knew what was going on. The two girls weren't trying to get away and the one wearing pedal pushers dropped the small jar of hair pomade onto the ground. Artie Jelinek swooped down into the fray and picked it up.

"They took something. I saw them!"

Artie glowered and yelled at Philomena Sukla to call the police.

"You don't have to get them arrested," Cookie yelled. "They're just little kids."

Artie had not seen what had happened. He scowled at Cookie and, without saying a word to anyone, scurried the girls away into his back office. The girls might have been younger than eleven or twelve, maybe ten. In the heat of the moment, Cookie had just reacted. She had done what she had been told to do to stop shoplifting. And then she realized what an awful, awful mistake she had made.

It was not clear how word about the busted black girls surged out of the store and into the street. In the aftermath of the parade, people were everywhere, breaking up into small clusters, gangs of four or five, swarming in front of the store, where there was a bus stop. The sidewalk was jam-packed with black bodies, spilling onto New Main Street.

The news spread as fast as a Yonkers fire. Big fires were common in South Yonkers. Old tenements and claptrap apartment buildings incinerated in the middle of the night. Buildings burned slow like molten lava or blew up into one old volcano at a time, throwing hot cinders into the air, crackling wood, melting asbestos walls and floorboards. Charred remains and chain link fences marked vacant lots—that's all that was left. No insurance was ever paid out. The banks never owned the buildings. No mortgages. Redlining. People lost everything they had. They were left homeless.

Arson, some said, paved the way for urban renewal, high-rise public housing projects. Corrupt politicians and their cronies made money. Dirty money. People knew what was going on, but there wasn't anything they could do about it. People were waiting to go wild. The threat has always been there. The threat had been there for years.

Within minutes, the door to the store was propped open. Guys kicked their black Pumas and red and white Adidas shelltoes against the storefront glass. Banging, leaning in together, butting their heads, they broke open a fire hydrant. Water gushed onto the sidewalk, flooding down New Main Street. Garbage cans were emptied on their sides. Dogs roamed, running around in circles within the growing angry mob. This was the only relief they would get from knowing two of their own young girls were being held in custody. Unfair! It was always the white folks who did nasty things to their kids—that's when the real trouble began.

Guys poured into the store, broke the glass on the display case holding Timex watches, and grabbed everything they could—looting. Mamas too, carrying armloads of small appliances and Tupperware, saying over and over "Honky Mutha Fucker," as they helped themselves to everything they could carry away in their arms.

Heat from the wave of bodies felt like fire. The store was as hot as hell. The heat was a form of blood simple. No one was dying and no one was killing anybody, but everyone was sick to death and that is the same thing. Delirious and out of control, the mob took what they could, kicking the rest, entire shelves of products, to the floor. Cookie thought of her black clouds swirling their diamond fingers, lashing like a whip, getting blown by fierce wind and turning into a tornado. Only the rain could put out the fire. There was hell to pay before the police arrived. Carole Zukowski ducked to the ground behind the cash register. The other two cashiers were gone. Only Cookie was in the front of the store in the direct line of fire and alone.

Then she figured out how the word hit the streets so fast. She came face to face with the scariest girl in the hood. The two young girls who had been shoplifting were working with a mentor. It was an inside job.

Once Cooke realized who she was dealing with, her face flamed as hot as the core of mercury. She was in a ball of fire too close to the sun to guess the shapes and colors of clouds. She could not see anything except for the beefy face of Mosella Moran, who had a whimsical green bow tied around her fro, which would have been disarming if it were not for her crazy-mean look in her eyes.

"What are doing, girl? I'll wipe your sorry ass on the ground and stomp on your face."

Her arms were folded across the bulk of her chest. She wasn't what you would call fat. She was large and wide, rippling with dense rubbery muscle that you could pound on. Beat her up bad, and she wouldn't feel a thing. Everyone in Yonkers knew Mosella Moran. Rumor had it that she carried a razor blade in her fro.

She clicked open a switch blade. "I'll cut you."

Giver of life. Giver of death. Cookie emitted a raspy gasp of fright. Adrenaline coiled up Cookie's back and left her head and neck tingling. She leapt into the air and kicked Mosella in the hand, knocking the switchblade to the ground. Mosella scrambled to get the knife but was unable to move fast enough. Cookie struck her on the head and shoulder. She swung back and tried to pull her hair but could not get a good grip and it only served to increase the force and fervor of Mosella's blows to Cookie's face. Cookie never flinched and did not back down. Backing down would mean death. She kneed Mosella in her stomach hard and took her to ground.

A bunch of guys broke them up, pounding on the counter in front of the cash registers. It was another way to vent. "Don't you know, the cops are gonna come here and both of you be going to Juvie."

Cookie stared at Mosella, not caring much, keeping her cool. It didn't mean a thing. Within moments, Mosella had latched onto Cookie's legs and dragged her to the ground. Her fall was cushioned by several pairs of handsome sneakered feet. She heard "Honky, Honky Mutha, Honky badass. Honky *yous* is having a bad dream."

Much to her surprise, she was picked up off the ground by a crowd that demonstrated their fondness for all things white by shoving her back up onto her feet like a pop-up doll ready to take two more blows to her face.

Cookie's mouth tasted like blood and her eye had puffed. Mosella had gotten the best of her but she wasn't going to die by giving up. Fists in front, elbows close to her body, she jabbed to the side and danced to keep Mosella away and off her game. Mosella was strong but Cookie was fast.

In the large crowd, shuffling ensued, pitting black against white, black against the nearest aisle's endcap, and black man against black man, as they formed a closed tight circle around the front counter and rocked a cash register violently, trying to get its cash drawer to open. The crowd and its animosity grew until the store became embroiled in violence that involved two opposing gangs using their fists and knives.

But there were no guns.

Cookie stood her ground, facing Mosella. She had taken a few hits and wasn't looking too good, maybe worse than Cookie. Her green bow had come undone and clung to the side of her head. There were no signs of her razor blade.

"My eyes play tricks in the rain," Cookie said.

"Uh-huh. My ears play tricks in the rain too. That don't mean I'm not gonna be coming after you!"

A cool, well-modulated voice came from the crowd. "Please let me pass. Let me through. Thank you, kindly." People paused, opening up, making room for the newcomer. A hush fell through the crowd, a low ripple of whispering in a hum that spoke to the importance of the person who was arriving. Everything stopped, like cold water poured on a fire. From the corner of Cookie's swollen eye, she saw the crowd changing its rhythm. Most of the black guys left. Two black mamas huffed, "Honky Mutha Fucker," and retreated, taking a basketful of stuff with them as they hurried out of the store.

The two young girls were scared out of their wits and their sweatshirts were askew, one torn, the other rumpled. Cookie wondered what Artie had done to them. Outside the store, there were pops and cracks that could have been firecrackers, cherry bombs, ash cans and M-80s, only this was not the Fourth of July; it was St. Patrick's Day, and it sounded like a big celebration, or a riot, both of which were the same thing in Getty Square.

As soon as Cookie saw Mrs. Kerry, she felt ashamed of herself. She used to have only a few streaks of grey in her dark brown hair but now she was turning white. Tired and fragile, she looked like she had rushed there from the library. Her sweater, thrown carelessly over her shoulders, had knobby knots of green and white yarn. She smiled at Cookie, but it was brief and felt uncomfortable—something was troubling her.

Mosella took the opportunity to grab her switchblade from the ground. With a venomous look in her eye, she flicked it open and snuffled, about to charge Cookie.

"I'll take that." Mrs. Kerry held out her hand.

Without saying a word, Mosella closed her switchblade and handed it to Mrs. Kerry.

"Thank you, Mosella." She slipped the knife into her large black leather pocketbook that had interlocking brass handles and snapped it shut. "I'll deal with you later."

Mosella frowned and rolled her eyes. "I be going now."

Mrs. Kerry nodded, then turned to Artie Jelinek. "I want to hear from the girls."

The girl in pedal pushers admitted her theft, said she was sorry, and bowed her head. Mosella eyed the girl, making sure she didn't rat her out. Polite scuttle, a repartee of calm between Mrs. Kerry and Artie Jelinek, rang throughout the store.

"I'll take the girls," she said. They will be under my care from here on out. They can help me in the library."

Artie Jelinek handed over the girls to Mrs. Kerry. His arm swept through the air. "I don't want no trouble with you folks down here."

"Thank you for your courtesy."

On the way out of the store, Mosella nudged Cookie in the stomach, not too hard, just a jab of things to come. "I be looking for you, girl, I know where you go and who you hang out with. I be finding you. I be finding you soon." Her pointer finger assumed the force and velocity of a knife. "I'm gonna hurt you real bad."

"That's enough, Mosella." Mrs. Kerry gave Cookie a once-over, mother-like and stern. "Cookie, I'm surprised at you. You look hurt. You better take care of your eye. Put some ice on it and get yourself home."

Cookie wiped her mouth and saw a trace of red on her hand, the same color as the blood Reenie left on the cot at the clinic.

Mrs. Kerry lowered her eyes and looked away. "I hope this is the last time I find you in this sort of situation."

The look she gave Cookie was one she would carry with her for the rest of her life. She had let her down. Mrs. Kerry was one of her owls—a person worthy of respect, her guide to the world beyond the cloying provincialism of Yonkers.

A trio of cops blustered into the store, but they were too late. The girls, Mosella Moran, Mrs. Kerry, everyone, had left. Artie Jelinek shook his head and leaned against the aisle end-cap across from the cash register that had been dislodged from the front counter. Weary and wan-faced, Artie removed his glasses and rubbed his rodent-colored eyes. He took a handkerchief from his pocket, using it to clean his glasses. Covering his hand over his mouth, he yawned. Scowling at Cookie, he explained what happened to the police, but it was a lie. He had never seen the two young girls take anything.

Monday April 16th 1973

A stool pigeon is a canary that sings. Informer. Rat. Rat fink. Snitch. Stoolie. Tattler. Tattletale. Squeaker. All of those words describe my little sister (who isn't so little anymore) Donny. I hate a snitch! Donny told Johnny that I was fired from my job at the drug store. He would never have known! I was trying to get a new job! She also told Johnny that I owe Arky Lovato two hundred dollars!

The cops took me home the night after the St. Patrick's Day riot. They said it was to protect me from getting hurt by *those people.* Johnny wasn't too happy to see me. He said I always brought trouble upon myself. Donny brought me a bag of Birdseye frozen peas to put on my eye. I didn't find out until later that she was telling Johnny all of these lies about me. Well. I guess. Donny isn't lying. She's just snitching. I have the feeling that one of these days Donny is going to get herself into a big mess on account of her butting into my business!

I'm in a bad way. Everyone is looking for me. Arky Lovato is looking for me cause he wants his money back. Mosella Moran is looking for me cause she wants to hurt me. Artie Jelinek fired me right after the riot for no good reason. He said it wouldn't look good to let me work there cause it would only invite trouble from *those people.* He wants everything to go back to normal.

My life is getting really complicated. Tony Amendolito is everywhere. I don't know what he wants.

Izzy likes me too much and I don't know why.

I can't go anywhere. I feel trapped.

I still think of Stanley and wonder if he knows that my life has fallen apart since he left. It's not like I only lived for him. I didn't build my life around him. I just wanted to be in love with him. He's gone and that's okay. I'm used to him being gone.

What is not okay is that who I used to be does not work

anymore. I do not know who I am. It seems like I am on a losing streak. Everything I touch seems to go wrong. I feel like I have forgotten how to put one foot in front of the other. Life has lost its meaning for me. Life has lost its meaning for everybody. It's 1973. The world has major problems. Blacks hate whites and whites hate blacks. We don't really hate each other but have to act like we do cause that's the way we get along with one another. Lots of kids want a come-up. Some move up. Some move down. Some are dead. Reenie's brother Billy Dee is still strung out on heroin and she is a mess over it.

I still write in my black & white notebook and I still write in cursive. I cross out lots of words that I change my mind about. I show my writing to Izzy. I also show my writing to Sister Mary Eau Claire. She's giving me extra credit for my English class. She likes it when I write about clouds. I think she likes when I write about clouds because it reminds her of God and heaven. Imagine that!

Clouds rolling by. Clouds rolling back on themselves. Clouds dissolving and drifting into a great sea of blue. Black clouds are definite proof that a storm is moving in. Black clouds stand strong in defiance of the storm and turn to white. The clouds are my dark veil of sorrow. (I was writing about Reenie and Billy Dee.)

I am very sorry for Reenie and her Nonna. They only have each other cause Billy Dee is so badly strung out. I guess that's better than having nobody. They give each other a gift of nothing and that's something.

-eee

Eleven

Cookie couldn't stay in hiding forever. Showing her face to the whole world was the only thing to do. She thought it was best to run headlong into confrontation—just to get it over and done. She found Arky Lovato's jeep parked in the lot next to Jimmy's Barber Shop Down the End on Palisade Avenue. Businesses would come and go in droves *Down the End*, long before 1954 when the Yonkers Trolley stopped running.

Presently inhabited by two grocery stores, two barber shops, two beauty shops, two luncheonettes with soda fountains, two drug stores, two liquor stores, and two dry cleaners, everything came in twos Down the End, but there was only one Arky Lovato, and she needed to find him fast.

Wearing green satin platform heels and a long flowery cotton skirt, she walked up and down the strip with the fierce energy of a moving target until her feet grew sore and began to swell.

She went into the parking lot on the side of Jimmy's Barber Shop that was marked with a red, white and blue barber shop kiosk. The shop was famous in Yonkers because next door there used to be a pizzeria named Vicky Lee's Villa, where the famous starlet Jayne Mansfield would visit. She'd get out of her long limo, all legs and smile, a brilliant bosomy blonde apparition after a long dark spell. Rumor had it, she was in love with a Yonkers cop named Nick Rossi.

It had been over seven years since Jayne Mansfield wowed the North End with her electrifying Hollywood beauty. Vicky Lee's Villa was gone under the cloud of a money laundering scandal and Jayne Mansfield had died in a horrible car crash— her Buick Electra slid under a trailer truck and her head got cut off.

There were times when Cookie wished she could have her head cut off, and today was one of those days.

The closest shop to Jimmy's Barber was Hedy's Luncheonette. Cookie peeked inside; the luncheonette was doing brisk late afternoon trade, but there was no sign of Arky Lovato. She was curious as to why he had parked there. He rarely walked because it took too much physical exertion—one reason why he was always good for a free ride. He rarely strayed from his jeep, or whatever loaner car he was driving. She sat on the concrete balustrade in the parking lot and lit a Marlboro. Her tinted sunglasses turned the world upside down, giving the grey buildings of Yonkers a greenish technicolor cast like the 1940s film *How Green was My Valley* that idealized a Welsh mining town.

Cookie blew smoke circles in the air. Yonkers had a lot in common with the Welsh mining town Gilfach Goch. Life was hard. Life was unfair. Back then the women wore dresses, and the men were men. People were happy in Yonkers, talking about their lives as idyllic romps through acres of pristine woodlands, full of wildflowers, foxglove and thistle. They'd have you believing the North End was a small happy town, always in the midst of making memories, vivid, heartfelt and wholesome. But thistle has thorns and the dying cycle of wildflowers and foxglove never did anyone much good. There was no harvest to speak of, among weeds and thin brown reeds. Plenty of people did not see what burbled beneath the surface—the intense pressure to conform by hating anyone different or new. Herman Lynch. Henry Kagan. Izzy.

A full sun spread the warmth of early Spring. People shed their coats, favoring short-sleeve shirts, cotton tees and soft knit tops. The scent of tender new leaves wafted through thick bands of carbon monoxide and diesel fumes. The combination made the air smell like the burnt pretzels sold by sidewalk vendors.

Cookie looked to the sky that was clear with a few scattered clouds, resembling green-tinged, succulent ground cover. Then she looked to the ground. An assembly of hens and chicks, the same shape as clouds, peeped between the sidewalk cracks. She scuffed her shoe on the ground. Beauty was found between the cracks of sadness and tragedy, but only if you worked hard, and if you worked yourself to death. She recognized that the sudden warmth made people smile and the earth tremble with new life, but that made her feel even more removed and lonely beyond the words she could scribble in her notebook.

Immediately overwhelmed with contempt for her own life that was so small and so insignificant, she could dismiss the reality of Yonkers or the illusion of what some people believed to be the truth about this small city sitting on the cusp of the city—Manhattan.

Man, am I in a bad way, she thought.

The day had grown as warm as it was going to get. Late afternoon. Maybe about four. Cookie had never owned a watch and reckoned she never would. Few cars passed by on Palisade Avenue. The ash on her Marlboro grew long, like a grey contrail slitting a gash behind a large white cloud in an anxious sky. She liked going back to the cloud stuff. It kept her mind away from the terrible things going on in her life. On a lark, she counted cars, betting in her mind about what kind of car she'd buy someday, but she couldn't come up with anything. Most cars were from the early 1960s, Chevy Bel Airs and Dodge Coronets.

With so many hills and narrow streets, she could not fathom why Yonkers was a car culture that had dumped its trolley system. With so few through-streets, it took forever to drive anywhere. Yet having a car was a sure sign of success. Some people bought a new car every other year, even if they were in a bad way. Shiny new Vegas and Honda Civics tied first place for being as yellow as a stop sign.

She also could not figure how Johnny had come up with the money to buy himself a fancy, expensive car. His life had changed. He worked fewer hours and made more money. Except she wasn't sure about the money. She didn't know what he was doing to make so much money.

If she ever came into money, she'd fasten her eyes on a yellow convertible, a Dodge Coronet with plush leatherette seats. She'd ride in that car all day long and clear across the country, if she had it in her mind to drive west into the setting sun. Maybe she'd wake up to see a mirage of an oasis in the distance with Stanley in its midst. She stubbed her Marlboro against the side of the wall behind the barber shop and let the half-smoked smoldering butt fall to the ground.

Then she saw a most awful thing. Arky Lovato was coming out of Donaghey's Pub. She never thought of looking for him in the bar. It was too early to be drinking. With him was Tony Amendolito.

Even though seeing the two of them together was an awful fright, it wasn't like she was going to run or anything. Cookie Colangelo didn't run from anyone. She sat there expecting them to come right at her. She was learning about who she was all over again—someone new, calm and mature, not easily rattled about anything.

Arky reeked of cigarettes, but not beer, and that's important to mention because he was so strung out, he didn't need to drink. He gave her a shy wave and a Howdy-Doody grin.

Tony Amendolito got right to the point. "What's this about you owing him two hundred dollars?"

"One-eighty," Arky objected. "She gave me a twenty last week."

"Who asked you?" Tony pulled out his switchblade and palmed it. "How'd you get a twenty? I hear you got no job no more."

"It's none of your business," Cookie told him. She thought he went out of his way to look tough and she was getting sick of it. He wore dark brown chinos and a yellow shirt that was left unbuttoned down his chest, revealing a heavy gold chain and an Italian gold horn charm. He was a Guido, dumber than shit, but thought he knew everything. Arky sniffed so much that Cookie felt sorry for him. She'd hate to see him end up as strung out as Billy Dee.

Tony flicked open the knife and smiled at Arky. "It's still two hundred. You forgot about the interest."

"You know nothing," Cookie said. "This was a loan, not a theft."

Arky nodded and sat down beside her on the wall. "I'm not mad at you, you know. This is his idea. I know you'll pay me back."

Intent on winning a staring match, Tony's eyes locked down on Cookie. "Any time I see you walking around here, I'm going to let it be known that you are a cocksucking, little whore, a no-good nothing low-life who likes to lie with scum. You suck black dick. Got that?"

"God!" Arky looked upset. "You don't have to talk to her like that! Geez!"

"What are you, stupid?! I'm trying to help you, you fucking moron!"

Cookie tapped the edge of the frame of her sunglasses. She knew he couldn't see the fear in her eyes, but she did find it difficult to swallow. The passageway in her throat was blocked. No one had ever talked to her that way. He was dangerous and she didn't know what he'd do next.

Arky put his arm around Cookie. "He doesn't really mean

that." His breath was mildly antiseptic, a lethal breath, not unpleasant nor strong; it was a derivative of cocaine, mixed together with other controlled white substances. "You're my friend, Cookie, and I know that."

"Don't tell her that. I know what I'm doing and if you keep messing with me, I'll cut you off."

Cookie got what was going on between them—Tony Amendolito kept an open supply line to Arky. More and more kids were getting strung out on heroin. Some were in a bad way, like Reenie's brother.

Eyeing him carefully through her green-tinted sunglasses made her feel like a gangster. Something wasn't right with his eyes. His eyes failed to catch light in the sun and looked black, two dark holes under the hood of protruding forehead. Off the beam, dangerous, he gave her a twisted smile and clenched his hand in a fist. She felt some of her old self returning. She'd like to cut his throat but handling a knife was out of her realm of experience.

"I think you're all talk. You keep messing with me. I don't think you know what you're doing, do you? Let's just see what happens to you." She wanted to light a Marlboro to show him how tough she was, but she knew her hands would shake. Cookie was more surprised at herself than she had ever been before. She had always stood up to people who had bullied her, but this Tony Amendolito was different, and he was everywhere.

Twelve

Cookie thought she should have gone to Louie Santamassino at the first sign of trouble. No job. No boyfriend. No schoolwork. She didn't have to be anywhere. The entire front of his house, including twenty steps (Cookie counted them), was constructed from large grey slabs of granite. Dappling late afternoon sunlight gave the dark stone the striated ebb and flow of warm glow. Cars moved at a steady clip in front of Louie's house. It was getting close to five. Soon rush hour would begin. The house sat high above North Broadway, the reigning king of the hill. All other homes sat low in comparison, as if they were kneeling before his majesty.

She didn't need to ring the bell. Louie Santamassino's German Shepherd Blackster barked as soon as she approached the Browning Vault Door. She knew Louie had already identified her from behind the small bulletproof glass window. He was the only person she knew who had cameras monitoring his home, a rarity in 1973. The moment Louie Santamassino opened the door, Blackster greeted her, nuzzled her legs, giving her a good welcoming sniff. He had not forgotten her.

Neither had Louie. Although he didn't open the door wide enough to extend an invitation.

"Hey, Kiddo, got a problem?"

Cookie nodded. "Big problem."

"I don't know if you should come in. I don't want no neighbors talking and stuff. Next thing I know Fran will think that I'm doing something wrong with you because you're starting to become a very attractive young lady. Then I've got a big problem too."

Fran Ochiogrosso was the widowed neighborhood gossip and Louie's main squeeze, a pairing made in heaven, and in hell. Since they had been together, Fran never let him out of her sight.

She called out from inside of the great stone house. "Who are you talking to out there?"

"She's here all the time and I can't get rid of her," Louie whispered. He threw his hands up. "She's starting to drive me nuts. Thank God, she's moving to Florida, or so she says. She says that all the time."

"Nobody," he called to Fran. "Nobody's here."

"I hear Cookie Colangelo," Fran said. "I know that sneaky little voice."

Fran tried to come to the front door, but Louie shook his head, and held her off, using his arm to block her. Fran craned her neck to get a good look at Cookie. Her shock of bright red hair stuck up over the top of Louie's head.

"Debbie's been looking for you. She wants to know what happened to Stanley. It's because of you he left Yonkers, you know!"

The mention of Stanley made Cookie feel sad. She remembered how he had looked that first day she saw him down on the Hudson River, all lean and sinewy muscle, smooth chest laid bare under his dog tags glinting in the sun, blonde hair streaming down his back. There were no clouds in the sky that day. Not one.

"What are you deaf or something?" Fran's voice had a bite. "Talk to me when I'm done asking you a question."

"Come on, Fran, go inside, tell Debbie to mind her own business and leave Cookie alone."

Cookie felt horrible when she remembered the way Debbie had stalked Stanley everywhere. So had Cookie, now that she thought about it, but Cookie had sincerely been in love. Debbie, on the other hand, was seeking someone to father her latest baby. She was known throughout the North End as the invincible baby machine. Rumor had it, Debbie was pregnant again—and had made her fourth trip to the unwed mother's home.

"I have a right to know!" Fran bickered with Louie. "I just want to know."

"Fran, look! Go back inside, already!"

Louie looked at Cookie, whispering, "What do I have to do to get rid of the broad? She gives me agita."

Fran screamed from inside the house. "Agita! The way I cook for you! I spoil you, you rotten bastard, and you don't even appreciate it!"

Clattering pots and pans was Fran's way of letting Louie know that she was not happy. Cookie swore she could hear plates crashing to the ground. Blackster barked, not in friendly or good way.

"And on top of that I've got to put up with that smelly mutt!" she yelled. "The way he sheds and barks at everything!"

It was unusual to see Louie look intimidated. "I don't have to see her face to know it's as red as her hair. And that's as red as it gets."

Cookie put her hands up to her mouth and started laughing. She found it hard to believe that Louie was scared of Fran Ochiogrosso. He wasn't scared of anyone.

"I'm going home," Fran yelled. "Right now! I'm going! I said I'm going!"

"Good, you do that," Louie said under his breath.

"I'll meet you somewhere. Just give me a few minutes to talk to Fran. How about I meet you at that pizza joint *Down the End*. You go there. She doesn't like you and she doesn't like your mother, but she likes your father, thank God. It gives me a headache just thinking about it."

Without waiting for Cookie to respond, he slammed the door shut.

There would be no walk in the park on this fine Spring day for Fran and Louie. The way they barked at one another was so incredibly *Yonkas*. Cookie denied that life in Yonkers was good, idyllic and wholesome, for no reason that she could fully understand—except to say, she knew the score. She knew what was real and what were fabricated concoctions, fanciful illusions, for the way some people wanted Yonkers to be—a quaint town with nice neighbors, good manners and clean streets, not a small working-class city that was gritty inside and out, and especially at the core of its rough and ready inhabitants.

On the side of Louie's house, close to his front door, a grove of lilac swelled with the splendor of tender shoots and newly hatched buds. Thick grey bark on the sturdy lilac tree trunk revealed its old age. From the nearest limb, she picked a small cluster of white flowers tinged with purple. This lilac tree was unusual in that it was burgeoning with both purple and white flowers. Pressing the small flowers to her nose, she inhaled their perfume and felt excitement travel through her body. In the Spring, the scent of lilac was as sacred as experiencing first love. She slipped the sprig of lilac into her saddlebag, planning to hold onto it for as long as it kept its scent. Maybe forever, she told herself, knowing that was not true.

She felt like slipping off her heels and skipping down the large granite steps but couldn't bring herself to do it. The temperature was going down and a light breeze rustled through Louie's bed of daffodils. The flowers had lost their heads, leaving gnarled wisps of brown petals like caterpillars. A year ago, she was madly in love with Stanley de Falco, tracking his every movement around town so she could always show up, coincidentally, wherever he happened to be. Now he was gone, off to California, lolling on the beach under a cloudless sky in full sun. She thought of herself as coming to the edge of death, the death of her former self. She was the same as the daffodils, all of them now shedding withered petals.

Off with their heads, she said to herself. She wanted to lose her own head. She wanted to lose the person who no longer existed. Her blooming season was over. The gangster, the carefree hippie, the *soigné* siren of the night so in love with Stanley de Falco, they were all dead. And she did not know who or what would take their place.

Thirteen

As she crossed Broadway, she saw Louie's Mercedes speeding onto Roberts Avenue, heading *Down the End*. He must have been preoccupied because Louie didn't beep his horn or acknowledge that he saw her.

She walked into Palisade Pizzeria and saw Pasquale wearing his chef's whites stained with tomato sauce. His clothes had been washed so many times that most of the stains had faded to yellow. He gave her a wink and a smile. "What have you got for me today, Doll?"

The pizza place was busier than it had been in the past. About half of the eight white Formica tabletops showed the remnants of people who had already eaten and left behind their paper plates and crumpled napkins.

Cookie didn't plan on having anything to eat, but now her stomach rumbled with the aroma of garlic, a touch of real parmesan cheese—the kind that has to be freshly grated, robust tomato sauce and pizza baking in the wood-fired brick oven.

"I don't have any money."

Pasquale scowled, but it was in jest. He nodded toward the window, where two tables were empty and clear of debris.

"Can't have you starving. You'll lose that figure you got. What do you want?"

"A slice. Plain."

"What other kind of pizza is there? When the pizza is good, you don't need no toppings."

Three metal rounds of pizza sat on the wood butcher block table below the counter. Pasquale used his pizza wheel to cut slices from the pie. He took a long-handled pizza peel, slid it under the slice and stuck it into the red brick oven. The heavy aluminum door slammed shut. He turned around and smiled at Cookie, motioning for her to take a seat.

She sat by the window, looking out to Palisade Avenue. Cars blazed by blaring music. Convertibles cruising with their tops down had their first showing under a warm honey-colored sun. Clusters of kids swarmed in the parking lot next to Jimmy's Barber Shop. Wrapping sweatshirts and sweaters around their waists, people had shed their clothes, yearning for the sun to warm their skin and root them to the earth, even if that earth only existed in between the cracks of the sidewalk.

No sign of Louie Santamassino. She sat there for a while, but he never showed. By the time her pizza came out of the oven, she started to think he meant a different pizza place and grew worried.

Pasquale slammed her slice into wax paper and onto a paper plate. "Here you go, Doll."

She took the plate and returned to her table, pulling a few napkins from the dispenser. Pasquale was a nice guy, a hard worker; he and his brother had only been in America for a few years and already they had their own pizza place. She took one tentative bite and let it sit to cool. Oil from the pizza left a puddle on her paper plate. Pasquale filled a small plastic-coated paper cup with water and set it on the counter for her.

"Case you're thirsty." He winked as though she was a good friend. She knew he didn't mean anything by it. It wasn't a come-on, it was just his way.

There was a time when Cookie, Reenie and Herman used to eat nothing but pizza. It was rumored that Yonkers had more pizza joints per capita than any other city in the world. The best pizza was found at the Raceway Pizzeria on Yonkers Avenue. Reenie disagreed, saying pizza joints like Dom & Vinnie's on Lockwood Avenue or The Donut Den in Getty Square had the best pizza. Herman loved Queens on McLean Avenue or Capri Pizza. The three of them used to travel extensively in search of good pizza, but those days were gone.

The place began to fill up. Pasquale jammed slices into the oven, gushed soda into cups, and also pounded the keys on the cash register. The rushing swell of activity made his face flush, with pride or exertion, Cookie couldn't tell for sure. Probably a little bit of both.

She squeezed her slice, firm enough to fold lengthwise in her hand, drawing the mozzarella into the crust, while she watched droplets of escaping olive oil drip onto the wax paper. A thin layer of red sauce was married to the crust, making it light enough to fold into two, and form a cone that became a natural cradle to catch the drizzle of pure olive oil and melting *mozzarelle'*.

Too early for supper, there was no explanation for an incoming surge of customers that came in all at once, crushing themselves between the front door and the service counter. The pizzeria became populated by men. Dark men. Italian men. Greek men. Hispanic men. Black men. And the whites— the Irish. Yonkers men. The natives. They were co-existing like they got along well with each other, and that was good. And yet Cookie couldn't shake the feeling that any second things could blow up and there'd be a knife fight, a fistfight, or someone would get clocked with a quick hit-and-run punch in the face.

She took two bites of her pizza and immediately felt self-conscious. Regardless of the color of their skin, every guy looked at her as though she was a stoplight that had stayed red for too long.

"Come on. Aren't you gonna eat your pizza?"

She had been so lost in thought, she didn't even see Louie push his way in through the crowd. On second thought, Louie didn't need to push his way in anywhere. Everyone in the North End knew who he was and gave him room to travel expansively.

"Louie, Louie," they called to him.

Tony Amendolito strutted toward Louie, giving him the high-five, nodding toward Cookie, raising his eyebrows. He didn't have the nerve to give Cookie shit in front of Louie.

"Nice day for the two of you having pizza together. Is this something special or what? What do you got going on for yourself, Cookie?"

Louie sat across from her. He didn't need to ask her what was wrong; his face was screwed-up, a deliberate question mark.

"How's the pizza, Kiddo?"

She knew he wasn't interested in pizza. He scratched the back of his head and gazed out the window. "I hope Fran doesn't follow me here. Jesus! Jesus! What if she does?"

Cookie kept an eye on Tony Amendolito, who stayed within earshot. She spoke, in a barely audible whisper. "I'm in trouble." Cookie dropped her pizza onto her plate.

Louie leaned forward and lowered his head, turning the side of his face closer to her. "I can't hear you too good."

"I'm in trouble," she repeated.

"Can't be that bad, cause you're a good girl, at least I think you're a good girl and that's all that matters." His eyebrows knitted together, but his mouth remained a solid straight line. "What kind of trouble?"

"Money. I need money. I need a job."

Louie shook his head. "I thought you had a job, down at that drugstore in the Square."

"I got fired."

"What's this about getting fired?" Tony Amendolito

laughed. "I heard you picked a fight with some huge black chick. Mosella Moran! Shame on you, Cookie Colangelo."

Louie shooed him away and looked taken aback. "Sorry." He turned away from Cookie and looked around, nodding to a dark guy wearing a suit and tie, another in coveralls looking like he walked off his shift from Con Ed. Nods, slaps on his back and greetings, "Yo, Louie," came from every corner of the crowded pizza place.

"Maybe we shouldn't have come here. Too many people. It's hard to have a conversation."

"I need money bad."

Louie made a clicking sound with his teeth, like he needed a toothpick. "You're a young pretty girl, you can get guys to take you on dates to pay for stuff. What do you need money for?"

"I borrowed two hundred dollars and I need to pay it back."

The perpetual straight line of Louie's mouth flipped down into a frown, showing deep displeasure. "That's a lot of money, Kiddo. What do you need so much money for? You're not doing those drugs? I hear all of these kids are on heroin now. The China Blue stuff. Doing that stuff is just nasty. You're not doing that stuff, are you?"

Louie turned all the way around in his seat to make sure they didn't have an audience. Tony Amendolito leaned over the jukebox, scanning songs, pretending not to listen, but he was.

Cookie shook her head, leaned forward and whispered. "I borrowed the money for a friend."

"Now let me get this straight, you want me to give you money for a friend?"

"I need a job."

"That I don't know about. There are tons of jobs. You just have to look. Go to the Square and put your applications in."

"I have." Cookie felt frightened and didn't know how to tell Louie that Arkie Jelinek was a creep, saying bad things about her.

"What's the money for?"

"My friend, Reenie, she was in trouble."

"What kind of trouble?"

Cookie felt a flush come to her cheeks. She turned away from Louie, wouldn't look at him and mumbled, "It's not easy to talk about."

"Oh, oh, now I get you. I think I do. You tell me."

Cookie still did not look at Louie. "She got herself in a family way."

"Huh? How do you like that? I remember Reenie when *yous*, you and Herman, you were all little kids. Now she's getting knocked up! What's she gonna do with the kid? Keep it? When's she gonna marry the father?"

Cookie hadn't thought through what could happen in a conversation like this. She didn't have an answer for him.

"She could talk to Fran, to go to that place with the nuns, where Debbie goes. Jesus, that girl can't keep her panties on. I'll tell Fran and you tell Reenie to give her a call. Okay?"

Cookie shook her head.

"Well, I don't know what else to tell you."

"There is no baby."

"I thought she was in a family way."

"She was." She looked where Tony had been standing by the jukebox, but he was gone. Most certainly he had to have been eavesdropping and had taken word of Reenie's plight as his cue to leave.

Louie shifted uncomfortably in his seat. His face had turned red. "Now I get it. I see what you mean. I don't like none of this stuff, like this. We shouldn't be talking about this." He shrugged. "It embarrasses me to even think about it. Sorry," he said, shaking his head. He leaned in and spoke in a gravelly hush. "I can't help you with that. It's not my thing. I won't go there."

He stood up and stared at Cookie. "I don't go to church or nothing, but I know when something's wrong. And that's wrong." He pushed his chair into the table.

"Your friend should have done the right thing and had the baby at that place with the nuns. Some people want a baby because they can't have kids."

"She didn't want to have a baby then have to give it away." Cookie heard her voice cracking. "She wouldn't be able to live with herself, not knowing what would happen to her baby."

"So she kills it? Is that what you're telling me? You have no business getting involved with stuff like that."

He turned back to look at her, giving her the hairy eyeball. "I'm not good with these kinds of things. You shouldn't come to me. Know what I mean? It's not that I think bad of you, Cookie, but this stuff is women's problems that I really don't want to hear about. Sorry I can't help you. I'm just glad you're not the one who did this terrible thing. Terrible thing!"

Cookie cried the smallest, "No," from the place deep inside where she rarely felt the onset of tears. She opened her saddlebag to reach for a Marlboro and a match. Her fingers curled around the lilac fronds until she felt the flower buds. Crumpling the tiny flowers, she tossed them onto her soiled paper plate where they splayed across a napkin stained with red sauce. Going to Louie for help had been the wrong thing to do. It was a mistake.

Louie left in a hail of people calling his name, giving him his due respect. These are the kind of men who feel obligated to beat people, not so much with their hands, but with their mouths, as if talking tough made them stronger. These are the kind of men, who are only intent on one thing: passing *Yonkers bravata* on to the next generation. Admittedly, Cookie was one of their children. And no matter how hard she tried, she did not know if she would ever shake her blue collar culture to become *So Not Yonkers*.

By the door, Louie turned back and looked at Cookie. His eyes gave her a warning, one of complete disappointment. He pointed his finger and looked as though he was about to say something, but he stopped himself, shook his head and left.

As he walked outside by the front window of the Pizzeria, he did not look at Cookie.

She couldn't define what she was feeling. Worse than the shame and the sting that accompanied being rejected by Louie Santamassino, she told herself she was a real jewel of a kid. A black diamond in the rough. Instead of glittering, she shined intermittently with crude flashes of grey light, the same dull but sparse sparkle of granite that was excavated from the Yonkers quarry. She knew herself by heart and was sick of the same old story. There are moments when she longed to be anyone else, anyone other than who she was. In her mind, she was unafraid to greet the strange, the different, the remote, but she had always stopped herself from pursuing new experiences. She was her own barrier to her change. The utmost reach of her imagination did not dare go beyond picturing her usual life in the same old setting, like a staged scene in a glossy teen magazine. She could not conjure her own vision for the future, her future, the world's future. Stuck, she was a victim of her own limited imagination, all except for the clouds. Only the clouds could set her free.

Saturday May 19 1973

The days seem longer now that the clocks have been turned an hour ahead. Clouds in the night sky move across a waning gibbous moon—that means the moon is still big but getting smaller. I read that description about the moon in some book. The light of the moon helps me to find my way home. I cannot count on the clouds.

I think I should forget the past. I have been thinking about Stanley de Falco less and less. I don't see the image of his face so much no more. I mean any more.

Reenie wants to see me and won't say why. I have to meet her at Yonkers General Hospital.

I'm shivering because it's only about 50 degrees and it's already the middle of May. The clouds keep masking the moon and that makes the night feel colder. I'm also getting older. My blood is getting thin. I'm in bed and my blankets are pulled up to my chin. My bedroom door is locked. It's Saturday night and I'm stuck home alone.

The big song on the radio this week is *The Sunshine Of My Life* by Stevie Wonder. I hate this song because the radio stations keep playing it over and over. And the fact that there is no sunshine in my life does not help. I know my attitude is real bad.

I don't have a new job yet. I keep applying for jobs but I'm not having luck. They seem to know that Arty Jelinek has accused me of something and I don't know what it is. I don't know how I'm going to pay back Arky Lovato. Donny told Johnny that I took money from Arky for an abortion. Now my father won't talk to me. Can you imagine what that's like? Well. Maybe. It's a good thing having Johnny not talk to me. Kitty giggles every time she sees me and rubs her nose with both hands. I think Johnny got her new drugs that work. No wonder why she smiles a lot. I thought of stealing her drugs and selling them as happy pills.

But my drug dealing days are over. I think. I hope.

I don't know what I'm going to do. I'm kind of desperate.

Let me count the ways to make money. Babysitter. Mother's helper. Coffee girl at Chock full o'Nuts. Department store salesgirl. Waitress in a Greek diner. A&P grocery store clerk. I could be a check-out clerk. I could join the checker's union and get paid time-and-a-half on extra-long days or double-time on Thanksgiving and Christmas. I could do this for the rest of my frigging life. Do you know how depressing this is?

This Tony Amendolito follows me everywhere. His red car shows up all of sudden. He doesn't say anything. He just rolls down his window and watches me.

Arky asked me for money again and he wasn't polite. I told him I didn't have any and this much was true. I don't have any money for a junkie. He seems intent on destroying his mind. A mind is a terrible thing to waste. Look at Kitty. My mother doesn't have a mind that works and that's sad.

I've been grown up as far back as I can remember. I'm going to be seventeen*years*old* later this year. I feel like a runaway freight train about to jump the tracks. I'm not looking to ball guys in all of the wrong places. I'm not looking for sex or love. But I'm sure as hell looking for money. The notion of money makes people do strange things. I'm no exception.

Money is important. There are a whole bunch of people that I know who have no money—that's the way it has been their whole lives. And it is the way it is always going to be. Why do some people have money and most have none or never enough? I can't think about it cause I don't know the answer. Money can save your life. Rich boys didn't go to Vietnam.

I visited Zelda the Gypsy. I put a slug into the slot and pulled the handle. Zelda's eyes opened and her crystal ball lit up. Zelda shot out my new fortune that said: *soon you will come into lots of money.* I don't know if she's telling the truth.

-*eee*

Fourteen

Cookie walked across Ashburton Avenue to meet Reenie at Yonkers General Hospital. Reenie had been waiting for her in the shadows under two large Sumac trees that had not yet begun to bloom. Cookie recognized the trees as Sumac by their fern-shaped leaves and conical clusters of snowy flowers. Come fall, the trees would be the color of raging fire, full of shiny leaves and plump berries. A brief lance of light from the moon edged across the side of Reenie's face. She didn't brighten when she saw Cookie. She looked sullen; all color had drained from her brown cheeks.

They walked up the steps and squeezed into a side entrance door. As they entered the hospital, no one was there to greet them except for a gleaming, yellow linoleum floor and a wet mop and a bucket. A sandwich board sign cautioned *wet floor*. Every so often a siren screamed outside. It was late on Saturday night in Yonkers. Anything could happen.

"They told me to use the side entrance and go down to the basement level."

The old yellow steps, speckled with black dots and tan amoeba-shaped blobs, weren't well lit. Cookie nudged Reenie's arm, tapping her gently, and held onto the yellow-painted steel handrail that felt too rough and too cold to touch. At the bottom of the steps, a narrow hall lacked signage. They walked in the direction of intense fluorescent light. Cookie still didn't have an inkling as to why she was here, but she knew whatever it was, that it wasn't good. Another dark cloud had formed on the horizon.

They did not walk far when they came upon a small, half-moon-shaped reception desk staffed by a lone man, wearing hospital greens and what appeared to be a white hairnet, similar to ones worn by old women who didn't want to muss their hair. He hardly looked up beyond the wire-framed eyeglasses that sat low on his red-freckled pug nose.

"Reenie Ruggiero." Reenie shifted her weight to one side, closer to Cookie, leaning for support. "We talked by phone."

The man frowned, a display of overt disapproval, as though he didn't like teenage girls. Cookie bolstered her, patting her arm, giving her a slight smile, more out of nervousness than out of compassion. The man handed Reenie a clipboard to sign while Cookie looked over her shoulder, watching what she wrote. There was a place for Reenie to print her name, sign in cursive, date, time and then a name she had to fill in under a category that said: *Name of the Deceased*. Reenie looked at Cookie, who nodded as though it was okay to write his name. In beautiful cursive, Reenie wrote *William Christopher de'Angelo* and in parentheses *Billy Dee*.

The man examined the clipboard, then got up from behind his desk. He handed the clipboard to Cookie, where she followed Reenie's example, but skipped formality and used her own fountain pen, instead of the hospital Bic, writing her own name as *CCC* and under Name of the Deceased Billy Dee, where she intentionally left two big blobs of ink.

"Black tears." She wiped away an irritating eyelash. Her eyes had begun to shed tears for the wrong reason.

If the man had a name, Cookie had not noticed, and neither

girl referenced him as being a genuine human being. The girls looked at each as if to ask *what the fuck?* He instructed them to follow him until they reached a door that appeared to be made from heavy reinforced steel in mustard yellow. The door had a slim band of window made from glass, embedded with a crisscross thatch of mesh wire.

Before the man opened the door, he looked at both girls with neutral eyes. "He didn't have any identification on him, but people in the North End who knew him were able to identify him. We haven't yet performed an autopsy, but the preliminary report said he still had a needle stuck in his vein and a tourniquet tied around his arm."

He paused, taking a couple of breaths before saying, "It appears to be an overdose." His voice lacked emotion. Even though the man tried to look like he cared, in Cookie's estimation, the whole process felt rote, mechanical, a perfunctory duty.

On the right side of the thick door, a sign said *Depository*, as though it was a bank to deposit money. The smell in the room was sweet but astringent, borne of powerful disinfectant. The room felt refrigerated, and there was the hum of motors. Cookie and Reenie shivered, drawing their arms to cross their chest. They stood there while the man read paperwork on his clipboard. The room, cold as a winter night, made Cookie's teeth chatter. She paced the length of the room, complaining, "I'm freezing."

Tiled floors beneath their feet were soaked with disinfectant, clouded with streaks and strokes of a mop. Everywhere she turned, she cowered in the fluorescent light. Her eyes began to hurt from too much light and a stench she could not fully define. She held her hands out and shook them, waving her arms to increase warmth. Her skin had turned to mottled pink. The room had eight metal sinks and tables made from dull stainless steel. She counted them all until it seemed pointless to have her mind consumed with playing numerical tricks to stay calm. Reenie leaned against a gurney in the corner. Her eyes were closed. She seemed to be praying or thinking—both can be the same thing.

Cookie lit a Marlboro, took a deep breath, drawing in as much smoke as she could, then offered it to Reenie, who shook her head.

"Put that out," the man said. "Can't you read the sign?"

A small yellow sign on the wall read: *Danger! Biohazard.* Cookie dropped the cigarette to the floor, stamped on it, and did not move her foot. She was pissed. Never in her life, had anyone told her to put out a cigarette. She was almost seventeen years old for Chrissakes!

The last Cookie saw of Billy Dee, he had been in the parking lot *Down the End.* So strung out, Billy was unaware of everything going on around him. He did not know Cookie watched him kneeling on the ground in between two parked cars, using the flame of his lighter to cook his works, getting ready to shoot up. She did not want him to die. Too many had already died.

There were lots of guys around that late summer night. Cookie was hell bent on kissing them, trying them all on for size. The other guys didn't pay much attention to her—they knew she was there, but did not want her to know that they knew she was there, the boy-girl chase thing. The other guys scoffed at her, except a glassy-eyed Billy Dee. Only Billy Dee treated her like a person. Amber light above the parking lot had shone on his pale skin and blonde hair, making his face glow. He was a fallen angel who had once been good.

"What do you want?" he asked. His speech was slurred, but he was alive.

"I hardly knew you, Billy." Cookie blurted, "I'm so sorry."

Reenie pressed her lips together hard, almost biting them to squelch a sob. "Me too! I hardly knew him and he was my brother."

Cookie stopped pacing at the sight of a black body bag sitting on a steel gurney that had been wheeled in by the man.

The bag had a number encased in black plastic as though it was clean laundry returned from the dry cleaner's.

The man snapped a gauze mask over his mouth and pulled on latex gloves, leaned over, unzipped the black bag, and revealed a small pale head. Blonde hair clumped on his forehead and clung to his neck. His skin had the unearthly sheen of the white candles held by Catholic altar boys. His mouth lay open, but frozen, as if he still wanted to breathe.

The man asked Reenie if it was her brother. She nodded and he quickly zippered the bag. "I have some paperwork for you to fill out."

Again, Reenie nodded with eyes dulled by shock; she looked too scared to move. Cookie took her arm and led her out of the refrigerated room. They followed the man into the hallway. The morgue's sickly sweet odor lingered with Cookie. She stopped and hugged her chest again, not due to the cold, but from a numbing fear that stopped her from thinking.

"I couldn't do this alone." Reenie stifled a sob, then stopped herself from doing anything close to crying. She was even less of a cry baby than Cookie. "Thanks." She sniffed.

Cookie stared at Reenie so hard that her eyes felt dry, lids heavy like stone. "Don't mention it."

The man handed Reenie the clipboard with more papers to sign. She glanced at the form. "Where am I going to have him buried? I don't know how to do any of this shit."

"Have him brought to Sacred Heart." Cookie's eyes redefined a harder edge, a pure, almost holy resentment. "Let them deal with it. He's one of their kids, isn't he? Tell them to come by and pick up what's left of him."

They left the hospital by a different door than the one they had entered and found themselves on Ashburton Avenue, close to the encroaching ghetto. Cookie didn't remember walking or where they were at first, but she heard every word of what Reenie told her.

"My mother was married when she had Billy, but that guy

left her. Not so much with my father. They never married. We had different fathers, that's why Billy's blonde and I'm black. I never told that to anyone before." Reenie looked at Cookie as if she had stunned herself. "Did you know that I was half-black?"

"Kinda figured that." Cookie poked her on the shoulder, then got right in her face. "Hey, none of that matters. It's about you, not where you came from, or who your parents are."

Reenie stared at her and grinned. "Know what you mean, but it's hard to feel that sometimes."

"Fuck that man for leaving your mother, girl. You could have been white too!" Cookie laughed. "White like me! And just look how great that is!"

Reenie laughed so hard, she started crying. Cookie stood back and let her go. Reenie's face swelled with sadness; tears streamed to her chin, leaving blotchy wet marks on her cheeks. Cookie thought of hugging her, but that would have been too much for Reenie. Cookie too.

Across Ashburton Avenue, Cookie looked toward the small strip of neighborhood shops: Restivo's Florist, Gene's Pizza, the Henry Bedard Drugstore that had an old-fashioned soda fountain counter, and the Café Trento—that had the best sfogliatelle and cannoli. It was the place where she would frequently visit, seeking a chance encounter with Stanley de Falco. As far as she knew, his mother still worked there. She missed going there. Big Bertha had been like a mother to her, but the notion of seeing her made her flinch and feel an old, worn-out, well-traveled route to a place where she became numb, raw, stripped down to nothing. The image of Stanley began to flit through her mind, but she immediately banished him, and stared into the distance, where two oak trees had sprung tender green leaves. She thought of sex, but the urge was quickly overtaken by her need for money. She wasn't looking for sex, but she was starved for money and she did not know how to reconcile the two. Maybe sex and money were joined at the hip.

Fifteen

It was not a good day for Cookie to talk to Reenie about money, but she tried. Cookie told Reenie that Artie Jelinek fired her right after the riot on Saint Patrick's Day. He thought firing her would quell the discord from black people in the neighborhood. Getting rid of Cookie was a symbolic gesture to restore peace, law and order, and goodwill. As ridiculous as that sounded, Reenie did not get the hint that she was also responsible for paying back the money to Arky Lovato.

"Now that I don't have money coming in, I was wondering if you could help."

"That's a bummer."

"For the both of us. I went out on the limb for you."

Reenie didn't get the message. She was more responsible for the debt than Cookie and not owning up to it.

Reenie stared her down with black-eyed intensity. "Girl, you need to get the money."

"So do you," Cookie reminded her.

"Maybe you could get a hot tip."

"I'm not understanding you."

"I'm talking about Wanda McGillicuddy. She used to be a waitress at Sal's Pizzeria."

"So?"

"Wanda played the horses at the Yonkers Raceway."

"Don't know nothing about no horses."

"She got a hot tip."

So much for Reenie's grief. She was acting fine, fine enough to forget about the debt to Arky Lovato.

"Wanda McGillicuddy shared the tip with Yonkers cop Nick Rossi, and they won a grand jackpot of over three hundred thousand dollars. In the beginning, they divvied up the money easily enough, but then things changed."

Cookie was cold, bored, and didn't want to hear Reenie's story.

"Funny stuff started happening to Wanda. She kept getting phone calls at the pizza place that made her cry. Then, she thought someone was following her. One night she was closing late and held up at gunpoint. The gunman didn't take what was in the cash register. He took her home and held her hostage until she forked over the dough. He kept her hostage for two whole days until she withdrew thousands of dollars from her bank."

"Okay. So?"

"After the gunman took Wanda's money, he let her go free—that's how everyone found out what had happened, but then, a couple of days later, she disappeared. Wanda McGillicuddy disappeared from Yonkers and was never heard from again."

Cookie offered her own recollection. "Nick Rossi used to be the cop who Jayne Mansfield used to come to see at Vicky Lee's Villa."

Reenie nodded. "It was too much money and putting it in the bank drew attention to the situation—the race was rigged. Nick Rossi knew the race was rigged. He's the one who gave Wanda the tip. She shouldn't have put the money in the bank."

"I wouldn't be dumb enough to put the money in the bank."

"Now do you remember?" Reenie asked. "Nick Rossi left the police department and became a *goombah* bodyguard hired by famous people in the city."

Cookie cut loose a loud yawn and made no secret of the fact that her eyes had glazed over. She hated the way everyone in Yonkers always called Manhattan *the city*, as if they were too unsophisticated to acknowledge that they lived in their own city. Everyone calls Manhattan *the city*. They don't call any of the other boroughs the city. Brooklyn, Queens, The Bronx and Staten Island are never called the city because that's where the working people live. They call Manhattan the city because that's where all the rich people live and those rich people think there is no other city in the world.

Yonkers is a city too, she meant to say but didn't. She was being polite and didn't want to be argumentative because of what Reenie had been through, but she definitely wanted to get away from her.

Sixteen

Getting away from Reenie wasn't easy. Reenie told Cookie she had something important to tell her. Cookie felt herself sinking into Reenie's cot, which was unmade. She sank like a grey stone dropping to the bottom of the Sprain Brook Reservoir. She remembered when Toni Ferlinghetti had pushed her into the reservoir and she had nearly drowned. She did everything she could do to breathe the day she almost drowned. Now listening to Reenie's story was a form of drowning too. Her so-called friends were suffocating her.

"Two hundred dollars." Cookie held up two fingers. "No way, you can help?"

"Here's the skinny," Reenie exclaimed. Her eyes were big and her nose was red and shiny, oily-looking like a teenager on the verge of breaking out with pimples. She was sniffing a lot and kept rubbing her face. "We live on social security, that's all we've got. The money comes every month because my mother died."

Cookie lit a Marlboro, sticking the match in a water glass that sat on Reenie's nightstand.

"There's hardly anything left after we pay for our rent and food."

"What about your grandmother?"

"My uncle was here for a while, but he's gone. Billy Dee used to get social security too but now he's dead. Less money coming in."

Reenie jumped off of her bed, walked to the window, and looked out into the night. Her hand glided over brown oil paint, a thick lacquer, covering the old window frame. She turned and looked at Cookie. "My Nonna doesn't get nothing. My money pays for her, and she's sick all the time."

Cookie dropped her head. "I'm sorry." She stared into the pile at the foot of the cot: sheets, a thin pillow and a blanket with holes.

"One day last week, my Nonna passed out. I saw her lying on the floor, face down on the shiny yellow linoleum. She looked like she wasn't breathing, that's all I know. I went to call for help. It reminded me of what happened to my mother. I was there with her when she died but I was too young to know any better."

Reenie's voice became thin and shrill as though she was trying to blow a street whistle, but she was unable to wet her lips enough to summon sound.

"It's okay, Reenie, you don't have to talk. You don't have to say nothing."

"But I do. I do want to talk."

"Nobody's stopping you."

"I wanted to get help for my mother, but I didn't know anyone close by. I thought if I took a washcloth and wet it that I could use it to cool her forehead. Maybe that would wake her up."

"That was a good thing to do."

"I found a washcloth and rinsed it in cold water. When I touched her forehead, she didn't move, not even a little. I pressed my face close to hers and I couldn't hear no breathing. I wanted to call someone, but I was too small to reach the phone. It was one of those heavy old black wall phones. I pushed a chair away from the kitchen table to a spot under the phone and climbed up. I had to stand on my tip toes to push the receiver away from the phone so that I could grab it. But it fell from the cradle. It hung straight down, with its springy cord bouncing. Bouncing. I still remember that black cord bouncing."

Reenie stopped talking and looked at Cookie. She opened her mouth and tried to access the right words. Small utterances, a pause, a breath, shallow breathing, she sniffed as though she had a runny nose. She wasn't going to cry even when crying would have been the best thing to do. "I wanted to help my mother. I knew something was wrong. I was too little. There was nothing I could do."

Reenie pressed her hands against her cheeks, tilted her head to one side, and avoided looking at Cookie, repeatedly swallowing, clearing her throat from phlegm. "Next..."

"Go on."

"Dialing the phone..." She shook her head with resignation. "I reached as high as I could go. I wasn't going to be able to dial a phone number because I didn't know any numbers except the one we had. I managed to dial a 0 to get the operator. I heard her voice. She was a real operator. I kept saying my phone number. BE7-9848. That was the number I always heard my mother say. She'd go BEVERLY 7-9848. I did not know why it could be BEVERLY 7 and not BE7. So, I tried saying them both. I kept saying the number BE7-9848. I told the operator my mother fell down on the ground. She asked me for my address."

Reenie lowered her eyes as though she was shamed. "But I didn't know it. See, I knew my phone number, but I didn't know our address."

Cookie couldn't bring herself to move. Her clouds could free her, but they could also engulf her, get caught in her throat, and take away her breath.

"They said they would send someone, but no one ever came. I kept poking her and kissing her but she never moved.

It wasn't until my Nonna came home that we knew. My mother had died."

Reenie took a deep breath. Cookie failed to find the right words to say. Only stuffy air in the room separated her from Reenie. Cookie went over to hug her, but Reenie stiffened and pushed her away.

"I've been dying to tell you for some time that what happened to my mother wasn't because of drugs. They said it was an aneurysm."

Cookie didn't know what to do. Whenever she thought about a kid who had been orphaned, stabs of pain traveled from her heart to her stomach and made her feel sick. She also felt bad for herself. She was stuck owing a lot of money and had no way out. She glanced around the room, seeking the door so she could escape. She had to keep moving to stay alive.

Reenie suddenly took on a cheery tone almost as if she had snapped herself into a different mood by the sheer force of will. Her quick transformation away from grief puzzled Cookie. Scared her too. Reenie owed it to herself to grieve but not at the expense of leaving Cookie with a hefty debt to pay.

"Sal's Pizzeria on Nepperhan Avenue has the best Italian food and pizza in Yonkers! It's owned by Sal Caro. His son Chet works there too sometimes. The address is 209 Nepperhan Avenue, got that?"

"Uh-huh."

"I don't know why I'm telling you this, except to say that Sal's Pizzeria has the best pizza, Zuppa di Pesce, Eggplant Parmesan Wedges—they call them *heros*, not wedges, and their Fra Diavalo sauce will make you scream. Steam comes out your ears. Burn you once, burn you twice, going in and going out. Know what I mean?"

Cookie knew Reenie was okay as soon as she began talking about food. She dropped her half-smoked Marlboro into the water glass, where it sizzled its last vestige of smoke and looked at Reenie. A hollow pain fanned through her heart and chest. Giving each other high-fives and harsh but still girlish *I've-got-your-back* nods and slaps, Cookie left Reenie. On the way out the door, she stopped to give Reenie's Nonna a kiss on the top of her curly grey-haired head. The old woman had fallen asleep in an armchair in front of an old, box-shaped console TV. The sound had been turned down. A flurry of black & white images flickering on the walls illuminated uneven cracks, splotchy pockmarks and strips of peeling paint.

Seventeen

Reenie's talk about Sal's Pizzeria made Cookie hungry.
Fighting back the rumble in her stomach, she headed to Getty
Square. She had no business being in *Ghetto Square*, the part
of town where whites weren't supposed to go after dark, but
the danger in Cookie's heart was far greater than anything
she would encounter in South Yonkers. Reenie's talk about
not owning up to the two-hundred dollar debt angered her, but
what could she do? The girl was totally down and out.

The RKO Theater had closed for the night. She saw the
marquee for *Pat Garrett & Billy the Kid*, directed by Sam
Peckinpah. Some Yonkers guys said Peckinpah's films told
the real story of the way the west was won. Cookie winced at
the notion of gun violence, even if it was only acted out in the
movies.

She headed to Johnny's office in the Yonkers Savings and
Loan Building. She used the spare set of keys, the one she
had made unbeknownst to Johnny, to unhitch the brass locks
in the old oak front door that was heavy, hard to pull open.
The hallway was dark, cold and deserted, a sharp contrast to
daylight hours when the inner sanctum swam in activity. But

in the middle of the night the only sound came from a rodent scurrying across the grey-veined marble floor. The chill in the building made her shiver. Marble floors and walls kept the old building from getting too cold or too hot. Winter or summer, the temperature in the building seemed to stay the same.

Stepping into the small elevator car, she closed the old fashioned brass accordion gate and pressed knobby white buttons. She felt like a bird trapped in a gilded cage. A relic from the glory days of Otis Elevator, the elevator creaked and groaned, rising ten floors on a pulley that squealed like it was hurt and in pain. The car jerked as it rose, with each floor hitting a keener note of anguish, like the wail of a bagpipe. Cookie imagined the pulley to be threadbare, on the verge of snapping. Any second the elevator would career to a crash landing, leaving her smashed flat in the basement. She smiled to herself for being overly dramatic, but it was her secret. No one else needed to know about her inner desire to be a very bad actress.

Johnny's office was tucked away, almost hidden, on the tenth floor. His business was not listed in the building directory or advertised in the yellow pages. Cookie tried to look in through a filmy pane of glass, but there was no light. She used a second key to let herself into Johnny's office. Now a blue patch of light came from the streetlamps on South Broadway. She moved through the office as though she was wading through murky water, avoiding empty liquor bottle boxes strewn all over the floor.

Her father had always kept a small cot in the back of the office in what was really a huge walk-in closet. He slept here when he couldn't put up with Kitty's spells. Lately though, he was spending his nights at home, and much to Cookie's annoyance, the springs of her parents' bed had begun to squeak again.

She needed a place away from the world to rest her weary head. The bed's dark comforter and top sheet had been turned down as though someone was looking out for her. But the bed linens were always turned down like that. It was one more way that Millie Mangano took care of Johnny. She would do anything for him, and that included making his bed and washing his dirty laundry.

It was no secret that Millie Mangano was in love with Johnny. Cookie hated the way her father double-crossed her. Behind Millie's back, he said that she was as ugly and as large as a Mack Truck, but to Millie's face he acted though he was madly in love with her. She was suspicious of anyone who came to see Johnny, even his daughters. She ran his office with the efficiency of a stern nun.

Cookie sat on the side of the bed, looking around to make sure she was alone. The sheets felt cool under her worn blue jeans. She crossed her legs and thought of how unpleasant it would be if Johnny suddenly showed up. She would be long gone in the morning before Millie Mangano arrived. Then she remembered it was almost Sunday. No one would be coming to work. Instead of wringing the top sheet for warmth and sliding under the covers, she lit a Marlboro.

The office was normally as loud and as busy as the Yonkers Raceway. Even if people weren't coming and going, Johnny and Millie made enough noise between the two of them to create the sound of a pre-recorded audience for a TV sitcom. That's what they were, Cookie thought, audio mimicry of cheap TV white noise, nothing more.

Johnny's massive oak desk sat in the far corner of the office. The big man needed a big desk. All of his desk drawers were always open. Cookie could not understand why he never closed them. Paper in every shape and size, folded, creased, ripped and crumpled, spilled from the drawers and lay strewn across the top of the desk. She didn't know how her father found anything. Some family photos were turned over, lying face down, not as though someone had done that intentionally; it was just part of the ever-evolving mess of Johnny Colangelo's life.

One thing that made sense was the picture of his beautiful but crazy Kitty wearing a blushing pink swimsuit, boasting movie star curves, dime-store red lipstick—her head tossed back in a cheesecake pose.

Another thing that explained the true essence of Johnny's personality was the portrait of Mayor Fiorello LaGuardia that was hung on the wall, albeit crookedly. Johnny didn't like politicians but because LaGuardia had been the first Italian who had ever acquired power—legitimately—he held a special place of honor in Johnny's heart.

Then something else caught Cookie's attention. She thought for sure her eyes were playing tricks on her. The lack of office light or too much light from a three-quarter moon struck just the right place on the seat of Johnny's large oak desk chair. The chair's leather seat was the color of a red delicious apple, but tonight the cushion was dark, and its entire shape and texture could not be fully discerned. On top of the seat sat a box without a cover and in the box sat money. Stacks of twenties. A lilac-colored band wrapped around each stack held each bundle together.

It could not be real. Her eyes had made a mistake. She wanted money so badly that she had begun to hallucinate. She was clearly losing her mind.

She walked over, picked up a stack and held it in her hand. It had the right weight. Having worked at the drugstore, she knew enough about money to know that one stack of twenties was two thousand dollars. She counted the stacks. Ten across. Three wide. Four deep. Lying right out in the open.

There was more light from the streetlamps than from the moon by the window. The stack felt hefty in her hand, a good weight to hold onto. In her mind, the lilac-colored band took on the same sweet fragrance as the lilac tree in the front of Louie Santamassino's front yard. She walked back to the box in the chair. Mesmerized by the sight of money, she ran her hand across the length of the stacks, trying to erase her shock, her doubt, her glee, her disbelief, her astonishment; all of these emotions converged as one, numbing her brain, a paralysis that stopped her from taking immediate action.

But not for long. She began to panic, adrenaline coursed through her veins, causing her heart to surge, then to skip beats. She would not stay stuck forever. She began to calculate the ramifications of finding so much money in a place where she was alone and no one could see her. It was late, in the middle of the night, and there were no eyewitnesses. Not one.

Unraveling from the shock of her discovery, almost hearing a song in her head, she moved about the room slowly and methodically, checking windows, opening the office door, poking her head into the hall, glancing at the elevator, which sat still in the dark with none of its buttons blinking. The song she began to hear in her head was of no rhythm, and no use, no value, a song she had never heard until now, her own song, coupled with both lyrics, but without distinct words or a voice. Then she began to hear a few choice words rising an octave or two above the melody. *If there was any money to be had, it's going to be mine.*

She did not know what she was going to do with the money. She had borne the whole weight of the world on her shoulders, but now she was free. Tough. Dangerous. Strong. Catching Zelda the Gypsy on a good day was just the lucky break that she needed: *soon you will come into lots of money.* Money bought privilege and life, a life worth living.

Most people would have turned away from the money, turning their backs from temptation. Good Samaritans would walk away, leave it there, because the money clearly belonged to someone else. Some would have taken a twenty or two, thinking it would never be missed. A small percentage would have taken a whole stack of twenties.

Should I take all of it? Part of it? None?

Regardless of what Zelda the Gypsy had spouted, it was beyond the realm of Cookie's imagination. She had never conjured a personal vision for stumbling upon a boatload of money. But she had never shied from taking a risk. She opened her rawhide saddlebag and stuffed it with as much money as she could take. When the bag was full, she removed the pillowcase from Johnny's cot and stuffed that too. She didn't see the point in leaving behind any money. It was all or nothing. She didn't worry about anyone finding out or anyone bothering her on the way home. No one was going to mess with her.

She had money. Lots of money. She had no choice but to go home. Johnny wouldn't even notice she had come home late, she would make sure of that, but eventually he would notice the money was gone. The streets grew darker as she walked with a pillowcase slung over her shoulder. The night air stank of diesel exhaust from buses on Broadway and raw sewage from the river. The big moon slid behind the clouds, exposing a narrow band of light as thin and as satisfied as her smile.

Friday June 8 1973

I had always been a good girl. I worked hard to get a good reputation. No one would believe I had done anything wrong. But that is not the complete truth. I am really a bad girl. I enjoy being bad. I don't enjoy talking about it too often cause I don't want to get caught at being bad. Let me tell you the truth: I have not forgotten what happened to me when I was a good girl and I played by the rules. Talk about unfair! I don't need to learn that lesson ever again!

I never had a larcenous heart. I'm not a thief. But things have changed. It's a matter of survival. Tough. Dangerous. Strong. Add determined to my list. I can't write too much about it here in my journal for fear of getting ratted out by Donny. Hear that Donny? You're nothing but a snitch.

I'll just tell you what I've been doing.

Reenie didn't have any money. Neither did her Nonna. It was real important to do the right thing by Billy Dee. His funeral mass was held at Sacred Heart Church. I paid for his funeral reception afterward at Sal's Pizzeria. The food is not nearly as good as Reenie said. It sucks compared to Louie's on South Broadway! Hardly anyone showed up at the restaurant. The bill came to sixty-eight bucks. I left the new waitress a twelve buck tip. Four twenties. Even Steven. I felt sorry for her. She might end up disappeared like Wanda McGillicuddy.

I might end up like Wanda McGillicuddy too.

I might end up like Wanda McGillicuddy cause I don't know where my money came from.

I gave Arky Lovato his two hundred bucks. I only owed him one hundred and eighty dollars but who's counting? He was real sick on the day that I gave him his money. Sniffing. Blowing his nose and rubbing his eyes. He stood there and looked like he had been bombed on in a heavy mortar attack.

Arky never mentioned Tony Amendolito. I didn't either.

The days of my wearing the same clothes as everyone else are over. It was bad enough having to wear a school uniform. But every time I bought something for fun—every other girl had on the same thing cause it was bought on sale. Lerner's. Genung's. Korvette's. Can't afford Gimbel's or Wanamaker's. We all shop at the same stores. It's like we're all the same big blob of teenage girls who have to work for a living.

The first thing I did was buy myself a pair of fancy shoes. I went to Manhattan and found this place across the street from Macy's on 34th Street. The 34th Street Bootery is in an old building that looks exactly like the Yonkers Savings and Loan Building in Getty Square. I could see lots of shoes in a basement-level window display. These shoes were like nothing I had seen before. Wild colors! Psychedelic! Leather and satin! Platform shoes with heels as high as stilts!

The funny thing is I had to walk up the stairs in this old fashioned building to get into the store. I almost stopped breathing as soon as I saw my shoes. They had one-inch velvet patches stitched together in every color under the sun. A rainbow of color. Even black. (I know black is not in the rainbow.) You better believe they had my size in stock! These rainbow platform shoes are mine! No other girl in Yonkers would have anything like them! Not ever!

I also bought these shoes called Springolators with open toes and open heels. Clear. Carved. Lucite. I could see my feet right through these shoes! They looked like something Kitty would wear! I caught a glimpse of a pair of red Pappagallos with impossibly high heels and added them to my haul. Peeling off twenties is easy. I'm starting to get used to it. The hard part is explaining my sudden wealth. I told myself I didn't think anyone would notice my shoes or anything else that I did with my money.

It was a mistake. It was not the first mistake that I would make.

-ccc

Eighteen

Donny locked Cookie in her bedroom. Being held in captivity had nothing to do with money. The bedroom door had long ago been fitted with a bronze Dutch bolt that slid into place, locking the door from outside. Johnny had installed the lock to keep her from going to Woodstock, but that was nearly four years ago, and it had not stopped her then, nor would it stop her from going anywhere now. Everyone seemed to have forgotten about the lock, except Donny.

Twelve going on twenty-five, wearing a lacy bra and matching tap pants, Donny had squeezed herself into Cookie's translucent Springolators, making a big point of clomping around the house, loud enough for Cookie to hear her along with Kitty breathlessly exclaiming, "Where did you get those shoes? Let me try on those shoes!"

Cookie imagined their bodies rocking and jamming together, hair bouncing, strutting and preening in her new shoes. She thought of calling to Johnny to let her out of her room, but she was doing everything to avoid him. She did not want to see the pain in his eyes over losing so much money.

Guys like Johnny have made an art form out of

complaining and you can't take it personally. He was so afraid of contemplating a different life, a life without brutality, that he complained about things totally unrelated to the source of pain. Bitching and moaning was just an excuse to give himself a beating.

Except Johnny wasn't acting like a guy who had lost thousands of dollars. He wasn't complaining at all. He wasn't upset. He didn't act like there was anything wrong. Cookie heard him whistling a tune that sounded an awful lot like *If I Were a Rich Man* from the Broadway Show *Fiddler on the Roof*. No one could whistle for as long or as loudly as Johnny. No shit, the man seemed happy, unbelievably happy, and that was too weird!

She had stashed her dough under her mattress. There was no safer place. No one slept on her bed or came into her room. If hiding money under the mattress had worked for Grandmother Delia during the Great Depression, it would work for her.

She opened her bedroom window. The warm night air bore traces of fresh cut grass combined with car exhaust, hovering a notch above the sweet fragrance of Lily of the Valley. It had been awhile since Cookie had jumped out of her bedroom window. She examined the ground below. The drop seemed far more precipitous than it had in the past. Years ago, she had just plunged out the window and latched onto the clothesline. Now she stood there weighing the alternatives like a plodding old man. *Jump!* she told herself, but her body didn't budge.

Cookie left the window, leaned against her bedroom door, and waited with infinite patience, waiting for something to happen in her favor.

Instead of being a quest for freedom, jumping out of the window felt like a suicide plunge. She was approaching seventeen, far too old to have to resort to desperate moves! How undignified it would be to jump out of her bedroom window!

She pressed her ear to the door, listening for the sounds of the house. Her mother's stereo, tuned in to WPAT-FM, played the *Moonlight Sonata*, in direct juxtaposition to Johnny's exuberant whistling of a show tune. The music defined them as two strange people, who were always at cross purposes with their different dreams and desires, and wholly incapable of one understanding the other.

She heard someone come to the front door. The man's voice was familiar but Cookie could not identify him. Few spare words passed, too muffled for Cookie to hear what he was saying. Although he put a stop to Johnny's whistling and Donny's clatter, he didn't stay long, and the front door slammed shut. There was an unnatural period of calm. No yelling, whistling or complaining, no noise, it was as if Johnny had died. Donny too.

Finally a brief opening appeared. Johnny was still alive. "Where's your sister?" he asked the snitch, who did not tell him what she had done to her older sister. "And would you please put some clothes on!"

Cookie's patience had paid off. "Johnny, Johnny, Donny locked me in," she hollered through the door. "Please let me out."

"Jesus Christ," she heard him say, climbing the steps. "What's the matter with you, Donny! That lock serves no good purpose unless I use it! What did you do that to your sister for?"

"There," he said, unlatching the bolt. He opened the door and looked at Cookie. "That kid is a pisser! How could you let her get away with that? You know she looks up to you. You need to be teaching her what's wrong from right."

Cookie could not comprehend what he was saying. He always said things that didn't make sense. "I didn't notice the door was locked until it was too late."

She especially hated when Johnny's eyes narrowed and his jaw hung loose. It was the facial expression of a fool who thought he was incredibly smart. Handsome too.

"What's the matter with you being home alone on a Friday night? Shouldn't you be out with friends?"

"I'm just chillin' at my pad." Cookie stared at her father. It was as if he did not know that thousands of dollars had been stolen from his office. She had expected some reaction, his concern, weeping and hollering, dry-mouthed fear, but there was nothing.

"Aren't you worried about money?"

"Huh?" Johnny looked confused.

"Money, money," she said in a sing-song voice. "You know the green stuff you never have enough of and always complain about? Money?"

Johnny's eyes had never looked so clear and blue. "This guy just came to the door, looking for you. He's nice. I like this guy. He's Italian. Not that Polack half-breed Stanley or the colored kid."

Cookie didn't know who the guy was or what Johnny was saying.

"Drives a nice car. Little red sports car. Said he'd wait out front for a while. He said his name is Tony Amendolito. Know him?"

A flash of cold paranoia crept up her back. She felt like she had been clocked. "How long ago was this?"

Johnny's eyes searched his daughter's face in a most loving way, a solemn moment to establish their deep father-daughter bond. He gave her the smile that he thought only belonged to the two of them. "Concetta," he paused. "Concetta."

He took a deep breath as if he was overcome with emotion and his voice grew gentle. "Concetta, this Tony Amendolito looks like the kind of guy I always imagined for you. Know what I mean?"

Cookie grew more despondent by the minute, not knowing what to do next, but certain of one thing: She had to get the hell out of here! "Would you close the door? I'm not feeling well."

Johnny looked concerned. "I'm starting to worry about you. Since you got rid of that Stanley guy, you never do anything fun! And where's that colored boy, Herman? I wish I was him, young, starting out in music again! If I was a musician and black, then I'd have made a name for myself by now."

"Like your color ever had anything to do with anything you've ever done! I never understood why you gave up your music! It used to be the only thing you cared about!"

"I can't believe you talk to me that way!" Johnny looked like he had been cut to the quick. "What's the matter with you? You're always moping around, not doing nothing with yourself. You've got no job and no friends! What kind of life is that for a young girl? You should go out with this Tony Amendolito. He would be good for you."

"I've got cramps. I've got my period." Cookie smiled. She knew that would get rid of him.

"Oh." He gave her a uneasy grin. "Oh that. I'm glad you got that," he said, muttering to himself, closing the door, giving her a wink. "I'm glad about that. Boy, am I glad about that! Geez! You wouldn't not want to not get that thing. I don't even want to think about that, for Chrissakes!"

Cookie leaned against the door until she was sure he was gone. She had not thought things through. Money was supposed to make her life better, not worse.

Nineteen

Stella d'Oro cookies are made in the Bronx. In the summer when the windows of the subway are open, you can take a bath in salt, flour, butter, eggs, sugar, anise and rum. Even in June, the core temperature of the subway can be as hot as hell. The open windows of the car did little to circulate the muggy air. It was one of those hot, almost summer nights, humid enough to make Cookie's hair curl around her face into a swirling mass so voluminous that her head felt as heavy as her legs. The steamy air thickened her skin, making her feel like she could drown on a night like this and nobody would notice.

Never wear nice clothes. No jewelry, she had told Izzy, but the girl had other ideas and paid no attention to Cookie's advice. She wore enormous gold hoop earrings. Her usual tiny cross was gone and replaced by a trio of thick, ropey gold chains and a gold bangle bracelet glittering on her arm. A skimpy pink crochet dress clung to her petite body, amplifying her small, pointy breasts.

As the subway trundled south, the aroma of Stella d'Oro cookies waned as surely as the half-moon that appeared in the hazy sky, 90 degrees to the north of a sullen sun. It was rare to see the sun and the moon settling in the same sky. Izzy's perfume flared in Cookie's nostrils as if it was a seductive balm, but in no way did it banish the demons from Cookie's soul.

"What are you wearing?"

"*Je Reviens.* It means I will return. It's made by Worth, one of the oldest couture houses in France." She looked at Cookie and smiled. Cookie didn't know whether Izzy was being patronizing, engaging in subtle flirtation or just being kind.

Izzy had expressed reservations about riding on the subway; she thought it was beneath her, but Cookie nudged her along for the ride. Now she was sorry because Izzy did everything wrong. The two girls sat pressed together, shoulder to shoulder, not speaking to one another, while the subway banged along the track.

Past rush hour, the car was light with passengers. At the other corner of the car, two guys crammed into a small two-seater. More brown than black, the lighter skinned guy wore a shirt unbuttoned to his navel. The other very dark guy had a big gleaming fro. A third guy wearing a Brooklyn Dodgers baseball cap and sweatpants stood over the other two guys. Exuding raw power and a high wattage, toothy grin, he seemed to be the one in charge. Doing his best to avoid holding onto the pole, he was surefooted and kept his balance, rocking his body in the same jarring rhythm as the subway. Cookie could feel the guys looking in their direction every so often, giving both girls the once over.

Up on the El, the subway cars swung side to side and scraped against the track, squealing metal, a sensational screech that threatened to split the cars apart in a great unraveling of rivets and bolts. The subway always felt unstable in this part of the Bronx, as though the entire train would derail, until it slipped down into the tunnel, and then everything would be okay. But they weren't there yet. They still had to get through the Bronx and Harlem.

Cookie took to staring. Staring was a good place to be. It was her favorite method to seal herself in a bubble, away from any danger. She wouldn't dare look at the guys at the other end of the car. What little she could see from the corner of her eye made her nervous. Gangs rode on the subway, mugging people, snatching gold chains from their necks, holding innocent people at gunpoint, screaming until they wished they could die.

Knowing she'd be on the subway, with the exception of her psychedelic platform shoes, Cookie had dressed conservatively. Her short-sleeve yellow peasant blouse was not a showstopper. Her new bell bottom jeans lacked frayed edges or patches—she was so done with patches.

Izzy turned and looked right at the three fellows, giving them a small friendly smile. Cookie elbowed her and whispered in her ear, "What are you nuts! Never make eye contact. Make eye contact here and you're dead!"

Izzy didn't like being reprimanded. She turned her head away as though she had been insulted. "My eyes play tricks in the heat," she whispered, giving Cookie baleful eyes and a coquettish smile. She took her hand into her own and caressed her fingers. "My, you have such long delicate fingers."

Cookie pulled her hand away. She felt uncomfortable talking so much. It would only draw attention. Shaking her head, grimacing, she felt nasty and nudged Izzy, whispering hoarsely into her ear. "You have to have an attitude. You have to show attitude that says, *Don't mess with me*, and at the same time, never, ever, make eye contact!"

Izzy laughed. "How do you show attitude without making eye contact?" She moved her face close to Cookie and smiled. "Haven't you noticed the way I look at you? I think you're one sexy Mama! A hot fox as they say!"

Cookie yanked the strap on her shoulder bag. "I'm serious!" she said in a harsh whisper. "The subway is a dangerous place!"

Pulling her ear, Izzy giggled. "You're tickling me. That tickles." She looked at the three guys, giggling. They didn't seem to think she was funny. One guy nodded his head; it was a look that said he knew what she was all about. *Crazy honky chick.*

Staring straight ahead, Cookie gritted her teeth together. "Stop drawing attention to yourself!"

"I don't see what the big problem is," Izzy protested.

Cookie rolled her eyes for effect and felt a tight sneer zipping across her mouth. She saw Izzy look at the guys again. "If you don't cut it out, you're going to get us killed or worse!"

Izzy laughed. "What could possibly be worse than death?" She dropped her pocketbook to the floor, pulled out her wallet and began counting dollar bills.

"What the fuck!" Cookie grabbed Izzy's wallet, stuffed the money back inside and plopped the bag into her lap.

It was useless to talk sense into Izzy. Scanning the banner ads that littered the horizontal space above the subway's windows, she saw an ad for the early entry program at New York University. She wouldn't mind going to a fancy college like NYU, but Harvard was her first choice! NYU wouldn't get to first base with the amazing Cookie Colangelo, not with Harvard and Yale clamoring to get her attention! She scoffed to herself. *I'll be the first girl from Yonkers who goes to Harvard.* But even at that moment, she knew it was a delusion, and just not possible. *Kids like me don't go to Ivy League schools.*

Yonkers was once full of factories that hired teenagers, The Alexander Smith & Sons Carpet Mills, the Sugar House or Otis Elevator, where there were no college recruiters from the Ivy League schools. Most of the factories had shut. Yonkers had once been the Queen of Manufacturing, but those days were gone. Working in the A&P or for New York City's utility company Con-Ed was as good as it got.

After the Dyckman Street stop, the subway descended into the tunnel and began moving faster on a more even keel. The girls jostled into one another with fluorescence flickering on and off across their faces. Izzy took Cookie's hand again and smiled sweetly.

The walls of the subway were brown. Most of the people getting on the subway in the Bronx were brown. Izzy might have been Hispanic and brown, but she was different—rich and totally clueless. Cookie was white alright, but not stupid. Stupid and white did not do well here. You might think that skin color should not matter, but it did in New York City, where in 1973 the battle lines were divided and the history was bitter.

The subway car had become swallowed by darkness in the tunnel. Overhead fluorescent light flickered, more often off than on. The car's windows gave passengers a mirror-like reflection of themselves. Izzy watched her own image in the subway window across from where she sat. She stuck out her tongue. Cookie saw her in the subway window and took note, thinking Izzy had a particle caught between her teeth.

Izzy's tongue darted to the side, back and forth, then up and down. Lolling round and round her mouth, her tongue spun languidly. Her tongue picked up speed, lapping and panting the way a dog drank water, then clamping down hard with the feral delight of a cat biting off the head of a bird. Her tongue picked up greater speed, turning into a whirling dervish. Flicking her tongue lizard-like, she made a sucking noise as though she was drinking the last bit of a milk shake through a drinking straw. Her tongue flattened, expanding into sponge, and ultimately widened into a mighty sword, with which she intended to dominate the universe.

"What are you doing?"

"I'm exercising my tongue. After all, it is a muscle."

"I don't get it."

Izzy smiled coquettishly. "Would you like to find out why I keep my tongue in shape?"

The dark guy with the big fro opened his mouth, then he

threw his head back and laughed, a mighty uproarious laugh. "What's going on, my man, my man?"

The black guy who had been standing, now gripped the steel pole for support. His other hand slid into the deep pocket of his black sweatpants, rummaging around for something large and convenient to pull out in case he needed to have it fast. He angled his body away from the girls and toward the two guys in the seat who looked dumbfounded.

All three guys stood up and walked over toward the girls, laughing, hitting and slapping each other so hard, Cookie thought they would collapse on the floor of the train, and clutch their bellies.

"You are one jive turkey!" One of them yelled.

The subway came to a grinding stop at 168th Street. The guys' bodies knocked into one another. Still laughing, they walked off the car. Cookie was horribly embarrassed and pulled her saddlebag closer to her chest. She feared Izzy's breach of subway etiquette had cast a spell as powerful as a fortune doled out by Zelda the Gypsy: *Soon you will lose all of your money.*

The three guys were still laughing as the subway pulled out of the station. One guy laughed so hard he clutched his chest and keeled over.

You can't tell a good guy from a bad guy by the color of his skin. The three guys on the subway who had made fun of them were nowhere near as dangerous as Cookie had become. She had stolen a lot of money and would do anything to keep it. Even kill somebody.

"You see, they were harmless," Izzy said. "And kind of cute. Although not top pick for an afternoon of delight." She patted Cookie's arm. "You're my first choice."

Cookie yelled above the subway thundering through the Bronx, toward Washington Heights and Harlem. "You need to wise up!"

"You need to talk properly." Izzy's long smile fanned the

conflict between them, but she never raised her voice. "If you want to get somewhere in life, you had better be well spoken."

Cookie started to think some people sailed through life unscathed, protected from reality. Izzy always seemed so self-assured, as if her life was golden, magical, and nothing could ever possibly go wrong. Everything worked out swell for people like Izzy. They enjoyed a special type of dumb luck.

From 137th Street, the subway came out of the tunnel and began climbing the El. It took tremendous effort for the subway to reach the flat plane of track en route to the Harlem station at 125th Street—the last station on the IRT line going south that was steeped in darkness and perched on top of the El like the empty nest of a raptor. Surrounded on all sides by slum dwellings, the buildings were close enough to reach out of the window and touch their soot-stained yellowing brick walls. The subway slowed to a crawl, taking the scenic tour through one of the most notorious slums on earth. The two girls were eye level with broken and boarded up windows, air conditioners blocking any sort of view from inside or out, and clotheslines strung with pants and shirts drying under the last trace of afternoon sun before night fell.

You could see people inside the buildings. Shadowy forms floated through time and space, never becoming fully defined enough to be the real human beings who were shaving, washing clothes, eating supper, opening the fridge. Jolts of music came in waves, blaring from a boom box, then quickly receding, falling away like sound made dismal by the static of poor radio reception. Real life was going on amid the squalor and the TV images melding into a wallpaper that flickered in darkening rooms. Every so often, somebody waved to the passengers passing by on the train as though it was nightly entertainment, a private TV show instead of a subway traveling through Harlem.

Cookie had the only white face in the car. Someone might think the only white face was ugly and want to shoot her.

From any window in the building, a gun could be fired at close range. She used to think a sniper sat in one of those windows and he'd be looking for a Honky Mutha Fucker to maim or kill. *That target would be me.* Cringing at the notion, Cookie bowed her head. If she kept her head down, she'd be safe. This part of the subway ride always made her hold her breath until the subway safely disappeared back into the tunnel.

Cookie wasn't sure if Izzy's persistent touch was sexual or romantic, just a girl thing—when girls hold hands because they love each other as friends, it's a flaming girl crush. Cookie was white in a sea of black and brown. So was Izzy, but who's counting—the girl could be white or brown, brown and white, or white and brown, depending how she identified herself when she was applying for a job or for a scholarship to a school, any school, NYU or Harvard or Yale. And that did matter. Race and ethnicity did matter. But it was money that mattered most of all.

Izzy's father worked as an investor in commercial real estate and traded stocks and bonds. Cookie no longer knew what Johnny did for a living or why there had been so much money in his office. It dawned on Cookie: Izzy had no idea she had stolen thousands of dollars.

The subway stopped at the station on 125th Street. The doors opened and stayed open. The composition of the air changed radically from the aroma of Stella d'Oro and Izzy's perfume to the miasma of car exhaust, rotten eggs, and rancid trash decomposing under a hazy June sun. The subway doors remained open at this station longer than any other on the IRT line. Cookie didn't know why. No one seemed to know why. Maybe it was time for the subway operators to take a smoke break on the subway platform out in the open in the fetid air before disappearing back into the tunnel—the bowels of earth—running underneath the west side of Manhattan.

Twenty

Isabella María Fernanda Donovan knew things about New York City that Cookie did not know: art, theater, libraries, museums, popular eateries and the clubs. What Izzy did not know about being streetwise in the big city was shocking. She looked up at the tall buildings, ogling them, pointing toward the sky with childish delight.

"The Gulf & Western Building always takes my breath away. Not because it's tall. There are much taller buildings. It's modern. So new!"

Only gaping country hicks and sad sack out-of-towners look up at tall buildings in New York City. Cookie nodded wryly to herself; she knew most of the buildings by heart, studying their pictures, attributes and dimensions in a book lent to her long ago, handpicked for her by Mrs. Kerry at the Carnegie Library in the Square.

So, she avoided looking toward the sky. She knew here, in the city, there were no clouds to speak of, not one. Her sky had gone dark, darker than the deepest shade of Yonkers granite, and her clouds had been sucked away into a secret vortex by a phantom hand.

Izzy stood on the corner of Columbus Circle and Central Park West and attempted to hail a cab. Cookie insisted on walking. Izzy's small mouth twitched with disapproval.

The girls ducked arm in arm into the subway station at Columbus Circle and got off two stops later in Times Square. Peep show arcades. Massage parlor storefronts. Cheap clubs promised lap dances and much more for fifty cents. Side acts and side shows offered girls, girls, girls, two for the price of one, 16 beautiful girls and 3 ugly ones. Pimps, hookers, and junkies, all looking the same, all of them could be one or the other, or all three, a pimp, a hooker, and a junkie, and all of them hustling.

Two New York City cops were huddled in the corner of a music store, looking like they didn't want to be seen or they were just trying to stay cool from the heat. A ruddy-faced man with long stringy hair smiled, flashed his two gold crowns, and bade them to come into his massage parlor. Its yellow awning spelled out nude flesh, as if naked flesh could be anything but nude. He opened his wide red mouth and flicked his tongue, mimicking cunnilingus.

"Where are we going?" Izzy wailed.

"How the fuck should I know!" Cookie yelled. "Just look like you know where you're going!"

The girls fumbled hastily, still holding onto one another. They began to walk faster, passing another nude live sex show storefront, where the man out front greeted them by massaging his balls.

"Hello, baby!"

Times Square was full of pimps, whores and drug addicts; there was something promising about low life because they were real people. The down and out, the criminals, the wannabees and the hipsters, all struggling for a come-up, hustling to get by in the big city.

They reached a gritty line of women in micro-mini-skirts and shiny platform shoes, beckoning them with pouty lips and air kisses. Cookie and Izzy began running, madly, blindly, arms linked together as strong as chain. They ran headlong into a woman with enough brute force to almost knock themselves silly.

"Excuse me!"

Cookie had no choice but to look up. She was not a tall building, but the tallest woman Cookie had ever seen. Blonde and black, she stood well over six-six in her silver spike heels.

"Excuse me!" She put her hands on her hips and said, "Yous is nasty! And rude!"

"I'm so sorry."

"I didn't mean to.

"Please excuse us," Izzy proffered, taking Cookie's arm.

Cookie stopped noticing anything on the street, tuning out blaring horns, doors slamming, smatterings of street Spanish, the echo of music from cars and ghetto blasters. All was lost on her. Cookie stood there, mesmerized, in awe, and did not dare move. She had never seen a woman like this, a neon blonde goddess after a long dark spell.

"What you got going on, Girl?" The blonde woman almost purred, winking at Cookie like they were old friends. "You've got yourself great shoes. I just love-love-love those crazy-ass-quilt shoes!"

Izzy grew so frightened, she feigned innocence, her eyes pled ignorance. She crossed her legs and feet as if she was trying to avoid peeing in her pants.

"I could make a lot of money with yous girls." Distinctly low and androgynous, her voice crooned a true contralto. "I be needing four new girls." She held up four curvy fingers, red fingernails as long as the talons on an owl. Her bright white teeth showed the distinct stroke marks of a small paintbrush.

She looked at Izzy's pointy breasts, then turned to Cookie. "You got yourself one of thems peach and creams complexions.

"Peaches and cream," Izzy chirped.

"Shut up, who asked you? With them pointy tits, you be

chillin' with them old men, the sorry kind that ain't got nobody to go home to, cause they be pervs of the worst kind!"

Cookie visibly brightened and nodded, giving her the high-five. "I've been looking for you."

The woman leaned down, gave Cookie a high five with her other hand, and bumped her broad beamed bottom against Cookie's shoulder. "Is that so? How'd you know me, Girl?"

Cookie tilted her face up, giving her a full dose of attitude. "I just know."

"I'm Gwendolyn, Sugar. Some niggas call me Wendy, but I don't listen much to them cause I don't respect them." She opened her beautiful gold lamé purse and pulled out a business card that sparkled with glitter and rhinestones. "Call me and leave your number. I gotta answering machine and I always call back."

Cookie gave her good smile, big, china white and profuse. "I'm Cookie. She's Izzy."

"Uh huh. Call me anytime. You got my number." She spun in her silver spike heels with the astonishing agility of a mighty ballerina, strutted down the street, and turned right on the corner of 42nd Street and Eighth Avenue.

The subway shuttle from Times Square to Grand Central Station took about eight minutes, long enough for a mangy old man to beg for money. He pulled out a ukulele, sang *Tiptoe Through the Tulips*, and passed around his grease-streaked grey cap. Abiding by her rule, *never pull out your money in public*, Cookie turned away from the beggar. She was appalled to see Izzy reach into her pocketbook and take out a dollar for the man. Cookie nudged her firmly in the shoulder, but all that did was raise Izzy's ire. She tossed the dollar into the man's cap, placed her pocketbook in between her legs, onto the floor of the subway.

"You were so brave. Oh my God! Wendy!"

"Gwendolyn," Cookie corrected her. "She doesn't like being called Wendy."

"She scared the bejeezus out of me." Wrinkling her pert nose, baring her chiclet-shaped teeth, Izzy squeezed Cookie's leg. "Mind if I feel you?"

She smiled with great intention as though she did not need to ask for permission. "Nice, firm muscles. You're so shapely. I feel too skinny compared to you! You must know by now that I'm very attracted to you."

Cookie did not know how to respond to her silly entreaties and felt embarrassed. No matter how big you think you are, Manhattan cuts you down to a small size. While Izzy loomed large in Cookie's life in Yonkers, in Manhattan Izzy was diminished by the size of the crowds swirling around them in a crush of mostly men, wearing business suits. Some women wore flowery summer dresses and strands of metallic beads or pearls. Rush hour had begun, a fact that did not go unnoticed by Izzy.

"I want to show you a real library." She led Cookie west on 42nd Street, passing the Daily News Building, which was once the fictional headquarters for the Daily Planet, employing the boyishly handsome, bookish-looking and well-mannered Clark Kent aka Superman. "The lobby has an enormous globe that rotates on its axis. I think I heard it is the world's largest. Would you like to see it?"

Cookie shook her head and frowned. As much as Izzy tried to impress her, the girl was totally lacking in street smarts. Plus, if it were not for Cookie, Izzy would have to sit in the last seat in history class. She was dumb alright, but would always be able to get by in life because she was rich.

A block away, Izzy gushed over the Chanin Building. "Look, at the bronze grills! It's so Art Deco. I bet you don't even know what that is?" She looked at Cookie with a sardonic grin.

If they were in the subway station, Cookie would think seriously about pushing Izzy into the track—she was so horribly condescending.

"It's a terra cotta skyscraper. One of the first in the city, built in the late 1920s." Cookie pointed to the bottom of the building. "That base there is black Belgian marble."

"You're so knowledgeable." Izzy raised her eyebrows. "Well, sort of." She winked.

Cookie did not tell her that for years she had pored over *The AIA Guide to New York City*. At the Yonkers Carnegie Library, Mrs. Kerry had loaned her an original copy that could only be checked out at the reference desk.

Cookie was oblivious of Izzy or anyone else around her. She looked straight ahead, walking west on 42nd Street, while she spoke about the Chanin Building. "The bronze frieze above the black marble shows scenes in evolution. The second frieze with lots of curvy leaves is made from terra-cotta."

Cookie stopped walking for a moment and shifted her saddlebag from her left shoulder, took a moment to rest and catch her breath before heaving the bag over her right shoulder. In the insufferable heat, the bag had grown heavy, but it contained her most important possessions: the black & white notebook that she never seemed to write in anymore, a tube of peach frost lipstick, and a small wad of cash.

Izzy poked her saddlebag. "You always think someone is trying to take your money."

"That's because someone always is!"

"You're not going to give me that dribble again about having an attitude."

Cookie stopped walking in the middle of the street and gazed at the sight of the grand New York Public Library on Fifth Avenue. As wide as a city block, its marble façade and ornate detailing represented the finest in beaux arts style architecture, the same architectural style as her beloved Carnegie Library in Getty Square. The steps leading up to the library were guarded by two stone lions like bookends. In Cookie's mind, she thought of them as literary lions, and they were formidable.

Izzy took off and skipped up the steps, proclaiming, "Now, that's a library."

"I've been here before," Cookie said, racing up the steps to catch up.

They rapidly climbed the steps toward the front entrance. "Don't know why you like that old library in Getty Square so much."

"That library will always be my first love."

"Kind of like Stanley?"

Cookie frowned. It hurt her to think about Stanley. She wasn't even going to bother to respond.

Both girls had reached the front entrance of the library. They stood facing one another. Despite the weight of her bag, climbing the steps made Cookie feel strong. She glanced at the lions as if they were familiar friends. She knew she needed to always have a couple of lions in her life. The library was much more than a library or a landmark from the past. The library represented all that was yet to come.

As they wandered up to the third floor to the Rose Reading Room, Cookie told Izzy, "I used to play hooky from school and come here."

"How strange that you'd play hooky from school and go to a library."

"Not just any library, but this library."

The Rose Reading Room was filled with generous light filtering in from windows that reached forever upward to a ceiling that appeared to be painted with clouds like a rich variation of heaven. The entire room was filled with the old card catalogs stored in heavy standing furniture with multitudes of narrow drawers that held a card for every book in the library. The drawers were made of dark wood and had brass pulls so highly burnished that they gleamed.

Cookie whispered in Izzy's ear. "When I was a kid I was scared that someone would tell me that I didn't belong here, but no one ever did."

"Why on earth would they say that?" Izzy looked baffled.

Cookie shrugged and smiled. There was no explanation

why she would feel that way and Izzy would never feel the same sting of rejection or experience a similar sense of not belonging, of being told you don't fit in somewhere where you want to be, when you have every right to be there. Cookie was still trying to figure that out. She only knew the library made her feel tender spiritual awareness, some sort of connection with something greater than herself. She did not know what that connection was, but she knew it had nothing to do with the dough she had stashed under her mattress, the small ream of twenties she carried in her bag, and of course, the clouds.

Izzy led her to an unexpected dark nook off of the main hallway outside of the reading room. The nook held a heavy glass case displaying a medieval manuscript. Cookie leaned closer, noting the manuscript had been handwritten by monks in the twelfth century. The parchment had yellowed and the cursive script seemed to be in another language, vaguely reminiscent of an old English font. Otherwise, the manuscript was in excellent condition and obviously had to be kept in the dark to prevent deterioration from natural light. Not all that light reveals is certain or good, nor was being kept safe in the dark always bad or forbidding.

Before Cookie could ascertain any change in her friend's movements or of the emotional dynamics between them, Izzy made a bee-line for her body. Her face moved as fast as a billy club and kissed Cookie squarely on the mouth. The kiss was neither hard nor soft, neither dry nor wet, somewhere in between mildly moist and sweet, and it disarmed her.

"Please stop." Cookie's soft voice sounded meek, even to herself. "You're crushing my bag."

Izzy looked down; realizing Cookie's saddlebag had come between them, she smiled. "You really ought to get over this money thing. You have a peasant mentality."

They descended down the steps to the main floor, each bearing a heavier burden than the lightness that had first led them into the library. Cookie was sure her clothes reeked of Izzy's perfume. *Je Reviens. Give me a fucking break.*

"How do you have money? You don't work. Is your family rich?"

"Why, that's so rude! Very rude! I get an allowance. Don't you?"

"An allowance!" Cookie scoffed. "What do you have to do to get an allowance?"

"I think, therefore I am." Izzy's tone was snotty as though she thought she was superior to Cookie and indignant over the fact that she had a crush on her.

Izzy turned her back on Cookie, swooping out of the library and into the street with the mercurial force of an apparition fleeing the scene of a haunting. The forced gaiety that was as contrived as her ability to fake foreign accents vanished. Izzy promptly hailed a cab on Fifth Avenue to take them both north. The cab driver wore a turban and never turned around, instead watching them in the rear view mirror. Izzy whispered to Cookie, "I don't like those people, they smell bad." Cookie felt embarrassed. "He's Sikh. Have some respect." She squirmed away from Izzy and her ridiculous pout. Izzy instructed the cabbie to take them to Riverdale. Cookie quipped, "Where the Bronx kisses Yonkers on the ass!"

Twenty-one

Everyone seemed to be gunning for Cookie: Johnny Colangelo, Mosella Moran, Tony Amendolito and now, the Yonkers City Police. A cop called Izzy at home and got a hot tip. She told him he would not find Cookie on the Number Two Bus. There was no way she'd travel through Getty Square when Mosella Moran, Tony Amendolito and possibly Toni Ferlinghetti were itching to hurt her. A New York City medallion taxi would not travel all the way to Yonkers. Cookie was about to hop into a local cab at 242nd Street in the Bronx when Detective Sergeant Ronan O'Hearn intercepted her.

The detective wore plain clothes. The appearance of his shield and badge number did little to reassure her that he was really a cop. Ever since she was a little kid, she had always been told never to get into a car with a stranger. The driver at the wheel of the cab she was about to climb into recognized O'Hearn and accorded him the politeness and respect befitting a cop.

Cookie got into the car with the detective, not knowing what he wanted from her, but suspecting his interest had something to do with money. She thought she'd make it easy by cooperating with him.

"Are you related to Pinky O'Hearn?"

"The little red-headed guy who hangs out at the Midget Bar?" The cop turned briefly to look at her. "I know who he is. No, we're not related."

A small green sign saying *Welcome to Yonkers* hung suspended on a metal pole above a balustrade like a neon reflection of the humid night. They were on South Broadway, going north. Detective Sergeant Ronan O'Hearn hugged the steering wheel of his canary yellow Ford Bronco, driving fast and hard on the offensive, not looking out for the other guy who, for all practical purposes, should be compelled to watch out for him. The windows were open, letting in warm fetid air, commingled with exhaust fumes. Cookie did not know where he was taking her and hoped it would not be to the police station in Getty Square, which was close, too close, to the Yonkers City Jail.

The road was empty. It was the middle of the night and in Cookie's estimation around two o'clock in the morning, but she wasn't tired. Izzy thought the Bronx was inhabited by slovenly low-life that existed in a subterranean world fathoms beneath her. After Cookie ditched Izzy in Riverdale, she went clubbing on her own. She cabbed herself to the Pick and Shovel on Webster Avenue. There were jams going on there all night long. Dancing in her crazy-quilt shoes was easy, but relaxing was impossible. Stowing her saddlebag filled with dough on a chair shoved under a table didn't give her much room to take a chance. She had to keep moving.

On 231st and Broadway, she ran back and forth from the Green Alligator to Johnny Mac's. When one band took a break, the other band next door started playing, and Cookie kept moving.

She had turned into a mover. Never staying in one place, never settling down, it was the only way to keep two steps ahead of the world, because every time you thought you were ahead, the world threw a curve ball that forced you to take a step or two back. She was racing against time, racing against a world that she knew was stacked against her, and racing against herself. She didn't know if she'd win and thought, in the end, she stood a good chance of losing, but she was going to do everything in her power to give it her best shot.

Four-wheel drive suited Detective Sergeant Ronan O'Hearn. He never knew when the terrain would turn treacherous. He needed some company. He had that vacant cadence in his voice men get when they're starved for conversation but are distracted by sexual fantasies of their own grand design and making. Cookie was as good a target as any. He rambled some inconsequential crime statistics that had long become familiar to Cookie in her normal but negative discourse of life so close to New York City.

"Do you gamble?" O'Hearn asked her.

Cookie wasn't going to bother to say one way or another. So much for cooperation. "Why do you ask?"

"Johnny Mac's Bar always has after-hours card games. I thought you knew that. Doesn't your father gamble?"

"Johnny? I don't know what he does."

O'Hearn was handsome, especially when he smiled. Irish looking, with his pug nose, fleshed-out cheeks, and round face, he was very unlike Stanley who had clean angular lines, an aquiline nose and high cheekbones. The cop's brown hair looked freshly cut, almost as clipped as a Marine Corps style crew cut. Stanley had worn his thick blonde hair down to the middle of his back. Despite their glaring physical differences, Cookie thought of them as similar, maybe because they were much older and seemed to know something she did not yet know. Maybe they needed to learn something from her. Maybe she was fooling herself again. She was good at that.

O'Hearn wanted to be helpful. "You can get a sloe gin fizz for seventy-five cents at the Leprechaun Bar on 238th."

"Cool. But I don't drink." And that much was true. She didn't crave the taste of alcohol. She didn't like to drink in bars, worrying some guy would try to take advantage of her, overpower her, especially now because she was in the money. The funny thing was, it had been a month since a guy had put the moves on her. Instead, she was still reeling from the pint-size lezzie who had stolen a kiss from her in broad daylight.

"What are you doing out in bars so late?"

"Dancing. I like to dance all by myself."

Cookie thought of the cop as an unformed lump of maleness, lean and ready to take charge, to take action over diddly-squat. He was trying to be somebody or something. Maybe if she was feeling generous, she'd help him out, but she wanted to get home so she could collapse, drift to sleep on her lumpy mattress and dream about leaving Yonkers.

She was relieved when he pulled up in front of the Broadway Diner on South Broadway. Even though it was late, it was Friday night and the diner would be full, but she'd have no trouble getting a seat. Everyone always wants to accommodate cops.

Cookie smiled sweetly at him. "Do you always work so late?"

"Only when I've got to." He winked at her.

The wink was all she needed to cast light on her foul suspicions about O'Hearn. He was just another Yonkers guy on the make.

"Well, might as well get this over," she said, jumping out of the Bronco.

Cookie took a seat in a booth across from the refrigerated bakery display case holding cake and pie. Apple Pie. Blueberry pie. Peach pie. Mounds of whipped cream fluffed on the top of a massive strawberry short cake. Now that she thought about it, she was hungry. It had been a long day. She had gone from being locked in her room to getting kissed romantically by a girl.

The waitress wore a peach-colored uniform and a hairnet. Under the hairnet her hair was brown, frizzy, with a few stray wisps of grey. Her face was lined but unremarkable. Her eyes were hooded, heavy lids weighing down dull eyes, neither brown nor blue, some undefined color. She fawned over the cop, calling him "Ronan" in a tone best reserved for saying the name of a lover. Her body pressed close to his shoulder. Any moment she would take a seat in his lap. Cookie wondered if, one day, she could turn out like the waitress, down on her luck, but not bad off, decent apartment, a string of ex-boyfriends, hustling for tips, getting to flirt with cops in the middle of the night.

"Coffee?" Without waiting for a response, she poured into two mugs, smiling at the cop, never once looking at Cookie.

What was it about waitresses that they never smiled at her? Scanning the menu proved to be a more favorable pursuit. Belgian waffles, eggs benedict and ordinary scrambled eggs, omelets. Her eyes feasted on the refrigerator case full of pie and cake. She had a sudden craving for Boston Cream Pie.

"Get what you want." O'Hearn smiled. "It's on me."

"Boston Cream Pie."

"You mean, Yankee Cream Pie." The cop's eyes betrayed his mischief; at least, he had a sense of fun.

This was a guy who liked to play practical jokes and drop puns. She liked the way his eyes weren't as blue as Stanley's eyes and seemed to change colors in the yellow light overhead or the fluorescent light shooting from the display freezer and the silver diner jukebox mounted on the wall inside of the booth.

Cookie's hair felt as large as the mane on a literary lion. She pushed her hair away from her face and stared at the cop. "Is this a date?" Cookie asked. "Do you have a girlfriend?

The cop looked taken aback.

Cookie's smile was effusive. "I just want to get a lay of the land."

She wondered if O'Hearn had a woman in his life to fancy his cheap cologne. She probably had large pendulous breasts, the kind that swung when she walked. And although she was extremely dumb, she had an answer for everything. Cookie knew all about Detective Sergeant Ronan O'Hearn. She could imagine his woman.

"I don't pay much attention to the routine stuff," he said. "It's the weird stuff I can't take."

"Murders?"

O'Hearn nodded. "That, yeah, I don't like murder, but it's the strange robberies that leave me cold. I don't like anyone playing me for a fool and people who steal always think they can get away with it. Murderers don't do that. They usually know they stand a good chance of getting caught, even when they're smart, because most murders are committed for a reason, and it's usually emotional, or it's business."

O'Hearn stared at her but she knew he could not read her face. No one could.

"Nine times out of ten, the murder victim will always know the perpetrator. That's not true of robbery. It can be completely random."

Cookie knew she was guilty of stealing, but certainly not murder. She knew being guilty for one crime made her guilty for every theft since the beginning of Yonkers history. Unequivocal and universal guilt was like original sin. And that was a Yonkers thing. These deep rooted feelings only hold true if you're not a real criminal. A real criminal has no conscience—and that was the ultimate form of protection.

"I'm having a bad day." She smiled at the cop and placed her saddlebag on her lap. She was very careful about diving into her bag to get her Marlboros. She didn't want stray twenty dollar bills to accidentally spill out.

She went to light a Marlboro, but O'Hearn was quick to light a match for her.

"Your old boss, Artie Jelinek, said you took money from the cash register."

Cookie was sincerely surprised. She knew Artie was a slime ball, but she never had considered that he would stoop this low.

"He's lying. He fired me because he called the cops on those young girls, not me. He wanted to send a message to the black community. He thought keeping me there would be bad for business. There are other reasons why he fired me too...." her voice trailed.

She thought of telling O'Hearn what Artie was doing to her, but she didn't know whether he'd believe her, and why should he? Guys did stuff like that to girls all of the time. For all that she knew, the cop might be angling to cop a feel too.

"How much did he say I took?"

"About a hundred dollars."

Cookie scoffed. "Give me a break."

Then he squinted his eyes. "Maybe two hundred."

"He's lying."

Cookie laughed even though she didn't feel like it. The accusation made her nervous, scared, reminding her how she had gotten beaten up by a nun for doing nothing wrong. She was the kind of person people accused unfairly. She had always stood out. People made false accusations against her. Usually, they were seeking a scapegoat or just wanted to cause her harm. She could not believe the irony of the situation. She had succeeded in hauling off a box full of money. Lots of money. And here she was being accused by a twerp of taking a hundred bucks. It was a joke. She laughed again.

"He must think I'm stupid or something!"

O'Hearn took a long drag from his own cigarette, a Chesterfield. "Everyone in Yonkers has a scam, a game, a take going on."

"If you say so." Cookie smiled. "But I'm just a young girl trying to get by in the big city."

Cookie flipped through the songs on the jukebox. She thought of Stanley, leaning over the full-size jukebox at the Midget Bar, and the way his hair had shone like a full moon, made pure and incandescent by the bar's signature black light. The bar was famous for making light colored and white objects glow in the dark. She barely heard the cop place the order for a piece of Yankee cream pie and ask for the check. She clammed up and could hardly swallow. Afraid that her hands would shake when she took a drag, she let her Marlboro burn down in the ashtray.

Johnny had always said, *You're better off not to talk. You see nothing. You hear nothing. You know nothing.* Sometimes, you're better off to hold the reins tight over your own personal mystique. She thought of it as protectionism. These were private thoughts and she kept them to herself.

Saturday June 30 1973

Artie Jelinek says I took money from the cash register at Rite Aid. Imagine that! He's a liar! The cop came looking for me cause money was missing from the cash register on the night of the riot and he wanted to talk to me. Detective Sergeant Ronan O'Hearn easily let me go cause he has nothing to go on. It's Artie Jelinek's word against mine. Now I see why no one would hire me. The other stores where I could have gotten a job talked to Artie. They believed Artie. They never even asked me. I can't tell you how angry that makes me feel! Why does this stuff keep happening to me?

I have been a lot of things during my short life. Being a thief is not big on my list. Oops! I guess things have changed! Most of my savings is hidden in the last place anybody would think to look. Oops! Money is beginning to be troublesome. A horrible burden. Maybe I'm not using money the right way. You'd think there would be a school somewhere to teach me how to use money.

I haven't thought about owls much lately. Remember me and my owls? I used to hide in the Owl Hole or the Owl Bowl. I stopped thinking so much about owls after the Blind Owl Alan Wilson died.

The Blind Owl Alan Wilson has been dead for almost three years. To this very day no one knows for sure why he died. Accidental overdose? Suicide? Owls haven't stopped coming into my life. Mrs. Kerry was an owl. I haven't seen her since St. Patrick's Day. Herman Lynch was an owl. Stanley de Falco was an owl. But both of them are gone now too. I thought my owls were going to live forever. I guess they don't. And I can't tell you how sad that makes. So sad. (Three blobs of ink).

I haven't seen Reenie Ruggerio or Herman Lynch in weeks. It's hard to believe that we used to be best friends. Things are weird between me and Izzy. I don't know if she thinks I'm bad cause the cops called her to track me down or she's mad at me cause I don't like kissing her. We still talk but she gives me a funny smile. Crooked. Lopsided. Loopy. And she stares me up and down like something's always wrong with my clothes. She doesn't seem to have many friends. I'm the only person at school who talks to her. I worked hard to catch up in history class and in all of my other classes. I know it's hard to believe but I was promoted to the twelfth grade. School is out for the summer.

Today there is a total eclipse of the sun. The moon is passing between the earth and the sun and that blocks the sun from being seen by people on earth. The total eclipse happens cause the moon looks larger from the earth and blocks the sun. Day turns into night. Good to know! But there will be no solar eclipse going on anywhere near Yonkers. You've got to be in the Sahara Desert to see the whole thing! I heard about a chartered plane leaving from Mount San Antonio College in Southern California to track the eclipse. I bet you anything Stanley is on that flight! He probably has a girlfriend by now! She's probably on that flight with him! I bet her hair is blonder than his. Longer too!

The eclipse is supposed to last for over seven minutes. There will not be a total solar eclipse longer than that until June 25 2150. We're all gonna be dead by then. I want to leave something behind to the world but first I have to live a normal life. I haven't been writing here in my journal too much. I'm going through this f-a-z-e. (I learned that's wrong. It's not faze. It's phase like phases of the moon.) Commas remind me of the moon. A crescent moon. Don't think of trying to steal a comma from me. My commas are not for the taking. I still don't use them.

-ccc

Twenty-two

Arky drove Cookie to the Yonkers Savings and Loan Building. The open windows of the limo let in the thick air of the night, bathing her face with gas fumes and the stench of raw sewage and dead fish from the Hudson River. She fished through her Boho bag for her keys, but Arky was quick. He produced keys to the building and let her in. It was strange that he had keys to Johnny's office. Cookie asked him how he got the keys. Arky smirked when he told her everybody had keys. Cookie did not know whether she should believe him. She knew her father was sloppy, but the revelation that everyone had keys to his office was preposterous.

She did not know if Arky knew about the big crime, the theft, a heist, otherwise known as the greatest windfall of her life. She had not been here since Saturday night on May 19th, the same night she and Reenie had identified Billy Dee's body at the morgue.

Cookie spied Arky from the corner of her eye. She could have been mistaken, but she thought she heard him say, "Haven't you ever heard of preservation? The sanctity of human life! My life!" Those were sophisticated sentiments for

Arky Lovato to express. Very emotional. She thought maybe she had underestimated him.

He flung open the windows behind Johnny's desk and poked his head out into the night. "I want to preserve my life! Don't you give a shit about that?" He waved toward a newly excavated black hole in the ground, marked by bright yellow cones that rerouted traffic through Getty Square. Most of the Arky that Cookie had become familiar with from the back seat of a car had been swallowed by the sultry night. His entire torso was hanging out of the window.

Cookie thought he might jump. She didn't know if there were onlookers below. If there were people on the street waiting for him to jump, it didn't matter. They'd never show mercy. They'd never catch him if he should crane his neck too far and fall. But as soon as he hit the ground, they'd pick his wallet clean. The human head weighs a lot, Cookie thought. Then it dawned on her, Arky was getting sick. Poor innocent bystanders. No one wants to get puked on. She asked him if he was feeling better.

"It was the tension," he said.

"You don't have to take the job," Cookie told him. "If I knew you were going to act this way, I would have never asked you to come to work for me."

Arky straightened and walked away from the window. He was starting to look better. A tinge of color rose to his forehead that was covered with a fine glaze of oil. He was sweating profusely.

"It's not the job. It's Tony Amendolito. He's everywhere. I don't know what he wants from me."

Arky pointed toward the street. "Take a look for yourself."

"Why bother? I know what his car looks like."

Cookie sat down at Johnny's big desk as if she had always wanted to try it on for size. Little had changed since she had last been here. All of Johnny's drawers were open, a surefire way of telling that Johnny was still doing business. She was astonished to see the cardboard box on Millie's small, collapsible doll-sized desk. The money had disappeared and was in very good hands now, but the box was still there. The notion made Cookie smile.

Millie was a large woman, too large for such a small desk. Then it occurred to Cookie that Millie never sat at her desk; she hovered over Johnny, a cyclonic force of adoration, with the pure devotion of a woman hopelessly and utterly in love, a love that would never be returned.

The uneasy calm of Johnny's inactive office was suddenly interrupted. Things began happening, simultaneously. The low rumble of the ancient elevator was moving up the shaft and Arky disappeared. Cookie called him, but he did not answer. Cookie slumped in Johnny's red leather chair, crossed her arms over her chest and waited. Waiting was the hardest part of her life. The sound of a saxophone playing jazz drifted in from a far corner of the building. Lonely discordant notes floated into the room like welcome strangers in the night. A ghost from Johnny's past. When Johnny lost his music, he lost his soul. Now he was in the money but dead in his heart. Music had been the only great love of his life. It was his life. And what a life it was! All gone now.

She cleared a space among Johnny's piles of documents and placed her latest acquisition in the middle of the desk. Carried exclusively at Henri Bendel, her new Boho bag was the most aristocratic of hippie fringe bags. Multi-color, multi-stitched leather, the Boho had become the focal point of her life. The bag was appliquéd with multi-color patches in the shapes of clouds. Eyeing it lovingly and carefully, she decided to practice locking down her money in its zippered compartments, so she would never get ripped off.

When the elevator reached the tenth floor, its doors opened for an indeterminable length of time, not unlike the Broadway IRT subway crawling slowly but rocking violently on the El to stop at 125th Street. Cookie wished she was normal enough to consider all of the scary or dire possibilities. It dawned on her that she knew what was coming. She was prescient that way. She'd be concerned if the newcomer wore skinny Italian loafers, the kind that make little noise and never leave footprints. She'd also be concerned if it was Detective Sergeant Ronan O'Hearn, but she knew he was done with her. Two hundred bucks. Geez. What kind of cop would bother messing around with a sixteen-year-old chick?

Her vague notions were quickly abandoned when she caught a glimpse of crazy-quilt wedge platform shoes, exactly like the ones she had bought at the 34th Street Bootery. The shoes were brand new, or used but in mint condition, and moved purposefully in her direction.

"Fuck, where did you get those shoes?"

Toni Ferlinghetti folded a paper airplane out of one of Johnny's past due bills and let it go in Cookie's direction. The paper airplane sailed across the room and dropped onto the floor, short of the oak desk.

"Where the fuck do you think I got them? Think you're the only one who knows about the Bootery?"

The way she said *Bootery* with phonetic emphasis on the long oooo vowels of Bootery made Cookie laugh. Big hair, big boobs and bats for brains, Toni Ferlinghetti was the quintessential Yonkers Italian girl. *So Yonkas.*

"Look who's here with me," she said in a snotty tone.

Tony Amendolito sauntered into the room as if he was the sole male heir of an old money scion on the Upper East Side. He leaned against the desk and sneered at Cookie.

"Better be nice to my boyfriend," Toni warned her.

"Get the fuck off the desk," Cookie shot back.

Tony Amendolito looked a little put off, not enough to get rattled, but still at a loss for words. He looked at Toni who gave him a big bright smile, showing a full set of white teeth about to bite her prey with fang-like intensity.

Without warning, Toni's face softened into the sulks. "How

could you do this to me? You were my friend," she accused in between sniffs.

Toni wouldn't look at Cookie directly. She had this thing about pride and not showing the cards on sympathy, compassion, warmth, and sadness—all of the crying emotions. Instead, she fiddled with the papers on Johnny's desk, of which there was no shortage. She would have loved to stomp on Cookie's face with the heels of her crazy-quilt shoes. Cookie slammed her hand on the desk close to the papers Toni had been thoughtlessly shuffling.

"Get the fuck out of here." Cookie never raised her voice. Showing anger was losing control. "Leave or I'll call the police."

"We'll call the police on you!" Tony growled, shaking his fist.

Toni rarely blinked. "You wouldn't dare. We'll get you in trouble."

"I said get out. Get the fuck out now."

Cookie imagined the worst thing that could happen. She wondered if there would be a round of pops, gun blasts, and a mess. She watched the floor carefully to see if she had the stamina to outlive by one breath the sight of her brains scrambled on the floor. She never raised her head to look at Tony and Toni.

"How many times do I have to tell you to get the fuck out of here."

She saw their feet moving, her crazy-quilt shoes and his cheap black leather penny loafers. Imagine a Guido like him wearing WASP-boy shoes! How gauche! The two of them were nothing but a *Gina* and a *Guido*, cheap Italian losers, thinking they were strong, trying to prey on the weak.

Cookie saw both sets of shoes walking out of the office. The door closed behind them. The sound of murmuring raged in low echoes in the hall, a dull snicker or two, though no laughter. Soon the elevator came and slowly descended the shaft.

"You can come out now, Arky. Tony's got nothing on me and I'm not going to let him think for a minute he can outfox me."

Arky came up for air. It was unthinkable that he could have rolled into a ball small enough to fit under Millie's desk. Unbeknownst to Cookie, Arky was incredibly flexible and had innate talent as a contortionist. Maybe he had talent in other ways too, she surmised.

She pulled a black cap from her Boho bag and tossed it to Arky. Even in his emotionally wrought state, he caught the cap. Holding his hat in his hands, he avoided making eye contact with her. He attempted to talk, but it came out as babble with his tongue growing thick and rolling back on itself.

Eyeing Arky, Cookie pulled out a Marlboro from her Boho. "You gotta be prompt, ready to take me wherever I want to go."

Arky nodded, pulled a lighter from his pocket and lit her Marlboro. "Got it."

"I like the limo you picked. It will work just fine." She took a long indrawn drag from her Marlboro and examined Arky, assessing his every movement.

"You show up here every Saturday night, and I'll pay you in cash. Two hundred bucks a week, plus tips. Plus gas. You stay in the car wherever we go. You wait. You wait for me as long as it takes."

She watched him carefully for any signs of trouble, but this was going to go real smooth. He took off his cap and scratched the back of his head. He was waiting on her, waiting for her every word.

"If you get yourself caught up in any expenses, just give me the bill. I'll always pay you cash."

"Got that?" Clenching the Marlboro between her lips, she stood up from the desk and held out her hand to shake on the deal.

Arky tripped over to the desk and clumsily faltered to the ground, but he rallied, quickly saving face by pretending he was just checking his shoelaces, which were unraveling but not completely untied. That is exactly how he would always conduct himself. He possessed the uncanny disposition to always catch himself in the nick of time. A lackey in possession of talent. Not too shabby. He had promise. He shook her hand. His palms were moist, but he had a good grip.

She looked toward the window into the night. She heard the sound of the saxophone bleeding the ache of loneliness and felt like Johnny was in the room with her. It made her remember Stanley too. A sharp but brief stab of sadness pierced her heart and stopped her breath. Then she laughed at the notion that her heart was only in one place, in the same place, and the only place to feel like crying and laughing and laughing and crying until she extinguished her grief. Blue neon from the street flashed a wide band of light across her Boho on the desk. The solar eclipse had come and gone. The moon lanced into the room from a dark sky. She was going to latch herself onto the back of that moon and cruise into the next phase of her life.

Twenty-three

Reenie and Izzy sat in the backseat of a black limousine, cruising south on the highway, bumper to bumper in a late-night squall of traffic. Each girl staked out her turf at opposite windows. Folded arms, obliquely turned away from each other, they stared into rows of blinking lights on the outer curve of the East River Drive. The infinite expanse of the black leather seat yawned between them like a gaping hole in the ground. There was nothing to do except study the punctured concrete walls, pitted white tiles, and rusting stanchions of the United Nations Tunnel. Structural decay and deterioration had created a chaotic pattern of industrial chicken pox ravaging concrete with the slow seething but sure signs of urban blight in New York City, circa 1973.

Nothing has changed much to this day, but on a sweltering night in June, Reenie and Izzy hated each other on contact, a small fact that was making Cookie miserable. She sat up front in the passenger seat, where she liked to be; it made her feel in command of the situation.

With no father, a dead mother, a dead brother and an ailing grandmother, Reenie lived on a slim payment of social security and food stamps, courtesy of her mother's death. Izzy, on the other hand, was a daughter of wealth and privilege, who had comfortably traveled around the world and had hinted at having a trust fund. Reenie mentioned that she had tie-dyed her own halter top. Izzy boasted that her pale lemon-and-white floral pinafore linen smock had been hand-stitched by Italian artisans in Trastevere.

"Designers," Izzy emphasized. "They are very Bohemian, and I've met them all."

"Probably fucked them all too," Cookie muttered under her breath. She clutched a tube of shiny softening geranium-colored lipstick from her purse and checked herself in a small compact mirror. Like everything else, she was melting in the heat.

"I bought it at Henri Bendel's." Izzy patted the front of her pinafore, smoothing its creases, admiring the fabric. "It was part of their spring collection."

Feigning a touch of concern, Izzy looked at Reenie. "It's probably on sale by now."

Reenie blew smoke in her face. "You be too rich for my blood."

"Honestly, where did you learn to speak that way?"

Reenie rolled her eyes and resumed her gaze out the window, ignoring Izzy's whining that the heat in the car was causing her to perspire. With her long slender fingers, she tapped the back of Cookie's head. Cookie didn't appreciate being poked from behind.

"You might never show fear," she said for Cookie's benefit. "But I never let them see me sweat."

Arky sighed because he had worked hard to get the air conditioning fixed. It was just like him to get a showy car that was as hot as hell but had enough room in its rear quarters to drag a coffin to the cemetery. Reenie said she was hungry. Arky Lovato was not. He needed some other form of sustenance. His nose was running. He didn't care enough to wipe it. Either that or he didn't know. Some guys are like that. They can't feel their nose running. Cookie conjured the image of the broken down street bum from Jethro Tull's song "Aqualung," *Snot's running down his nose.*

Cookie could offer Arky sympathy, but she didn't feel like going out of her way to be kind. It doesn't matter how old you are or how much you've learned about life. All the cogs come back into place and dictate the way you behave.

I'm from Yonkers. Lord have no mercy on my wicked soul.

The limo rose in a lumbering assault to a viaduct around 28th Street, then headed south on Second Avenue. Streetlight flashed in desultory waves along the side of Arky's face. She could only see his profile, noting he had a rather straight nose. If his nose hadn't been running, it might have been one of his only redeeming characteristics aside from his astute sense of direction. He always seemed to know where he was going.

He pulled up behind a row of cars and double-parked in front of the club. Other cars dropped off people, scrambling onto the sidewalk. Throngs stood outside, waiting, hanging out. No line to get in. No line to get out. The crowd melded into a rambling army, coming and going with no governable size or shape. Everyone was in a state of constant flux, even those sitting on the curb, nodding off, about to pass out, waiting, getting stoned, smoking, shooting up.

Reenie saw a needle, shuddered and turned away.

The joint's name, *Max's Kansas City*, weirdly positioned on its awning, foreshadowed the trouble yet to come. A sign as small as a black postage stamp had white letters that ran vertically on the awning and encompassed a food menu: *Steak* on top of *Lobster*, and *Chick* above *Peas*. A trickle of thick adrenaline coursed through Cookie's chest, settled in her throat, getting her tongue-tied, afraid she would not be able to talk. There is no way she'd be nodding off on this street. There's no way she'd ever be a down-and-out junkie like Billy Dee. She knew Reenie was quaking every time she spotted used needles in the gutter, pushed against the curb into piles, amounting to a puddle of pain and broken dreams, reminding her of Billy Dee's untimely death.

Cookie felt tall in her chunky four-inch heels but not tall enough to stand out amid a mass of campy bodies in heels, camo and silver jumpsuits spilling across the sidewalk as far as the curb. Lots of chicks in halter tops. The guy at the door had a massive chest, glistening with oil, and thick forearms. He wore jeans with suspenders over his bare chest. He held the door open, letting some people in, but not everyone. He seemed to know who was who and who was nobody.

The guy with suspenders looked over the three girls. He didn't ask them for their ID, but he didn't let them in either. Izzy came up to his side and squeezed his pumped-up bicep, letting her fingers linger with the force of a tender hook. "Hello, Mr. Bonhomie. Nice muscles you have there."

Freshly shaved and wearing the jaunty Chauffeur's cap gave Arky less of a glassy-eyed look and plainly accentuated his baby-face. Left behind on the street, he leaned against the door of the limo.

"He's my man," Cookie told the burly guy at the door.

He ignored her, letting in two hot blonde girls, one with a feather boa covering her tiny breasts, and a diminutive elfin girl whose head was disproportionately large for her emaciated body. Twin sets of eyes, rimmed with black eyeliner, too stoned to know where they were or where they were going— Mr. Bonhomie ushered them into the club. Cookie had been passed over.

Then Cookie got it: this guy *Bonhomie, whatever the fuck that meant*, was the gatekeeper, deciding who got in and who had to wait. No need to form two clean lines for the hip and not hip. This guy was the sole arbiter deciding if Cookie was cool enough to get into the club. His *fuck you smile* told her he thought she was from the Bridge and Tunnel crowd; the doofus kids from New Jersey, Long Island and Connecticut stepping out for a night in the big city, who could never hold their liquor, mixed with drugs; they'd puke all night long, then pass out somewhere inconvenient, a bathroom, the doorway of a fleabag hotel or a birdshit-covered bench in Union Square Park.

Cookie yanked the guy's suspender and gave it a sharp snap. "I'm from Yonkers."

"Isn't that upstate?" The guy shook his head and laughed uproariously showing his row of uneven teeth and a stubby red tongue.

Cookie turned her head and cocked her ear to the traffic on the street, pretending what he said had not registered in her primitive but proud brain. If she did acknowledge his insult, she'd have to kill him. Then, they'd never get in. She pulled a twenty out of her bag and handed it to the big fucking dickhead.

He smiled, shrugged and turned away. Humiliated, she felt the same way the day Fangs beat her and made her stand in the center of the playground while two lines of students exiting the school, during the fire drill, had circled around her. She stood red-faced, head hanging in shame. More than anything in the world, she hated being humiliated in public for all the world to see. *So ashamed.*

Sometimes you have to suck up and stay strong. Here she was stuck in a public situation. Freaks coming and going, staring at her, shunning her. A dark dude wearing knickers in a crazy-quilt pattern and lace-up brown leather boots twisted the end of his moustache and stuck his tongue out. Make no mistake, a slur directed toward Cookie. She gave him the finger.

"Be nice," Izzy told her. "Consider this. His pantaloons look exactly like your shoes."

Cookie pulled two more twenties from her bag, but Izzy slapped her hand back. "Don't insult him. He doesn't want money. He wants to be charmed."

She turned to the dude. "Hello, Mr. Bonhomie, how about doing us a little favor and letting us in. We just want to see what it's like. We won't get into trouble. Promise. Please. Pretty please." She held her hands, praying. "Please," she implored him. "Promise I'll be good to you."

He winked, scanned her breasts and shrugged. She returned his wink and caressed his arm. But it was a no-go.

Izzy struck Cookie's bag, giving it a good whack. "I see you got rid of those crazy-quilt shoes but now you've got a patchwork bag with fringe no less. "Where did you get that thing?" She stamped her petite feet in a girlish tantrum. "No wonder why he won't let us in! You are so uncool!"

Reenie's face gleamed whiter than the full moon that was left behind in Yonkers and could not be seen in the Manhattan sky. She had not said a word since they left the limo. Scared to death by the crowd, the uncertainty of it all was more than Reenie had bargained for. Her arms cradled her chest, locked in an embrace for self-protection.

Cookie's Boho fringe bag was big; zippered compartments held cash and its colorful leather bottom dripped with a rainbow of tassels. She didn't bother to tell Izzy she had bought her Emanuel Ungaro Fringe Bag at Bloomingdale's for $295 and it was not on sale.

Cookie felt like an idiot standing on the sidewalk. She did a quick mental inventory of what she presented to the world, a package of hair, skin, teeth and nails; her physique: legs, torso, breasts and neck, the shape of her shoulders, the v-slope of her back, and of course, her ass.

"I'm supposed to be perfect, but I'm not!" she called out.

A man came along her side, exhaling smoke from his nose, squeezed her arm. "I dig chicks who are a challenge," he said, passing her by, a late night fanciful remark, taking a potshot and dropping a F-bomb in one casual remark.

"And even when some fucking interloper from afar sweeps into the fray and steals away my heart, my uneven features are freakish and so far from perfect."

Izzy slugged her in the shoulder. "Stop talking nonsense."

Milky eyes behind the lens of thick black-frame eyeglasses betrayed one man's startled but accusatory gaze—either he thought she was young and stupid, or he had no feelings at all. She thought of his hair as decidedly red, more carrot colored than coppery or earth-toned, and very thick and curly. He didn't seem up for a chat and quickly walked into Max's holding his black hat in his hands.

Mr. Bonhomie never gave him so much as a nod. Cookie felt another sting. She shut down her feelings. Leaving now would be total defeat. She wasn't going to give up, but standing there made her feel rejected, a June bug waiting to get stepped on. Someone was bound to enjoy the crunching sound of her dead beetle carcass. *Fuck, what am I doing here?*

Searching the fringe of the crowd, she found the moment she had been waiting for. The chance of a lifetime. A freak occurrence appeared in the form of a woman wearing thigh-high silver lamé boots. Her silver metallic skirt glittered like magic in the night. She strutted with the uneven gate of a man who had been galloping on the back of a horse for too long. Her hair was blonde and much longer than Cookie remembered.

"Gwendolyn!" Cookie was so thrilled that she found herself shaking, almost crying.

The woman's height commanded serious attention from the crowd; she clearly loved being noticed. She placed her hands on her hips, sashaying in a precise but large circle around the three girls.

"Gwendolyn," she enunciated with her hands in the air. "Yes, that is my name. How'd yous know dat?"

Cookie gave her the best smile of her life. "You don't like being called Wendy."

Her white painted teeth lit up an exuberant smile. "Ain't life a bitch! How'd yous know dat, Girl? Who sent yous girls to me?"

"I just know things. Remember?" Cookie thought for sure she must have made an impression when they bumped into her, almost running her over, in Times Square.

Gwendolyn used her hand for emphasis, blinking her silver glitter encrusted eyelashes. "No, don't know what you're talking about, Girl."

Cookie embraced Izzy to show they were together. "Remember us? Pointy tits and peach and creams?"

"Peaches and cream." Izzy lolled back and forth on her small feet.

"Lotsa girls look like yous. Ain't no big deal that you got going on there." She gave her head a violent shake, filling the air with a swirling blonde mane, giving Mr. Bonhomie a nod, admonishing him to let them into the club. "They be with me."

Cookie latched her arms with Reenie on one side and Izzy and the other. If looks could kill, Cookie would have killed Mr. Bonhomie.

"Come on, pointy tits and creamy peach, let's go."

Reenie had no idea what she was talking about or what was going on, but she didn't let go of Cookie's arm, firmly locked in position. *Yonkers girls forever.*

Gwendolyn swished around to Reenie, bent over and stared down into her face. "What's with the sad sack, Girl?"

Bonhomie held up his hand and waved them in. He looked so nonchalant, but he was the worst kind of dumbass— pretending to be so cool that money didn't matter; but if that was the case, what was he doing working as a fucking bouncer for a dive night club?

"You should have taken the money," Cookie told him. "Money will keep you honest."

Gwendolyn put her arm around Bonhomie to soothe him. "I'm not doing nothing cept minding my own business, but ain't she a bad ass?"

Jutting her chin upward to the place where a sky would be if it wasn't so damn dark, Cookie glared at Bonhomie and gave him the finger. "You fucking poseur, you probably grew up in Kentucky and spent your wonder years fucking cows up the ass."

Gwendolyn immediately intervened. "No, Honey, that's my job. The harder you ride them the more they like it, Honey. Ain't that so?" She asked Bonhomie whose face sat even with her massive bosom.

"Know them?" He nodded to Cookie.

"Don't I ever!" Moving right past Bonhomie, giving him a wink, she prodded Cookie into the club, and squeezed her shoulder. "Now you be talking to the man real nice, so he gonna be looking out for yous. Hear what I'm saying to yous?"

"See that man over there. That be Robert Motherwell. You know, the artist, the painter."

Izzy fanned her hands across her eyes and shrilled into Cookie's ear. "The abstract expressionist! He's a legend!" She put her hands over her mouth, buffering her gasp of awe.

"He be talking to Willem de Kooning," Gwendolyn crooned in Cookie's ear. "They talk here but they hate each other so bad, so bad I tell you, and that's good. Bad too."

"All these people in here, they be famous. Cept me and cept yous." She laughed hard enough to split the seam in her metallic skirt. "Cept they let me in cause they know I'm famous in my own right on a hot night like tonight. Don't you know it. I think I'm gonna be a poet. And so it goes. I be dancing on my toes. And I'm outta here. Gonna get myself a beer. See you squeaky, titty and creams."

Gwendolyn gave the girls a big smile, raised her arms over her head in a hallelujah show of praise, before completely turning her back on them. "I'm bitching cause that's who I am. Now yous be off to your own party show. I'm done with yous girls. Got to do my own thing and strike some gold. Be bold. Be right. Go gladly into the night."

Sidling her large body up to the bar, she wedged herself in between the two artists who hated each other and flagged the bartender, a girl with a pink polka dot rag wrapped around her tousled black hair. The artist who was not Robert Motherwell pulled away from the bar, stood up in his perfectly pressed striped seersucker jacket, circumspectly draped over a cotton tee—the only way to look, to be, to pose, to make the scene, any scene, in art, in a bar, on the street or in a show. A long ash head trailing from his cigarette conjured the image of a snake slithering in the air. Pure art and intentionally so. He casually flicked the long ash to the floor. A moment of pure theater. He knew he had an audience.

Twenty-four

Izzy was pretentious and Reenie was in over her head. Cookie wished she had not brought them along. She operated best when she was alone. No baggage. The girls clung to her side; a warm beacon casting a rudder to navigate the congested smoke-filled bar, breathing narco gusts of smack, speed, speedball combos, ordinary pot, Marlboros and French cigarettes as strong smelling as cigars, leaning into the juddering chaotic freakish force of backs, hips, faces, heads, arms and legs, a frenzy of flesh, clattering drinks, beer bottles and a band performing reggae on a stage that wasn't a stage but somewhere on the floor in the midst of everyday lowlife and lost souls clamoring hard to get the attention they had been craving all of their life.

Yes, this was, from Cookie's perspective—Max's Kansas City.

Acting as a fat cushion, Cookie's Boho fringe bag did more than carry wads of money and cheap lipstick. The Boho protected her from getting crushed against the bar where she slapped a twenty, no, on second thought… two twenties lay flat on the bar. She ordered scotch on the rocks. She knew she could make scotch last all night long. Izzy jumped, hovering over to her side and cast her two cents without putting forth actual money.

"I want a glass of Pouilly-Fuissé, please."

"What's that?"

"White wine." Izzy looked at her with mild disdain. "It's from the Mâconnais district in the Burgundy region of Central France."

The rag-headed bartender's sardonic smile won first prize in Cookie's heart.

"Make it a carafe." Cookie dropped another twenty on the bar. "Take care of us and I'll take care of you," she told the bartender. She knew Reenie wouldn't want to drink and ordered bowls of pretzels and chips. She knew she was paying way too much but flinging away money on this night was a matter of survival. She laughed to herself because she had forgotten that she had so much money that it didn't matter.

Reenie fell backwards, disappearing into the arms of a docile boy wearing false eyelashes, tips fluttering with glitter, tons of black eyeliner, few clothes, a baby diaper loincloth resembling attire worn by Tarzan in the original movie with Johnny Weissmuller, along with Maureen O'Sullivan as Jane. Cookie wrinkled her nose, looking for the two artists, the red-headed dude, and Gwendolyn, whose massive height made it certain she would be seen lording above this crowd that loomed large and dark like a mob of crows.

In Cookie's mind, Gwendolyn was a neon god that she created to protect them with her secret powers as an oracle, an Amazon, and an angel, all wrapped into one. Why, now that Cookie thought about it, Gwendolyn was almost in possession of the absolute power of a rare owl, a strange and beautiful creature, worthy of awe and admiration.

No epicenter, nowhere to go, Cookie allowed the crowd's momentum to carry her to the back room. Her rock glass, closely held against her arm and away from her precious Boho bag, left her too uncoordinated to gracefully balance the bowls of chips.

She felt strands of Izzy's hair grazing her cheek and Reenie's stodgy pant, a breathy wheeze borne of high anxiety; the two girls were as annoying as gnats, following her everywhere. She was nobody's epicenter, just a cog in a whole wheel or sphere or cycle of life that did not even know she existed. She was neutral, a benign force in the universe. Nobody.

The servile looking boy in diapers had laid his body across the lap of two girls tangled in a mass of their long hair strewn along a stiff and hard backed wooden bench, resembling a pew in a church. Bohemian, arty and intellectual, they were leftovers who used to be called beatniks.

Then Cookie quickly and inadvertently made a new friend. She felt his bowl-shaped hair dyed silver, frosted with pink, to be fetching, sad though; he offered her a line to snort on an exquisitely carved, oblong-shaped sterling compact mirror.

Cookie gently pushed his hand away. "I'm done with all of that."

"That doesn't mean you can't do some more."

She looked into his eyes, so soft, so welcoming. "But I'm done."

She turned away from his gaze, thinking it was strange he cared to comment at all. She pushed through the passageway, dropping pretzels from her precariously balanced bowl. She didn't mind losing pretzels, which augured as well as the breadcrumbs of Hansel and Gretel, just in case they needed a trail to find their way back. Snagging her bag on shards of metal, something had caught her, and didn't know what exactly, except she began to suffer from a mild, almost dislocated, form of claustrophobia and fancied herself as being in an auto wreck, trapped inside a crushed car that was about to explode into fire.

Cookie hated being in a nightclub where she could not see the exit signs. No Exit is more than the name of a French existentialist play. Cookie had learned as a little kid that too many fires had happened in old buildings. Old buildings were killing fields for working people, and especially for their children.

This building that housed Max's Kansas City was old.

In the 1876 Brooklyn Theater fire, a canvas backdrop caught sparks from a gas stage light and exploded into fire during a sold-out performance. With no fire escapes and only one staircase out of the building, people were trampled to death, bodies piled on top of heaps of bodies, and a total of 278 people died.

The doors to the stairwells and exits were locked, killing 146 young girls in the 1911 Triangle Shirtwaist Factory. The managers had locked those doors because they thought the young girls would steal bobbins of thread.

The fire Cookie held closest to her fondest nightmares happened in Yonkers in 1965 when she was a little kid. Nine children and three adults attending a music class died in a fire that swept through the Yonkers Jewish Community Center. Kids stampeding to get out. Doors locked or no doors at all. Cross ventilation fanning flames. One staircase. One way in and one way out. Overcome by heat and smoke. She thought she could still hear their terrible screams. No way out is not the name of a bad French existentialist play.

No way out is what happens to girls like me!

She turned to look behind in the passageway. Izzy and Reenie walked in a single file line like schoolgirls exiting a burning building. People cramming against them in the passageway turned sideways, every which way, trying to pass. The span was not that long, just unfamiliar to them. Ahead, the narrow passage opened into a back room bathed with pink light, the shade of a rose colored gold, where they were free to roam.

They sat at an ordinary round wooden table, not quite all the way in the back of the room but close enough. Cookie did not know where Gwendolyn had gone but a man swiftly sat at the table with them, extended his hand and peered up at her from beneath the brim of his black fedora. His eyes were magnified behind thick-lensed, black-framed eyeglasses. And even though she didn't know him, she knew that she had seen those eyes before. He drank from a glass tumbler that smoked and offered her sip.

"It's on fire," he said.

"How strange!"

"It's better than what you've got there." He pushed the tumbler toward her. "Give it a try."

Cookie's gingerly sip meant to taste but not swallow, like a Catholic schoolgirl's loose interpretation of giving a boy a blow job. She visibly grimaced once her tongue touched the liquid fire.

"Never had that before?" The man smiled. "It's green chartreuse and rum. It's the rum that's on fire. One-fifty-one proof rum."

Cookie pushed the glass back toward her gentleman friend, wondering what he wanted from her, as if she didn't know. She tried to guess his age and when she grew tired of guessing, she hoped he wasn't bald and decided to find out. She reached forward and pushed his fedora off of his head. It was a rude thing to do, but she didn't care. He didn't seem to mind either. He laughed, showing his off-color teeth bathed in the red neon light. His hair was not brown, black or blonde, but looked distinctly orangey-red, but his hair might have taken on a red cast from the light.

At least he had hair. The only thing worse than an older guy pandering to young girls is an old guy who is bald. She imagined having to polish his head with a soft cloth the way a cobbler shines shoes, a notion that made her laugh. A private joke.

Izzy and Reenie were not laughing and had pushed their simple chairs close together, leg to leg, side to side, their very faces almost blended together as a single unit, twin thalidomide babies, two heads in one body, stuck together for life.

She knew such a small sip of chartreuse was not making her feel crazy. She was intoxicated by virtue of being in the moment, a moment that throbbed madly, pounding her brain, robbing her of rational thought, only impulse existed, the wild craziness of not knowing anyone here except her two friends that she wished she had not brought along.

In the far corner of the room, torn pages from magazines were spread across a square table. Occasionally she heard snatches of conversation about designing costumes for bands and groovy ideas for record covers, but she never heard enough to form a definitive story. The sound of the Reggae band had been replaced by the whining of a steel guitar and a lead singer whose scream exploded as hot as a big smoking fire in a burning building with no way out. The noise of the band muted the crash of glass glittering across the floor, but amplified the shards of broken glass. Under the crazy red light, glass on the floor sparkled like jewels under a setting sun. Someone had thrown a bottle of beer and someone else threw another bottle. Both shattered into bits and pieces, spreading across the floor like liquid fire.

Most of crowd looked to be in their twenties, and by Cookie's reckoning, some looked real old—in their thirties or forties, much older than the three girls. Women jousted freely with each other, rousing fear, envy and awe, dancing around the room, stomping, arching backs, thrusting asses high in the air. A herd of bitches. Bitches in heat. Tongues wagging and tongues tied. Fashionistas, queers, musicians, junkies or losers; it was hard to tell. And no signs of Gwendolyn.

The guy in the black fedora pushed his plate with a half-eaten hamburger and onion rings in front of Cookie, but she not so politely demurred, and shoved the plate onto the floor. The plate shattered and found a home among the litter of glass. It thrilled her to be bad.

Why would she want the guy's leftover food? He had insulted her. She got up to dance, gyrating her hips the way she used to back in the days when she first felt the sure signs of adolescent heat. Only this dance was angry. She was joined by a longish haired hippie-looking guy who had a dime-store smile and a bashed-in face.

He screamed, "We can't find any guys good enough on pipes, man," and threw himself into the crowd, knocking into anyone within his reach. Wearing silver thong bikini briefs and thigh-high silver boots, he rocked back and forth, coming down on his knees in front of Cookie, and tugged at her crotch. Then he stuck out his tongue.

It was much more than she could take. She stood her ground in her chunky black heels, kicked him in the head and dove for safety at her table, but lost her footing on the slimy remnants of a burger and felt the resurgence of her trick knee going out from under her. She cried out in pain, but no one came to her rescue, a small detail she found irksome. Her friends did not seem to notice or care. Reenie and Izzy were holding hands, staring agape at the hippie guy who was licking ketchup from the broken plate on the ground. He was working hard to be as outrageous as he could be. It was live theater and not his only performance.

She remembered the hokey black light in the Midget Bar in Yonkers and how it made white appear to be almost translucent and everyone was beautiful. Here, everyone was beautiful or outrageous, maybe both, and not in need of the flattering, rose-colored light. She pulled a Marlboro from her purse and tried to strike a match, but the man in the fedora was quick and got there first.

The lead singer of the band screamed obscenities as loud as the noise amplified by the convulsive tumult of a bass guitar and drums. People drank glasses of rosé and sangria, or under the glare of the pink light, it might have been white wine sloshing into glasses from an accompanying carafe. She studied the light sculpture in the farthest corner of the room. Two fluorescent bars formed a V-shape, a shorter band of fluorescence formed a cross beam; the effect of the two bars of light created an imperfect triangle. There is no such thing as an imperfect triangle. All triangles are perfect. She might have flunked high school geometry, but she had embraced the perfection of triangles, the same way she embraced clouds, which were never perfect but always beautiful.

Suddenly she knew the light was an ephemeral masterpiece, important in the moment, but not so in the whole grand scheme of things—a bloody sobering thing that she would soon forget. It seemed to match her mood, defying reality, defying the laws of math, defying the conventional life. But the light was not pink. It was red. The glow emanating from the light sculpture turned most flesh tones rosy-pink and warmed dark skin, giving it a protective sheen of quick-drying lamination. Regardless of skin color, all faces turned into masks under the throw of red light.

Her eyes followed a trail of red light straight to Reenie's face. The girl looked aglow, on fire, but sick, clutching her stomach, on the verge of vomiting. She saw what Reenie was seeing: a young pretty boy with a blonde helmet of hair had a needle stuck in his arm. She saw Reenie stand, retching, covering her hands over her mouth, running toward the passageway, running blindly, passing people, getting knocked about, running for her life, and out of the back room. She hardly felt the man's hand traveling along her thigh to stop her from following Reenie. His fingers probed the inside of her thigh. His hand was like fire.

Twenty-five

Reenie and Izzy sped ahead to Union Square Park where they found Arky snoozing on a bench. His cap lay over his face. He struggled to wake and get into an upright position. He told them he had found a spot on East 17th Street to park the limo. Then he stretched and sighed. It was easy finding a place to park for free late at night, close to sunup, even in Manhattan. He picked up his bottle of Yoo-hoo from the ground, close to the leg of the park bench, drank what remained of the chocolaty drink in one thirsty chug, and let go of a loud belch.

"Do you have to be so disgusting?" Izzy complained. She leaned against Reenie, cozying her head into the girl's neck for love, sex or solace—all the same to Izzy.

Park benches, set in the curving line of the shape of a half moon, encircled the north end of the park's entrance where 17th Street linked together with Park Avenue South and Broadway—the same Broadway that led to Times Square and farther north Uptown, through the Bronx, eventually reaching Yonkers.

The two girls sat on another park bench, away from Arky but still within earshot. Reenie had recovered from her grief.

"Cookie left us." Izzy sniffed. "Just when I was starting to like her." She giggled.

"Cookie and me, we go way back and she's pretty tough. You gotta be tough to be from Yonkers, tougher than most people in the city. That's my word to you, Izzy. You're from the city, but you're not tough."

"Sure." Izzy nodded. "Got it." Her pert nose twitched with amusement. "When have I not been tough?"

Reenie laughed. "Being tough is not an act. It's what you feel deep inside. Maybe one day, you'll get it."

From behind the shadows of a double line of towering trees, Cookie had been listening to them. She didn't mean to eavesdrop. It was the way things had worked out with the girls zooming ahead of her to get away from Max's Kansas City. Disappointed about how the night had turned out, she had taken her own sweet time to catch up. The man trailed along talking to her about things she knew nothing about. Art. Abstract Expressionism. He dropped the names of the many famous artists who frequented Max's and lamented how Andy Warhol never came back to the nightclub after, in a newsworthy event, he had been shot by Valerie Solanas.

"He rarely goes out in public."

Cookie could care less. Clattering her shoes on the cobblestone pavement, she stood in front of her two friends. "I didn't leave you. In case you haven't noticed, I've been following you guys, watching your every move. And I don't like you talking trash about me."

The carrot-top dude moved to stand by her side, balancing his black fedora on the top of his fingers. "What have we here, a few young girls who have managed to escape the terrifying jaws of Max's Kansas City?"

Izzy and Reenie smiled at one another. They could tell he might be a freak.

"Oh, yes," the man went on. His accent was mildly British, or maybe not. Cookie could not pinpoint where this guy was from.

He seemed friendly enough, harmless. "Everyone wants to make the scene at Max's, all the young girls."

The guy gave Reenie the creeps. She knew for sure he was a freak. She nudged Izzy. "We'll wait in the car."

"Where's the car, Arky?"

Arky sprang to his red-sneakered feet and stood at attention. He was the perfect chauffeur. "I'm parked by the Everett building."

"Where?"

"200 Park Avenue South," said the man with red hair. He pointed to the sixteen-story concrete block of a building in the distance.

It reminded Cookie of the Yonkers Savings and Loan Building in Getty Square. She could never shake that building from her mind, especially since it had become the scene of a crime and the source of her newfound wealth.

She wanted to follow the girls and Arky, but the man bade her to stay. "Please, I'd like to talk to you for a minute. Let them go. You'll catch up with them soon enough."

He nodded in the direction of the chalky-looking box of the Everett Building. "They'll wait for you."

He pulled a cigarette from his own pack, a red and gold box. The label read *Dunhill, the new luxury length cigarette.* He handed the cigarette to Cookie and lit it for her. It tasted odd, a bit bitter, but it was tobacco just the same. She preferred her Marlboros.

"Got a name?"

He looked at her, mildly surprised, a bit taken aback. "Do I have a name?" Then he began to laugh loudly, heartily, and it was at her expense. "Yes, I do have a name."

A cloud of smoke came from his mouth as thick as exhaust from a stalled car. His smoke rose high in the humid air. Hers too. The temperature had not cooled. The night had grown warmer. Faint blue light illuminated the outline of the park and the man. Blue light cast no shadows. Soon the sun would appear. The man's face did not look good or kind or anything.

He held out his hand. She surprised herself and took it. He leaned forward and spoke in a clipped whisper. "My name is Farley Stewart."

Cookie laughed. "What do they call you for short? Stewie?"

She pulled her hand from his and eyed him carefully. He didn't seem up for a long chat. This was more of a chance encounter, one that would lead nowhere. Cookie had no intention of going anywhere with him and wasn't concerned about being accosted. It was late at night or early in the morning depending on your perspective. People strolled through the park night and day. Broadway was always a busy street.

"Where are you going?"

"Uptown."

"Where uptown?"

"North."

He looked alarmed. "The Bronx?"

"Yonkers."

"Yonkers?" He raised the bushy band of his blonde eyebrows and laughed.

"I don't see what's so funny."

"What do you do for fun in Yonkers?"

Cookie gave him the stink eye. She was flattered by his attention but didn't really like him.

"You're a long way from home."

She caught a whiff of his fancy men's cologne. It wasn't a clean, natural scent the way Stanley's skin was warm, an earthy fragrance blending caramel and honey. This man smelled expensive. He carried himself well, holding an aura of sexiness, a mystical attraction as if he was wholly in possession of himself and superior to everyone else in the world. He was different from Stanley, much more sophisticated, friendly enough, but there was an element of something out of whack, a degree of danger or dishonesty.

"Is this a high school prom outing?"

Cookie's gaze focused on the man who called himself Farley and waited for his reaction. "No. I don't go to proms. Proms are for hicks and wannabees. Those girls are just my friends. Arky's my driver. I pay him. He works for me."

"He works for you, eh?" He touched her neck. His hand lingered on her shoulder longer than it needed to. "How'd you like the music at the club?"

He yelled above the procession of garbage trucks rumbling down the street. She could hardly hear him. He waited for the garbage trucks to pass.

"I really prefer Motown, the Four Tops, the Marvelettes, or classical music. Any classical composers that you care to listen to?"

Cookie shrugged. She didn't know how much further she wanted to go with him. There was no mistaken notion about the color of his hair. It was red and she told him so. "I thought your hair just looked red at Max's because of the light. It really is red."

"As red as the light?" He laughed. "Did you know that light, as you call it, is actually a sculpture that commemorates the bloodshed in the Vietnam war?"

The mention of Vietnam made Cookie go silent. She stopped talking. Stopped thinking too.

"The sculpture is by the artist Dan Flavin."

She could care less about a neon light in the shape of a cross. An ache settled in her heart, brief but biting, a sting with an edge, a tinge of a memory hinting at Stanley—remembering his grief. But she was strong. She was tough. She banished Stanley from her mind as if he had never existed. He had been gone for over six months. No word from him. He was gone. She was certain.

"The tragedy is all of those boys who had to go to Vietnam. Sad. Isn't it?"

Cookie didn't respond. Farley asked her if she had something to write on. She sat down on the park bench and opened her Boho. She produced her black & white notebook from her bag, opened it to a page in the middle of the notebook and handed him a pen.

"What's the notebook for?"

"I write stuff."

He opened the cap of her green fountain pen and held it in the air for him to grab. "Do people still really write with these things?" He laughed while he scribbled on the page.

"How the hell should I know."

"Of course, you write with a fountain pen. You're a schoolgirl. I bet you wear a uniform too." He snapped the cap back on the pen and handed it to her.

"You're the one with the funny cigarettes that I've never heard of before."

"Would you like another?"

She shook her head and gazed into the street where traffic was picking up. The sky turned from black to blue-grey light, leaving no shadows in between the trees or along the low rows of hedges bordering the half-moon circle of park benches. The wrought-iron streetlamps were still illuminated, but their light was no longer needed or made a difference as the night gave way to the day.

He had written his name in cursive, small expansive letters linked together in the shape of the outer fronds of an overgrown fern plant. His phone number did not include New York City's area code 212. It was so like New Yorkers to think the entire world was in their area code, their time zone, and always all about them. He seemed annoyed at having to make small talk with her or anyone. Cookie had never met anyone like Farley Stewart. He watched her every move, yet he maintained a detached air, as if he was bored by every word she said. He had some other reason for wanting to be with her. She asked him if she could wear his hat home. He put his hat on her head, telling her how pretty she looked. She could wear the hat for as long as she liked, so long as she promised to see him again.

Saturday July 28 1973

My first memory of a rock concert is Woodstock. Nothing is better than that! There was a big summer jam at Watkins Glen this weekend. I was supposed to go but I changed my mind. I'm so not into psychedelic light shows and rock concerts. The Allman Brothers. The Grateful Dead. The Band. I don't care about that stuff no more. I mean anymore. Folk. Rock. Heavy Metal. Americana. New music is coming along. Garage rock. Glam Rock. Underground. Music is changing.

I'm changing too and I don't know who I'm going to be. I don't know what's going to happen to me. I quit doing drugs long ago. I don't like to drink. People I know are getting into this stuff for the very first time in their lives and they are way older than me. The doofs! I've always been ahead of everyone else! I do like to dance. I've been going to other clubs. The Cafe Wha? is small and stuffy. A firetrap. The Back Fence. I kept worrying fire would break out. The Bitter End is supposed to be the oldest rock club in New York City. Another firetrap. It's nowhere near as crazy as Max's Kansas City.

I keep thinking about the light sculpture with the red glow in the back room of Max's Kansas City. I keep wondering if the artist had gone to Vietnam. I wonder if he saw the things that Stanley saw. The color of the light is the same blood red color of Kitty's glass objects that are on the shelf in her picture window. She sits in front of her picture window and stares at her many colored glass things. The light filtering through the glass speaks to her in a way only she can understand.

Kitty's picture window is art. Shapeshifting prisms of glass refract and reflect light the same way her moods change for no reason. No reason at all. Her colored glass catches jagged shards of red light from the sun in a bleed of the nightmarish thoughts that keep her agitated and awake at night and sleepwalking like a zombie during the day. Her thoughts could get stuck in the back of her throat or fall onto the ground and burn up in a raging fire. I swear this is the way she is through no fault of her own. She turns her anguish and fear into something wondrous and beautiful. My mother could be an artist.

Kitty is doing okay. She'll never be normal. I want to be normal. I know I look like I'm doing okay. I'm really not okay. What else is going on? Johnny is happy. I've never seen him so happy. He's playing music again. Every night he practices playing the vibraphone in the basement. He doesn't play music for money at weddings and bar mitzvahs. Funny thing is he never asks me how I can spend my nights running around the city cause I don't have a job and never ask him for money. Now that's weird.

Donny had a birthday. I don't really know how old she is. Twelve? Thirteen? I've lost track. I never see Herman or Mrs. Kerry. Reenie and Izzie see more of each other than they see of me. I heard Happy House went out of business. I don't know what happened to Giorgio DeSutter. I miss him. I stay away from Getty Square. I don't want to run into Mosella Moran or Tony and Toni.

I want to visit Zelda the Gypsy. Arky can drive me there and wait outside Greens in case I need to make a quick getaway.

I've been spending mostly every day and night in the city. I hate the way I'm starting to call Manhattan the city. I don't want to be like everybody else.

I forgot to mention that Farley Stewart has been going to different places with me. I think I like him. I don't know. I can't get used to his flaming red hair. He's so white and has freckles everywhere. Yes everywhere. He smells good. He wears a cologne called Guerlain Vetiver that comes in an evergreen glass bottle. I can always smell him coming into a room before I see him.

-ccc

Twenty-six

He asked Cookie if she wanted to share his Cadbury chocolate bar with hazelnuts and raisins that had softened in the July heat but wasn't quite melting. He confessed he didn't like nuts and raisins in his chocolate because it took up too much space. Furthermore, dark particles became stuck in his teeth and could easily be mistaken for cavities, rot, poor hygiene, as if he were someone born in the Bronx or Yonkers.

He picked up the receiver of a heavy black telephone, dialed a number, strumming his fingers on his desk while he waited for the phone to ring. His strumming fingers turned into a solo tap dance routine rounding out his impatience, hardly a bedeviled state for him. He often mistook impatience for boredom. He seemed unaware of Cookie, but she was very aware of him.

No one answered. Cookie had no idea who he had been phoning. It was late in the afternoon, almost five. He dropped the receiver into its cradle and appraised Cookie lounging on the floor with both mild amusement and annoyance. She felt his gaze traveling the backs of her legs, up over the slight rounded hill of her bottom to her gently curved arched back.

She had propped herself on her elbows to read excerpts from her black & white notebook. Her latest journal entry had been written this morning before she left home. She thought it was funny that she could smell Stewie's cologne before she heard him, or detected his movement, or actually laid eyes on him.

Farley Stewart hated being called *Stewie*, yet he continued to invite her to his place until she took it upon herself to come and go on her own accord, which meant whenever she pleased. He never did anything. He didn't move in on her. She was trying to grow into the idea of wanting him. Physical urge, her raw desire for him could not be summoned no matter how much she wished it would take her by surprise. Nothing ever happened. No one made the first move. A strange awkwardness prevailed between them.

There were no clouds visible from his apartment, a studio efficiency in the Remington Hotel at 129 W. 46th Street, between Sixth and Seventh. The sky, the sun, the moon or stars, and of course the clouds, none of these things were visible from the one tiny window above the sink in his apartment kitchenette. The hotel itself was small, with wrought iron fire escapes that ran up the vertical facing of the building's primary exposure to the street. Even from the street the front of the building looked like a dump, an eyesore if placed anywhere else in the world, even in Yonkers, but totally befitting its proximity to the Hell's Kitchen neighborhood of Manhattan.

Farley talked to her very little and most of what he said had a faintly condescending tone. Cookie put up with him because she wanted something from him. She was onto a new adventure. She sat in his apartment or by his side in a popular eatery or bar, as if she was holding vigil. He made her feel girlish and more restrained than her natural self would have otherwise allowed; it was the same way Giorgio DeSutter used to make her feel, a bit more polished, almost refined and much more knowledgeable about the world than most Yonkers girls. One minute she behaved like a little kid and in the next instant she adopted the haughty, mature and knowing air of an older woman. She was out of her league and knew it.

Giving him the nickname *Stewie* slightly diminished the disparity of wealth, age and class that existed between them. Still, it was a wide gulf; and so far, he had the edge.

He called her *Bell Bottom* because he detested her nickname Cookie and Concetta was too much of an ethnic mouthful for a man of the WASP persuasion. In fact, Stewie was the first WASP she had ever known. Everyone she knew in Yonkers was either Catholic or Jewish.

"Bell Bottom, are you sure you don't want a bite of chocolate?" He held up the half-eaten chocolate bar as if he was presenting her with a gift, alms for someone not as well off as he was.

He was teaching her things, about what she wasn't quite sure—art, she guessed. The man spent an unusual amount of time grooming his carrot-colored hair. Say whatever you want about the man, plus or minus, but he wasn't very passionate; of men he was the least aggressive she had ever known. No, he was not a guy's guy or a man's man or anything like the Yonkers boys she had long grown to detest.

She considered the possibility that he was similarly dispositioned to be very much like Herman Lynch—not attracted to girls. The moment she had seen Herman with Henry she had understood what he had been trying to say to her for so long. Now she was beginning to understand. This thing called sex was confounding her more than ever.

Cookie ruminated out loud so Farley could hear her. "Reenie was dating a white guy, got pregnant and ends up being consoled by Izzy. Can you imagine that?"

"Bell Bottom, this Izzy creature is exactly the type of person who comes into your life when you need a relief pitcher, a lover on the rebound who will be gone in three days or less." He picked up the phone, again dialing a number to no avail, no one was answering.

"Isabella María Fernanda Donovan, Izzy," Cookie emphasized, "would have sex with anyone or anything, any day or night."

"Why don't you invite her over, Bell Bottom?" Farley plopped into the aqua velveteen couch. "We could use some fun around here."

She didn't know what he meant by that. She only knew he got around the city quite well—theater, libraries, clubs, museums, art galleries—the places where Cookie wanted to go.

A pile of brochures heaped haphazardly on the floor caught her attention—some covered with dust or stained by coffee that had formed concurrent rings from cumulative coffee cups as if they were rings around Saturn. Some brochures had been ripped, torn or poked with holes as if they had been angrily stabbed with a small knife. One brochure, far larger than all of the others, as large as a Life Magazine, assumed last place on the bottom of the pile. Its cover bore an ominous warning written with a ballpoint pen: *Do Not Touch!*

A series of black & white paintings, "The Stations of the Cross" by an artist, Barnett Newman, who obviously liked biblical themes such as "Adam and Eve" and "Uriel the Archangel." Cookie was totally turned off by the waxy feel of the brochure and its graphic representations of churchiness. A three-dimensional collage, spirogyra-shaped in the odious psychedelic colors of the 1960s, was on the cover of a brochure printed by the Museum of Modern Art: Frank Stella, a retrospective, 1970.

A Xerox copy of a black & white photograph of three men wearing tweedy jackets struck her as odd. One man held his hat in his hand. The men stood in front of a marble plinth that supported a sculpture of beneficent cherubs, toddler angels or perhaps fairies. The photo meant nothing to Cookie but obviously held fascination for Stewie, so much so that he had written the words, *I am superior*, above the head of the man holding his hat in his hand.

She asked him why he cared enough to make a copy of a photograph, but he did not respond to her question. He told her mornings were his finest hours to work, to entrench himself within the contours of the art he often created which he often talked about, but never showed to anyone. His apartment was small. There were no signs of his art. Amply lit by two brass lamps, the ornate base of one lamp suggested the face of a lion, including its mane, and the other lamp bore the head of a bull. The lamps sat on the two mahogany end tables on either side of Farley's couch. The lamps were undoubtedly a pair. She asked him about the lamps because she liked to learn about unusual things—the things she would never have found in the homes of friends and family in Yonkers.

"I bought them at a flea market in Soho. I didn't mean to buy anything that day, but one thing led to another and before I knew it, the lamps were mine. They are quite heavy, and I had to haul them home on the subway. I was quite embarrassed. I don't like to draw attention to myself."

His explanation sounded like a confession. "As you well know, I'm quite self-contained. I really don't need anything except my work."

"I still haven't seen your work. Where is it?"

"I have a studio here in this hotel, a separate room."

She was thinking about sex and confused by that. She wasn't looking for love, but she was starved for sex. She knew it was going to happen—the search had begun—trying on men the way she tried on shoes. She thought of Stewie as a pair of oxblood penny loafers that she fully intended to try on for size.

"Even my parents still have sex." Cookie turned away from her notebook as though her thoughts were making her shy. She stashed the notebook in her Boho and sat forward, placing her arms around her knees as if she meant to rock backwards into a somersault.

"Your parents are very unusual." Farley laughed and lit a Dunhill. He didn't offer one to Cookie. "Most married people stop having sex eventually, no, on second thought, most stop having sex within a year after they get married."

"Fran Occhiogrosso is always following Louie."

"Who?" Farley had taken off his glasses. His eyes were puny and blue, rheumy looking. "Bell Bottom, what on earth are you talking about?"

"Fran is always following Louie Santamassino. I caught the two of them in the act once. She was on top of him, flailing around like this—" Cookie swung her body facedown onto his red and gold oriental carpet, spreading her arms and legs, as though she was swimming in a breaststroke. She swam on the carpet while Stewie watched.

"I take it, she's very dominant."

Cookie did rock backwards into a complete somersault and came to a standing position. She reached for the sky in a stance intended to be jumping jacks.

"Please don't. No jumping, please. I'll have the neighbors complaining. They are the most unfriendly, loathsome creatures as it is."

She stood very still, not comprehending why he was rearranging a few oversized art books on his mahogany coffee table.

"Should I know these people? This Fran and what on earth is the man's name?"

Cookie read the title of a big book on the table and flipped it open. "Marlborough-Gerson?"

"The gallery's on 57th Street. They've recently moved from Madison, closer to 6th." His tone of voice was curt; he sounded annoyed. "You have not answered my question about the name of the man. Must I ask you again?"

"Louie Santamassino has nothing to do with you. He's a Yonkers guy, that's all." She plunked herself on the couch next to him. "Donny is starting to attract boys and flirts with them." She wished he would make the first move, just to get it over and done with. She inched closer to him. He did not seem to notice.

"Donny?"

"My younger sister."

"How old is your sister?"

"I forget."

"You forget? It's funny how we forget things." He paused for a moment and pondered the name. "Donny. Why is it that all of you Yonkers people have nicknames instead of complete first names? What is it about you that you need to have monikers like silly pets? It's like the whole lot of you are from the *East Side Comedies. Little Rascals. Spanky and Our Gang?* Remember those old black & white comedies? You can still catch the reruns on Channel 5."

"How old are you?" Cookie's voice turned snotty. "I know you're older than me but how much older?"

"I'll turn the TV on for you if you like."

He turned to Cookie and smiled mischievously. "Oops, pardon me. I forgot. I don't own a TV."

He looked directly at her as though she had just arrived at his apartment. "Bring your sister here. I'd love to meet her. If she's anything like you, I'm sure I'd find her interesting."

"Johnny is always following Donny."

"Johnny?"

"My father. That's what Italian fathers do. They follow their daughters to make sure boys aren't taking advantage of them."

"I hope to God he's not following you here."

"Nope, he's given up on me. Now he wants to get rid of me." Cookie gave him a wary smile. "He's open to bids. Do you want to be the first taker?"

"Oh, Bell Bottom…"

He stood and groaned, an aching sigh, stretching his arms to the ceiling. His mouth fell open. He knelt before her in front of the couch and looked at Cookie, admiring her, as if seeing her age or her innocence for the first time. He pulled her forward and gave her a chaste kiss, too lukewarm to be erotic. Cookie tumbled to the floor beside him. He tugged her head back, tilting his mouth toward hers, probing her mouth with his sandpapery tongue. He held her tight, kissing her face with urgency that felt rigid, forced. He leaned into Cookie, pressing his pelvis into her. His vetiver scent commingled with his sweat and washed over her. She felt his hardness come between them. He gripped her hard for a moment, then let go. As suddenly as his hardness had come between them, it softened and went away altogether, a strange sensation of energy surging, then going down a drain in a rhythm as certain as a fulsome cloud discreetly breaking apart in the sky.

Twenty-seven

Farley Stewart greeted the large woman by the door. "Elaine," he called her, the same name as the restaurant. She wore yards of flowery fabric that could have been measured by the bolt in an uptown sewing store.

Elaine reminded Cookie of Millie Mangano, her father's right arm and caretaker—his office manager. Although Elaine was not larger than Millie, she carried significantly more heft in her extraordinary double chin. A fat band of jowls covered any semblance of her neck. She wore a long ropey necklace in five cascading tiers of copper and gold, the kind that are often favored by large women. She put her arms around Farley, giving him an effusive greeting but appeared to be skeptical of the two girls in tow.

Farley introduced Cookie as "Bell Bottom" and Izzy as "Isabella María Fernanda Donovan." Elaine ignored Cookie and popped Izzy a slight nod. By Cookie's reckoning, Izzy's full name made her sound royal—as if she was *somebody*.

Elaine Kaufman was loud, obnoxious and cast her roving eye around the restaurant with a wide net. She clearly preferred men and deigned the company of women unless they were someone fabulous or accompanied by a man worthy of her lavish ministrations. She explained her Number One ground rule in coarse New York squawk. "They know enough not to bother nobody?" she asked Farley. "No asking nobody for autographs!"

Izzy elbowed Cookie in her side and rolled her eyes. "How gauche."

Cookie felt offended by Elaine's implication that she'd disturb celebrity guests by doing something as uncool as asking for an autograph. Fawning over celebrities was akin to sucking up and so not Yonkers.

She stared at Elaine's necklace as though it was a prop in a traveling Broadway show, wondering if being huge meant having to wear accessories that diverted attention away from owning an amazing abundance of flesh.

Elaine motioned them to sit at a table for four by the window that looked out onto Second Avenue. The restaurant's black awning spelling out Elaine's in white cursive script, casting a long shadow that blocked any light, kept the table in the dark. White on Black. Black & White, the same as Cookie's composition book, which she never thought of pulling out, not for a moment, not in a place like this, known for its pageant of celebrity writers. She knew she was nobody. She knew she would never be somebody. It wasn't in the cards, the stars, the sun, the moon, or the clouds that she could no longer see on the Upper East Side of Manhattan.

She was a cheap hustler, a thief. Sooner or later her crime would be uncovered. She would be found out and sent to jail.

Izzy squeezed Farley's arm. "This place is so perfect. Look at all the dark wood and the book jackets all over the walls. Cookie, you like to read. Look at all the book covers!"

Cookie leaned forward, resting her elbows on the checkered tablecloth, and stared upward at the pendant-shaped lights overhead. She scanned the menu, full of Italian fare. "Looks like overpriced Italian food to me."

Puffing on a Dunhill, Farley shook his head. "It's not about the food."

"It's the company one keeps." Izzy winked.

"The atmosphere." Farley glanced surreptitiously around the room, exhaling smoke from his nose and mouth.

Cookie stood in her wobbly Springolators and waved her arms gracefully. She felt invincible. "It's the greatest place in the city, maybe the world? Isn't New York City the world?"

"Go on, make a spectacle of yourself. See how long it will take for Elaine to kick you out." Farley laughed. "All the paparazzi are here. Not everyone is a great writer," he whispered. "They'll write about Farley Stewart in a most dismissive and mocking way that I will not only take to my heart, but I will also commit the nasty things they write to memory and take them with me to my grave."

"Oh, my." Cookie clutched her chest.

"Oh, no." Izzy apologized for Cookie. "She doesn't really mean to be irreverent. She's just in awe. As am I."

Peeking out the window, Cookie smiled. She saw Arky double-parked in a long lazy line of limos. He wore his chauffeur's cap, which lent an air of importance to his persona. The notion made her smile. Aside from the business deal between them, she had given him a come-up, and for sure that was the Yonkers way.

She turned back to Farley whose eyes ricocheted along a row of tables, called the line, that sat Elaine's favorites, the regulars, the famous and the boys on the way up. Izzy's puckish mouth and sweet smile did not betray her intentions— her hand had dropped into Farley's lap. Cookie felt a twinge, quick and sharp like the bite of a mosquito, certainly not lethal but still a sting. She did not know whether to feel relieved or to give full reign to a dramatic bout of jealousy.

"I'll be right back." She pushed her chair into the table and smiled at Farley who looked dapper in a freshly pressed orange and white checked cotton shirt.

"Order me chocolate ice cream. Promise, I'll pick up the tab."

"Don't you want something to drink?"

Cookie motioned to him, using her hand to mimic slitting her neck. She'd rather give him the Heimlich maneuver, or possibly decapitate him. Farley Stewart was wearing on her frazzled nerves. Izzy had repossessed her wandering hand, at least for the moment.

"Whatever you want, Dear."

Farley motioned toward the back of the restaurant where Elaine hovered by the bar. Everyone was under her scrutiny. Elaine rose to her feet from her lookout perch. On high alert, she watched Cookie to see where she was going. Cookie stared straight ahead and avoided making eye contact with anyone. It was exactly like riding on a subway. Looking neither right nor left, nothing broke her concentration or caught her fancy as she sauntered through the restaurant, not knowing where to go, cruising to take in the scenery along the way.

Adrift, she fancied herself as being captured by pirates, walking the gangplank. One false step would cause her to fall into the water and become surrounded by hungry sharks. She would be torn to pieces. She did not want to be here! Yet, she did have to walk through the restaurant! She did have to cavort among celebrities whose names failed to rise to the tip of her tongue even if her life depended on it! One woman looked like Carole Channing, but she could have been Phyllis Diller or Joan Rivers. Cookie could not distinguish one person from another. She did not want to look anyone in the eye or, God forbid, stare, and knew the moment she did, she would turn to dust and be swept away by the street cleaner in the morning.

Mostly, she felt embarrassed for being there. Annoyed with herself. Annoyed at them. Annoyed with the whole damn world.

A few sets of eyes threw darts at her. She became conscious of the way she looked. Too hot to wear something dark and unseen, her pants were light and airy, a turquoise patterned sarong, sort of a gaucho look, under a diminutive knit halter top the color of putty. She liked not wearing a bra and knew the cool air from the air conditioner made her nipples hard. She remembered Stanley. One night at the Midget Bar, he tied her halter top tight to stop Pinky O' Hearn from undoing her knot.

But what was the use of remembering Stanley de Falco!

She felt terribly self-conscious and succumbed to the spell of male gaze as long as the mahogany bar. She imagined seeing herself the way she thought they saw her. Her breasts were small but well-formed and firm. Slinky fabric swathed her legs, caressing her fine white skin as she walked.

The rounded curves of her shoulders rose and fell when she turned slightly to the side, avoiding direct eye contact, and allowing someone with unseen eyes to pass. Her bare midriff exposed a navel as round and as perfectly formed as a bull's eye. She was somebody. She was young. She was pretty. She felt perfect. She wanted to be touched. She dared someone to touch her. She dared someone to touch her, but only if she wanted to be touched.

She refocused her eyes to see where she was within the context of the infinitely long bar. No one was looking at her. The sensation of being admired in the midst of a crowd of celebrities was in her head, a fixation. She was not quite perfect. Her ratty brown hair had curled excessively in the heat and felt heavy in the cool room; horsetail hair needing to be groomed. Her skin felt hot and oily as if she wore a plastic Halloween mask. Her nails were ragged, uneven in length and texture. Her teeth hid behind her lips pursed into a comely pout. She had not become familiar with the habit of getting manicures and had not been to a dentist in years.

There were many beautiful women crammed close to the bar, faces she recognized but whose names she failed to remember. Her confidence plummeted. She felt alone, ungainly, ugly. She wanted to run or maybe scream. Despite her inner terror, she held onto her composure.

A strange interloper swept into the fray. Grabbing her bare shoulder, he nudged her to his side and into a small service kitchen with hard tile floor. The man was very tall, wore black rimmed glasses like the ones Farley wore, but his hair was dirty blonde, exceedingly curly and messy, sprigs poking up on the back of his head. He could also stand a clean shirt, a shave and a spritz of cologne. Her back pressed against a row of stainless steel refrigeration units with heavy handles. He leaned over her.

"What have we here?" He slurred, stumbling over his words. "Sometimes you have to let somebody inside of the terrible wall between us."

She smelled the alcohol on his breath and looked at him as if he was stupid, but it was she who was the one really feeling stupid. She didn't trust herself to be with an older guy, especially a guy as old as Mr. Blondie. She was doing her best, trying to be like all of the other swell people passing by. She just wanted to be normal, like other girls, to fawn all over him and get down on her hands and knees to worship him in the manner befitting his celebrity-hood, his royal status and his manhood.

"You look so terribly afraid. What are you afraid of?" The man smiled, tilting her chin up.

"Silly wonkish white people just don't get it. They're not street smart. Know what I mean?"

He stared at her and laughed, a full belly laugh, redolent of a grandee from a bygone era. He was so very sure of himself and he reeked of alcohol.

He mimicked her. "Silly wonkish white people."

He touched her on the arm. "I'm Will," he told her, "as if you didn't already know."

Will! She keened inside and laughed, a laughter that no one could hear except herself. Will the WASP! No one, not one person in Yonkers had a one-syllable name. In Yonkers, he'd be called Willy, Billy, Willy-Billy, Willy-Nilly, Willy Chills, Chill Willy, Billy Club, Billy Bro, a name that showed he was tough. Will, she wanted to die laughing. She did not know the joke was on her.

He touched her again on a different part of her arm, closer to her shoulder. Chuckling to himself, he squinted his eyes and stared at her. "Where are you from?"

She didn't know what to say. She was just a girl from Yonkers, trying to get by in the big city. She wasn't going to tell him that. It was none of his business. She didn't need to take shit from him. She looked at him as if he is was really stupid.

"I hear the food here is lousy."

"No one comes here for the food." His finger traced a line along the side of her bare midriff. He found her navel and pushed his finger in, a little poke. He was in and out of her navel before she could even protest. His touch was as cool as the air conditioning. His hand moved inside around the waistband of her flowy pants.

"Listen kid, what is it that you want?"

She didn't know what she wanted but began to figure out what he wanted. It was a sad reminder that her innocence was gone.

"Everyone who comes here wants to become famous or stay famous. Or maybe they just want to look at the famous. Which are you?"

His drunken smile told her he already knew the answer. She was a blank slate waiting for him to write her a letter of introduction. He could easily peg her to be whatever he wanted.

He knew she was a nobody, but he feigned interest. "What do you do, Missy?"

She felt young, out of her realm or comfort zone. She also felt his hand probing under the elastic of her waistband. His fingers found his way inside and inched down below the side of her tender pubis bone, which would normally be ticklish, but his touch was cold, rough, and unwanted. No one had ever touched her there like that. She pulled away from him, but he did not altogether remove his hand.

"Sing? Dance? Write? Tell me you want to be actress. Am I right?"

Cookie shook her head and shrugged.

"All of the above? None of the above?"

"I'm just a girl from Yonkers."

"I can see it now...The girl from Yonkers!" he exclaimed in a loud theatrical voice, sweeping his one arm in the air, forming the arced trajectory of the *Lights On Broadway*.

"What do you do with yourself, Sweetheart?"

She pushed his hand away from her waistband. He immediately lost interest in her and became distracted. Activity in the restaurant peaked, an insular swell of waiters, each of whom had their place and role in a dance as dynamic and as tight-knit as any family's, rushing in and out of the service kitchen from the other end, careful not to disturb the star and his quarry, carrying trays and pitchers, clattering utensils, clinking water glasses in a chaotic kaleidoscope wreaking havoc on her senses, creating a perpetual din, an overload of noise and fast-talking commands that saved Cookie from having to talk. She certainly wasn't going to shout.

The man seemed to know that and despite his drunkenness, he did the talking for the two of them. For the moment, Cookie was exonerated from any other certitude other than silently ogling this man's greatness. She had a funny notion that if she had a mirror, she would gladly hold it up for him so he could admire himself, unshaven, unkempt, and all.

Suddenly he blurted, "I could make you a star." He said it with such jollity that she was sure he was toying with her.

"I can't sing. I can't dance. I can't play an instrument." Cookie bit her lip and debated whether she should admit the truth. "I can't really do anything. Nothing. I have no talent."

"Think Janis Joplin could sing?" Will moved a little closer to her and whispered, blowing out his foul alcoholic breath. "Janis Joplin couldn't sing. Trust me, I know."

Tongue-tied, a fleshy knot welled in her throat. Her stomach turned, burbling a noise that she hoped only she could hear. Will's eyes magnified in size, always roving, scanning her body, her face, her hair and settling on her eyes. She kept looking at him, though. Looking away from him would have been a sure sign of weakness. His face had dark brown and grey stubble as if he had forgotten to shave not for a day or two but much longer. There was no denying his hooded eyes, narrowing, then opening, sloping, all to see himself through her eyes more clearly.

Much to her dismay, he leaned forward and kissed her. A big, wet, sloppy kiss. Embarrassed, she pulled away from him.

Feeling like her lips had been bruised, kissing him was the last thing in the world she wanted to do! An unwanted kiss is a fierce sentence to purgatory. She dared not press her lips together. She did not want to taste him or revel in his drunkenness, no matter how famous he was, or if he was famous at all.

"You're blocking the kitchen! What do you have to say for yourself? Didn't I tell you not to bother anyone?" The force of a cyclone hurled into the kitchen and nearly knocked Cookie over.

"You, out!"

"I didn't mean to do nothing...anything wrong!" Cookie looked for Will to help her, to provide an explanation, but he had gone and left her standing there.

Elaine's huge body shook with rage. "Out! Get out! Get out now!"

"Wow!" Cookie was so flustered that she could not think but felt a red-hot stain cover her body with so much shame she wanted to die. She felt all eyes on her, but every face melded and blurred as a single distorted picture on a jumpy black & white screen.

The mammoth woman seethed in her face. "I warned you not to bother the guests! You're not supposed to bother the guests! Get out!"

"Oh my God. Oh, wow! I can't believe this." She cringed, moving quickly through the crowded bar, passing tables, vaguely seeing Izzy and Farley.

Izzy jumping to her feet, exclaiming, "What happened?"

Farley's face turned the same shade as his hair.

Cookie shuddered, clutching her hands to her shoulders, a breastplate protecting herself from a battle she had not knowingly cast herself into, a game she had not bargained on losing. Every pore of her body felt scrutinized, legs, torso, breasts, the nape of her neck, her cowering back, and especially her ass. She had no lover, no friend, no wish except to flee into the night. Suffering from the oddity of having been a newcomer, out of her league, away from her turf, she had been caught unaware, not knowing the rules were made in favor of only a few to shun the many. She was among the many. Ostracized! She flinched at the thought of the unseen faces, surprised, curious and horrified, who had seen her fleeing, a bad dog getting kicked to the curb.

Twenty-eight

Arky's limo was no longer among the limos double-parked in front of Elaine's. Cookie had no way of getting in touch with him and prayed that if he had been forced to move, he stayed close by and was circling the block. She began walking on Second Avenue, a one-way street going south.

She could not shake the terrible shame that had been foisted upon her. The faster she walked, the faster she would rid herself of her embarrassment. Being shamed in public destroyed her semblance of self. She could think of nothing other than the raging red face of Elaine Kaufman, treating her like scum, white trash, throwing her out of the restaurant!

Cars passing by on the badly rutted road roared their engines, blasted horns and the music of the Number One hit song of the week *Bad, Bad Leroy Brown* by Jim Croce. No amount of city noise could drown the reality that she had been a laughingstock at Elaine's. A grand spectacle. The burn had not left her cheeks. Searing pain throbbed from her toes to the top of her head. A thousand pin pricks needled her bare skin.

She didn't know where she was going. She didn't know the Upper East Side. A row of yellowing five-story buildings, dismal in their decay, stared at her. Two buildings had fire escapes mounted on the middle window of every floor as if the safest defensive posture in the world was by staying in the middle. She thought about that for a minute—staying in the middle, choosing safety over truth, not choosing black or white, even if black & white was as plain as day.

The stoplight on 88th Street hung suspended from a long galvanized steel pole, resembling an arc-shaped arm. She didn't know any neighborhood in New York that well. Whenever she had come up from the subway, she had always become confused, turned around, not knowing east from west or north from south.

Her feet hurt. She wanted to pull off her Springolators and walk barefoot but knew her feet would turn black from city grime. She felt as though the last trace of who she had once been, fearless and indomitable, was gone. She was getting beaten down by life.

She was trying to understand what had happened. She was trying to make sense of this world. Any sort of clarity or insight eluded her. She remembered the red glow of the light sculpture at Max's Kansas City commemorating the bloodshed of the Vietnam war. The war in Vietnam was coming to an end. Each day the number of casualties was diminishing. Still, death continued, innocent people were victims of a war they did not want, a war that they did not create. It was so unfair.

Life was unfair. She had been thrown out of Elaine's because some jerk had been putting the moves on her. He was exonerated, but she had to pay the price! She had done nothing wrong! She reached for her Boho, usually slung casually over her shoulder. Feeling for the bag behind her, thinking it had fallen to the side, another mini shock wave numbed her heart. She sobbed, oh no, realizing she had left her bag behind on her seat at the table with Stewie and Izzy. She could only hope and pray, it would be recovered. Much to her horror, her black &

white notebook contained her innermost thoughts, the things she wrote, never intending to share with anyone.

Then a funny thought occurred to her and she began to laugh. If Elaine confiscated her Boho, she'd be stuck holding a bag stuffed with cash. She could not imagine the look on the brassy woman's face upon discovering the truth about Cookie—her rambling writing and wads of dough.

Cookie did not know why but she began to laugh and could not stop. It was so absurd. She had plenty more money hidden under her mattress. And her notebook? That is what she wanted more than anything in the world. It was more precious than the clouds in the sky that she had once thought she owned, and the love she once had for Stanley de Falco. Of all things in this world, her silly prattle on paper with ink blots, smeared words and crossed-out patches mattered more to her than life itself.

She didn't need commas and could write without them. She didn't need her notebook. New words would come. Better words. A bare trace of moon as thin as a comma slipped away behind a cloud darker than the black sky.

She had no choice but to return to Elaine's. Arky was nowhere to be found on Second Avenue, but she knew sooner or later he would appear. Another restaurant next door, smaller than Elaine's, had outdoor seating, blocks of white wicker chairs set around square glass tables. Nice night for dining outside to feel the balm of warm air and to look upon an inky sky with only the slightest sliver of a moon and no stars. She leaned against the wall of the outdoor enclosure, took off her shoes, held them in her hand and resolved to wait patiently.

Izzy had no other way home. She was not fit to ride a subway. She could cab it home but never had any money and it was doubtful that Farley Stewart would pay for her. Stewie never paid for anything. He would nurse his drink long enough to assuage the wound he had suffered in having been seen with a loser—the young girl he called Bell Bottom. Consorting with her had been a tragic mistake, a mistake any man could make. Bell Bottom was young and pretty, but terribly ill-behaved due to bad breeding. A Yonkers girl.

Cookie imagined Stewie sipping his precious elixir, savoring every drop, nonchalantly nodding to anyone who passed by his table so he could stake a claim in his own smug self-importance. She sensed an ugly secret there, within him and kept in the dark, but it was muscular and had been well worked out. He kept his emotions under control, the same way he could effortlessly flex and contract his biceps under his crisp orange and white checkered shirt.

Hands came from behind Cookie, covering her eyes, startling her. She had been shocked enough to gasp. Whoever it was sensed her distress. The hands immediately let go. Herman Lynch lit into her face, grinning and laughing, and gave her a most endearing kiss.

"Didn't mean to scare you, Cookie girl. It's been awhile hasn't it?"

Herman hugged Cookie. "What are the chances of running into you, Cookie girl!"

"It's so *Yonkas* to run into somebody you know in the middle of the city."

"But it happens all the time," Cookie and Herman said in unison. "It's a Yonkas thing."

Herman's brown skin gleamed in the night. Henry Kagan stood beside him, beaming a slim moon of a smile. His pale blonde hair shone under the streetlight. Since Cookie had last seen him, he had grown soft bangs, a fringe fell into his pale blue eyes. He gave Cookie a hug. "Nice to see you, again. Herman talks about you so much. I should be jealous."

"But he's not." Herman put his arm around Henry's waist. Henry gave him a sultry smile and kissed the side of his neck.

They wore identical ribbed cotton tank tops, except Herman's top was white, Henry's black. Matching bellbottom blue jeans, cowhide fringed belts. Lean bodied and agile,

Herman more muscular and Henry less so, slender and lithe. Two halves of the same person, they were one half of the other, yet distinctly individual.

"How are you? What are you doing here? We just came from the 92nd Street Y."

The 92nd Street Y was a cultural and community center on the Upper East Side of Manhattan at the corner of East 92nd Street and Lexington Avenue. Known for its live performances and lectures, an icon in city life, and especially prominent in New York City's Jewish Community.

"Dance." Henry said. "Alvin Ailey."

"You in the show?"

"I've been dancing at Alvin Ailey. Henry too."

"But he's white."

"It's not about color," Herman said. "It's about talent."

"Right on. You got that straight." Cookie looked around, musing to herself, "I wish I had a Marlboro."

Herman took out a pack of Marlboros from his back pocket and offered her one. Her hand shook when Herman went to give her a light. She still wasn't over the shock of what had happened.

"Are you okay?" Herman looked concerned. "I've never seen you shake like that. You're not using, are you?"

"Come on, Herman, you know me better than that." Cookie shook her head and closed her eyes. She took a long drag, then nodded toward Elaine's.

"I'm upset cause I got kicked out and my handbag is still in there."

She watched her smoke rise, curling in the air, then dissipating quickly, a brief spell of fog in the night. She shook her head to let Herman know she was okay, and handed the Marlboro to him, just like old times.

"You got kicked out! Oh, bummer." Herman's eyes grew huge. "What happened?"

"An old drunk guy, some celebrity, was hitting on me."

She looked away embarrassed. "I guess it's my fault for being there, for being a girl."

"Don't give me that guff, Cookie girl. You know better than that."

Henry laughed. "From what I hear you don't put up with stuff like that."

He smiled and nodded, changing the subject. "It's a nice night. We needed to chill after the show and decided to walk downtown."

"Staying in shape." Herman grinned at Henry.

"Cruising," Henry quipped.

"Just looking."

"Want to hang out with us?" Henry gave her a hug. "I'd love it if you did."

"I can't walk very far in these." She held up her Springolators. "Besides, my friends are still in there. And I've got to wait for Arky."

"No sir," Herman's eyes grew huge. "Still hanging out with Arky?

"He's my chauffeur now."

"What were you doing in there, anyway? Cookie girl, what's come over you? Are you going to put up with that? You are not the same Cookie girl. You get your bag back now. Want us to help? I'll go in there and ask for your purse. What does it look like?"

Cookie shook her head. "I'm not going to drag you into this. You guys, go on. I'll be fine. I'll call you. Check ya later."

"Promise?"

"Promise."

She didn't tell Herman she worried that if he went to get her Boho, he wouldn't be treated well. She had not seen another black face anywhere inside and felt sure the only black person allowed in would have to be famous. Fame, like money, changes things. New York was New York, the most diverse city in the world, but there was still a pecking order, the illogic of privilege and the logic of wealth, as to who got to be accepted and who was shut out. She felt protective of Herman. Henry too. The three of them hugged one another, still promising to catch up soon, and she knew they would make good on their word—the unspoken bond between them had not been broken. As much as she had feared that Herman was gone forever because of Henry, she realized Henry was now her friend too.

Twenty-nine

On the corner of East 88th Street, Arky jumped out of the limo and opened the door for Cookie. Instead of behaving like a strung out junkie, a waste-of-life from Yonkers, he had become a true gentleman. His soothing voice calmed her jangled nerves and began to heal her wounded pride. She was never so glad to see anyone in her life.

"How ya all doin?" His voice had taken on the slight affectation of a southern accent. He told her he got the name Arky because his mother had conceived him during her honeymoon trip to the Ozark Mountains in Arkansas. He pronounced Arkansas *Are-Kansas*.

A pale glimmer of light from the streetlamp illuminated his eyes, round and kind. She caught a glimpse of his face, peering at her from under his chauffeur's cap. He told her he had been concerned about her. He was freshly shaven.

Once she was inside the limo, she detected the subtle aroma of his aftershave. The hair she could see that poked out from under his cap appeared to have been washed and clipped into a page-boy style that framed his face.

She was seeing Arky Lovato as a new man who had

suddenly burst into her life. He had changed and until now she had not noticed.

She told him about her missing Boho, her humiliating eviction from Elaine's, and her friends, who had stayed behind, flatleaving her. She told him these things in no particular order, offering him the essential facts out of the time sequence in which they had actually occurred. He bared his teeth, that lacked the tartar and yellow stains of the past, in a conspiratorial smile.

"If there is anything I can do to make things right, I'm your man."

He avoided the queue of limos parked out front of Elaine's and circled the block, probably for the umpteenth time that night. "We'll need to get your purse."

Talking about inconsequential things such as crime in the subway that really did not affect him, he began to drone about all the things in the world that really did impact his life. Riots. Looting. Welfare. Slums. Urban Renewal. The high cost of living. The lack of good jobs. No way to pay for education without racking up gigantic amounts of student loans—debt. He wasn't offensive and he did not lack good judgment.

He did fail to provide Cookie with a quiet moment of reflection. A private moment of mourning for the death of her former self. She half-expected to hear the wail and trill of bagpipes to commemorate her inability to rise quickly from the dead.

She heard the low hum of news on the car radio. France performed a nuclear test at Mururoa atoll, Skylab launched three astronauts into space, and Led Zeppelin had performed to a sell-out crowd at Madison Square Garden.

She asked Arky for a Marlboro. He told her he had quit smoking and let go of the steering wheel to show her his hands. "Look, hands free." He laughed.

He circled the block, watching her in the rearview mirror. "I'm sorry about what happened, Cookie. I know that you've always been a proud person. Who was the guy hitting on you?"

Cookie stared at the back of his head. His soft hair fell in a gentle wave below the nape of his neck. She watched other cars moving seamlessly alongside the limo. Light from the street flickered across the back of Arky's cap.

"I wish I had a Marlboro."

He sat up straight, watching her in the mirror. "You really ought to think about quitting. It's not like you to have a ball and chain dragging you down."

She thought she was hearing things. Was this really Arky Lovato or had he been snatched by aliens and replaced by an imposter? "Come on, you're jiving me."

"No, sir, I am not. I mean what I say and I say what I mean." He pulled alongside another limo in front of Elaine's, idled the engine into park and locked down the emergency brake. "No sir. I've always admired you, Cookie. You've always been someone to watch."

He turned around and looked at her. "Wait here, I'll get your purse."

"No." She opened the car door. "No," she said again. "The day when I have somebody fighting my own battles is the day I stop having a reason for living."

She gave Arky a cautionary look and got out of the limo.

Arky also got out of the limo, ran to her side and stood at attention. "I expected you to say something like that."

With a shrewd gleam in his eye, he tipped his cap.

Cookie gave him the thumbs up and walked under the longish awning leading toward the front entrance of Elaine's. Like mostly every place in Yonkers, there was only one way in and one way out. New York, the so-called city, wasn't much different, in many ways, from Yonkers.

She didn't look back at Arky, but felt sure he was keeping an eye on her. Before she got to the front door, Izzy spilled out of the restaurant. Her movements were tiny and frantic, a colorful songbird in distress.

"Here!" She sacked Cookie on the shoulder with her Boho. "I know how important this is to you!"

"What's wrong with you?"

Izzy was indignant. "Elaine needed my table and told me to leave."

"What about Stewie?"

"Farley," she emphasized as though his name was a euphemism for contempt. "Farley's in there somewhere at the bar. I don't know where, exactly, not that it matters."

She looked at Cookie. "I want to go home. Now. I've never been so mistreated in my life!" She began to cry, tiny tears gathered in the creases under her eyes as though they had been placed there by an eyedropper. She sniffed, placed her arm on Cookie's shoulder and held her breath.

"Geez, Kid."

Cookie felt bad for her. Crying! Crying in public! Crying at all! It was unthinkable to watch the girl sniffling. Her small body shook. She began to hiccup.

"Don't let them get you down. They ain't worth it."

"What you meant to say is that 'they're not worth it.'"

Cookie pulled a Marlboro from her bag and struck a match. She took a slow, lingering drag, eyeing Izzy who looked utterly humiliated and had run out of words to say. She drew her rail thin arms around herself in a closed knot. "I'm cold." She shivered even though the air was excessively warm, humid, and there was no breeze.

Mr. Blondie stumbled out of the restaurant onto the walkway beside Izzy and staggered into her, almost knocking her over. He saw Cookie and began laughing. He was so drunk that he couldn't keep his head upright. He smashed his cigarette to his lips, inhaling and exhaling in syncopated gusts, clouds of smoke flaring from his mouth and nose. Cookie grabbed his cigarette from his hand, tossed it to the sidewalk and stomped on it.

"That wasn't very nice, was it? I should have you arrested.

Technically that was an assault." Then he laughed. He wasn't so drunk that he had not remembered her.

"You're a funny girl. I thought I liked you very much. Well, not very much. Just a little bit." He showed a small space between two of his fingers. "This much."

Arky inserted himself between the girls and Mr. Blondie. Cookie nodded. "Yes," she said softly. "It's him. He's the one."

She didn't have to spell out what she meant.

Arky took the cue. "I think I've seen him before on TV."

Mr. Blondie never saw it coming. Arky punched him in the nose. In the stillness of the night, despite traffic on Second Avenue, the stray noise of people walking in and out of Elaine's, and random voices from the sidewalk, the blow sounded like a pop of flesh, a small slap—not hard enough to knock him out, knock him over, or to draw blood. Mr. Blondie cursed and clutched his nose. It all happened so fast that any potential witnesses had little chance to react.

They fled from the sidewalk, jumped into the limo, slamming doors, locking them for good measure. They sped into the night, going crosstown on 88th Street.

"C'est la vie," said Izzy.

"Why do you always have to talk in French? You're Hispanic."

"Half. The better half, I might add."

"Why don't you talk English."

"Everyone speaks English. It's so boring."

Izzy nuzzled her face into Cookie's neck and sighed. Cookie placed her arm around the petite girl and consoled her. She felt protective of Izzy. Delicate and light, as tender as a child, Izzy tended to be haughty, but she was still a teenage girl, trying to find her way in the world. She didn't deserve to be humiliated in public.

No one knows us, Cookie thought, and no one cares. If clouds could be seen, they would bleed dark red for the many wounds she had suffered and collected like old postage stamps bearing images of battle wounds and containing them in her cold heart. She thought fleetingly of getting revenge on Elaine, but why bother? The woman had made a career of relying on the kindness of strangers, the rich, the famous, and the beautiful, calling them her friends. In the end, she was nobody, the smallest of moons, less moon and more of an atomic meteorite, orbiting around a dying, illusory sun, an infinite speck of dust.

Cookie was proud of Arky and told him so. He smiled at her in the rearview mirror. "It's Saturday. It's pay day."

Wednesday August 15 1973

A full moon happened Monday night at 10:17 p.m. I don't know why that's important. A full moon makes it easier for me to see at night. I watched the outline of Stewie's body in the moonlight. He's very white. He's the whitest person I've ever known. I'm still seeing him and hang around his apartment in the Remington Hotel. He still calls me Bell Bottom. We go to lots of places together. We have not gone back to Elaine's. Someone told me he used to live in the Chelsea Hotel and got kicked out. I don't know if its's true. He still hasn't shown me his art or his studio. Sad.

Sometimes I think he's not an artist at all. You wouldn't believe how many people lie about who they really are.

I hate August in New York City cause it's so hot that my hair curls and my face feels oily. My feet get so dirty just walking on the street. The smell of garbage is everywhere. Piss too. Little has changed at home. Johnny mostly ignores me. Kitty is still trapped inside of the red glass in her picture window. I can't understand why Johnny isn't upset about the money that was stolen from his office. It's as if he does not know about it. Kitty is acting loonier than usual. She thinks the church bells are sending her secret messages. The church bells ring a lot. Every hour on the hour. The bells ring extra-long at noon and six. That's a lot of secret messages.

Schizophrenia is a terrible sickness. Illness. Disease. I hope I don't catch it. I love my parents. I guess. A part of me has always wished that I was adopted. I would not have to be related to them if I was adopted. I couldn't catch stupidity from (Johnny) or schizophrenia from (Kitty).

You should see Donny. She's the most beautiful girl in the north end. She's tall and has long curly blonde hair. Her eyes are as blue as the pictures I've seen of the Mediterranean Sea. Her skin is smooth and creamy. Soft looking. The color of honey. She looks old and very young at the same time. I can't explain how she looks both old and very young. I imagine her getting old like Kitty. Kitty looks both very young and very old. I don't know how to explain that either.

Where do I want to go? How the hell should I know? Why do I ask myself such difficult questions! I do know being a good girl is not all it's cracked up to be. Sainthood is not for me.

You can be a good girl and end up getting turned on the wheel like Saint Catherine of Alexandria—and that ain't no fun ride in a limo.

Something really weird happened the night after I got kicked out of Elaine's. Led Zeppelin had a ton of money stolen from their safety-deposit box at the New York Hilton. More than two hundred thousand dollars in cash was stolen! Can you believe that? It's hard to believe someone noticed that and Johnny didn't notice the money in his office was gone!

Money is supposed to change things. Money also makes sure that things stay the same. I don't know how to spend money. I don't know what to do with all of my money! Maybe I should buy a car. I will need to have a car someday. I do like having Arky chauffeur me around. He's more than a chauffeur. He's become my friend. I never see his sister Lizzie around no more. Anymore. She's gotten into the early college entry program at Columbia University to study physics. She's a genius. It's hard to believe she and Arky are brother and sister.

But wait a minute! Arky has changed. He's gotten smarter. Better looking too. He does a very good job working for me. He is always on the lookout for Mosella Moran. Tony and Toni. Anybody who could cause me trouble.

I know I look like I'm doing okay. I'm really not okay. I feel like the world is coming to an end. I don't know if it is my world or the whole world. I'm going to visit Zelda today. Maybe she has the answer.

-CCC

Thirty

The radio in the limo played *Touch Me In The Morning*, sung by Diana Ross, which was kind of funny because it was about ten in the morning and early for Cookie to be up and about. It was August and it was so hot that the air conditioning running on high failed to cool the car. Cookie kept asking Arky if he had fixed the air conditioning. He assured her that although it was working, it failed to counter the fact that it was as hot as hell.

"Concrete holds the heat," he yelled above the motor of the air conditioner.

The limo pulled up on Palisade Avenue in front of Greens. Cookie pushed open the car door and was engulfed by a thuggish blast of humidity.

Arky stayed behind the wheel in case they needed to make a quick getaway. He didn't do the chauffeur protocol, opening the door for her, standing at attention, and holding his cap close to this chest. The routine wasn't part of his job description when he was in Yonkers. The limo already drew too much attention. People gawked at the long black car, wondering what was in progress, a funeral or a wedding.

Under the cloak of humidity, Cookie's hair had sprung into Methuselah locks. She sprinted from the limo to the front entrance of the store, pulled open the heavy glass door, and immediately saw Zelda. Soothsayer, oracle, fake friend, the gypsy mannequin was all of these things, and she was a far better bet than giving alms to the Catholic Church. Cookie slipped a quarter into Zelda's coin slot. The Gypsy's eyes opened, her crystal ball lit up and out shot a fortune.

Watch your back!

Cookie dropped the slip of paper to the floor.

"Come on," she shouted at the Gypsy. "Give me something good."

She pushed another quarter into the coin slot. This fortune was a little better, but not what Cookie had in mind. *Observe all men, but most of all yourself.*

She looked at Zelda to get a clue of why she was being difficult, but as only could be expected, the fake gypsy had closed her hard plastic eyes. She needed to try again. She shook a quarter in her hand and kissed it like she was about to roll dice, before sliding it into the slot. This fortune was the worst one yet.

The fortune you seek is in another cookie.

"What do you think this is, a fucking Chinese restaurant?!"

She hit the metal side of the coin-op machine box and immediately felt ridiculous. The Gypsy bore no expression but had opened her eyes. Cookie thumped the side of the gypsy's coin-operated box. Zelda's eyes shut.

"Thanks a lot!"

"You're welcome," Cookie thought she heard the Gypsy say, but knew it was all in her head. The scent of popcorn from the coin-op machine next to Zelda overwhelmed her. She felt hungry, but not for popcorn.

Outside on the street, she eyed Woolworth's and thought of going there for breakfast but knew it was too risky to stay in Ghetto Square. Also, rumors were flying that Woolworth's would soon remove its restaurant counter. No more banana splits, ice cream sundaes, overcooked rubbery hot dogs or fried eggs and ham. It was the end of the five-and-dime store era. It was only a question of when Zelda would be gone too. She felt bad for bullying the gypsy to get a good fortune and fretted that she might have broken the coin-op machine.

She was desperate for some small inkling of which way she should turn and what she should do for the rest of her life. She had always been decisive, so purposeful in all of her actions. Something had changed that had little or nothing to do with money because she had all of the money in the world and that wasn't helping because she didn't know what to do with it. She was adrift, going nowhere, going nowhere fast.

When she returned to the limo, she told Arky she was hungry and needed to eat. He heard her alright, but he also detected that trouble was looming on the horizon.

Toni Ferlinghetti's hand was on her hip. She gave Arky a breathtaking smile and offered him a smoke. She wore a red knit halter top that was too small to cover her large breasts. Very short and tight, the knitted fabric of her white high-waist hot pants stuck to her legs with the tenacity of glue. She quickly scanned Cookie's hot pants ensemble that was rather conservative, a red onesie with pockets above the hips and white piping edging the bottom of the shorts, the cap sleeves and her modest scoop neck that showed the barest hint of décolletage.

Toni eyed Cookie playfully and broke into a fit of laughter. "Want some ice cream?" she asked. "You look like you need to stay cool. It's going to be a real scorcher today. It's already pushing ninety."

She walked up to Cookie and examined her face. "I hear you been hitting on Zelda the Gypsy to give you good fortunes. Someone I know was just in there and saw you beating on the machine. Don't you know that gypsy's not real! And even if she was a real gypsy, she'd lie to you just to get your money."

She took a deep drag from her cigarette and blew smoke toward the side of Cookie's head. "People are starting to talk about you." She rolled her eyes. "What I meant to say is people have always talked about you. Only now it's even worse. There's talk that you're crazy and you're gonna go to jail for stealing money from Rite Aid."

She took a break from talking to Cookie and looked at her as if she was trying to make up her mind about something. "You know what I think? I think you've done something really bad, and I think I know what it is. Guess what? You're not going to get away with it. It's all gonna catch up with you."

Cookie felt tears come to her eyes. She was scared but in no way would she ever show fear, certainly not to Toni Ferlinghetti. She turned around and walked away from her.

"Where did you get that outfit," Toni called after her. "You look ridiculous."

Cookie had bought what she had considered to be her demure summer outfit at Bonwit Teller on 57th Street. According to Izzy, who had accompanied her there, the store's facade was a replica of its parent on the Faubourg Saint-Honoré.

"Paris," Izzy had emphasized triumphantly.

Cookie's new outfit had cost nearly three hundred dollars and had been featured in the July issue of Vogue. Cookie especially loved the fabric covered snaps on the inner thighs to her crotch that allowed easy access to go to the bathroom instead of having to take off her entire suit. Her outfit was outré, unlike any other garb worn by a Yonkers girl.

But Toni insisted. "You look like a freak."

All of Toni's cruel remarks got to Cookie. As much as she didn't want to admit it, she was susceptible to criticism. A part of her felt like ripping off her onesie because Toni had been implying that it looked ugly on her. Toni had no concept of style or sophistication. The clothes Toni wore were cheap, meant to shock old women and titillate guys. What else would you do if you had breasts that big and a brain that small?

Observe all men, but most of all yourself—that was the only one of Zelda's fortunes that mattered.

Thirty-one

Menstruation is a gift from our lady, not a curse. Each month the arrival of her period was a joyful occasion, a reminder that she had not, in Johnny's words, *gotten herself knocked up.*

Today was the Feast of the Assumption of the Blessed Virgin Mary, a holy day of obligation that commemorates Mary, the mother of Jesus Christ, ascending into heaven to be with God, the father, the son and the holy ghost, a pure transition from earth to the afterlife that did not involve the loss of bodily functions, decomposition, rot, and maggots.

No suffering here. Mother Mary had done all of her suffering at the foot of the cross. She had even conceived a child without sin. No pleasure here too. Despite Cookie's deep antipathy toward the Catholic Church, there was no harm in going to confession. Cookie needed all of the help she could get.

The sight of the limo parked in front of Christ the King Church made it appear as though there was an unscheduled funeral about to take place. Any moment a casket would be dragged out of the back of the limo and into the church, which was as small as a church could be, the size of a little brown chapel stuck in the middle of nowhere.

Cookie was neither a casket nor a cadaver as she alighted from the shiny black limo with the panache of a megawatt celebrity. Big hair, wearing a spectacular hot pants ensemble and a tentative smile, she knew what she was about, at least for the moment. All around her there were familiar faces, but she said hello to no one. She was willing to try anything to regain her equanimity, even if that meant giving alms to the Catholic Church.

No sermon. Mass was not in progress. This was the peep show, the movie trailer, the prequel and the opening act before the grand event. She heard the tinkling of bells coming from the altar boys who knelt like second-string cornerbacks on the sidelines of a football field. One boy spewed clouds of incense from a golden thurible. Gleaming candelabras with tall white candles guarded the Blessed Sacrament, which remained in the tabernacle, an omnipotent oracle gazing upon an unruly, sinful flock.

Images of Christ's ordeal walking to Calvary were depicted in the Stations of the Cross, small wooden plaques that were indifferent to the carnage that might have really taken place. She walked the red carpet toward the back of the church as if she was washing herself in the red blood shed by Christ. Cookie's ordeal was no different than what Jesus had endured; teenage angst was right up there with crucifixion. Anyone in this world who is different is persecuted. Jesus was different. So are teenagers—all of them struggling to grow up in a world that is rigged against them.

Among the many clouds in the sky that were her friends, here the clouds of incense congested her throat. Her eyes watered, yet she could see that the church was in full swing. People praying in the pews. A line of two queued in front of the confessional box. Soon Cookie would be next.

On the verge of turning seventeen, something was changing in Cookie and it wasn't necessarily for the better. She was not at all certain of her own place in the world. She was young, Italian, Irish, Catholic and some, even Stewie, called her beautiful. It was a lethal combination, especially the Catholic aspect. She liked to do bad things, strange things, naughty things. She knew she would always be forgiven.

And she needed to be forgiven for stealing so much money. Mostly, she felt bad about stealing the money because it might be hurting Johnny in some unknown way. He had endured enough pain for one life. Broken in battle on the front lines of Korea. One of a few Marines surviving the battle of the Chosin Reservoir. Failing in his pursuit to be a musician. Losing his passion for what he loved more than anything. Losing his music. Losing his soul. Trying to love a wife who could never love him back. She did not want to be the one to further hurt him. The guilt in her heart felt as heavy as her hair.

She ushered herself into the confessional booth that had just been vacated by Millie Mangano. When she saw Cookie, the large woman tripped all over herself, scuffing her foot on the red carpet. Millie pretended not to see her, hurriedly blessed herself and left the church. It was one more moment of unbidden anguish for Cookie. She had often thought that Millie would have made a better wife for Johnny than her own mother.

She entered the confessional booth, knelt on a padded footrest and made the sign of the cross. Although it was dark, everything could be seen, the silhouette of shapes and sizes, yet a form of twilight protected the identities of the priest and his repentant sinner. The drapery partitioning the booth from the vestibule of the church was a rich shade of burgundy. Cookie touched the drapes, caressing the velvet with her hand. The texture was smooth and sensuous, thick with cumulative incense and dust.

The priest opened his window, revealing a dark screen that obscured his features but not the shape of his head. Cookie was sure it was Father Dunn, the same priest who took money from her father, hush money to put up with Kitty's crazy antics. He was the same priest who had come to her home snooping, to learn of Donny's whereabouts. Rumor had it that Father Dunn had an ongoing illicit relationship with the church organist Mrs. Myrtle Shep. But it was a ruse. The plump blonde Myrtle Shep lacked sufficient allure to rouse passion in any man, and certainly not in the priest. The true litmus test of his lack of attraction toward women resided in the priest's succession of blonde, blue-eyed altar boys.

The priest had a sidekick, Sully, a red-faced, drunken pedophile, who often cornered young boys in the north end. Taking the boys into wooded areas and back street alleyways, Sully raped them, intimidating them to never tell. He took them to the priest to offer them forgiveness, purification and protection in return for their silence. Whispering and fever-pitch rumors that took place behind closed doors proclaimed a dark message: *The priest and Sully were in cahoots.*

After Father Dunn said his mumbo jumbo, casting a rote opening prayer, the priest cleared his throat and hesitated before he went on. "Today is the Feast of the Assumption of the Blessed Virgin Mary, a holy day instructing young women in the way of our Lord. Let us pray to our Mother Mary for guidance and our willingness to serve Jesus in all ways."

While the priest admonished her for all of the sins a young woman could possibly commit, as well as some she had not yet thought of, she realized the error of her ways, the grievous folly she had undertaken. She had come here to confess her sin; it was not possible—she could not reconcile her small sins within the context of the much greater sins of the world that went unpunished and were swept under the carpet.

"Father, forgive me, but I don't understand. I've committed small sins, but I do not know why rich people get away with really big sins. Know what I mean?"

The priest did not respond except to clear his throat again.

She, too, remained silent. She glanced around the semi-darkness of the cramped booth. The little crucifix above the screened-in window to the priest's booth was wooden.

The anguished statuette of Jesus, also carved from wood, stared upon her with his generous, outstretched arms. She envisioned herself as being in the wooden heart of the man who was impaled on the cross like a slab of meat. Blood, wooden wounds, the smallness of the cubicle, made her feel claustrophobic. The drapes and their accompanying fittings were strong enough to hold onto if she wished to swing cheetah-like on a trapeze.

"What do you mean by big sins?" The priest whispered.

Obviously, she had struck a chord and felt a bit of mischief overtake her. "Little boys," she whispered back. "Sully."

The priest closed his window, further diminishing light. There were ledges for elbows and benches for knees in the cubicle. She could climb in the booth if she wanted to, holding onto the sturdy drapes that were hung from a powerful beam. And she wanted to climb to see how far she could go. The priest came around to her door, opened it and gave her the stink eye. Baring his teeth, he nodded as if he had all along known that the person could be none other than Cookie Colangelo. Satisfied that he had uncovered her identify, he returned to his own cubicle and resumed his role as Father-Confessor.

Cookie knew he had desecrated the inviolable sanctity of preserving anonymity between the sinner and a holy, sanctified priest. The screened-in window to the priest's booth was the direct route to heaven, the path to God's ear, and for once she wanted to see how much God could take. She detected that the priest had composed himself to resume his duties because he opened the window, leaving only the fine mesh screen to separate himself from Cookie.

The silhouette of his head showed he had turned to the side, showing his profile. In repose, even in the dark, he lowered his head, giving the impression he was deep in thought, engaged in a moment of prayerful contemplation. "I will pray for you," the priest hissed. "May God have mercy on you. May you find everlasting peace."

Cookie erupted into schoolgirl laughter. She climbed as high as she could go. The priest did not see the silhouette of her head. Instead of bothering God, she wanted to see how much the priest could take.

She twisted her supple body into an intentional posture of defiance and rage. Undoing the four snaps on her onesie was easy. One for the nun Fangs who had beaten her as a child. Snap! Two for her mother who no one could help. Snap! Three for her father who had been put in the untenable position of having to pay vast sums of money to the priest. Snap! Four for the many reasons she would never be as pious as Mother Mary—the woman who conceived a child without having sex! As if she and all other young girls were supposed to believe the impossibility of a virgin birth! Snap!

The priest saw white flesh, two orbs of equal strength and intensity, firm and of matching size. "Oh My God!" the priest moaned. Father Dunn had good reason to be upset. Cookie Colangelo had taken the liberty of showing him the moon.

Thirty-two

Her heart raced in a swim through a stew of conflicting emotions over what she had done to the priest: shame and embarrassment, crazy glee and satisfaction. She felt guilty pleasure over mooning the priest, but she was high on adrenaline; her emotional scoreboard stopped meandering all over the place and registered extreme delight. Even if it had been the wrong thing to do, the phony priest deserved it. She hated him and could not stop laughing. In the back of the limo, she crossed her legs, fingered her snaps which were now securely fastened, lit a Marlboro and opened the window.

Arky had no idea what she had done. She did not feel the need to tell him. He chewed on a toothpick, his new habit that had replaced smoking cigarettes. The news on the radio was all about Vietnam. The U.S. had stopped bombing Cambodia, officially ending twelve years of combat in Southeast Asia. In the Gulf of Tonkin, the U.S. Navy aircraft carrier USS Constellation departed Yankee Station for the last time. American aircraft carriers had been deployed from Yankee Station since 1964. The USS Constellation was the last aircraft carrier to leave and return home.

Her heart skipped, a slight twinge, the same old dull ache of having known and loved Stanley de Falco. She opened the limo's window and blew a stream of smoke, hoping, wherever Stanley was, that he was okay, and she wished him well.

She bowed her head in a moment of silent prayer, praying to a God who she did not know for sure if he existed, but just in case he did, she really wanted to ask: Why is there so much pain in life?

The limo cruised south on South Broadway through what used to be the old Irish-Italian-Polish-Jewish-Ukrainian-German neighborhood of old Yonkers. The buildings belonging to St. John's Episcopal Church sat on the right side of Broadway. Constructed in 1752 from red brick and slabs of smooth granite, the church, its rectory and other accompanying buildings were as old as the seven hills of Yonkers. The church dominated the corner, giving it the stately air of a private estate, somewhat out of place in the midst of drab pre-war buildings and schlocky, glass-window-front department stores, all of them with one door, one way in and one way out.

Directly across the street lay the old Yonkers Savings and Loan Building, the scene of Cookie's crime. Stopped at a light, from the limo she watched the entrance of the building for signs of Johnny. She did see Millie squeeze herself through the brass fitted oak door and into the building's cool marble lobby. Tony Amendolito slithered into the building and wrapped himself in a stiff squat pose behind Millie. She saw them standing side by side waiting for the elevator, not talking to one another, and yet it was obvious that they were together. They were an unlikely duo and she wondered how they had come to know one other.

The Church of the Immaculate Conception, known by everyone as St. Mary's Church, was the oldest Catholic Church in Yonkers. Serving mostly Irish immigrants, many whom came to the United States during Ireland's great potato famine, the church's exterior granite façade favored the texture and shade of dark dried mud. Its copper trim, sconces and the cross that sat atop a sharp peaked roof had turned green with corrosion. Cookie's Grandmother Delia went to mass there every day. Even if she had not been a daily churchgoer, most certainly Delia would be there on this holy day of obligation—the Feast of the Assumption of the Blessed Virgin Mary.

She really wanted to talk to her grandmother about the virgin thing and ask why women were expected to be pure, unblemished and without sin, but men could do anything that they wanted to do. Cookie had no idea what time it was until she heard the radio announce it was 12:20. Shortly after noon, mass was still in progress. Cookie could not bring herself to walk into the church to find her grandmother. She did not want to give the old woman a heart attack.

The library came into view, drifting by as if it were a boat, rocking and weaving in between the waves of intense heat building up on the pavement. The limo picked up speed on South Broadway. The library was in the distance now, but always there, an image to hold onto. The place she had always held sacred had a calming effect on her frayed nerves. She remembered carrying armloads of books home on the bus, trudging through inclement weather, snow, rain, intense heat or cold. Nothing stood in the way of her love of books and the stories transporting her to faraway places and magical worlds, giving her a love for people, all kinds of people, and a love of life. The library would always be her lifeline. And it would always be there. She wasn't sure of many things in life, but she was sure that her library would be there forever.

Loew's Theater on South Broadway, now officially renamed Brandt's Yonkers after an ill-begotten legal dispute, was still called Loew's *Lowees* as a tribute to its grand past as a palace theater. The theater had stood strong since the 1920s, offering movies, live shows and vaudeville to the ordinary people who had endured the Great Depression, World War II, and the post-war boom that had uplifted them, giving them better jobs and homes and hope for the future.

An older woman in a royal blue floral dress stood outside the theater, almost blending into the building's stippled blue and white lines carved into red bricks. She wore white gloves, a straw sunhat and carried a matching straw pocketbook large enough to carry a book or two. Despite the heat, a pale yellow cashmere sweater sat on her shoulders as if she anticipated encountering a chill from too much air conditioning.

She was protected from the hot August sun by the theater's ornate gilded awning that harkened back to the days when the men wore britches and the women wore dresses with a full arsenal of foundational garments: slips, girdles, garters, stockings, a brassiere and full-size underpants. Smart looking, the woman possessed a certain air of propriety and seemed sure of herself as she unlocked the front door of the theater.

Then the woman stepped slightly to the side, turning her profile to the street. Cookie recognized Mrs. Kerry. Cookie had not meant to tell Arky to stop the limo, but Mrs. Kerry had her full attention.

"Hey, let me out here and wait for me."

Mrs. Kerry had already gone into the theater. Cookie followed her into the lobby. With its high ceilings, balconies, chandeliers and intricate artwork, the grand interior had a bearing as regal as Mrs. Kerry.

Upon seeing Cookie, Mrs. Kerry's eyes misted over. "I was starting to think I'd never see you again."

It was a difficult moment for Cookie. She lifted her head toward the ornate ceiling and its double-orbed chandelier dripping with diamonds of shimmering light.

"That would never happen. Do you know how much you mean to me?"

She rushed to hug Mrs. Kerry who gladly took her into her arms.

"And you know how much you mean to me." Her black-framed eyeglasses dangled from a turquoise beaded chain around her neck. She lifted her glasses, placing them on the bridge of her nose, scrutinizing Cookie. "You're looking good. Healthy, nice clothes, you look like you're being good to yourself."

Cookie pulled away and looked at her. "Why are you here in this old theater?"

Mrs. Kerry sighed. "I can't believe they want to tear down this theater. They want to tear the whole thing down. All of it. Those developers get greedier by the day and I'm trying to stop them."

Waving her hand, turning completely in a circle, clearly gesturing toward the enormity and grandeur of the auditorium.

"This theater runs the entire long block of South Broadway from Vark Street to Herriot Street. It was built to be magnificent enough to make every person who walked in feel special just for being here."

Mrs. Kerry removed her delicate sweater and placed it in her straw bag. She also removed her gloves. "It's hot in here and musty." She sniffed. "I thought it would be cool, but I guess the air circulation hasn't been turned on in months. They've closed the theater, you know."

"No, I didn't know. Why?"

"Last March after they showed the remake of *National Velvet*, they closed it. They say it's for good."

She eyed Cookie with grave certainty. "They want to do the same thing to the library."

"No way. That will never happen!"

"Some say the people down here don't need a theater." She paused. "Or a library."

"What does that mean?"

"The color of the people has changed." She paused again and took a deep breath. "The people have changed from white to brown and black."

"The library?" Cookie was incredulous. "They'll never get away with it!"

"You'd be surprised at what some of those white folk can get away with. Put a little money behind it and they always seem to win."

Mrs. Kerry stepped to the side, walking in front of an empty popcorn machine and thick glass candy counters coated with dust. "It's a shame what's happening to Yonkers. I never know what building will come down next."

She touched Cookie below her chin and lifted her face to her own, taking a few moments to examine her eyes as though she found them beautiful.

"Come, that has nothing to do with us. Let's sit and enjoy each other."

She led Cookie through the lobby lined with tall standing torchiere floor lamps set inside of the recessed hollows in between commanding Grecian colonnades. Heavy brocade draperies cinched with gold ties and tassels gave formal definition or clarity to the golden opulence of each hollow. Queen Anne style settees and armchairs were serenely tucked within each hollow to create the impression of having a private room of one's own.

Together they walked along a floor of black marble, listening only to the squeak of their shoes. Occasionally the sounds of their footsteps were buffered by an assortment of Oriental and Spanish themed carpets that differentiated one alcove from another.

Mrs. Kerry opened two doors and walked into the auditorium that had a large balcony, a proscenium-arch stage with three opera boxes on each side, an orchestra pit, and comfortable seating for nearly 3,000 people. She pointed toward an enormous pipe organ that had four ascending rows of black & white keys.

Her voice trebled in the cavernous auditorium. "That's a Robert Morgan Theatre Pipe Organ. Its sound is exquisite. It's like listening to an entire symphony."

She eyed Cookie and folded her arms tightly, almost up to her shoulders. "There are only about thirty of these organs left in this whole country."

"Looks complicated to play. So many keys in black & white."

Mrs. Kerry turned around, away from the stage. "There used to be more than movies here. Live shows. Years ago, this theater was the very first stop for Al Jolson on his legendary tours called 'Jolson Sings Again.'"

Cookie listened and watched the floor carefully. Traversing from marble and tile to carpet, she did not want to catch her shiny white platform heels in the thick nap of the carpet.

"He used to perform in blackface showing only the whites of his eyes."

"Singing Sonny Boy." Cookie quipped, "I don't think I know the lyrics to that one."

"With his thick flesh-lipped white mouth. Or maybe it just looked that way with that dreadful black face makeup."

"He's the poster boy for blackface."

"He took what he wanted from African American music and made it his own. He made it popular too. White people wouldn't listen to African American music when it was performed by black people."

She shrugged. "Can't say I blame Al Jolson."

"Times have changed."

"Have they?" Mrs. Kerry looked at her quizzically. "If you ask me, the more things change, the more they stay the same, especially when it comes to race. Some say racism is a two-way street, but that's not necessarily true. Racism is a white-man's game where the stakes are drawn so only white people can win. That's why we have to remember what happened, so we don't do it again. We've got to learn by our mistakes."

Her eyes bore deeply into Cookie with quicksilver precision. "And I hope you are learning by your mistakes."

"I'm still trying on shoes…"

"What's that supposed to mean?"

"Trying on things to see what I like and what I don't want."

"As long as you don't trip and fall off of your high heels. When you fall hard, it can be a mighty fall. Beauty always does a magnificent job of falling from grace."

Cookie looked away from Mrs. Kerry, knowing what she said was the truth. She had an uncanny knack for always saying the right thing with heart and verve.

She led Cookie into a small sitting lounge with stiff-backed Chippendale-style mahogany chairs. Its seats were upholstered in brilliant colors of diamond and rectangular shapes, a subtle variation of art deco design.

"Come, Cookie, sit, tell me what's been going on with you."

Cookie sat on the chair and crossed her legs. "Mind if I smoke?"

"I do. I can't stand the smell of it. Herman doesn't smoke at home. Can you wait a bit?"

Cookie nodded and set her Boho on the back of the chair.

"That outfit must have set you back a pretty penny."

"You always had an eye for quality."

"And I always saw quality in you."

Cookie felt herself blushing and hoped it was dim enough for Mrs. Kerry not to notice.

"What's with the fancy outfit? I hear you're being squired all over town in a limousine by that Arky fellow. Herman said you ran into him in the city. You were standing in front of one of those celebrity restaurants. So please tell me what's going on with you?"

"It's just a phase I'm going through. I miss Herman. I want to see him."

"He misses you too. You ought to try to get together. Soon," she emphasized.

She took Cookie's hand and patted it. "None of us ever know how much time we have. Speaking of which, have you seen your Grandmother Delia?"

Cookie shook her head.

"Every day I see her walking on South Broadway, going to noon mass. I run into her at Finast. She loves to buy bananas, pears and chocolate box cakes."

"Entenmann's." Cookie laughed. "I swear that's all she eats."

"Your grandmother is a lovely woman, but she seems lonely."

Cookie shrugged. She wasn't willing to tell Mrs. Kerry that the notion of talking to her grandmother right now was not a good thing. She couldn't see herself lapsing into a conversation about the Virgin Mary and the Holy Roman Catholic Church.

"How about Reenie?"

Cookie shook her head. She twisted her ankle in a complete rotation, testing her flexibility. She felt embarrassed over Reenie on account of flatleaving her and all.

"I'm not sure her Nonna is well. I hear she's been sick. Heart problems. Cancer. Something's wrong. She's getting up in years."

Cookie pressed her lips together. She couldn't bear to say what they both knew to be true—Reenie had no one else in the world.

"Something tells me you are off sowing yourself wild oats." She stared at Cookie, thoroughly assessing her. "Are you sure you're okay?" She looked at Cookie with a small measure of transparency, as though nothing Cookie could say or do would stop her from seeing right through her. "Are you sure there's something that you're not telling me?"

Mrs. Kerry's question was one she could not respond to, nor did she care to insist that everything was okay when it was not. Cookie let the question dangle in the air, the wrong tense of a verb, a lost adverb, a succession of poorly placed adjectives, a misplaced comma or two—the commas she refused to use in her black & white notebook.

She thought the keys on the Robert Morgan Theatre Pipe Organ were like the pages of her black & white composition book. She thought of taking the notebook out of her Boho to write stuff, but then she chuckled to herself. Only this morning, she had written a journal entry, but it seemed like years ago, light years before she had mooned the priest. And now here she was on good behavior with Mrs. Kerry. Why was it that her owls brought out the best in her? The Blind Owl Alan Wilson. Herman Lynch. Stanley de Falco. Mrs. Kerry. They were her owls. There were no new owls on the horizon. Not one.

Thirty-three

Farley Stewart was not an owl. He was a necessary but expensive accoutrement, waking up and fulfilling Cookie's ambition to imbibe in the many cultural activities in Manhattan that would forsake her ties to Yonkers. He took her to galleries, museums, concerts and nightclubs. Izzy often accompanied them. Cookie always paid their way. Long on culture and breeding, but short on cash, Farley Stewart and Isabella María Fernanda Donovan were freeloaders.

Giving them the nicknames Stewie and Izzy did not make them regular hardworking Yonkers kids. As fate would have it, they didn't see themselves as freeloading sponges. Well mannered, they spoke in clipped, grammatically correct sentences, dripping with bon mots. They acted as if the world owed them something, as a birthright. Besides, they thought they were simply wonderful. Izzy described herself as Super Fantástico. Strangely enough, Izzy and Stewie never went to private parties together. Cookie found it was odd that they didn't really seem to know anyone except their financial sponsor—Cookie.

The Library for the Performing Arts at Lincoln Center was

high on Cookie's list of places to explore. She sat in between two stacks of record albums: Chopin and Debussy. This library was one of the few places in the world where people could check out music, borrow albums to take home, or listen to whatever gave them immense pleasure in a small soundproof cubicle.

From inside the nearest cubicle, Stewie watched her. The way he looked at her told her that he was smitten with her. She did not consider that she was nobody special, and that he held a fascination for all teenage girls. Redheaded, pale-skinned Stewie was not young, not old, something in between. He had not at first seemed like a lech, a perv or a screwball, but he was getting increasingly weird. The dynamics between them had started to become a game.

She regretted looking in his direction because now he would not stop staring. She ignored him for a lengthy period of time, every so often giving him a nonchalant side-eye glance. She began to play a little game of cat and mouse and swore she would not return his gaze, but eventually she did and broke into an effusive grin and giggled. She loved being given massive amounts of attention from a man who appeared to be sophisticated and definitely not a Yonkers guy. Who was the cat and who was the mouse? One can never tell for sure.

He did not approach her in the library—that was part of the game. It wasn't until she stepped outside onto the wet planes of mottled beige and grey pavement that she became aware of him. The waning sun could not be seen in the sky from her vantage point, only the diminishing grey light told Cookie it was close to six. At first it seemed as though they were strolling in the same direction through Lincoln Center Plaza. The protective concrete awning arching over a passageway, marked by massive stanchions, shielded them from other pedestrians passing by. As they crossed 60th Street against traffic, zigzagging in between delivery trucks emitting noise and diesel fumes, he was keeping stride with her. It had also begun to rain, not a heavy thundering shower, but a fine mist coating the street.

The sidewalk was thronging with dense bodies amid the careless toss of umbrellas collectively brimming far too wide for anyone to pass without turning sideways. She wasn't dressed properly for the rain and regretted wearing her onesie and its companion, a light blue knitted shawl that she pulled out from her Boho. The thin wool shawl was no match for the rain. Tiny pinprick beads of water gathered on her arms and bodice. Her exposed legs and her bare feet tucked in platform sandals felt wet.

When they reached the corner, he sprang forward, said hello, touched her arm and pressed a folded square of paper in her hand that was slightly larger than the one spat out by Zelda in Greens' arcade. She blinked back rain from her eyelashes as though they were tears and hoped her mascara had not begun to run. She could hardly see what he wrote and the fact that he wrote anything made her feel strangely sad. She was wishing in the form of a short prayer how badly she wanted this game to end but, unknown to her, it had scarcely begun.

At his lead they took cover under the yellow awning of a small Hispanic grocery store. She looked at the small square of paper, which read: *A pleasant surprise is waiting for you.* It was a better prospect than the fortunes she had recently received from Zelda the Gypsy. Cookie pressed the paper into her Boho and walked away.

She was learning her way around the city and knew vaguely she was close to a subway station. Under normal circumstances, she would have counted on Arky, but he had not been included in this game. Stewie had insisted so. Arky had been sidelined, left behind in the Riverdale section of the Bronx, close to the subway line. She knew she could catch a train, if she needed to, but she wasn't sure of her next moves, or what Stewie had in mind.

The drizzle had thinned to a transparent mist, indistinguishable from the usual summer humidity that made her face feel hot and oily, expanding her hair into random ringlets.

She kept moving, hitting sharp strides against the hard concrete that jostled her body, inviting the mist to blur her vision. She followed the signs into the tunnel for the Broadway IRT train, going north to the end of the line at 242nd Street. All the way down, down, down into the subway station, she felt a big mad coming on. She didn't notice until she stepped into the car and the doors slammed shut behind her that Farley had followed her.

The car lurched, swaying from one side to the other in a terrible groan, squealing along the tracks. Farley yelled above the noise, "You need to take better directions. You keep going off on your own. Stop doing your own thing. You're going south, not north."

The game continued between them. He convinced her over the clang and roar of the subway that she needed to get off at the next stop on 59th Street.

Once she exited the train, he led her out to the street, crossing to the other side, so she could catch the train going north. She started walking away from him, but he followed her, then walked alongside her, stopping every now and then to spin around on the pavement, turn around and face her. She ran in a mad dash, fearful that her knees would give out. He ran like a crazy man until he caught up with her.

"I'm not going to hurt you." He looked at her with what appeared to be sincerity, half dim-witted, slanted eyes and smiled. "But the reality is, I'd like to."

Cookie revaluated him and the situation. Too stymied to say anything, the way he gushed made her feel off-balance. He did not do anything that made her detect that he could be dangerous. He seemed to be befuddled by his own actions. He was distracted not by her or the incessant activity of the street but by a distraction of his own making.

"Should we stop somewhere and have coffee? There's a Chock Full o' Nuts around the corner."

Cookie imagined the narrow half-moon, circle-shaped

white counter and the spare, built-in stools of Chock Full o'
Nuts, where they could sit, and she could figure out what was
going on and where this game was going to end up. She also
didn't want to know this part of him. It was getting too weird.
She avoided looking at him.

"Okay, I'm sorry to trouble you, I'll be on my way. I usually
don't do things like this. I was struck by something. I don't
know what. You tell me. Tell me why I'm making a fool out
of myself."

He put out his hand. "You can come with me."

He seemed to know where he was going, which was good
because Cookie did not know. She kept up with him as he took
long strides on the street. They changed trains at 42nd Street
and took the shuttle from the West Side over to Grand Central
Station. From there he nudged her onto an East Side subway
going Uptown, where they exited the stop at 86th Street where
the Metropolitan Museum of Art, The MET, was located.

Cookie had no idea where she was, definitely off of her
beaten trek. She vaguely knew the West Side of Manhattan
but now on the East Side, with the exception of knowing where
Elaine's was located, she was in uncharted territory. Farley
blithely nodded to a row of town homes on 5th Avenue across
from the MET, announcing that was his home, but she did not
look, nor did she stare at him for too long—because he had told
her not to look at him.

He led her into an alley between two residential buildings,
one a Beaux-Arts style manse, and down into a lower floor that
appeared to be a basement apartment. She grew concerned
now and would not take another step into this strange place
with this red-headed man of an undetermined age.

"Stop," she told him. "I'm not going inside there with you."

Paused by the alley that looked like it was going nowhere,
she came to a dead stop. The building had numerous entrances.

Stewie got the picture and told her to wait by the wrought
iron fence that ribbed around the house environs. Once he

walked in, he never came out. She was standing there, not knowing where she was, not knowing whether she should leave or stay. People walked dogs, most on a short leash. A few dogs were led by their masters on long leashes. All seemed normal until she saw a woman leading a man by a black leather leash. He wore a thick matching black collar with silver studs and had a vacant look in his eyes.

She suddenly became filled with self-loathing and despair at her own paralysis. She stood there, twisting her toe, stabbing it into the soil beneath a small ornamental tree that had been planted close to the entrance leading into a shabby brownstone. The rain had stopped but the temperature stayed the same and the air thickened with insufferable moisture. She didn't know where she was and felt so depressed and alone. She was lost but too embarrassed to ask anyone for directions. She refused to break the cardinal rule of the city. *Always act like you know what you're doing even when you don't.*

Noise assailed her ears, the bellow of snare drums, missed beats on a construction chain gang, and she could not hear herself think. Above the exhaustive scrape of tin, the peal of car horns, and the rumble of delivery trucks, she heard distinct sounds, a sneeze, a cough and random voices.

She noticed other trees on the street. Stunted in growth, not even three feet high, old and withered as though they had been cut off at their knees. She thought if the trees tried to walk, they would grow legs, the kind that had once suffered from polio, crooked and trembling. She thought of her father cutting down all of the Sumac trees and how he believed they were poisonous no matter how hard she had tried to tell him otherwise. Two scruffy sparrows flitted among the stunted trees and danced on small patches of soil covered with weeds. She reckoned the birds were street smart, far more savvy than most people who were not from New York City.

There were no hills anywhere here, unlike Yonkers that was called *the city of hills*. Manhattan was flat and logically constructed, the eternal proposition of an even grid in a geometric equation. Even without the presence of hills, she felt that she was on the edge of a steep slope that would cause her to slip away, with a force that was nameless and unknown.

She was acting as though the city was new and forbidden to her, when it was not. No one had ever told her she was not allowed to go to the city. She did not know why standing on Fifth Avenue across the street from the MET made her feel off-kilter. Fleetingly she thought of being a kid again when she had more guts than she did now. Here she was at sixteen, too unsure of herself to move in one direction or the other.

Farley returned and took her by the hand. She gladly took his hand. It was the most ordinary thing she could do. She could not bear to stand there a minute longer. He led her through a black wrought iron gate, down a short flight of steps and into a basement apartment. Despite the grandeur of the building's ornate exterior, the basement room was sparsely furnished and smelled of mildew. A love seat sofa with frayed orange corduroy fabric and a thinly veneered coffee table stained with watermarks were the only pieces of furniture to catch her eye. She didn't know why but she thought of the moon drifting in and out behind clouds, waning gibbous, waning spiritually—the distinct sign that she needed to move on to a new phase of her life.

Cookie wanted to be anywhere but here but did not know where else to go. She had waited patiently to feel good again. One day she would go where no one knew her and she could start all over again. He led her to the sofa and pushed her down. He sank to the floor and pushed his red head between her legs.

"Snaps, I love it."

His long bellowing laugh engulfed the room and was punctuated with a howl. She was a comic who had hit the mark. Ever since she met Farley Stewart, she had been feeling as though she was deeply flawed, not quite good enough for him. It was definitely not love or infatuation. He represented a world away from anything she had ever known or seen. He left her sitting there on the edge.

Then they left the 5th Avenue apartment. He never brought her back there again. On the way back to the Remington Hotel, he spoke to her about his life. They rode in a cab, but it was Cookie who paid the fare, not Farley Stewart, despite his claim to having been brought up in the lap of luxury.

"I'm not in the habit of slumming," he said in an almost apologetic tone.

Farley's largest gaffe was the fact that his family never had a milkman. He had a personal milkmaid, a wet nurse. A woman of color, more white than black, breast fed him as an infant. He was born in the Grand Cayman Islands. His father had gone there to set up an immutable tax shelter, one that would one day pass on to Farley and his said issue. He thought he was entitled to privilege. The poor and working classes on the other hand got that way due to their own moral failure and ineptitude. He always thought that, even after he went to high school at Dalton and met kids of great talent and sportsmanship who had come from humble homes in Queens or the Bronx. Although they had been granted access to private school due to sheer talent and ability, Farley dismissed them as freaks of nature.

Back at the Remington Hotel, they tried again to have sex. There were no witnesses to his parlayed expression of lust. He was more interested in sniffing her crotch than he was in kissing her. One fleeting encounter after another felt like a series of bets, wages she had staked in a game, a contest of sorts, only she did not know if it was her game or his.

He touches her on the top of her head, using his long fingers to deliver a lingering stroke from her brow to the nape of her neck. It makes her shiver. She was moving through the incoherence of a dream. He stares at her, not gentle or kind. He is invading her, peeling away the layers to reveal where she is the most raw and vulnerable. This is no longer child's play.

He pulls his pillow out of the closet and drops it onto the bed, carefully watching her, waiting for reaction. She gives him nothing. It was too exhausting to pretend that she cared.

Out of the blue, he says things to her that are mildly cruel. "You can kill the curls on those Cs," he tells her. "They are quite unbecoming."

He is criticizing her signature in her journal entries in her black & white notebook. He wasn't supposed to read her notebook. She never gave him permission to delve into her Boho. Nor did she give him permission to take a thin sheaf of twenties. Now she will have to hide her notebook and her money from him.

He also makes comments that are slightly rude, insulting. "You look a bit addled. Maybe you're tired, huh, Kiddo? Or perhaps you are getting old before your time."

He has this odd obsession with youth, with girls who are real young, younger than Cookie.

One day he asks her: "Do you have to work?" The way he said it made her feel as though she was a peasant or a feudal serf toiling on the field for a bit of gruel.

Later they make another attempt of some grand form of lovemaking. She could say that she loves him, but she can't bring herself to stoop so low. Somehow, she knows that he is the one who is really beneath her. She knows this because he moves his body in bed, shifting toward her as if she owes him something. Cookie knows she owes him nothing and she is not going to pretend that that she does. Still, she feels self-conscious and a tad uncomfortable. She can't summon desire for him as if it can be conjured on demand. Physical Attraction exists in the form of two categorical imperatives. Either it is or it isn't. It's on or off. Black or white. Crystal clear or opaque, as dense as coal or as meaningful as a cloud.

She wanted to know her new self by heart too and would do anything to gain that knowledge, that insight. She had been sick of her old story—the story she told herself about who she was and who she was not. There had been moments when she longed blindly for anything different, anything strange, remote and previously untried, but the utmost limits of her imagination had prevented her from picturing her life in a new setting. But things had changed. She broke through. All of what she was experiencing was new to her. Untried and unsettling. She had broken new ground.

Monday September 24 1973

My love for Farley Stewart STEWIE isn't love at all. It's weird and sad. (I ALWAYS WANT HIS APPROVAL.) I'm so embarrassed and I don't know how to get away from him. Sometimes I feel smart. Sometimes I feel like the dumbest girl alive. I think I am the dumbest girl alive. I feel like I am on a runaway roller coaster at Playland! Remember when I went there with Arky and dropped acid? We were tripping on ORANGE SUNSHINE while we rode on the Dragon Coaster!

Farley is obsessed with his art. Guess what? I still haven't seen any of it. He's been very upset lately cause Jackson Pollock (another artist) sold a painting for two million dollars. The painting is called "Blue Poles." I haven't seen it. I don't really want to see it. I can't believe that a painting would sell for that much money. Can you? I don't understand how money works. People are starving and don't have homes. I guess people can't eat a painting or put a small bed in its picture frame and call it a home.

Farley is a jealous guy. He's jealous of me. He's jealous of everything. He thinks he should have a better life. I feel like I'm suffocating. There are too many strange things about him. I don't know whether I'm coming or going. The world is spinning. The walls are closing in on me. Winds blow hot and cold. Clouds are passing me by in the sky. I try to capture the clouds the same way I want to write about what love is and what love is not. I think about sex a lot and why it's tough for Farley to make a go of that. Why do I put up with it? Why do I think it is always my fault? He says I'm old enough to do better. Then he says I'm too old. What does that mean?

I try to imagine myself as impossibly sexy to shrink the huge distance between us. He puts up a wall and I don't know how to take it down. I don't know if I want to take it down. We get together and fall apart just as easily for no reason. He likes

Izzy well enough. He says she looks younger than me and he likes that. He calls her by her real name. Isabella.

I think Farley Stewart is my fantasy of a man that I want to love too much to ever make it happen in real life. I don't love him that much. I will never love him like the way I loved Stanley. I will never love him the way I loved the Blind Owl Alan Wilson.

I haven't seen Tony and Toni or Mosella Moran. I still haven't seen Herman Lynch. Reenie and I go to different schools. I haven't made it a point to go and see her. I hear Reenie's Nonna is very sick. I see Izzy in class. Her grades are worse than ever.

The money is starting to be a big problem. I don't know what to do with it. I can't talk about it. No way would I tell anybody!! Doesn't that sound funny? Think about it. I took a lot of money and nobody seems to notice that it's gone. Ha-Ha! It's hard to get rid of money. It's just as hard to hold onto it. Shopping is boring. A girl can only buy so many pairs of shoes. I can't put it in a bank. I thought of hiding it in the Owl Hole.

I have to go to bed now. I am so tired of sleeping on a lumpy mattress. My back hurts! It's almost TWO and I have to get up in the morning and go to school.

-ccc

Thirty-four

Everything that was real and true in Cookie's life often seemed to be at first a dream. She was not sure if she was awake or asleep. Her nose tickled, a sensation that had no origin in reality because now she thought for sure she was having a dream. She rubbed her nose to take away the itch. In the dream her nose continued to tickle. She heard the rustle of paper and felt a slight breeze that was not wind.

Opening her eyes, one then the other, two eyes seeing the same thing—Donny fanning a wad of twenty dollar bills in her face, wearing an evil grin as wide and as polluted as the Hudson River. Pink creamy skin as smooth as a satin bedspread. Eyes bugged, bursting full of mischief. Donny giggled and giggled, turning red, hiccupping involuntarily from too much laughter.

"Give me that!" Cookie snatched the stack of bills from her sister's hot hand.

Donny retaliated swiftly. She cocked her transistor radio in Cookie's ear, pumped the volume as high as it would go, blasting *We're An American Band* by Grand Funk Railroad. Cookie tumbled out of bed and crashed to the floor. Landing on top of Donny, she wrestled with her, fully intending to kill her. Interlocking arms and legs banged across the floor in a succession of loud wooden shocks and jolts. Rolling on her back, Cookie tried to get underneath Donny to flip her onto the floor but was stopped by Donny's size and strength. The girl did not put up much of a fight. Donny simply held the line, a defensive posture to save her life and to finally get the attention she craved.

"I know there's a lot of money under your mattress," the girl said knowingly, defiantly.

Cookie throttled her. "You've always been a troublemaker!"

Donny gyrated, squirming along the floor, deliberately setting herself underneath Cookie, surrendering.

"Where'd you get so much money?"

Cookie yanked her by the hair and shook her. "Say that again and I will kill you! Tell anyone and I will kill you!"

Donny curled her body into a ball, playing possum, hardly breathing while she took a pounding from Cookie. Whatever rage Cookie felt quickly petered away. It alarmed her to see Donny's face turning red, tears pooling in her blue eyes, playing dead as she pleaded for her life.

Donny's sheer nightgown had bunched into a bundle of cloth under her chin. Cookie let go of her. She had no choice but to kill her.

She glanced at the window where the grim morning light revealed air swollen with humidity. The clothesline loomed in the distance, reminding Cookie she could use the rope to strangle Donny. She glanced at the rumpled pillow on her bed that could be used to smother her. Panic beset her. She could take her fountain pen and stab her in the temple. She had once heard that even a swift simple blow to the temple could instantly kill someone.

Cookie pulled herself into a closed heap, a lump of despair. "I have no choice but to kill you, but how can I kill my own sister?"

"My death could be an accident," Donny suggested.

Her impish, evil grin remained intact. She rose from the floor and stood over Cookie.

"I promise I won't tell nobody. Nobody will ever know. Promise, Cookie."

Donny's voice turned sugary. "Did you rob a bank?"

No further entanglements were necessary. Cookie was screwed. There was no way out. "Do you understand what I'm saying? I'll go to jail or get killed, or both. Someone in jail will kill me."

"Now I know how you got such nice shoes and all those fancy clothes."

"You're always snooping through my things!"

"Your money's good but your journal sucks!"

Cookie stood to face her sister, but realized Donny exceeded her own height by several inches. Her nightgown, still askew, revealed a svelte body, lean and sinuous, longer-than-ordinary legs and two cup-size breasts equally matched, perfect symmetry. Little Donny was no more. She was all grown up, a juicy peach ripe for the plucking.

Utterly defeated, Cookie slumped to the side of her bed and threw her face into her hands. She had always been unable to cry, but she was going to make herself learn how to do it! She tried forcing tears, rubbing her eyes to make them red and irritated, but nothing happened. Even now in complete despair, she could not cry.

"I just want to know why you never let me alone. Why have you stalked me my entire life? Why? That's all I want to know is why."

"Because she wants to be just like you, Cookie."

Kitty stood in the doorway showing all of the outward signs that she was having a spell. Disheveled hair poked from under an old blue cotton kerchief. Her eyes had darkened to black pools swimming in madness. She rubbed her hands as though she wanted to warm them, which was improbable, given the intense heat and extreme humidity of this September morning. Despite her obvious psychoses, Kitty was undeniably a truthteller.

"Why can't you girls be nice and just get along with one another?"

"Does she know?"

Donny shook her head. "What, do you think that I'm crazy too?!"

"If you say one word, I will kill you."

"It's going to be eighty degrees today," Kitty hissed. "And you know what that means?" She peered into Cookie's face as though she was intent on charming a snake. "My lipstick melts in the heat!"

Both girls stared and froze in place. From past experience, they knew to expect anything from their mother, from outlandish behavior to extraordinary violence.

Their mother held a gold tube of lipstick, examining its finer details in the light of the morning. "They've discontinued my lipstick!"

Both girls nodded. "We know."

"Now I can't steal it no more."

Kitty Colangelo might have been crazy, but she had confidence in two things, her beauty and her talent as a petty thief. Thieving was the latest manifestation of her chronic schizophrenia. She had worn the same shade of *Stop Red* by Elizabeth Arden for twenty years.

"How'd you like that? Geez, just when a girl's got it good, she gets stabbed in the back."

"Think of all of the fun you'll have trying on new lipsticks to see which one you like."

Cookie poked Donny in the arm. Muting her voice to a notch above a whisper, "Wrong thing to say."

"I only have a little bit left. Can I put some on you? I want to see how it looks."

Kitty unsheathed the lipstick from its gold tube and walked toward them, bearing the lipstick, weapon-like, a benign force that suddenly hinted of danger, crazy malevolence. The lipstick case glowed like a torch in a medieval sconce.

The girls sprang to their feet from the floor and leapt toward Cookie's bedroom door. They ran from the room, slammed the door shut and snapped the bronze Dutch bolt lock into place. Breathing heavily, Cookie leaned up against the door and released a weary sigh. It was only seven in the morning, but she had stayed up too late and was exhausted. Being smeared with red lipstick did not go well with her school uniform. Locking their crazy mother in the bedroom seemed to be a good thing to do, except for one minor but very important detail—the money stashed under her mattress.

Thundering words erupted from Johnny. It was evident that Johnny wasn't alone. Darek, a Polish plumber from M. Fraitag Plumbing and Heating on Riverdale Avenue, ambled beside him, carrying an open-socket tool chest. Huffing and puffing up his barrel chest, the bald plumber had once boasted of escaping from Auschwitz by jumping into the back of the last armored vehicle in a German military convoy exiting the concentration camp. He claimed to have laid himself flat on his back, hurling himself into the woods once the truck cleared the camp. No one had any reason to believe him or disbelieve him and gave him the benefit of the doubt until proven otherwise— it was a Yonkers thing.

Cookie wondered if he would be as lucky in his attempt to escape the Colangelos. She gave Darek a flighty little wave of recognition.

Johnny looked apologetic and shrugged. "Your mother's been flushing tubes of lipstick down the toilet."

Darek smiled, showing gleaming yellow teeth and arched his bushy eyebrows that compensated nicely for his baldness. Cookie wondered if he knew that it was in his best interest to escape while he still had a chance. His eyes scanned the entire length of Donny's body and stopped, on her breasts. Johnny noticed the same thing and grunted. He was not happy, man to man, looking away as though he had not seen Darek ogling Donny, and sought a respectable distraction.

"What's that?" Johnny squinted his eyes as though he was seeing things.

"Oh that." Donny had held on with all of her might. She gripped the stack of twenties the same way she used to clutch stuffed animals.

"Monopoly money."

"Play money."

"Oh."

"Looks real to me." Darek raised his eyebrows with expanding certainty. There was something weird going on here. He couldn't tell what exactly, but something was out of whack. Johnny paid double what he charged for his plumbing services—in cash, otherwise, he wouldn't be here at seven in the morning. Johnny drove a new Casablanca Yellow Cadillac and got any drug he wanted—without a prescription—from Nicky Santoro at the Nepperhan Avenue Pharmacy. Kitty habitually stole from every store in Getty Square but never got arrested for shoplifting.

Kitty knocked on Cookie's bedroom door. "I'm going to miss *As the World Turns*."

Darek might have misgivings about the Colangelo family but this was Yonkers. Everyone was on the take.

As of late, Kitty habitually watched soap operas. It seemed to mesh with her shoplifting habit. The older daughter rode around town, chauffeured in a limousine. The younger one was on the fast track to becoming the next Jayne Mansfield. The way the Colangelos pretended to be a happy family when they weren't was not a red flag; it didn't mean anything. Most of the families in Yonkers were like that. They cohabitated and coexisted in chaos, leading lives of desperation. Not quiet desperation. Complaining, criticizing, kvetching, squeezing the lifeblood from their oppressive lives, they were loud and obnoxious about foisting their misery upon the world. The Colangelos were no exception.

Thirty-five

Cookie did not want to explain the limo or her sudden wealth to Sister Mary Eau Claire or anyone. Arky dropped her off on St. Joseph's Avenue, a side street that ran parallel with Park Avenue, close to Blessed Sacrament Academy. Lightly trafficked, off the beaten path of where BSA girls walked to school, St. Joseph's Avenue was cramped with small, rundown wooden three-story walkups—firetraps—and a prime area in Yonkers that would one day be targeted by arsonists.

The limo parked close to Grant Park, a Yonkers city park spanning larger than it looked from its playground area that only had a small swing set and monkey bars. The park's lawn had become overrun with weeds and its straw-like grass looked burnt from the strong summer sun. Weather worn park benches dotted the perimeter of a walkway that cut through the park under a leafy cloud created by red oak and littleleaf linden trees. Leaves had dried, brittle as old yellow paper about to decompose into splintery dust. The air reeked of impending rain, a prospect further predicted by a darkening grey sky.

Cookie's teal blue uniform lacked the crisp edges of having made a trip to the dry cleaners. Her white cotton blouse was clean but had not been pressed with an iron. Carrying textbooks was for show. She never read assigned coursework and preferred to bask in the archaic Russian literature of Tolstoy or Dostoevsky. She had told Stewie she was reading *Anna Karenina* and he had made fun of her, suggesting one day, she, too, would throw herself in front of a train. She ruminated about him for a moment, but kept that private thought to herself, as if anyone could know what she was thinking.

Up ahead the triangular roof of the school jutted forth as if it were an awning with a peaked cap protecting the front entrance, a wall of glass, from ever getting doused by the sun, wind or rain. The odd-shaped roof was an endless source of irritation for Sister Mary Eau Claire. Whenever it rained, the roof leaked, drenching halls, carpets, two classrooms and the school's cafeteria. Students took refuge in the school's auditorium where a slow steady drip plundered the tops of the walls close to the ceiling, but miraculously left the floors dry.

Cookie looked toward the sky where steamy clouds were congealing into a solid bank of storm-colored grey. Gusts of wind kicked up in irregular volleys. Then the rain began; dense droplets hit the ground furiously, creating the rhythm of syncopated sound and instant ripples of water.

Just as she broke into a run, that very instant, something hit her on the head hard, startling her, hurting her. For a moment she thought she had been shot, but when she touched the top of her head, there was no sticky wetness, no apparent blood. In the next instant, she thought someone had thrown a rock. She had been popped in the noggin, alright. Looking toward the ground she saw the object of her mayhem. A jumbo acorn sat on the path that exited from the park.

She picked up the acorn and ran across Park Avenue to the front entrance of the school. She stood under the awning that shielded her from the rain. Larger than a half-dollar, closer to the size of a golf ball, the acorn's shiny green bottom was as round as a human face. A small thatched brown cap crowned its head like a small rain cloud. She flipped the acorn right side up and now it looked like an avocado jammed into a ceramic drip plate so it could stand upright on its own merits, as proud as a shiny-leafed houseplant soaking up sun. Turning it around in the palm of her hand, the acorn resembled a toy top taking a spin. On further examination the acorn blossomed under the tutelage of her wild imagery becoming Russian nesting dolls for kids, a silvery green thimble, a cup-shaped bell apart and adrift from a carillon in a friar's belfry, and the nón lá (conical leaf hat) worn on the head of a peasant picking rice in the paddies of Bien Hoa.

The acorn was a chameleon, a bit player in life, taking chances to be anything it wanted.

This is the way Kitty would see the acorn, from more than one angle, through the prism of her artistic vision, but that vison was held captive within the prison of her insanity. Kitty didn't have a creative outlet, a way to channel or express her vision. Kitty remained trapped inside of the red glass in her picture window.

Getting hit in the head by a large, random acorn was a wake-up call. Cookie told herself she was not going to be crazy! She told herself to stop thinking that way, and instead she began to breathe freely. In that instant, she experienced an epiphany. So long as she could find a way to express her vision, artistically, she would never be held captive within the prison of insanity. She was not destined to suffer from the same crazy fate as her mother. She fingered the acorn as if it was a powerful talisman, dropped it into her Boho and walked into the building.

Sister Mary Eau Claire stood in the school's lobby, greeting Cookie as though they had made a formal appointment. Arms folded, grim-faced and stony-eyed, she nodded to Cookie to follow her into her office. Cookie could barely keep up with the nun who walked at breakneck speed, swishing her habit, fanning the air with yards of black & white cloth.

Sister Mary Eau Claire rushed Cookie into her office.

"What's taking you so long?"

The nun motioned for Cookie to sit in the chair closest to the window.

Cookie sat and gave the nun a wan smile and a querulous groan. "Why am I here?"

She had not done a thing to invite a scolding.

"I've been to school every day, well almost…"

She thought of the morning she had slept until noon, lingering behind in Stewie's bed at the Remington Hotel. Another disappointing experience, one among a string of many. Morning or night, mid-afternoon on the fly, or an impulsive attempt made in the back of the dark bar at the Remington hotel, every time they tried to get it on, he had trouble. At first Cookie had blamed herself. Now she felt great embarrassment.

Gazing toward the rain-streaked window, Cookie felt strangely unsettled, uncertain as to why the nun who had once been one of her greatest advocates was now unapologetically cold and seething with anger. She heard a dripping sound and searched around the room, trying to find the source.

The nun pointed to a large stainless steel bowl full of water on the floor beside her desk.

"It's coming from the ceiling. The diocese doesn't have the money to fix it right now, but they have plenty of money to provide their priests with new cars and live-in chefs. Fancy that."

A row of asbestos tiles, stained with splotchy watermarks, had separated from the ceiling and were on the brink of falling down. Cookie remembered the wall clock had always shown signs of water damage. The stained grey face of the clock read 3:15, but its black hands no longer moved. The clock had stopped working.

She felt the nun's eyes probing her face, perhaps looking for symptoms of madness, the same madness as her mother.

"I'm not crazy."

"I never said you were." She cleared her throat, obviously having difficulty with what she was about to say. "There's been a lot of talk. Normally, I can often discern the truth from rumors, but in this case, there is too much evidence that is not in your favor."

"What do you want to know?"

"Some of the girls have said that suddenly you have a lot of money, that you had been working at Rite Aid but you were fired for stealing."

The nun leaned forward and pushed her wire frame glasses higher on the bridge of her nose. "I checked into that with the police. The money reportedly missing at Rite Aid only amounted to several hundred dollars. I'm hearing, from more than one source, that you are easily burning through several hundred dollars on a weekly if not daily basis."

She cared about the nun and didn't want to let her down, but the money was really none of her business. Cookie stared at the nun. It was a confrontational move, one that made the nun take umbrage and get right to the point.

"Where is the money coming from?"

Cookie decided to play dumb. "I don't know what you're talking about."

"Do you deny that you've been traveling all over the city in a limousine, buying new clothes, dropping money in bars and restaurants?"

"Who told you that?"

"Your friend Isabella María Fernanda Donovan."

"Exactly what did she say?"

"You travel all over the city in a limo and usually you pay for everything."

"Usually," Cookie scoffed. "I always pay for everything."

Sister Mary Eau Claire smiled at Cookie. Years of interrogating young girls gave her a special knack for getting to the truth. The nun had Cookie right where she wanted her.

"Are you dealing drugs?"

Cookie shook her head.

The nun avoided making eye contact. She stood up from her desk, turned her back to Cookie, and stared at the damaged industrial clock mounted on the wall above the window.

"Some young women get mixed up with the wrong kind of men. Older men. There are men who prey on young girls…they take advantage of them. They're usually sick in some way. And they usually have a lot of money."

The nun turned to look at Cookie. Her reddening face did not hide her sadness, nor disguise her eyes welling with tears.

"Is that what's happening with you, Cookie? Is there an older man who's taking advantage of you?"

Dumbfounded, Cookie shook her head. "How laughable this is."

"How so?"

"I thought you were worried about my sanity!"

"I'm worried about your safety, for God sakes!"

"God! Maybe I am losing my mind!"

"That's highly unlikely."

"No one pays my way in this world." Cookie stood and looked defiantly at the nun. "You should know that by now!"

"Are you involved in some sort of prostitution? Maybe a prostitution ring?"

Cookie was aghast. "Do you mind my asking if you sit around here and worry about the world ruining your students? Because if that's the case, you're undergoing a losing proposition. Sooner or later the world ruins everybody."

Sister Mary's face flushed. She pursed her lips, bowed her head and closed her eyes.

"Here are my questions! Why does there has to be so much suffering, so much pain? Why is the world so fucked up?! I've asked these questions of your God and all I can say is I don't know why the world is so fucking unfair! So tonight, when you return to your little cloistered convent, and you get down on your knees, and say your evening prayers, ask God! And if you find out the answers, please tell me."

"There is no easy answer for any of these things, Cookie. Don't you think I know that?"

"May I leave now?"

The nun nodded.

"I promise you, there will not be any problems with my grades or my attendance. I need to graduate and get out of here."

"Whatever you're doing... I'll pray that no one harms you."

Cookie heard a tick-tock and looked for the nun's other clock. A relic from the 1950s, the ceramic clock sitting on the nun's desk bore the actual time—8:15 a.m. Her class had begun.

An uncomfortable silence came between them and settled with the same finality as the end of the rainstorm that had erupted earlier. Small beads of water spread across the ceiling and scattered, no longer dripping as fast. Outside the rain had stopped. Come winter, heavy snow with its inevitable thaw might cause the roof to cave in. Cookie knew the nun worried that, indeed, one day the roof would collapse.

But the nun had not mentioned her other fears. Damage to the school was the least of her worries. Students and teachers could get hurt, or worse. Once the roof collapsed, the diocese would close the school, and that would be the end of Blessed Sacrament Academy. Cookie opened her Boho and offered the nun a Marlboro. The nun closed her eyes and shook her head. Sharing a ciggy butt had always been a thing between them. For the moment, all that remained between Cookie and Sister Mary was an unspeakable void. Beyond understanding, beyond the edge of reason, with no bridge toward rapprochement, they no longer knew what to think of one another. Cookie left the pack of Marlboros on the nun's desk and walked out of her office.

Thirty-six

Cookie changed into a sleeveless cotton-knit tank dress that had been acquired during her latest shopping spree at Henri Bendel. The pink dress bore an unusual decorative feature that added charm to its elegance but complicated its simplicity. A fake flower corsage was pinned to the dress above her right breast. She thought of the showy corsage as a symbol for Amazonian courage because it was above one breast and not the other. She knew Amazons shaved off one breast to make it more efficient to wield a bow and arrow, and other weapons.

"Spot me a twenty, would you, Cookie?" She gave Stewie two twenties so he would leave her alone for a while.

Stewie liked all types of young girls. As they rode in the limo, not one girl escaped the notice of the troubled hunger artist: blondes, brunettes, and redheads, tall, short, curvy, rail thin and deliciously pale, all shades of skin from creamy white to ebony, and everything in between. He called ugly women *ugly beautiful* and thought they were as stunning as the classic Italian girl that until now he had never met.

Toni Ferlighetti stood in front of the limo, looking as pure as a Botticelli angel sinking into quicksand. Humidity lingered despite the flashes of rain that had come on and off all day.

Toni's brief stab at innocence soon turned to rancor. Blocking traffic, shaking her fist, she pounded on the hood of the limo.

"I must be in Yonkers," Stewie fumed. "The women are so violent here. What a fucking nightmare."

The unexpected encounter with Toni Ferlinghetti didn't last long. Arky got out of the limo, pulled open the passenger door and insisted that she climb in. "Yo, Toni, join the party. Have some fun! We're going to The Playroom."

"What the fuck is The Playroom?" Toni dove her head into the limo, looked toward the backseat and wrinkled her nose, sniffing the contents of the car as though she expected to find trouble. "What's that smell?"

The limo was flooded with the scent of Stewie's expensive cologne, Vetiver by Guerlain.

"And what's that brat doing in the car? Isn't she a little too young to be tagging along?"

Donny shrugged and gave Toni the finger. "What's it to you, anyway?"

"You're wearing too much aftershave," Toni told Stewie. "You oughta go easy on that stuff. It's not going to help you pick up girls if that's what you're thinking!"

Stewie's thin-lipped smile curved like an ordinary garden snake.

"What's with the dead flower on your lapel?" She plucked at Cookie's corsage pinned to the top of her dress. "I don't get the clothes you got on these days. They look like they came from your grandmother's basement. Notice I said basement, not attic! That's where you belong! In the basement! Outta sight! Ha Ha!"

Cookie bristled at the mention of her grandmother, brushed away Toni's hand, and smoothed the flowers on her corsage.

"You didn't notice, did you?!" Toni held up her hand. "Look

at what I've got! A rock! Tony asked me to marry him! I wasn't expecting it or nothing. He came onto me like this. I swear he got down on one knee and looked up at me with big eyes that begged. He was begging me. I swear to God, he was begging me. And then he popped the question. I was gonna make him wait for my answer. But I'm seventeen and I've got no time left to play hard to get. We're gonna get married in June right after I graduate. Can you believe that? Can you believe that I've got this!" She shook her hand wildly, showing off her diamond ring, as if she meant to disperse many fragments of light into the muggy air.

"Wow! Now that is a big diamond!" Stewie laughed so hard he became slightly hysterical, overwhelmed with giddiness.

"What's so funny, Carrot Top?"

"You're a Yonkers girl! Every inch of you is raw with mind blowing authenticity. Squawking girl. You don't talk. Or should I say *tawk*? You squawk."

"Where'd you get this red-headed faggot?" Toni asked Cookie. "I'll not be joining no party tonight. Think I'll be minding my own B-I business. Don't think my fiancé would want me around that cretin anyway."

She slammed the door shut and clattered away in her four-inch platform heels on the wet pavement in front of Grants. Stewie watched her walk away, riveting his eyes to the movement of her curvaceous bottom.

"She is without a doubt a very attractive girl, but far too much trouble to take on."

Come to think of it, Stewie did look like a cretin. His hair, slicked back from rain and humidity, had grown longish, not hippie long; his hair was an odd length for a man of presumed wealth and sophistication. He wore a shiny green shirt. Cookie didn't notice his pants. As of late, she avoided even the slightest glance directed toward his lower body. He had been letting his appearance go, appearing posh but disheveled, presumably to enhance his mystique.

Cookie signaled Arky to stop the limo on New Main Street and bade him to wait for her while she slid into Greens to visit Zelda.

"What on earth are you doing?" Stewie called after her but she paid him no mind.

Greens' entrance had a sloping floor that required climbing a small mound to get into the store. Whisking by the red and white striped popcorn machine, she stopped in front of the mysterious gypsy who spouted fortunes from her mouth and put a quarter into her coin slot. Zelda's eyes shot open, looking blacker than usual. Her mouth locked into a tight line. Nothing came out. Cookie hit the side of the coin-op machine and pushed another quarter into the slot. Zelda's eyes failed to open, but her crystal ball lit up as bright as the diamond in Toni Ferlinghetti's ring. A fortune shot out of her mouth.

The best way to get rid of an enemy is to make a friend.

The Gypsy's fortune made Cookie smile. This was a fortune to keep and hold close to her heart. She could count her lucky stars. She had already begun to make Zelda's fortune come true. Her pesky sister Donny had indeed become her new best friend. Keeping Donny by her side was the only way to ensure she would not spill the beans about the money.

In the limo, Stewie had completely turned his attention to Donny. He was captivated by her, and she with him. Gazing at Cookie's kid sister with adoration, he placed his arm around her in a friendly, big brother sort of way.

The limo cruised the back streets east of Getty Square, bumping along potholes, lurching to a stop at lights, not a smooth ride at all. Cookie felt a major change taking place in her life. With Toni and Tony bound for marriage, she need not worry about him hassling her anymore. Stewie had a way of keeping Donny entertained and out of her hair. She felt as though she had gained control over her life and pulled her black & white notebook from her Boho. Quickly flipping the ink-smudged pages, she arrived at the last entries she had written, but she couldn't concentrate on her words. Farley's pompous voice intruded upon the voices she read on the pages as well as those she heard in her head.

"Those girls from Yonkers are incredibly beautiful, but it is a beauty that is spoiled the moment they open their mouths revealing the sound of a nasal squawk that is so childish and so piercing, it can drive a stake through the heart of any beast and quell the movement of ships traveling from afar. This is all a polite way of saying that the way Yonkers girls look is wildly out of sync with what comes out of their mouths."

He patted the top of Donny's honey-colored thigh. "Let me tell you, you are nothing like those Italian girls. I'd say you are quite refined."

The attention he lavished on Donny was both egregious and solicitous; he really wanted the young girl to like him. Farley had begun to tickle Donny. She squirmed in her seat, giggling, then she started to hiccup.

None of his actions went unnoticed by Cookie, but they did not register in her mind as serious enough to warrant concern. The rain that had come and gone in squalls throughout the day had cleaned the streets as thoroughly as owls devour prey. She felt around in her Boho for the acorn that had dinged her in the head. For some strange reason she now regarded the acorn as very lucky and imagined it had been knocked from the tree by an owl who had wanted to get her attention. How she longed for a chance encounter with an owl!

The limo came to a stop in front of a bar named The Playroom on the corner of Nepperhan and Lake Avenue. In a stroke of common sense, Cookie told Arky to take Donny to Friendly's for a cheeseburger and chips and then to Carvel Ice Cream for a vanilla-chocolate twist in a cone.

There were many popular bars in Yonkers: The Getty house aka the Port of Missing Men, Keller's, Gaelic, Riordan's, Donaghey's Pub, Emerald Isle, Judge Roy Beans, Jackie's Corner, Fitzpatrick's, Tremark's, Harp and Eagle, Hanratty's,

Hughes aka The Glue Pot...to name a few, but there was only one Playroom.

The Playroom was in the industrial part of town where the trees no longer grew. Most streets in Yonkers were named for the trees that grew there. Oak, Elm, Spruce, Maple, Sumac, Cedar, Walnut, Linden, Birch, Maple, and Chestnut. The last of the chestnut trees had been taken down long ago. Trees all gone now. Gangs of people stood in for the trees, chilling on Lake Avenue, looking for drugs or drug users to roll for their money.

Below Nepperhan Avenue, a row of steep granite steps led to Saw Mill River Road, where buildings paid tribute to Yonkers' industrial past. Factories and warehouses lined the street. The only other dwellings were ramshackle houses and shanty-town shacks. Parked cars jammed the parking lot catty corner to The Playroom. Along with many cars bearing license plates from New York, cars had come from as far away as New Hampshire and Maine. License plates read: New Jersey, Connecticut, Massachusetts, Pennsylvania, Delaware; cars had come from all over the eastern seaboard. Clearly The Playroom, the only gay bar in Yonkers, was a happening place, popular far beyond the city's limits.

Thirty-seven

Two of Cookie's fingers gripped a Marlboro with a long ash. Drink and cigarette in one hand left her other hand free to guard her purse. Her Boho cradled a stack of crisp twenties and she wasn't taking any chances that she could be ripped off in the crowded bar. She told herself, *I am the epitome of cool,* even though in her heart she knew she was so uncool, faking it, playing a role she had yet to define and playing it badly. She was nobody. Invisible.

Her chunky black rubber peep-toe platforms added five inches to her height, enough to keep her head on par with the crowd. The girl standing at the bar locked her arms and grinned. Izzy gave Cookie a crooked smile that was at once both sardonic and shy.

"I knew you were coming." Izzy wore a short-short yellow skirt and a castaway white T-shirt that had the words *Fairy Princess* scrawled in curly letters across her chest. She fluttered up to Cookie, stood on her tiptoes and gave her a kiss on the cheek. "I've missed you, My Love. Guess who's here?" She sidled around the curve of Cookie's waist, stood behind her, again rising on the balls of her feet.

She pressed her hands over Cookie's eyes. "Don't look until I tell you to."

With her eyes closed, Cookie picked up the floral fragrance of Izzy's *Je Reviens*, then the scent of *Vetiver* came into play. Without looking, she knew that Stewie had moved in between them.

"Okay, look."

She smiled at Stewie while he tweaked the larger petals in her corsage.

"Not him. Over there on the dance floor."

She couldn't see too far in the smoky bar. Most of the interior of The Playroom had been painted black to enhance its ultra-violet light and strobe lights from the dance floor, throbbing with dancing bodies, grinding hips and flailing arms all undulating to the heavy metal tune *Smoke on the Water* by Deep Purple. The house band had four guys, playing drums, keyboard, guitar; one guy sang and played the bass guitar. All band members were familiar faces from the high school dance and Yonkers local club circuit. Three of the guys had long shaggy brown hair. The guy playing the keyboard wore glasses and was bald.

A wild-eyed woman sat at a table in the back of the bar doing a tarot card reading. A crazed-energy melee was happening, twenty or so kids in tight jeans and T-shirts spilled away from the dance floor, frenetically dancing into the aisle, knocking into booths and tables, wild-eyed and grinning, wearing a stoned grin that said *I'm going to party all night*. Guys danced with guys and girls with girls, guys and girls, openly kissing, fucked up and stoned, grinding and getting it on right on the dance floor.

Izzy yelled into Cookie's ear, "Don't you see him?"

"Who?" Cookie squinted her eyes.

"The great love of your life, Stanley. Isn't that him?"

The jolt to her body took the edge off of cool and made her face flush and her hands shake. Cookie was prepared for anything, but she had not imagined seeing Stanley de Falco at The Playroom. Izzy grabbed her by the arm, pushed through the crowd, passing a sloe-eyed drag queen and a mélange of doped-up girls wearing gauzy see-through tops, grinning through smeared frosted pink lipstick. Strobe lights from the floor dazzled her eyes. She saw the back of a blonde head dipping, sweeping and rocking. The guy had short blonde hair and he could really dance.

"Isn't that Stanley?"

Izzy was sorely mistaken. It was as if she could not discern one blonde guy from another. She couldn't have been more wrong. The sweet blonde boy's black, kohl-rimmed eyes were familiar. Henry Kagan used his eyes, his head, his torso, his entire slight body to make love to Herman Lynch. Their luscious tongues disappeared into their mouths as if they drank from one another. Groins tucked, grinding rhythmically, Henry wrapped his legs around Herman in an erotic embrace, and would not let go. Nor did Herman want to let go.

Undoing their coupling came fluidly, a brief parting, love wrapping and unwrapping itself in the climax of a song that was reaching for a higher octave. Matching their leaps and turns in a blend of grace and guile, the air became water they lustfully took unto themselves. Club kids watched them, rocking in the sidelines. The house band dove into Deep Purple's *Hush* that opened with guys in the audience bolstering the band's intro—howling like wolves the same way the song sounded in Deep Purple's original studio recording.

"Say something. Say something. Say anything," Izzy whispered in her ear.

"I can't." Cookie beamed. "I'm so happy! It's not Stanley!" Cookie didn't bother to tell her how bad she would feel if she found Stanley here without first letting her know that he had come home.

"I know you really want to be with me." Izzy's face hovered by her ear. She used this intimate moment to slowly kiss her neck. Her kisses felt ticklish like small insect bites and made Cookie laugh. Her laughter was infectious. Izzy laughed too. As much as she tried, she knew she wasn't getting anywhere with Cookie.

"Silly girl," she chastised her.

Cookie broke free from Izzy's stinging little kisses to join Herman and Henry on the dance floor. Herman was so excited, he jumped in the air and spun in a double-axle turn. Henry caught him on the rebound, turned around his waist in a complete circle, launching into a triumphant pas de deux, dropping into featherlight hitch kicks in a marvelous lightness of two beings rising and falling in the air. The music was deafening but Herman and Henry's eyes welcomed Cookie. The three of them rushed repeatedly into each other in tempo with the heavy metal music, chanting the song's refrain, *Hush. Hush.*

Swiveling her hips, bending her knees, she rotated side to side in rhythm with the deafening pounding of the bass guitar and drums. Rocking hips, dragging her body lower, dipping and pivoting her feet, she launched into a wild dance. Stomping her feet, extending her arms far longer than wings and flailing open as wide as sails on a boat, she swiveled her head and spun wantonly around on the dance floor in between Henry and Herman. Izzy joined them, twisting herself into knots, waving her arms over her head, taking Cookie by the waist leading her into a foot stomping frenzy. *Hush. Hush. Na na na na na na.*

Everything was so perfect, Cookie wanted to rock the night away, but the music stopped. The band was taking a break in between sets. Herman nudged Cookie to follow him. She wasn't sure where Henry and Herman were heading. Their movement flowed into a single file line, reining in the out-of-control energy that had previously swept them away on the dance floor.

Feeling hot, sweaty, and exhilarated, high on the energy that can only come from dance, Cookie followed Herman through the bar. Every pore in her body felt alive, making her tremble. Dancing made her hungry. She felt a craving coming on, and wanted to eat something sweet, fluffier than a jelly donut, lighter than sfogliatelle, richer than cannoli or sweeter than a standard black & white cookie. She tried to catch Herman's ear to suggest they head over to the Broadway Diner, but he was moving too fast.

Henry had taken the lead in their line, cruising through tiers of bench-style seating, waves of people getting up, moving to the bar, taking a breather before the band started up again. Booths and tables clustered together across the room from the bar, all full, nowhere to squeeze in and sit. Cookie sniffed the air; the familiar stream of weed filtered through the room. Stewie flagged her down from the bar.

"During the entire time you were on the dance floor, I've been sitting here, nursing my drink."

"Nursing." Cookie eyed his drink and blinked. Blinding light from the dance floor lit up the green liquid in his glass.

"Absinthe is a precious elixir." He pushed the drink under her nose. "Take a sip."

She wrinkled her nose at the subtle spicy taste, a subtle twinge of licorice and something vaguely minty like Vick's VapoRub. "What's that taste?"

"What is it that you taste?" Stewie mimicked her voice.

"You don't have to be an asshole, you know."

Stewie's smile was mildly condescending but turned friendlier with the arrival of Izzy who offered breathless quirky movements, darting her small hands like pincers all over Stewie's chest.

Stewie's glasses did not make his face appear owlish. Instead, his eyes seemed smaller and increasingly un-trustworthy.

"Absinthe has delicate threads of saffron, a touch of anise, a hint of eucalyptus amid the three Bs: blackberries, basil and black currants. Keep in mind that absinthe is extremely high in alcohol. It can positively sear your taste buds. It can even kill you if you drink too much. For a time, absinthe was banned. Have I failed to mention that it is made from wormwood?"

He held up his glass in the next wave of strobe light. "Wormwood is what gives absinthe its lovely green color."

On the surface, Cookie demurred to Stewie, but despite his sophistication, she was getting sick of him. She was starting to think that he was a poseur.

His stare lit into Cookie's eyes. "Wormwood can make you crazy, as if you're not already crazy enough."

His mention of crazy stabbed Cookie in her heart. Obviously, he knew how to get to her. But it didn't matter. If she was going to go crazy like Kitty, she would probably never know it. Besides, she had her lucky acorn.

"Amazing!" Izzy squeezed Stewie's shoulder. Her fingers skedaddled along his pale, freckled arm. "You always know so much. And that makes me happy."

Of all of the things Stewie noticed among women, in particular he loved to look at Izzy's points. None of that mattered to Cookie because she had catapulted over the breaking point—she was done with Stewie. She looked for Herman and Henry, but they had moved on.

Stewie offered Cookie another sip from his glass. "It's supposed to make you feel sexy, but I guess that might be too much trouble for you."

She smiled sweetly and took a sip. "There's someone I want you to meet. I'll be back."

"Not true. What's wrong with your friends? Where did they go? Did they leave you behind, Cookie?"

She plunged through the crowd. She did not look back to see Izzy or Stewie. The band returned. She looked toward the stage where Herman and Henry had inadvertently put on a show, taking to the dance floor with professional flair. The music changed, still heavy metal. The next song, Black

Sabbath's *Children of the Grave,* earsplitting and ominous, slowed the tempo of the dancers on the floor to a repetition of jarring beats.

Something weird began to happen. Cookie couldn't put her finger on it. She walked out of The Playroom and found herself excitedly walking toward Herman and Henry. It was impossible not to see Henry's brilliant white blonde hair and Herman's glistening brown skin catching light from streetlamps on Lake Avenue. They smiled and waved to her. They had been standing there, waiting for her. Arky would soon come back. She imagined everyone piling into the limo, heading for the diner to get some late night breakfast. She drove herself forward, almost running in their direction, but her heavy platform shoes slowed her down.

Late on Monday night, hardly any traffic. A passing car or two, that's all. She called to Henry and Herman, asking them to look for Arky. Henry stepped from the worn curb onto Nepperhan Avenue. He walked into the oncoming lane. Herman trailed behind Henry, not trying too hard to catch up. There were no signs of Arky or the limo.

A car zoomed into view. As quickly as the car appeared, it picked up speed, moving faster. The driver gunned the gas, going full throttle as though the car was in the throes of a drag race. Only there were no other contenders. No other dragsters. No compelling reason to drive so fast. A thrill seeker. A thrilling ride. The car revved its engine, speeding even faster. Cookie saw the whole thing happening and screamed, but it was too late to stop the carnage.

Without a moment's hesitation, no braking action, no skidding tires, the car slammed into Henry, making a brutal impact, and tossed him up in the air. Herman's screams rose above the crush of heavy metal music. Onlookers asked what happened. No one seemed to understand how the driver of the car had not seen Henry. The car was gone. The driver had left the scene.

Henry landed face down on the pavement in a position so contorted there was no doubt that his body had been broken. He lay unconscious. Precious little blood. Herman tried to cover himself over Henry's crumpled body. People warned him not to touch Henry. *Neck and back injuries, you never know. You can't touch him without knowing what to do. You could cause greater injury. Paralyze him or worse.*

Lying on the ground next to Henry, Herman cried like a baby. Among those who spilled out from inside of the bar, some did not know what had happened and those who saw the impact were in shock. The metallic hammering of Black Sabbath's *Children of the Grave* persisted along with Herman's sobs and the scream of sirens.

Thursday October 4 1973

I was very nervous on my way to school today. I keep hearing the crack of metal against bone. I never saw the color of the car. It all happened so fast. They still haven't found the driver or the car. The car had to have dents after hitting somebody. I think the car was blue or black. It definitely wasn't red or white. I feel like it was all my fault. It wouldn't have happened if I didn't ask Henry and Herman to look for Arky.

Herman's a mess. I sat with him and I held his hand. We hug each other a lot. I didn't know what to say to him. I don't know what to say to Mrs. Kerry. I don't know what to say to anyone. Henry's neck was broken. His back was broken in three places. Some say he's lucky to be dead. He would never have danced again.

Stewie disappeared from The Playroom that night and got into the backseat of the limo to be with Donny. He said he did not want her to see what had happened cause she's too young. Izzy got home on her own. I never did find out how she did it. She's clueless about everything.

I still have money. I still don't know what to do with it. And I still don't know where the money came from. The money is not doing me much good. It's starting to become an awful burden cause I don't know what to do with it and have to worry about it all the time.

I haven't heard from Reenie. I'm going to make a point to see her. Maybe later today. I hear her Nonna isn't doing too good. Millie Mangano told Johnny that Reenie's Nonna is dying. That would be very bad for Reenie. She'd have nobody. She'd be an orphan. The thought of Reenie having nobody makes me feel sick inside.

I do feel sick. I could be depressed cause of what happened to Henry. I tell myself that I'm never going to get sick like my mother. I have my big acorn to hold onto when I get to feeling that way. I don't blame things on my mother. It's not her fault. She was born that way. I just hope I wasn't born that way too.

I hate all of this stuff that's happening. I'm going to be seventeen this month. I thought getting older meant I would be free. Things are getting worse and I don't know why. I don't want to be here anymore. I don't want to be anywhere.

I'm still not using commas. I don't need to use commas. Nobody can make me use commas. I think using commas is weak. I think it's pretty cool that I can make up my mind about something and nobody can change that!

Millie Mangano is hitting on Johnny real hard. I don't know if I ever mentioned that Johnny is very good looking. I'd say he's going to be 42. I don't know for sure how old he is. I do know that my father's birthday is the same day as mine in October.

I can't say I ever liked Millie. There is something very dishonest about her. She's doubling down trying to get into Johnny's pants again. She does this all the time but does it even harder whenever Kitty's missing in action. (Kitty is doing a short stint in the nuthouse.) And this Tony Amendolito seems to be everywhere with either Millie or Toni Ferlinghetti!

My father is a mystery to me. I still don't know why he gave up his music. And I don't know what he does for a living. I don't know him. I really don't know him.

Remember Detective Sergeant Ronan O'Hearn? He keeps asking me about fifty million questions. I don't seem to be giving him the right answers. I'm starting to think there are no right answers to anything in life. Send me a postcard if you know the answers. I'm all ears.

-ccc

Thirty-eight

Someone knocked on the front door. It was too early in the morning for an unannounced guest, unless the Polish plumber Darek was making another emergency house call. Cookie heard Johnny singing in the shower. He had turned into someone completely unrecognizable, a parody of his former self—a happy-go-lucky, hot-blooded Italian guy.

Johnny liked quality sausage from Trunz Butcher Shop in Ghetto Square. He liked to cook sausage that was blood red, spicy hot and loaded with anise, slowly and meticulously, with tender loving care that he did not expend on any other activity or life form. He liked full bodied wine. Dago red. He liked his pasta cooked al dente. He'd let it boil vigorously for four minutes, then turn it off and let it sit for eight minutes, giving it a couple of stirs. In the average stainless steel pot, it took exactly twelve minutes. He also liked to sip anisette and a double espresso with his cannoli at the Italian American Club on Lockwood Avenue.

The knocking on the front door had not let up.

The bathroom door opened. Johnny appeared in a gush of steam. Still crooning *That's Life* by Frank Sinatra, his feet squeaked as he padded through the narrow hall, a towel wrapped around his waist.

Cookie stumbled out of bed. The last thing she wanted was to run into Johnny, wearing a skimpy silk teddy. He'd turn red and grunt.

It was almost eight—time to get to school. Not much time to spare, she moved quickly, letting her hair hang wild and free, so unlike the terrible bondage that gripped her mind, heart and soul. She eschewed makeup; it took too much time to apply lip gloss, the only makeup that she thought she needed. She jumped into her wrinkled schoolgirl uniform. Just as she zipped up her ugly culottes skirt, banging thundered through the house.

There was no question that whoever was at the front door badly wanted to get inside of the house.

Kitty's expansive picture window took in the entire frontage of the house and street. Aside from Arky's long black limo, a red Alpha Romeo sat double-parked alongside Johnny's yellow Cadillac.

Cookie slipped behind the picture window's curtains while Johnny opened the front door. She positioned herself in an optimal vantage point to see what was going on while remaining hidden.

"Why don't you ring the bell for Chrissakes?!"

Tony was not alone. Millie Mangano was with him. Tony was polite to Johnny, asking him, in a roundabout way, what happened to the money.

Johnny was confused. "What money?" His hair was wet, combed back. Wearing dark trousers and a sleeveless cotton muscle shirt, he looked like he had dressed in a hurry, which wasn't good because nobody rushed Johnny Colangelo. He also didn't like being caught off-guard.

"You come to my house and talk to me like this! I don't even know you! Who the fuck are you? I thought you wanted to date my daughter. Instead, you're asking me about money!!!"

Tony sprung his body forward, showing Johnny he wasn't going to take no for an answer. Millie Mangano pushed herself close to Tony but closer to Johnny. Tony had that look Yonkers guys get in their eyes when they are intent on taking someone by surprise and by brutal force. It's not that he meant to hit Johnny—that would be a huge mistake! He wanted to show how tough he was.

"I wanna know what happened to the money. I've been looking for money that was left in your office and now it's gone. No one knows what happened to it."

Johnny grabbed Tony by the collar and shoved him.

"Don't you be talking to me like that, you punk!"

An immovable force, Millie sacrificed herself, pushing between them to create a barricade against potential violence. Tony looked upset, but there was no question that he would not take on Johnny Colangelo.

"I don't know why you come here to my house and talk nonsense to me! Who the fuck do you think you are, you dumb fucking punk! I'll fucking kill you!"

"He doesn't mean nothing by that, Tony," Millie gushed. "It's just his way. It's how he's always been. I'm used to it by now."

She sank her hands into her jumbo hips and shook. "Come on, Johnny. Give Tony a chance to talk, why don't you?"

Johnny looked at Tony, then Millie, backed away from the two of them and laughed. "I don't know what's wrong with you, Millie. I don't know nothing about no money."

He wiped his hand under his chin like he was slitting his own throat with a knife. "And I'm up to here with all of this stupid talk about money for Jesus Christ. What do you think I am? A fucking bank?"

Tony breathed heavily; he was in over his head and looked scared. "Somebody left money on the chair in your office."

"And it's gone," Millie chimed in.

"When?"

"May?"

"And you're just coming to me now with this shit." Johnny laughed. "Money can't just disappear. It can't just get up and walk away."

"Well, it did. We've looked everywhere for it. Didn't we, Tony?"

"What are you telling me this for? I told you once and I'm telling you again. I don't know nothing about no money."

Then he took a pause as though he had a big revelation.

"Where'd the money come from?"

Millie looked embarrassed and shook her head. She was about to cry and couldn't talk.

Tony came as close as he could to saying something that sounded like an apology.

"She made a bet."

"You gotta good tip?"

Millie nodded.

Johnny searched Millie's face, then growled. "From who?"

A veil of tiny tears rolled down Millie's face. "I can't say."

Tony looked at Millie. "Okay, we gotta problem."

Johnny shrugged. "You gotta problem. I can see that. But it's your problem. I don't need another headache. You gotta fix your own problem."

What Johnny didn't like could be lumped together in one category—he didn't like people who caused him trouble: priests, fat women (Millie Mangano was an exception) and wise guys who tried to fuck with him. (Tony Amendolito was dead meat.) They were all—in Johnny's eyes—expendable life forms.

It was weird that Johnny didn't seem worried about the money. He could care less. In fact, he started to laugh, a chuckle at first, that grew to be full-bodied, a deep belly laugh, and he kept shaking his head, alternating his laughter with a quirky smile as though the situation was incredulous, preposterous, unthinkable.

"Everybody has a key to my office! Whoever took the money..." He threw his hands up in mock resignation—the circumstances were beyond his control.

"It could have been anybody. Anybody. Anybody who has a key to the office and that's everybody. Somebody got lucky and you two are stoolies, patsies, dumbasses. I feel sorry for you but I don't feel sorry for you. Know what I mean? Eh?"

Cookie took a deep breath to restrain herself from laughing or crying; maybe in this instance, laughing and crying were both born of the same emotion—terror. Apparently, no one suspected that she was the *somebody* who had taken the money. She had always known it would be hard to hide that much money. It's not like she could deposit it in a bank. She still kept the bulk of the money under her mattress. That would have to change. There was something to be said for not putting all of one's money in one place. It was similar to not letting one guy have all of your eggs.

Thirty-nine

The whites of Ronan O'Hearn's eyes were too cloudy for someone with exceptionally blue eyes. He looked like he never got enough sleep. Admittedly, Cookie had an uncanny number of important blue-eyed men in her life: Johnny Colangelo, The Blind Owl Alan Wilson, Stanley de Falco and Farley Stewart.

She imagined she saw the entire sky in the cop's eyes, clouds and all. Everything was there except for the sun, the moon, and the stars only seen in a clear sky at night. He didn't seem up for a long chat today. Yesterday he had wanted to talk, and as much as she tried, Cookie could not get rid of him.

She couldn't get used to him either. She would never be foolish enough to let her guard down with a Yonkers cop.

"Sure you're not related to Pinky O'Hearn?"

"Do I look like I've got red hair and I'm a drunk?"

"You're kind of cute, certainly hunkier than Pinky."

If Detective Sergeant Ronan O'Hearn appreciated her flattery, he was not an easy mark. The smile he gave her told her that he was amused. This was one more routine interrogation, one that would lead nowhere because Cookie really did not know anything.

She sat in the passenger seat of his Ford Bronco. They were parked in front of The Playroom. She saw the place on the road, marked by crime tape and bouquets of withered flowers, where Henry Kagan had been killed. During the day, the bar looked like another warehouse, blending in with all of the other industrial sites on Nepperhan Avenue. She pulled out a Marlboro from her Boho. Before she lit it, he pushed the car's cigarette lighter in the console and pulled open the car's built in ashtray that only contained a couple of butts.

"Didn't know you smoked."

"I don't. It's only for my favorite passengers."

He smiled long enough to let her know that he liked her.

Now they were getting somewhere. She had O'Hearn just where she wanted him, thinking she might be an easy lay, but she wasn't about to ball a cop—that was Toni Ferlinghetti's job and all of the girls just like her who thought marrying a cop was a good bet for the future.

"Do you think someday you'll get a good pension?" She laughed.

"I hope so." His voice softened and sounded intimate.

The lighter popped out of the Bronco's console. He lit her Marlboro.

"Thanks." She found herself smiling at him. She could be intimate too. She did find him to be good looking, but not enough to get stuck in Yonkers. There were all kinds of short-term arrangements, ranging from a one-night stand to two hot weekends in Atlantic City, but guys like him always wanted ownership over a girl. It was a Yonkers guy thing. She knew if she got involved with Detective Sergeant Ronan O'Hearn, it would be hard to get rid of him.

"Let me ask you something."

"I would have said you asked me enough already, but go on. Shoot."

"There is the possibility that the driver of that car never intended to kill Henry Kagan, maybe he wanted to give him a scare, or never saw him until it was too late. What do you think?"

"I saw the car speed up." She rolled down the window and flicked her ash.

"You can use the ashtray if you want."

"He did it on purpose."

"How do you know the driver was a he?"

"I don't."

"Maybe it was hatred. Maybe the driver hated homosexuals."

"Herman and Henry preferred to be called gay."

The cop stretched his legs, rolled down the window, stuck out his arm, and patted the outside of his car door. "Maybe Henry was in the wrong place at the wrong time."

He looked at Cookie and smiled as though he had a crush on her.

"Here's another thing I've been thinking about. Do you think somebody wanted to get you instead of Henry Kagan? Maybe Henry was in the way and the driver really wanted to get you. Did you ever think about that?"

Cookie hadn't thought of it that way and the thought unnerved her. All of that money tucked under her mattress. All of the money she had already spent. Whoever lost the money might want to get her and get her good. Cookie nodded, but she didn't have anything to say.

"I hear there are a couple of people who have it out for you. Does the name Mosella Moran ring a bell?"

"She's into knives and razor blades. Can't afford no car."

"Tony Amendolito?"

Cookie shook her head no. "He got engaged to Toni Ferlinghetti. I'm sure to never hear from the likes of him again."

"Sure?"

"Sure."

She didn't tell O'Hearn that Tony Amendolito had been

by her house that morning looking for money because it was too much trouble.

"I don't like murder," he said. "I'd rather think that someone drove too fast and left the scene of an accident. Like I've said before, most murders are either emotional or it's just business. Murder can be accidental, but the anger was always there to begin with. Murderers come in flavors. It's the Irish wife, the Italian boyfriend, the Black junkie, the Puerto Rican pimp, the Guido Goombah, the rich hedge fund guy, the celebrity, the crooner, or the whacked-out musician, and the Jews always hire somebody."

"Sounds like you've got this murder stuff all figured out."

"I do have it figured out. That's my job. But I don't have you figured out."

"You've checked me out. What do you think?"

"I think somebody's out to get you."

Cookie stubbed out her cigarette in the ashtray. Noise assailed her ears: the bellow of horns blaring from delivery trucks, and the repetitive beat of a construction crew. She could not hear herself think. Above the exhaustive scrape of tin, pealing car horns, the rumble of delivery trucks, she heard the cop telling her that he would drive her home. She knew Arky would be waiting there for her. Donny too. No one else mattered except, maybe, Reenie Ruggerio.

She knew the truth about O'Hearn and eyed him warily. He liked to alternate between good cop and bad cop. Too bad he didn't have a partner that would cut him some slack, so he could take a break and exclusively play one role or the other. She was not too concerned about what he had said.

In a quick flash, she decided it could not be true. *No one was out to get her.*

She leaned over and kissed him on the cheek. His face reddened all the way to the tips of his ears. He seemed to like her kiss and would not mind another one. There was no harm in checking him out the same way she'd check out a book from the library.

O'Hearn started the engine and they were driving toward the north end, but his Ford Bronco did not move fast enough to get her mind away from The Playroom, a place she swore she would never visit again. There were no hills anywhere in the world like Yonkers, the city of hills. The Bronco climbed Lockwood Avenue, then up the steeper hill of Roberts Avenue. By comparison Manhattan was flat, oh so flat.

Here in Yonkers, she felt as though she was on the edge of a steep slope that would make her slip away, with a force that was reckless, nameless and unknown. She remembered the parting words of Stanley de Falco: "Always remember where you are going and never forget where you've been."

Friday October 5 1973

I remember Izzy phoning me to tell me she was with Stewie at the bar in the Remington Hotel and how much the ladies loved running their fingers through his red hair. She caught him looking at himself in the mirror and fluffing his curls. I think Izzy is exaggerating. Girls do not chase Stewie. It's the other way around.

He gets interested in a girl and follows her everywhere. He makes a girl feel like she's the prettiest thing in the whole world. He knows how to pour on the flattery. He gives Izzy and Donny so many compliments. He did that to me. I know what it feels like.

I phoned Arky to bring me to the bar. Stewie and Izzy had gone home by the time we got there. Too late. I would have done anything to be there. I don't like being left out of things.

We're spending more and more time apart. The worst part is that it's hard to be in school. I have to go to school! Stewie sleeps every day until noon. Sometime later. Much later.

I tell myself that we both look up at the same sun in the same sky. The same clouds form snow cone and animal shapes around us in shades of blue and gold. We breathe the same motionless air and inhale the same misty rain. We walk the same jagged and rutted streets in the city and see the same dry leaves left limp on the trees in Central Park. We experience the same things. Same.

I like being in my own bed at night. My bed feels unbelievably rich. Ha-Ha! I like to stay in my room to think about what it means to be rich and alone. I'm not afraid of being alone. I am afraid of being rich. I don't like it.

Money hasn't done all that much for me. I have thought of standing on a street corner and giving it all away. I was going to do that one day. But I lost my nerve. I'm also not that stupid. Really! Think about it. Who would take money from a young girl for no reason? And why would anybody give money away for no reason?

I'm about to turn seventeen. I guess I could say that I'm grown up. Nothing's really changed. I guess I could say that I've always been grown up. It's just that the stakes are more serious now. It's like placing a very bad bet at the Yonkers Raceway. One false move and I'm done for.

I'm still more determined than ever to write a novel. I still name the novel *Beneath the Passion of the Angelic Mystery Rose*. I have ten black & white notebooks full of rambling thoughts. Mutterings. Poetry. Journal entries. I write in both print and in cursive. I change my mind about what I mean to say. I get brutal with my words. Sometimes I wound my words and even kill them. I often cross out my words or blot them with splotches of blue ink. And I still hate commas.

-ccc

Forty

Stewie mocked her notebook, calling it a palimpsest of bad writing. She did not know what palimpsest meant. It was a snob word. Stewie claimed a palimpsest was a piece of writing on paper in which the original writing had been erased to make room for later writing, but the traces of the original words remained on the page like ghosts. He further claimed monks often wrote over the entrails of former manuscripts.

Cookie remembered the medieval manuscripts on display under glass at the library on 42nd Street. There were no ghosts on the parchment.

"Palimpsest," he suggested.

"Palimpsest?" Cookie screwed up her plum of a nose and squinted her eyes as though she didn't quite believe him.

"Your words appear to have succumbed to brutal revision. You write new words on top of the inky erasures of old words."

"Palimpsest." She nodded but still did not believe him.

"Someday if you get good at it, you won't make so many mistakes. But I seriously doubt that will ever happen."

Now that stung, but she did not say anything. She waited, trying to think of what she should do. Aside from her "pages" in her notebook, one of the few places she found solace was in Stewie's apartment at the Remington Hotel. Being there made her feel so grown up. He had shown her a sophisticated world beyond Yonkers. Yearning for and treasuring these learning moments, she ignored his dishonesty as well as his infidelity.

She could not dispute Stewie's cheating. It was perfectly acceptable. There had never been a formal pronouncement between them. Nor was there an emotion as grand as love. The relationship was betwixt and between sex and friendship, neither one nor the other. Yet the way he behaved caused her to feel queasy. He held power over her. Something was terribly wrong, and for that she could not forgive him or herself.

The stray sounds of whispering and giggling came from his bedroom that was actually a closet where Stewie had plunked down a double-size box spring and mattress to make it a cozy sleeping quarters. Cookie had been in the closet with Stewie, but now someone had taken her place. She waited patiently for the erotic hissing and laughter to end. She did not have to wonder who was in the closet. The soft tittering belonged to a teen girl.

Cookie ruminated, brooding really, over the art brochures strewn everywhere. She picked up a large brochure from the floor where it had been casually tossed, or worse, angrily thrown onto the ground and perhaps stomped on. She flipped through the brochure, examining paintings by an artist named Clyfford Still. His work was being shown at the Marlborough-Gerson Gallery on 57th Street. The gallery was showing eight works of art, all abstract with bold clarity and all different in meaning. Given the dimensions listed in the brochure, each painting was massive in scale.

Izzy tumbled into the living room with a sheet wrapped around her tiny body. Cookie sat on the couch. Izzy's long brown hair fell disheveled, covering her face.

"Care to join us?"

She whispered and nodded toward the closet. "He's having

trouble." She raised her eyebrows under the wooly mat of her messy hair. "Maybe you could help? The two of us working in tandem as a team?"

Cookie ignored her and continued to peruse the overly large brochure that was presumably created in an attempt to capture the massive scale of Clyfford Still's work.

Not to oversimplify Clyfford Still's intentions as an artist, but she did not understand why his work lacked conventional titles such as *Madwoman in Blue* or *Owl in the Woods* or *Sunset on the Hudson River*. Each work was defined by or named according to a series of letters and numbers. It was hard enough to understand abstract art, but even more difficult when the artist did not name his paintings. Titles often provided clues for understanding the artist's vision that had been freed from a prison of insanity.

What did he mean? she wondered.

Then one oil painting, identified as PH-372, took her breath away. Clouds unfurled across the sky in an endless band of navy ribbons, melding into coal, zigzagging into a hammer, an axe and the head of a very bad and dangerous man. The sky beribboned sheaths of black clouds, growing blacker and blacker, burgeoning into a black hole from which there was no way out. Balloons and rivulets, both slender and fat, broke through the dense black. Glowing yellow light edged with twists of muted orange the shade of an apricot rained upon panes of black and navy glass, forming wisps of steam like human breath rising in cold air. A rutilant skein, the color of yellow yarn, sat in slim patches of light in the upper right corner.

Stewie's heavy breathing broke her spell. His breathing wasn't erratic or erotic but agitated. He was running out of patience with her. Worse, he was thumbing through her notebook, first smirking, then laughing.

Izzy stood there, dumbfounded, not saying a word, which was unusual for her, and stared at Cookie.

"Are you back here on earth with us?" Stewie inquired.

"I wanted to know what you thought of my writing."

Cookie surreptitiously tucked the gallery brochure into her Boho.

"Do you think I could write a book someday?" she asked him.

Stewie shook his head as if the notion made him infinitely sad.

Izzy pressed her lips together, sighed, sat on the couch next to Cookie and rubbed her shoulder. "You know you really should let yourself go. You'll be surprised at how much fun you'll have. You're just fooling yourself. I know you really want to be with me."

She paused and looked at Stewie."With us. The three of us together. It would be so much fun."

"Ahem or I should say Amen." Stewie stood at the foot of the couch gaping at her.

Cookie didn't feel like she had to tell Izzy that she wasn't into having sex with the two of them, or either one of them individually. She was tired of Stewie's inability to function and she did not enjoy being kissed by Izzy. Nor did she want to kiss her. In fact, the thought of having sex with Izzy revolted her. She did not care what they thought. Right or wrong; call it denial of her own purported bisexuality or a denial of the sexual complexity of every human being, she just did not crave the scent of a woman.

But the scent of a man was a different matter altogether. She adored the way men reeked of sweat, glans, earth, bold, a bit of fragrant clay, warm sand, wind and newly turned soil—reeking pure testosterone. And she loved to stare at their bodies. Without a doubt, the surety and certainty of being in close proximity to a man who turned her on sent her reeling, wanting him and wanting him again.

Izzy began to massage the nape of her neck then her hand fell to Cookie's lap. "Give it a try. Just once." Her brown eyes grew huge and needy. "What have you got to lose?"

Cookie sat mute, seemingly blasé, inattentive, yet she watched every little thing and committed every nuance to memory.

Izzy moved closer to her on the couch and kissed Cookie's cheek. "I think it's sad that you won't admit the truth to yourself so we can try something new."

She pushed a few strands of Cookie's hair behind her ears. "I'm just suggesting you try being playful for a change. Playful is one more way you can be expansive and grow as a human being. What's so bad about being playful?"

Cookie's eyes hardened. She was feeling like an idiot, not because of Izzy, not because of Stewie. She was being penalized, censured for her childish instincts and her limited sense of erotic desire. She was a square, out of step with the reality of what was supremely cool and sublime.

"I thought you liked my perfume."

Cookie yelled, "When is it going to stop? I don't want to be with you that way!"

Stewie was noisily thumbing through the pages of Cookie's notebook. "Check this out."

With the booming voice of a great orator, Stewie declared, "Look at this poem...It's called called *My Owl*."

He read aloud: "His one eye is a jewel seeing through a prism transcending time. Distance. Light. And the motion of the night to reach two halves of the same leaf. I see the ghost of this pale leaf sitting beside my owl. He hears a chorale of birds unseen in the copse of trees. Peace. War. Blood. Wooden limbs. Arteries. Skin. Veins. Flesh and bones. His one eye is blind. The other sees too much. Is my owl dead or alive? I will never forget him."

Stewie closed her notebook. No one said a word. Utter and uncomfortable silence permeated the stuffy room. Izzy twirled a thick strand of her hair in her fingers. Stewie appeared to be sweating. His red hair looked damp and had flattened across the top of his head. They were unable to drop a polite comment.

Stalled in a dreadful lacuna, stuck nowhere, unable to transition from Stewie's patronizing reading of Cookie's poem and onto something else, the silence grew insufferable.

Cookie had no problem being blindly brave. "Well, what do you think?"

Stewie answered her with his signature bellowing laugh that engulfed his small apartment. Once again, Cookie was a comic who had hit the mark.

"I don't see what's so funny."

With his smile aimed precisely at Cookie, he emitted a strange whinnying from both his nose and his mouth that became a whistling, rustling sound as though he was overwhelmed with emotion and trying to catch his breath. He practically spluttered his words. "It doesn't matter whether you are any good. What matters is if I say you're good."

Cookie stood and reached for her notebook, but he clutched it in his hand, pulling it away from her.

"Not so fast. I'm not finished commenting on your writing."

This was not the first time someone tried to take her notebook and it would not be the last. She picked up the ornate brass lamp that looked like a bull and shook it, threatening to throw it at him.

"Give it to me now."

"You're so Yonkers." He looked at her contemptuously and handed her the notebook. "Haven't you ever heard of a comma, for God's sake?"

She slammed the lamp onto the table, hearing Stewie's indignant yelling and Izzy's girlishly soft apologies. Cookie offered no mercy. She opened her Boho and felt around the bottom of the bag until she was able to retrieve what she had been searching for—the acorn with the shiny green bottom as round as a human face had now become a green orb bent on revenge. With the precision of a star relief pitcher, she threw the acorn at Stewie, hitting him smack in the middle of his forehead, where it immediately left a red welt the size of a quarter.

"Crazy low-class bitch!" He laughed.

"You can take the girl out of Yonkers, but you can't take Yonkers out of the girl!"

Cookie bolted from his apartment and did not stop to look back.

"Cookie, don't be this way," Izzy called after her. "Hey, I thought we were going to the Russian Tea Room for dinner!"

Cookie bolted across the distressed orange shag rug in the hall to the elevator but decided not to wait and headed into the fire stairwell, where her platform heels clattered on the metal steps. Her head pounded madly with the metallic echo of her own footsteps. Round and round she clomped, passing steel-thatched windows that let in grey light but were too opaque to see out. On the ground floor, she pushed open a thick industrial door that set off a fire alarm, but she did not care, and she did not slow her panicky steps to get out of there.

Forty-one

The fire alarm screeched into the sulfurous, sooty air of the street. Heavy construction machinery belched smoke from a yellow smokestack that rose ten feet above a manhole. She imagined the manhole led below the concrete hell of Sixth Avenue. As she turned the corner, her heart raced in exhilaration; she was so excited to be leaving Stewie. Leaving him didn't mean they couldn't remain friends, but deep down inside, she knew she would never see him again.

She dodged between construction workers and men pushing small handcarts on the sidewalk, blocking her view. She stepped around them, hardly seeing anyone's face, instead fixated on the image in her mind: Clyfford Still's oil painting PH-372.

More than a painting, it was the story of her life.

She turned the corner onto Seventh Avenue, searching for Arky and the limo. She pulled the brochure from her Boho to find the address of the Marlborough-Gerson Gallery. Reading aloud the address 40 West 57th Street from the brochure, she did not watch where she was going and collided with a grey metal dumpster, its lid unhinged, and its innards exposed.

She looked inside of the dumpster. It was as empty as her broken heart. Soggy crushed cartons and cigarette butts floated in rusty-brown water pooling on one side. She tried yelling "hello" to see if it would talk back to her. She wanted to have a conversation with the dumpster; even if she only heard an echo of her own words, it might have been her only friend.

In an ultimate act of finality and despair, she took her black & white notebook and impulsively tossed it into the dumpster as though it was a mock suicide attempt and a plea for help.

She stared hard at the notebook that sat on the bottom of the dumpster, still intact, saved from drowning in dirty water by a flotilla of rotting banana peels.

Then she screamed inwardly, crying out "no." What had she done? She dove into the dumpster to retrieve her notebook.

"What am I thinking? What am I doing?"

"You got me," a voice answered back.

Cookie looked up, grabbed the notebook, hurdled herself over the side, and climbed out of the dumpster. She came eye to eye with the cinched waist of a big black woman draped from head to toe in copper lamé.

Gwendolyn gave her a dazzling, slightly dangerous smile.

"Honey, yous in a bad way. *Whatch* you doing that dumpster diving for when you've got yourself plenty of money? Yous looks like yous been sleeping with nasty-assed men who are real, real bad in bed. There are a lotta dem out there. I know."

Cookie clutched the notebook to her chest. "I am never ever going to let go of this notebook, even if I face a firing squad and die sixteen times. Seventeen times. I'm almost seventeen."

"Yous getting mighty old, Girl. Yous gotta get yourself grownup and do something with yourself. Yous only got one life to live. Quit acting whorish all the time."

"Whorish? Isn't that kind of a weird thing for a drag queen to say?!"

"I ain't nobody's queen except a queen to my own self!"

She pointed to hardcore junkies on the street. "They worked the junk real hard and dat ain't me. They be junkies through thick and thin. I'm all about sexing and showmanship."

She stared hard at Cookie, giving her the once over.

"Yous got dat sexy long hair. Nice smile. Dats a plus. Whatch you doing with that red-head guy. You be kicking that guy hard to get away from him. Sugar, you are a loose cannon. I keep my eyes on yous."

Cookie shouted above the jackhammer, close to the manhole. "I'm never going to fit in anywhere! That's just the way it's going to be! I'm an odd duck! A nobody going nowhere fast."

Gwendolyn put her arms on her wide hips and shook, vibrating with laughter.

"I'm not talking over dat thing. It's too loud."

She tapped the toe of her huge platform shoe on the pavement, staring at Cookie with big black eyes, while she waited for the jackhammer to stop. She looked dangerous, full of murderous intent, shifting her weight from one foot to the other. She pretended to be oblivious to the come-ons and leers of men passing by on the street, but it was all a fantastic show. She savored every glance, every obscene gesture, and every moment when she caught some man's roving eye. She was an out-and-out attention whore.

"Girl, what the hell is it that yous want?" Wanna a man? Wanna a job? Maybe you wanna get ed-du-ca-ted."

"I just want to be normal!"

"Good luck with dat. Ain't nobody normal cept for, maybe, me." She gave Cookie a big cocky nod, an expression of complete confidence, and hummed a song to herself, a glorious hymn that only belonged to her.

She laughed and started to walk away. "Like I said, Girl, I could make a lot of money with yous. And yous know where to find me. Morning or night."

She winked. "I be coming and going all day and all night long."

With one long glittering nail, she pointed toward the Remington Hotel, where an expansive network of fire escapes rode roughshod up the front façade, making the hotel look old and seedy.

"I've got the nicest digs up there, better than that loser you been messing around with. Dat red-head dude is real bad and I don't mean bad in a good way. He be real bad, as bad as they come, and then some."

Gwendolyn flashed her white-painted-tooth smile and sashayed away. Too huge to disappear into the crowd, she towered over everyone else on the sidewalk. Strutting on her four-inch, coppery-colored platforms, she moved her ass side-to-side, rocking it like Jell-O, generously showing off her big booty, the biggest booty Cookie had ever seen. Whistles and catcalls followed her all the way down Sixth Avenue. Gwendolyn had it going on.

Friday October 19 1973

I looked to the sky to join the clouds. I own the clouds and the clouds own me. I'm seventeen. My birthday has come and gone. Johnny's birthday has come and gone. Clyfford Still's exhibition has come and gone. I went to the gallery. The painting wasn't there.

I don't know if I told you about the Marlborough-Gerson Gallery. It's located between Fifth and Sixth on West 57th Street. Arky dropped me off right in front of the gallery. Hardly anyone was there. This snooty woman walked across the gallery's wide open space. The walls were white. She wore black. Head-to-toe in black. I swear the woman's face and brain was black and blue like it had been bruised in a head-banging contest with Mosella Moran. I didn't like her. She didn't like me. I asked her about the exhibition for Clyfford Still and she gave me a snobby look. She was a bitch.

She acted like I didn't know what I was talking about.

I showed her my wrinkled brochure. She looked at me as though I was a sorry-assed girl from Yonkers. I didn't like that. She told me to read the dates of the exhibition on the brochure.

She acted like I did not know how to read.

The art gallery brochure that I found in Stewie's apartment was over two years old. What a pisser!

I saw lots of glass in the gallery. No clouds.

I don't know if I will ever see that painting for real. I will have to keep seeing it in my mind. The shapes in the painting are really without a shape. They are the clouds that I have to travel through before I reach a small band of light in the sky. It's like I'm trying to find myself. It's like trying to find God. Good luck to me!

I know I'm weird. I know I think strange things. So what!

I'll always keep the Clyfford Still brochure in my Boho. I am saving the painting in my mind's eye forever. I also save my fortunes from Zelda the Gypsy. I want my big acorn back. It's lucky. But it means having to deal with Stewie. Bummer! Seeing him again would be like writing new words to cover old words on an Etch-A-Sketch tablet! I want to lift the page on the Etch-A-Sketch tablet to make him disappear for good. Palimpsest! He's such a fucking asshole!

Donny cut off all of her hair. It's not like her hair was the only thing she had going for her. She's been hiding in her room a lot. I don't know what's wrong with her. I always thought she was the worst sister in the world. A snitch. But now I have second thoughts.

I think I will never hear from Stanley de Falco again and I'm okay with that. I'm over him. I'm off to the races. I'm chasing new clouds. I sigh from the depth of my soul. Can you hear my sigh? My mouth quivers non-stop. My heart does leaps and turns. Fuck! Have you noticed that I like to say fuck a lot? It's a Yonkers thing. Don't get me wrong. Yonkers girls know how to use plain English. But there is something tough and fearless about exclaiming fuck. It makes the point. Know what I mean?

-ccc

Forty-two

Code Red. Johnny was beside himself. Cookie hadn't seen her father this angry since the day he had cut down all of the Sumac trees. Back then, Cookie had tried to tell him how the Sumac trees and the Sumac weeds were different, but he would not listen to her. He could not distinguish between poison Sumac, the weed, and the beautiful, crimson-leaved Sumac trees, which were gifts from nature, a glorious sight to behold, far from lethal and not the cause of Donny's extreme allergic reaction.

Donny, much younger then, swelled with welts, bumps, stinging lesions, and was slathered in pink calamine lotion. The sight of her sent Johnny over the edge. Say what you want about the guy. He did have a big head! Cookie swore he was full of hot air. He could be dumb, foolish, loud, crass...but he loved his daughters and could not cope with any harm that could possibly befall them.

Once again something bad had happened to Donny and it turned Johnny into a madman. His face looked as red as the fall leaves on a Sumac tree. Sweat poured from his body, running down his face and neck, dripping from his nose. His features contorted with hatred and he screamed.

"Look what she did to her hair! She cut it off and put her blonde curls into a paper bag! Your mother's not here. You're never here! Nobody stopped her from doing this to herself! Look what she's done to herself!"

He turned to Cookie and yelled, "Will you look at her hair! It's all chopped off!"

He threw his face into his hands and babbled softly as though he was about to cry. "She had such beautiful hair! How could she have done such a thing to her beautiful hair? Nobody has hair like that! Know how much most women would pay to have hair like that? Men too probably. I don't know. Jesus Christ!"

Donny sat at the dining room table. With her head bowed, her face was hidden from Cookie's curious gaze. Not crying. Not smiling. She did not move. Cookie could not be sure if her sister was breathing. She touched Donny on her arm, but she did not respond.

"Can't you see how ragged she is?! She's been hurt! Some guy's hurt her!"

He held up her white satin panties that had obviously been ripped at the crotch. "Look! And I found this! What does this mean?!" He shook the panties in the air. "What does this mean?! Don't tell me she's having sex already at her age!"

"I'm sure there's a perfectly reasonable explanation." Cookie could not believe the words uttered from her mouth, as if she was trying to remain calm in the midst of her father's rage, which was impossible.

"I can't understand things too good, especially girls. I always feel like I'm doing everything wrong."

He put his hands up to cover his eyes and sniffed. Johnny screwed up his face into a knot and swallowed hard. Then, he began to cry.

"I just want to do the right thing," he blubbered. "That's all I ever wanted to do. The right thing. I just don't know what it is. What is the right thing to do? What am I supposed to do?"

Cookie stared at him in horror. *Oh my god, please don't cry*, Cookie prayed. *If he cries, it's all over. I'm done.* She could take anything, but not that. She could not take the sight of Johnny Colangelo crying.

She did her best to stop him. "If I can't cry, neither can you. Got that, Johnny? She confronted him, stood up to him, and talked directly into his face. "I don't cry. You don't cry. That's the deal we have! Got that?!"

Johnny's eyes had turned more red than blue and watered. "I have to trust in the end, you're gonna be okay. I gotta believe that, even if it's not true. I gotta believe that. And if I don't believe that, it's gonna kill me. Okay? Don't you think I know how it is out there?"

He waved his hand toward the back door. "Don't you think I know how hard it is for girls to grow up in this world, the way men try to take advantage of them! Don't you think I know the world is rigged against girls?! Don't you think I know what men do to young girls?! You think I haven't been watching and noticing things?! And then I end up having nothing but girls. If I had boys, then I could relax, thinking everything would be even-steven, but that didn't happen! Did it?"

"You can't act this way! You're acting the same way you did the day you cut down all the trees!"

"The trees are growing back, but what about her hair?"

Johnny paced the olive-green Formica floor with an uneven gait, and stopped talking, which was the scariest thing of all. He walked out of the room and into the kitchen, but Cookie could still see him as he reached for the black wall phone and dialed a number.

"Who are you calling?"

"None of your business."

"Why?"

"I'm calling the guy who can help me figure this out. He always figures out things. Usually for a price, but it's worth it."

"Louie Santamassino?"

Her father grunted.

Cookie put her arm around Donny and kissed her on the top of her ragged head. She wondered why Donny had done such a thing to her hair, but that was a conversation for another day. Other matters were more urgent.

She whispered, "Are you going to tell on me?"

Donny shook her head and looked up at her with defiance. "You know I wouldn't do that to you, Cookie."

"It's not like you haven't ratted me out before."

Donny pushed Cookie away. "Don't touch me."

"Please tell me what's wrong."

"I can't."

Cookie heard Johnny responding in simple one word responses and grunts acknowledging he understood. She thought Johnny wasn't listening to them.

"Tell me."

"Stewie made me stare at his lava lamp."

"He doesn't have a lava lamp."

"Yes, he does. I looked at it with my own eyes. He made me stare at his lava lamp. Then he did things to me."

Cookie knelt on the floor beside her chair and looked up.

"What kinds of things?"

Donny shrugged. Her shoulders sagged, then she shuddered. She stopped speaking, reached toward the table to get her Etch-A-Sketch. Cookie's eyes followed the trail of the stylus that drew a crude shape, the form of banana. An added stroke gave the banana a small eye. A small curly line flowed from the eye.

"He did things to me." Donny lifted the plastic page and the image disappeared.

Cookie looked at Johnny. He looked at her. He had heard every word that had passed between his daughters. Italian men had a way of engaging in dual activities—keeping one eye open, one eye shut, pretending not to notice a thing. One ear closed, the other ear open and hearing everything.

Johnny continued his conversation with Louie Santamassino, giving him one-word responses—the code between men who do not want anyone else to know what they are talking about. Code Red.

Cookie knew something terrible was going to happen. Something terrible was going to happen, not to her, not to Donny, but to Farley Stewart. *Stewie.*

She confronted her father the moment he hung up the phone. "What are you going to do?"

"What can I do? My hands are tied." He held up his hands, fanning all ten of his fingers.

"You think I don't hear things, but I do."

His voice dropped. "Lava Lamp." His anger had taken a darker turn. She had never seen Johnny become so cold, seemingly unfeeling. The only thing worse than his rage, was when he became calm, cool and reasonable. Cookie was petrified at what Johnny was going to do.

"As much as I've always tried to protect my daughters, it's never been enough."

Although his body shook in a quiet rage, he had stopped sweating. For a man who was powerfully built, he shrank in stature, grace coursed through his body; he appeared to relax, and he smiled at Cookie. She had never seen him smile like that before and did not know what it meant.

He put his arm around her shoulder and looked into her eyes. His eyes blazed blue, bluer and softer than she had ever known. He used his shirt to mop sweat from his forehead and wiped his eyes. His tears had slowed. He was at peace with himself and had become a sizeable force in the world. Far from being an innocent, he was imbued with a purity of love that forgave all prior malfeasance, including sins and mistakes, regardless if they were intentional or not.

He drew Cookie forward into his arms, gave her a great bear hug, holding onto his daughter as if he would never let go. And, ultimately, he never would let go.

Nothing like this had ever happened between them and it stunned Cookie. Something beautiful and very loving had been living inside of Johnny Colangelo. She did not know what to say or what to do and slowly withdrew from his embrace. She didn't know what to do with his enormous display of love and affection. She was so overwhelmed that she forgot who she was, a tough Yonkers girl. But she could not let go of her armor, not for him, not for anyone. He patted her on the arm as though he understood. She understood too. Johnny put his hand on the top of Donny's head and let it linger there; he was blessing her like a good priest, the way priests ought to be. Looking at Cookie again, he nodded as if his silence would speak great wisdom to her. Then he winked, turned around and walked out of the room.

Forty-three

Cookie knew what she would find in her mailbox: bills, bank statements, overdue library notices, school reports, and grocery coupons. Johnny got paid weekly in cash through an unknown source, which made her stop to think that the nature of his business was a mystery. Since Kitty had married Johnny, she had never worked. Johnny was proud of that. He was the breadwinner—the fella who wore the pants and kept a roof over their heads, at the expense of his music, which he had loved so much.

On this Friday afternoon, she found an unexpected parcel that had been addressed to her. Wrapped in brown paper, the box bore eight *Oriental* postage stamps and was postmarked from the Republic of Vietnam. She carried the mail into the house and set it on small bench in the hall. Then she pried open the package, revealing a small hand-carved wooden box. The lid, attached to the box with tongue and groove precision, lifted easily. Inside of the box, a small black & white ceramic owl sat on a paper-mâché nest that resembled thatched straw and twigs.

She held the owl in her hand, examining its white eyes that were proportionately huge and not blinking. She immediately fell in love with the owl and deemed it to be a sign, a talisman, a harbinger indicating the next phase of her life would soon appear in front of her with unexpected ramifications that would be complicated but ultimately lead her to her destiny. Whatever that destiny might be did not matter. She only knew soon she would be leaving Yonkers. She and the Blind Owl Alan Wilson would be on the road again.

A slip of delicate paper folded into a square had been tucked alongside the owl's nest. One line ran down the center of the blue-lined paper. Thinking of you on your birthday. Signed /S/.

It didn't matter if she ever again saw Stanley de Falco. It was too late. Her birthday had been three days ago. Besides, she had long ago stopped thinking of him. Basking on the beach under the sun in Malibu is the final image of him that she held firmly in her mind. It is this image that allowed her to make the break with him.

Now she could not reconcile that image with the arrival of the owl. She needed to see Bertha Sokól. Stanley's mother would know why an owl had materialized strangely and magically from Vietnam.

The urgency to get to the Café Trento took precedence over wanting to bash in Stewie's face. She put Donny's dilemma on hold, then shook down Arky Lovato; he was waiting out front for her anyway, and hightailed it to the bakery.

Arky did not understand why it was so important to get to the bakery before it closed for the day. Cookie did not feel like she owed him an explanation. They left it like that for the duration of a rushed silent ride.

She didn't want Bertha to see her getting dropped off by a limo and asked Arky to pull into the alley between Café Trento and Restivo's Florist. The last time she had been here was on Valentine's Day when Tony Amendolito screamed at her to keep her hands off of his shiny red car. An ancient memory now, blurry and distant, along with Reenie's abortion, Billy

Dee's death, her shitty job at the drugstore, the riot and Mosella Moran. She no longer felt as though she was in danger from what had happened to her in the past. Those days were gone.

The warmth of the bakery calmed her. She had been on edge ever since she had made contact with the small owl that she fingered in her pocket. The owl was too precious to sink into the bottom of her Boho under the dreck of chewing gum, lip gloss, her black & white notebook, the crumpled Clyfford Still brochure, and a wad of money.

The woman behind the bakery counter had her back turned toward Cookie. Unlike the broad-beamed Bertha Sokól, this woman was slender by comparison and very blonde. Cookie felt faint from the overwhelming aroma of fresh baked bread comingled with almond, cinnamon, butter and anise. She realized she was hungry and had not eaten for hours. She traced her fingers along the glass display case.

"Where's Bertha? I came to see Bertha Sokól."

"Long time, no see." The woman's laugh was hearty, long-lasting. "What can I get for you? We're closing soon and I can't be waiting on customers who can't make up their mind, even you, Miss Cookie!"

"Bertha?" Cookie had not recognized her. Her hair, dyed pale canary-blonde, framed her face in ringlets. The creamy skin on her face had softened instead of creasing deeper with age. She had lost weight and was about half the size of what she used to be. Bertha Sokól had changed, for the better.

Her smile was as warm as the sweet pastries she formed by hand and baked to the hues of honey and gold. She came from behind the counter to the front of the pastry case and hugged Cookie.

"I hear things about you," she said, in her husky Polish accent, "that I can't believe are true. That you've got yourself a lot of money and ride around town in a fancy car."

She whispered in a throaty accent. "I hope you're not doing something bad to get your hands on some money."

Cookie looked up where the ceiling fan that had always been on, but it was now still.

"Gotta get that fixed.... But I don't need it now, the weather's cooled."

Cookie nodded, smiling. Today had been one of the first pure-blue-sky days, crisp, slightly cool air, full sun, the scent of fall, dried leaves crunching under her feet. It was a day like this the first time she had made love with Stanley. She fingered the owl in the pocket of her plaid woolen jacket. Thinking about the weather was a nice, but brief, distraction.

"Where's Stanley?"

"I knew you were going to ask that!"

Cookie's eyes followed Bertha as she set her arms on top of the counter and dropped her face into her two hands. She looked uncomfortable as though she did not want to talk. Cookie noticed that Bertha was wearing a wedding band. Her eyes followed Bertha's eyes wandering across the room where they settled on a new bakery counter that stood where the café area used to be. The new counter was small and hardly filled the space that used to be occupied by an intimate café that resembled an ice cream parlor with small tables and ornate wrought iron chairs.

She finally blurted, "He went back to Vietnam. He didn't want you to know."

"Why? I don't understand. Why?!"

"He wanted to be there for the final evacuation." She waved her arms. "I say, 'Stanislaus, I never heard of such a thing. I never hear of any young man going back there once they got home. You must have something wrong with your head.'"

Bertha sighed and tried to force a smile, but it would not come. "You know how stubborn he can be? Remember?"

Cookie pressed her hand to cover her mouth, not to stop from talking but because she did not know what to say. She was too stunned to know if she cared.

"He tells me he could not live with himself so long as American boys were still there. He said he'd stay until everyone comes home." She looked at Cookie. "I know that war is ending. Soon, he will come home. I pray and I pray."

She blessed herself. "I pray for him all day long. I go to St. Casmir's Church and I light all the candles. I have masses said. I do everything I can to make sure he comes home with his two arms, his two legs and his head screwed on straight."

Cookie went around the counter, reached for Bertha and hugged her. "That's every mother's wish." She sniffed. "I'll pray too, if I remember how."

Bertha wiped a faint trace of tears from her eyes and looked at Cookie. "How's the black boy? He used to come here with you?"

Cookie nodded. She didn't want to talk about Herman Lynch. The pain was too new and raw, the opening of a childhood scab on her knee.

"And the girl, she used to come here with you too, the one with the curly dark hair? I can't remember her name. The one who lost the brother. Now I hear her grandmother's dying."

Fleeing from the thought of Reenie's pain, leaving the bakery was the only assured escape route. As she moved toward the door, Bertha hastily packed a pink cardboard box with a sfogliatelle and cannoli.

"No matter what, you've gotta eat."

At the mention of Herman and Reenie, Cookie's body had stiffened with guilt. She bade Bertha a hasty but faint-hearted farewell. She told Arky to wait for her in front of the Café Trento. She headed directly to Reenie's apartment, which was within walking distance. It was a fine day to walk, kicking up piles of russet colored leaves beneath her feet. She remembered jumping in the leaves, the day Herman had caught her in the act, chastising her for acting like a little kid. She still felt that way, wanting to jump into the air to see how high she could go.

Cookie was mad at herself for not going out of her way to see Reenie. She tried to tell herself that because they went to different schools that Reenie was out of sight, out of mind, but it wasn't true. Reenie's losing streak made her feel queasy, as though she could catch her bad luck. There are some people who think bad luck is a disease as contagious as leprosy, tuberculosis or insanity. There were days in the past when she felt she could catch schizophrenia from Kitty, but no longer. Getting hit by that big acorn was a small, sure thing to hold onto.

Forty-four

The buildings on Ashburton Avenue were rundown. Dogs barked
behind chain-link fences or ran in the road, stopping or slowing
a meager procession of battered cars that beeped their horns.
Mattresses sat on stoops like grand outdoor seating, spitting
out stuffing, springs and foam. A lumpy old armchair looked as
comfortable as an old throne to sit and watch the world go by.
Dellwood Dairy milk crates had been turned upside down and
were being used as small tables or footrests. Empty beer cans
and liquor bottles littered the sidewalk, between alleys, tucked
against the curb. It was a neighborhood people thought of as
their own private dump, and it was also home.

Herman Lynch lived in the same building as Reenie.
Cookie dreaded running into him. She didn't know what to
say. She had not seen him much since Henry had been killed.
She didn't know what to do with grief or loss or sadness and
had no place inside of herself to make it her own.

The old brick building where Reenie lived had been
cleaned up. The façade of the building had been cleansed
of soot and had resumed the color of red brick. The autumn
sun filtered light through the few old oak trees that stood in

front of the apartment building. A muffler backfired on the street in a succession of throaty pops, mini-explosions. The entrance to the building had been restored. Vintage wood cornices and decorative crown molding around the front door had been sanded and polished to achieve high luster. All of these improvements had been made at the behest of Herman's grandmother. Mabel Kerry was highly respected, a force to be reckoned with, a pillar in the community.

The interior of the building still smelled of old wood that had been saturated with cumulative cooking odors. She raced to the third floor with renewed impatience. She really didn't want to be here and wanted to get this visit with Reenie over and done with as soon as possible. She knocked on the door of Apartment 3A. She knocked for what felt like three minutes. No one answered. She heard the phone ringing in the apartment, or maybe it was in the adjacent apartment, but no one answered.

Cookie left the box of pastry in front of the door. She reached in her Boho and ripped a sheet of paper from her black & white notebook. She hastily scrawled a note to Reenie to let her know she had been by. It was the least she could do, but it felt wrong. She was troubled by her inability to know what she should do, and even if she did know, she wondered whether she could summon the courage to be there for Reenie.

That night she was troubled by dreams that kept her from sleeping. She was terrified, wondering why with every passing year, things became so much worse instead of better.

She lay awake, staring into shadows. The slant of light under the door showed itself as sharp enough to slice her heart in two. While she drifted, the light grew fainter and fainter, as soft as a slim cloud until it finally disappeared. She had left her door opened a crack.

She heard Kitty wandering in the hall outside her door. She knew it was Kitty because she had come home from the hospital and wandered around the house, staying up all night, trying to get used to her new medication.

"Kitty? Close the door, please, Kitty."

It was a command which her mother did not oblige. Kitty wanted reassuring words, or a kiss from her daughter, both of which were the same. They both knew the truth. Cookie was the grown-up, and her mother was the child.

Cookie got up and shut the door tight. Locked it too. Left in darkness falling all around, she didn't need light. She had never been afraid of the dark and wasn't about to start worrying now. She glanced out her bedroom window and saw the crescent of a moon so slender that it might as well have disappeared into the black sky.

She did not sleep for long but stayed awake, whispering to herself, a weeping that lacked tears. She gnashed her teeth, grinding her molars and groaning. She was guilty, guilty, guilty. She was guilty for having all of that money and all of the ways she had betrayed the people she held closest to her heart. Herman. Reenie. Donny. Stanley.

She knew on one level she did not care what happened to Stanley; it was too long ago and she had made the break as surely as she had declared him dead on the beach in Malibu. He was her first love. Every girl has to have a love that is so big that no one can ever take it away from her. He was her first. But too much had happened, and she had changed, but not for the better.

She had abandoned everyone during their time of trial.

She had stolen the money, but the money, in turn, had stolen her soul.

She was not afraid of the dark. Never would be. Darkness is an expression of the simple absence of light, she told herself. Another way of looking at the same thing in a different way. She sees the crack on the wall. A thin band of light is as thin as the blade of a knife. She watches the band until it is completely gone. Then she looks toward the ceiling where not a thing can be seen.

Sunday November 11 1973

Zelda the Gypsy has never been cooperative. One fortune said: *An old love will come back to you.* I swear someone stuffs her mouth with cheap fortunes leftover from a Chinese restaurant. I kept putting slugs into the coin slot to get the right fortune to pop out of this bitch's mouth.

Another fortune said: *You will know it when you see it. It will know you when it sees you.* What the fuck does that mean?

I was losing my patience with the Gypsy. I never thought of her as too bright anyway. She's a coin-operated machine. I was about to give up and was down to my last slug. The last fortune she spouted from her mouth was the most interesting thing that I've ever thought about.

Hate is never conquered by hate. Hate is conquered by love.

I thought about hate and love for at least an hour after I got that fortune. I thought about all sorts of things. Money. My crazy family. My schizophrenic mother. My father showing his feelings and acting like a human being. The situation with Donny. She's recovering from whatever Stewie did to her. Thank you very much. I thought about Stanley and the owl he sent to me. I thought about the Carnegie Library in Getty Square—my favorite place in the whole world. And I thought about Mrs. Kerry. I thought about Reenie and Herman and the bad stuff that's happened to them.

I forgot to tell you that Reenie's Nonna died. Reenie is all alone now. An orphan.

I forgot to tell you about other things too. I thought about Yonkers and why I wanted to leave so badly.

We have major problems in Yonkers. The city of seven hills. The blacks hate whites and the whites hate blacks. Now here's the thing to think about. We didn't really hate each other but have to act as though we do. It's sort of an act that we put on. Lots of kids want a come-up. Some move up.

Some move down. Some are dead. And some will be long gone someday. I don't know what is going to happen to everyone else. There isn't anything I can do. It's not my job to figure it out.

I hope that I live to tell.

Most of the money is still stuffed under my mattress. Notice I didn't say my money. Having so much money makes me feel that I am living on borrowed time. The money is more of a burden than it is the ticket to freedom. I just don't know what to do with the money. Things would be different I guess if I had been raised to be rich. I would know what to do with it. I'm thinking about giving most of it away. Giving away money is tricky!

I am trying to find my way out of here. I live in a no man's land. A white man's ghetto. Why doesn't the world understand that white people live in ghettos too? And some black and brown people have fancy homes. Some black and brown people have money and know what to do with it. I don't know what to do with money. Maybe I should give it back?

It is very clear to me that I am crazy. Only a crazy person gives away money.

I light another Marlboro. Smoking keeps my head on straight. Ever wonder why crazy people smoke so much? I'm smoking and looking at the night sky. Clouds of charcoal ink blots pepper the sky between dismal smoky lines and faint stars. I cannot see the moon that is growing smaller every night this week. A full moon would still fade in and out of the clouds. Tonight's moon can hardly be seen. There are parts of the world that do not have any clouds tonight. I wish I knew where there are no clouds. Clouds are like the demons I am trying to squash from the depths of my soul. My darkness falls so softly that it cannot be heard.

-ccc

Forty-five

Her eyes traveled to the old Kennedy Marina, where the ramshackle wharf was a deteriorating eyesore, a wreck of uneven wooden boards and tarred rafters, a splintered mess of rotten chunks and gaping holes. She walked close to the river's edge and waited. She refrained from taking a deep breath of the air that smelled of a blend of raw sewage and creosote. Another current of colder air blowing from the river brought a scent as foul as a dead animal that had been left to rot.

She had instructed Arky to leave her there alone on the marina while she waited. It might have been a foolish decision to remain alone on a dilapidated dock on this cold night in November. The water of the river lashed against the edge of the wharf with thick tongues as black as ink.

She told herself she might be exceptional in some way because she dared to wait here alone and unafraid so late at night. She didn't wear a watch and had no way to tell the time, other than remembering what time it had been when she had left the limo and how much time might have elapsed since then. She had enough experience in life to know that a few minutes standing around in the freezing cold can seem like an eternity. Contrarily, many hours of clubbing and dancing can feel fleeting, a passage of time as rapid as the blink of an eye.

A car sped down the driveway. Its tires crunched along gravel in a gratingly unpleasant approach toward the marina. The car stopped and let a woman out of the car. As the car drove away, the shadow of a woman appeared on the road. She waved her hand gaily, calling Cookie's name.

Reenie had changed, but depending on your perspective, not for the better. Her magnificent hair had been shorn, slick to her skull, a shiny brown cap with flat waves catching a scintilla of light from the slim moon.

"You cut your hair."

Cookie stepped forward to examine Reenie more closely. She wasn't going to lie and tell her that her hair looked good. The girl bore a pinched expression, more defiant than grief-stricken.

"I've cut a lot of things." She took a long drag from her Marlboro and passed the cigarette to Cookie. "Thanks for meeting me here."

"Why here?" With her arms, she cinched her navy woolen maxi coat around her waist to stave off the cold. She clenched her teeth and shivered.

"I know it's creepy being here in the dark. They don't have lights down here on purpose."

She looked at Cookie as though she was privy to secrets and nodded as though she knew something Cookie did not. Reenie's posturing didn't convince Cookie. She knew Reenie was dodging the truth.

"They don't want people hanging around down here at night. You've got to admit, it's creepy, but people come here anyway, especially when it's hot outside."

She dropped a few paces away from Cookie, walked in a circle, then turned back and came closer to where Cookie stood than where she had been before.

"But tonight, it's Sunday. Nobody's here except me and you. Look around. See. No cars."

Cookie handed back the Marlboro. Reenie examined the cigarette's stub close enough to the filter to be done; she dropped it to the ground and stepped on it.

Reenie's close-to-the-scalp haircut made her eyes look enormous. Dramatic too. Her taut cheekbones sharpened the long oval shape of her face into lean lines. Gamin-faced but beautiful, she looked as though sadness had purified her.

"I can't stay in the apartment. Nonna died there. I just can't stay there. She had been in bed for a while. The place smells like a sick room. I knew it was coming, but I didn't know when. I kept hoping she'd get better and be okay."

Her voice faltered. "I thought she'd be okay. She was a tough old bird. But in the end, it got her. It was cancer, you know."

Cookie placed her arm around Reenie's shoulder and leaned in to hug her. Reenie shrugged and shifted away from her embrace; she did not want to be touched.

"By the way, I'm staying with Herman and Mrs. Kerry until I find a new place to live."

Agonizing moments passed in the strained silence between them.

On second thought, Reenie moved closer to Cookie and hugged her. "You've always been my friend. I want to thank you for that. You and Herman, you've been there when no one else cared. No one else mattered. I mean that, Cookie."

"I didn't do anything, really."

Cookie felt enormous guilt. She had done so little and had avoided Reenie like the plague over the summer, probably when Reenie needed her the most.

Reenie spoke directly into Cookie's face. "You were there when I had to go and get Billy Dee's body. You were there when I had to have an abortion. Just think of where I'd be if I had to have a kid right now. With that crazy guy threatening to kill me!"

"Has he been bothering you?"

She sniffed. "I haven't seen him around at all."

Cookie shook her head. "He's gotten engaged to Toni Ferlinghetti."

"He won't be treating her like garbage. Guys like him always handpick their victims. The ones they know they can get away with it. He went after me because I'm half black."

"He messed with me too."

"Yeah... well." Reenie rolled her eyes. "Guys like him have a radar for knowing who they can mess with."

"Knowing Toni, she'll be beating him for the rest of his life."

They erupted into laughter that got carried away, turning into a howl, sweeping them away, filling the vacant lot. Laughing led to sniffling and a sob. No tears though. Reenie wiped her eyes anyway.

The rain that had come earlier had blown across the Palisades to blanket northern New Jersey with black clouds. The red light on top of the broadcast tower steadily blinked, the one stable icon in Cookie's life. She could always count on that light to be there. The tiny jewel of red light lived far across the river but stayed as near and dear to her as her acorn, her owl, her notebook, some small thing that gave her own life meaning but meant nothing to anyone else.

"What you don't know is sometimes you might not be with me, but I feel you inside here." Reenie crossed her heart. "You were always so tough, but I know that you've got feelings. Big feelings that you don't show."

Cookie's lips kept moving, smiling, grinning, trying to scowl, anything to ward off a sob. No way in hell would she ever cry.

"I'm going to go to college," Reenie said. "I'm going to make something of myself. I owe that to Billy Dee. I owe that to Nonna. And I owe it to myself."

When Cookie reached into her Boho, she realized her fingers had stiffened from the cold. There was no colder spot in Yonkers than the brink of the Hudson River. It was not yet winter, but it was the first cold night since summer. An oily slick of yellow fog scudded across the top of the water as if it had been traveling, looking for home.

She handed Reenie a stack of twenties. "This will help you get a new place."

Reenie fanned the bills in the stack and slapped the bundle of bills against her wrist. "Are you serious? What did you do, rob a bank?"

"No." She slung her Boho across her shoulder and looked toward the road, hoping Arky would come soon.

"I want to be out in the open with you. I want to talk truthfully."

Reenie looked at her feet as if she meant to avoid making eye contact with Cookie. "Everyone talks about you having money. Now I know you've got a lot more than I thought if you you're trying to give me so much."

She looked incredulous. "What's going on with you, girl? Where'd you get all this money?"

Cookie could not talk. Words would not come. It was really none of Reenie's business. She wished she would take the money and shut up.

"You won't tell me where?"

"I found it in a box." She scratched her head. "I don't know where it came from. That's all I can say."

"You found it in Johnny's office, didn't you? Somebody left that money there for a pickup. Everyone's got a key to Johnny's office. That money that you've done got there, those are winnings. Someone rigged a bet at the racetrack. Remember Wanda McGillicuddy? She was too stupid to leave the money where she was supposed to. She put it in the bank. And that's why she got herself done and gone. Disappeared."

The night was beckoning Cookie to barrel her way out of the prison that Reenie had created for her. She had no idea that she had been living high on the dole—winnings from the Yonkers Raceway. Reenie took the stack of money and stuffed it into Cookie's Boho.

"Wanda McGillicuddy isn't the only stoolie who places bets. Others have been doing what she did. Nonna was gonna do it to make a quick buck but she got too old and sick."

Reenie lit a Marlboro and inadvertently blew smoke into Cookie's face. "You see, what they do is find a stoolie. They pick women who are old and all alone in the world. They tell the stoolie to place a big bet on a handicap, the horse that's predicted to lose by a longshot, but they make that horse win. The race is rigged. The payout can be enormous."

"God, it's cold. I wish Arky would get here."

"They don't throw the race too often. If they did that would be the end of the Yonkers Raceway. Know what I mean?"

Cookie shivered. "Sure, I know what you mean."

"Why are you ignoring what I'm telling you? What are you going to do with the money?"

"Give it away? Use it? I don't know."

"Not to me, you ain't. I'll share my ciggies with you, I'll even take a ride from you, but that's as far as it goes. I don't want no dirty money. I don't want that kind of responsibility. That's why I wanted to meet you down here. I don't want to be seen with you right now. Know what I mean? You've gone too far, Cookie, and I don't know how to help you."

Stunned, Cookie didn't say anything. Reenie had conveniently forgotten about the two hundred dollars Cookie had borrowed from Arky. Owing Arky is what led her to take the money in the first place.

Reenie took a deep breath and went on. "Herman and Mrs. Kerry are really worried about you, but they don't want no part of your money either."

She stopped for a second and stared hard at Cookie. "But both of them said to say hello and to send you their love. They love you, Cookie."

"There's no bullshitting me. Don't mess with me. Mess with me and you're done for."

"That's the Cookie that I know." Reenie smiled. "In the

long run, you're going to be fine. I've have faith in you and I always will."

It was ironic. Cookie thought she was here to help Reenie, but it was the other way around. In all of the tragedy Reenie had suffered, she thought she was the one who needed to help Cookie. Stunned, disappointed, she didn't hold it against Reenie and could not understand why. She had every reason to resent Reenie talking to her about people being mad at her for taking the money.

"Wouldn't you have done the same thing?"

"No." Reenie looked at her like she had three heads. "I would have known it was not mine to take."

She didn't say anything when she lit a Marlboro and handed it to Cookie. Cookie's hands were shaking, more from fright than from the cold, although she would never admit that.

Puddles of light from a pale thread of moon revealed small whirlpools swilling in the river. Unable to form currents or make waves, watery downdrafts trapped by suction were disappearing down a dark drain. The Hudson River had a long history as a catch-all net for slime, debris and toxic waste, a dump site for garbage, salvage, solvents and chemicals. Stench rising to the river's surface brought to bear the danger that had been lurking there are all along, purposefully hidden for a few days or, maybe, centuries—that was the river for you, it was the keeper of many secrets.

Monday November 19 1973

I only have two memories of the Hudson River: seeing Stanley for the first time and saying goodbye to Reenie for good.

I told Reenie goodbye that night on the river. I knew I'd never see her again. She told me I'd be back one day. I know in my heart that's not true. I am going to leave Yonkers and I'm not ever going to look back. I'll turn to a pillar of salt like Lot's Wife if I look back and I don't want that to happen to me.

The funny thing about the river is how it looked that day when I saw Stanley. He stood there in the sun. His long blonde hair clung to the middle of his back. He wasn't wearing a shirt. His body was lean and sculpted. His metal dog tags caught light from the sun. He looked like a work of art. Stanley de Falco is a work of art and a part of me will always love him.

I'm feeling sore about art. Stewie said he was an artist. He never really created anything. He's a complete fake. I still look at the picture of PH-372 and wonder what the letters stand for. I haven't been able to find the painting anywhere and I don't know where it could be. I don't know how to find Clyfford Still. He's a real artist. And what would happen if I found him? I wouldn't know what to say to him. I can be bashful when I respect somebody. I call Clyfford Still's painting "My Clouds of Meaning."

My Clouds of Meaning could be wrapped as a present and given away as a gift. Or maybe I'll just keep My Clouds of Meaning to myself.

I tried to find out what happened the night Johnny and Donny took off and went somewhere without telling me. Donny said Johnny took her out for ice cream. She swears she didn't tell Johnny about the money. I believe her for once.

Johnny's office is kind of everybody's office. There is something really weird going on there. I think it has something to do with Millie Mangano. She's always been nasty. I used to think it was cause she loved Johnny. Now I'm not so sure. I think she's running numbers for the Yonkers Raceway and other things.

No wonder why Johnny didn't know about the money that was stolen.

I know I should be scared of winding up like Wanda McGillicuddy. But I don't think about it. Don't ask me to explain why. People might think I'm wrong for taking the money. But a girl's got to do what she's got to do. I'm turning out to be more of a gangster than I ever thought I would be. I break the rules that were made by other people cause those rules were made to benefit them. Not me. Playing by other people's rules will not get me the life I want for myself. Playing by other people's rules will not get me to where I want to go in life.

I'm getting sick of my Boho. I've carried around a lot of money in that bag. It's getting worn looking. I was thinking of buying a Char Patchwork Bag. Do you know who Char is? She's a leather artist who designs bags for rock stars. Pretty cool! The problem is if I get a Char that will be the end of my Boho. I won't use my Boho anymore. I could never throw it away. It will sit around looking like a sad sack in the trunk of my car.

Did I tell you that I'm getting a car? It's my getaway from Yonkers car. Arky is going to New Jersey to buy it for me. A 1970 Dodge Coronet 500 convertible. The car had a few dents. We had it freshly painted yellow. Yellow is a big color for cars right now. Special delivery. An all cash deal. I can't wait to drive through the clouds and into the gash of a setting sun.

-eee

Forty-six

Sister Mary Eau Claire greeted Cookie the same way she greeted everyone, standing behind the desk that she used as a barricade between herself and the outside—the secular world beyond the walls of the convent, which was a grave disappointment to her natural optimism. Here, living within the fortress of the Roman Catholic Church, she was able to aspire to goodness, but it was a practical goodness she pursued and toward that end, she often recognized opportunity and seized it in a snap.

The nun pretended not to stare at Cookie's huge shopping bag. Two bags in one, or rather double-bagged, the shopping bag, embossed with Bloomingdale's signature logo, looked heavy. The nun pointed to the designated hot seat chair, where Cookie sat and lit a Marlboro. Sniffing slightly, the nun got a whiff of the smoke and smiled. She slid a squat square-shaped green glass vase across the desk for Cookie to use as an ashtray.

"I guess I should start right off by telling you that I've been very pleased with your grades, and your attendance has been exceptional, at least for you. And I'm very proud of your accomplishments."

"I'm still curious about your apparent wealth. Do you mind telling me where your money came from?"

"I don't know. I'm not sure."

The nun followed Cookie's eyes glancing up at the cheeseboard texture of the ceiling where watermarks deposited the distinct presence of black mold. Streaks of red mold had collected in the ceiling's corners. Brown mold, also known as dry rot, danced in waves along the highest part of the walls behind the nun's desk. Mold comes in many colors.

The nun had been dealing with teenage girls for years and she could always tell when they weren't telling the truth. She knew Cookie was lying.

But Cookie didn't think that she was lying. She had no proof that the money came from a rigged bet made at the Yonkers Raceway. Yet there was no other explanation.

The nun eyed the half full pack of Marlboros lying on the desk.

"Would you like one?"

The nun smiled appreciatively. "Not right now."

Gentle knocking interrupted their conversation that was haltingly familiar—the nun did most of the talking. She seemed to be the one in control, but it was illusory. Cookie was always going to do whatever she wanted. The knocking persisted; although it was not loud, it was an intrusion, as though someone was about to step on their collective souls. For the moment, Cookie and the nun were of one mind.

"Come in," the nun announced.

Beaming a chiclet-toothed smile, Izzy poked her head inside of the office. "Bloomies," she exclaimed. "What did you buy at Bloomingdale's? Can I see?"

"Not right now," the nun said. "It seems as though I'm repeating myself. I always say 'not right now.' Maybe that is the lesson in life that I need to learn. Not right now."

The nun waved her hand dismissively. "Later," she told Izzy.

They both watched the door and waited before resuming conversation.

"Would you check to see if she's gone?"

Cookie did the nun's bidding. Opening the door, she looked for Izzy and found her sitting on the floor outside of the nun's office. Her navy culottes rode up her hips. With her knees pulled up to her chest, she flexed her hips, opening and closing her legs in another sort of physical exercise.

"What are you doing, Izzy? Trying to catch a ball with your pussy?"

Izzy pressed her fingers over her lips, kissed them, then blew Cookie an air kiss. "I still love you," she mouthed. She flicked her tongue as if she was performing cunnilingus.

Cookie lashed out her own tongue as an insult. "I don't love you and never will. You're not my type."

Cookie closed the door and eyed Sister Mary.

"What's that all about?"

Cookie shrugged. "Not right now," she told the nun.

Before returning to her designated hot seat, she picked up another chair and propped it against the door.

The nun nodded in approval. "We were talking about money."

"I'm not trying to evade your question, Sister. If you want to know the truth, I'm trying to get rid of the money. It's done nothing but cause me trouble since the day I laid my hands on it."

The expression on the nun's face told Cookie she did not entirely believe her.

"I tried to do nice things for my family, but it always backfired. I tried giving it away to my friends, but no one wanted it. Well, that's not entirely true."

She was thinking of Stewie and Izzy. "Rich people were happy to take my money. Did you know that most rich people are freeloaders?"

"That's how they get rich and stay rich," the nun snapped.

"Spending it? I got sick of that. I never had so much money and don't know what to do with it. It's not like I could take it to the bank. Know what I mean?"

The nun folded her arms across her chest as if she aimed to protect herself or maybe she had a bad back or was preternaturally stiff; she closed her eyes momentarily to obtain relief.

"Many things are difficult in life but that's when we try harder, that's when we give it all we've got! We get through it. I've done things that were hard. I've felt like giving up. I might have even given up once or twice."

Cookie thought the nun was trying too hard to be clever and stifled a yawn. The sound of a clock ticking reminded Cookie that she wanted to get out of here with no further delay. She glanced at the antique ceramic clock on the nun's desk. Creamy white, plated with gold gilt, for such a small clock it ticked loudly, and compensated for the industrial clock on the wall that was dead.

"I used to want money," the nun said. "But when I took a vow of poverty, I gave up the notion of desire, especially desiring worldly goods. The church has been good to me," she said cautiously, and hesitated, growing quiet for a moment.

"After all, I have a place to live, simple apparel," she stroked her white bib, "good food. I serve God, all the faces of God, that includes you."

She looked up at the stained ceiling. "And I can never overestimate how important it is to have a good roof over one's head."

Cookie stared at the clock. Smiling snidely, she said nothing while the nun droned on. She knew where this was going.

Sister Mary rose from her desk and walked around to greet Cookie. "What is it that you want, dear Concetta?" She arched her eyebrows. "Cookie? What can I do for you?"

"I need to graduate early. There isn't anything to gain by staying in school until June."

The nun nodded.

"I need to go now."

"Where will you go?"

"I'm on the road again, me and the Blind Owl Alan Wilson."

"Practically speaking? Speak to me in practical terms. Tell me where you are going in a way that I can understand."

"I aim to travel the country. I'm going to make something of myself."

"You've already made something of yourself. Quite a spectacle, I'd say." The nun gave Cookie a chaste hug, drawing the girl to her warm bosom, enveloping her in a fresh scent as clean as Ivory soap and as sweet as Downy Fabric Softener.

The nun was the first to break the embrace. "And you'll stay in touch? You'll let me know how you're doing?"

Cookie took the shopping bag, turned it upside down, spilling the contents on the nun's desk—stacks of twenties wrapped with lilac-colored bands held each bundle together.

"Where'd the money come from?"

Cookie looked away. She was done talking.

"Drugs?"

Cookie shook her head no.

"Sex? A prostitution ring?"

"Of course not."

"Then what?"

"The Yonkers Raceway."

The nun smiled. "I like horses."

Sister Mary Eau Claire hovered over her desk with her white tunic spreading open as wide as the wings of an owl preparing to hunt. The outer black fabric of her habit puffed in layers and folds, formidable plumage to protect her in flight. She stared at the stacks of twenties as if they were magnificent prey, a slow-moving rodent, an unsuspecting snake, or a small plump bird. She opened the lower drawer on her desk, the one drawer as large as a filing cabinet. In one fell swoop, she swept the money into the drawer, closed it with a bang and locked it shut.

Forty-seven

Arky's chauffeur's cap was perched on the side of his head like a dead blue fish. The rain came down hard, obstructing the limo's windshield with waves of water. Arky turned the dial for the windshield wipers as far as it would go. The thrumming of the wipers did not make it easier to see. The limo's motor ebbed to an even lower hum as if it was an expectant, but miraculous, ache waiting for Cookie's attention—that is how their relationship began—miraculous and slightly painful—and that is how it would end. There was no doubt in Cookie's mind that the end was near.

Something was troubling Arky.

Cookie had asked him if he wanted a raise, but he declined the offer, and he didn't seem to know how to articulate what he really wanted. He might have been concerned because they had practically kidnapped Kitty and Grandmother Delia. Cookie was intent on giving them the most luxurious dining experience that they had ever experienced. The tab was on her.

It was her goodbye dinner.

She had tried to include Donny and Johnny in the festivities, but they had both vanished for the afternoon, in a normal way, not cause for major worry. Although Donny had always been a snitch, Cookie felt for sure that Donny would not rat her out. Cookie had hauled away some of the money in a pillowcase and stuffed it into the trunk of the limo—just a precaution that Arky didn't know about.

From Midtown, the large sign atop Prospect Tower read: Tudor City. Most people don't get that Tudor City is not a city but a neighborhood on the east side of Manhattan that borders Murray Hill and is walking distance to Grand Central Station.

Kitty and Grandmother Delia scuttled together, scared and crab-like, in the back seat of the limo. Delia had pulled out her rosary and was mumbling to herself. Her silver pageboy hairstyle framed her soft white skin and accentuated her piercing blue eyes, which could be lethal or kind, depending on her mood. Cookie recognized most of her Grandmother's prayers, but she could not make out exactly what she was saying. It would be fine if the mumbo-jumbo was coming from Kitty, but it wasn't. Until now Delia had always acted somewhat normal, but now half of what she said could not be deciphered to be anything other than a rash of rants.

Kitty examined her face in the mirror of her plastic pressed powder compact. Failing to see her spectacular beauty, she concocted imaginary flaws. "I have those spots again. I'm not going anywhere looking like this."

"I don't see nothing." Delia cringed. Her face was ashen, the same pallor as the corpses of her dead relatives laid out for a wake at Whelan's Funeral home.

"Shush, Ma, nobody asked you."

Delia fidgeted with her rosary; her fingers danced along the string of beads faster than anyone could utter prayer. "I'll say it once and I'll say it again. Nothing's wrong with your face. It's all in your head."

"Oh, shut up, Ma! You're a silly old woman. I've had enough of you."

Cookie lit a Marlboro and rolled down the window. It had been raining heavily but now it had petered out. A crack of lightning zapped the sky over the East River. They were located on the southern edge of Turtle Bay on the east side of Manhattan. The lightning strike, followed by a distant drum roll of thunder, set off a chain reaction. Delia gasped. Arky clutched his chest. Kitty dropped her compact onto the floor of the limo. Cookie took a deep drag of her Marlboro. The car squealed to a stop at a light.

"We're going to crash," Delia squealed. "I just know we're going to crash."

What began as an unpleasant jaunt into the city took a turn for the worse. Delia held onto the arm rest with two hands, riding sidesaddle, as though she was about to be thrown from a horse. Kitty slid out of her seat to the floor of the car and huddled over her mirror, chattering that she wanted to see how she looked in less harsh light.

The limo parked in front of the Tudor City Greens, a small park on Tudor City Place. Kitty and Delia huddled together, timidly looking out the window, lamenting over the rain which had clearly stopped.

"I'm not getting my hair wet." Kitty had pulled her knees up to her chest, hugging them.

"Me either," Delia snorted. She put her hand up against the back of Arky's seat, pushing hard with both her feet, acting as though she had jammed on the brakes, even though the limo had already parked.

The neighborhood was named for its Tudor Revival architecture, making its quaint cooperative apartment buildings appear as though they were from merry old England instead of being a stone's throw from United Nations Plaza. Both women shifted and squirmed in their seat like young children who were unable to sit still.

Delia rambled about her father, Tynan O'Toole, who was called Tiny Ten Pint because he was a hopeless drunk.

Everyone said he had a curse on him until the day he was struck by lightning and got cured from the drink.

"That reminds me." Arky pulled a flask from the glove compartment and passed it back to Delia. He thought he was being considerate, thoughtful.

Delia was appalled at Arky's magnanimous gesture. "You're done trying to poison me! What do you think I am? A stinking sot?! Tiny Ten Pint is back. I can feel his evil spirit. I can feel the rattle of death! Someone is going to die tonight. You mark my words, someone is going to die tonight."

Cookie corrected Arky. "You shouldn't have done that! Don't try to ply them with liquor. That's the worst thing you could have done."

Arky tipped his cap to set it straight and stowed his flask back in the glove compartment.

"I thought it would calm their nerves."

"They don't have nerves. They're both twisted, mad as a shad, spooked, nutso, crazy!"

Cookie had wanted to take them to the fancy French restaurant La Bibliothèque. It was her idea of an expensive dinner. She didn't know how to find a good restaurant, or how to distinguish one from another. She had seen an ad for La Bibliothèque on the back cover of an art gallery brochure.

She had not considered that both women rarely left Yonkers and were oh so obviously out of their comfort zone.

Kitty pouted in her mirror and freshened her lips with a dab of lipstick. "It's not the right shade. It's not red enough." She examined her teeth in the mirror and licked her lips. She shut her brown plastic compact with odd finality. A small cloud of face powder puffed into the air.

"Someone will die tonight," Delia insisted.

Arky whispered to Cookie. "Is there any way we can get them stoned? I'll give them anything. I'll do whatever we need to do."

Delia massaged her calves and moaned. "This car floats like a boat and it's given me really bad restless leg syndrome!"

The storm had passed, but no one mentioned it. The rain had completely stopped. The drum roll of distant thunder had ceased. Cookie opened the passenger door of the limo and stepped out into the cool night. A light autumn haze illuminated the space beneath the Tudor-style streetlamps set atop stately black poles.

Cookie helped both women out of the back seat of the limo. Kitty jumped out with the athleticism of a schoolgirl trying to hold onto her bloomers. Bugged-eyes, trembling lips, her face was starchy white, yet she giggled as though she meant to dish out a delicious practical joke.

It took extra effort to get Delia out of the limo and prod her to stand, then walk. Arky stood at attention, but it was clear he did not want to touch either woman. He meant to protect himself from their mercurial bouts, which could be capricious and mean-spirited. He cowered as if he felt that at any moment Delia would slug him.

Delia spun a macabre story about how lightning strikes can come out of nowhere long after a storm has passed. "Don't be fooled by no rain. Lightning can strike just like that."

"You're right, Ma. An avalanche of water can roll down this street before you even see it coming and we'd all be drowned."

Delia stood still, lifted her feet out of her dodgy shoes and rubbed them, one foot in front of the other, on the sidewalk. "Swear my feet have gone numb."

"Stop complaining, Ma. Cookie doesn't like it when you talk that way. Right, Cookie?"

Cookie looked at the two women; they were clinging to one another, so scared they were ready to jump to their death into the East River.

"Why am I doing this to myself?"

In Cookie's estimation, Arky was on the verge of quitting. No amount of money on earth would make him stay on the job.

Kitty looked at Cookie with a rueful expression and spoke plainly. "We've had enough excitement for one day. Would you take us both home?"

Delia's eyes looked earnest and icy blue, as calm as the end of a winter storm, as though she was innocent of all wrongdoing, especially her foul disposition.

"We want to eat lasagna at Louie's."

Cookie looked at Arky and nodded. "Let's head back to Yonkers."

So much for a festive goodbye dinner in the city. Arky pulled out his flask and took a slug of expensive whiskey. He offered the flask to Cookie, but she frowned, turned away and stared into the Tudor City Greens, where park benches were ensconced among the sculpted gardens, under maple trees that had dropped their leaves. A big mound of leaves sat under a solitary oak tree. Bare branches rose high upon its trunk as though its primary limbs had no choice but to reach for the sun. The leaves that had scattered under the trees had been drenched by the rain, too heavy to fly with the wind, shining on the ground, embellished by the Tudor lamplights and the night. Cookie remembered the oak acorn that had come from nowhere and popped her in the head.

Forty-eight

Farley Stewart or *Stewie* did have a studio in the Remington Hotel, a separate apartment as small as a closet, but according to Donny it was large enough for paint supplies, assorted blank canvases, a daybed-convertible sofa, and an orangey red lava lamp. Cookie arrived at the hotel in the twilight hour before sunup. Neither dark nor completely light, this magical period without shadows in dim grey light was the best time to stage a surprise visit.

Donny told Cookie the precise location of the clandestine apartment, quasi art studio, but she did not want to go there ever again. One good thing, though, Donny's hair was growing back into a crown of thick blonde curls with the vengeance of Samson, or Delilah? In Cookie's estimation, Donny was like every other girl who had suffered at the hands of a guy and lived to tell. So many girls just go on in life, living strong like Samson and as cunning as Delilah.

When Cookie arrived at Stewie's art studio apartment, a legal notice had been posted on the door. She read the document, which was a judgment. The Remington Hotel was listed as the creditor, Farley Stewart the debtor. The hotel had been authorized to seize Stewie's personal property to satisfy all or part of a money judgment.

Strange that the door was unlocked. Cookie walked in to find cockroaches everywhere, a perfectly mean sprawl spreading across the floor away from window. She turned on the light to get rid of them. The cockroaches scampered away in a tight brigade, taking refuge under the daybed, leaving behind trails of excrement that resembled used coffee grounds. She turned off the light and left the studio. What she was looking for could not be found here.

Returning to Stewie's residential apartment, the same type of legal notice was also posted on this door, which was locked. She knocked first softly, then more forcefully, growing louder, until it was clear that Stewie was not home.

"Quit knocking so loud! You're so rude, Girl!"

Cookie detected a tremendous presence; a large dark cloud appeared at the far end of the hall and made its way toward where she stood. Mouth agape, startled, Cookie was not too tired to fight, but wanted to reserve her angry energy for another more critical moment, like kicking the shit out of Farley Stewart.

"Leave something there, Babe? Yous want in?"

Cookie did not know if she was relieved or petrified to see Gwendolyn strolling down the hall, wearing a sky blue, see-through negligee. It was unavoidable not to notice that underneath her negligee, she wore silver lamé panties and a matching brassiere with cups big enough to encase boulders. Her hair had been coifed in a silver-blonde pageboy wig.

"It's early. Myself, I get up early. Got work to do." She winked.

She gave Cookie the fisheye. "Whatcha looking for? If it's those lamps..." She shook her head, but her hair did not move. "Those lamps be mine."

"I don't want the lamps," Cookie assured her. "I want what is mine that I left behind and it's not worth nothing."

Gwendolyn looked relieved. Her gaze turned slightly pensive. "I know yous is real different."

From the cleavage of her silver brassiere, she pulled out a metal pick, not the kind to comb hair. Her pick had a straight slender rod that came to a sharp point like an arrow. She inserted the pick in an old-fashioned keyhole lock, maneuvered the rod fastened to its black rubber grip, turned the pick right, bumped the door with her hip and easily sprung it open.

Cookie followed her into Stewie's apartment. "Me, myself, I got those lamps before the debt-collector shows. I's been eyeing them for weeks."

She sat on the couch and patted her hand along its aqua velveteen surface. "Took the lava lamp from upstairs. Might be taking this couch too. Wanna help me move it?"

"I don't think we can get it through the door."

"What about that fellow that's got that long black limo?"

Cookie nodded, walked the path around the couch, never letting Gwendolyn out of her line of sight. "I'll ask him."

"Whatcha say you be looking for? Might have seen it. Might not. You never know."

Cookie scrutinized the floor. She got down on her hands and knees and crawled. "Just a silly acorn from an old oak tree."

"I know every square inch of this place, case I want something else."

Gwendolyn plucked the acorn from under the couch. She held the acorn up to her eye. "This be what you're looking for?"

"Yes!" Cookie smiled brightly and sat next to Gwendolyn who had crossed her long brown legs, the longest pair of legs she had ever seen.

Cookie opened her hand.

Gwendolyn dropped the acorn into her palm. "What's this thing mean to you?"

"It means I'm not crazy."

"Oh, come on, Girl!" she scoffed. "I could have told yous that! I know you be thinking you're crazy. I know dat. I know yous. I knows what's wrong with yous. Yous got the virgin complex."

Cookie scoffed, "Virgin complex! I don't think so!"

"The virgin complex ain't got *nothin* to do with sex, Honey. Yous think yous gotta do something special that nobodys done before. Yous wanna be first. Well, let me tell yous something. I know crazy and you ain't dat."

Tossing the acorn from one hand to the other, Cookie held it like a precious jewel and leaned back into the soft couch. Staring at Gwendolyn, she noticed her huge head, thick lips, a thin pale scar ran outside the corner of her left eye.

"Where's Stewie?"

"He'd done and gone disappeared."

"Disappeared?" Cookie felt chilled. She drew her sweater close, cinching it clear up to her throat and buttoned up. She knew Stewie had not disappeared due to an accident or whim.

"Just like dat." She snapped her impossibly long black fingers. Her nails sparkled with silver polish. "I's seen dat happen before. When somebody disappears just like dat, you know they be gone for good."

She looked at Cookie as if she was a conspiratorial sister.

"Yous know whose made him disappear?"

Cookie didn't know, but she did know. She had her suspicions but no proof. When some fucking interloper from afar sweeps into our lives and does damage to our hearts, there is a heavy price to pay. It's a Yonkers thing.

Cookie rolled the acorn back and forth in between her hands, warming it up as if she meant to toss it again, but she was never going to let it go.

"Looks like yous gonna roll dice."

She stood up and smiled at Gwendolyn. "This is goodbye." She held out her hand.

Gwendolyn took Cookie's hand in her own hands and held onto her. "Where yous be going, Girl?"

"I'm going to get into my car and keep driving into every sunset I see."

Gwendolyn let go a hollow whoop, a whistle, a grunt of "Uh huh," and dropped Cookie's hand.

Cookie noted that for such a huge person, Gwendolyn was surprisingly gentle.

"All these peeps come to New York City trying to make it big or find themselves. Yous be leaving while all those other peeps are thinking this is the place to be. What's with dat? All those peeps come here cause they don't fit nowhere else. And yous leaving. Why?"

"I'm never going to fit in anywhere," Cookie said. "That's just the way it's always going to be."

"What's so wrong with dat?"

Cookie shrugged. "I get lonely sometimes."

Gwendolyn looked indignant. "There ain't nobody but nobody who ain't lonely and the more true yous are to yourselves, the more lonely you're gonna be!"

She stood up and put her hands on her hips. Even without heels, she towered over Cookie with the grace and majesty of a Great Horned Owl.

"Not fitting in is good. Real good. We're all lost souls, Sugar." She pointed her finger. "As soon as you admit how lost yous are, dats when you have the greatest chance of finding out who yous really are. Otherwise, you'd be cleaning public toilets as if they are your own."

She pointed her finger at Cookie and shook it. "Don't matter if you're a honky or a nigger, it's all the same. Being like all the other peeps....conforming to that bullshit! Letting them tell yous who yous gotta be! Selling your soul to those dudes who wears the suits and the peeps who suck their dicks. Don't matter if they be men...women or something else in between. Un huh, Honey. Let me tell yous something. You gotta fight to be who yous really are and when the day comes that yous can't do the fight no more, don't ever let nobody know!"

Gwendolyn walked toward the door and turned around. "Yous be surprised how much fight is gonna be inside of yous for the rest of your life."

"Man, you sure have got attitude."

"Don't call me dat. I ain't no man."

Cookie squinted her eyes, trying to figure her out. "Where'd you say you're from?"

"Yonkers, Honey. Not *Yonkas* like the honkies say. I'm from Yonkers and I'm not scared of nobody."

She put her hand to her mouth as if she was sworn to secrecy. "Shhh! Got that? Don't let nobody tell yous nothing different than what I say."

"Okay yous. Gotta go." She held the door open for Cookie.

"Yous be going now too. Gotta make sure it's all locked up tight. I's don't want nothing missing that I might want to have for myself."

Gwendolyn wasn't the kind of girl you hug goodbye. Cookie didn't bother to try. Touching Gwendolyn, without paying her or asking for her permission, seemed like the wrong thing to do, a major breach of etiquette. Gwendolyn pressed the button for the elevator. They rode down together, not looking at each other, not saying anything.

When the doors opened, Arky was waiting for Cookie in the lobby. He grinned and got all tongue-tied when he saw Cookie with Gwendolyn. No doubt, he was in awe. As a show of respect, he took off his cap, held it in his hand, and pressed it against his heart. Arky could be funny that way—he's always been attracted to strong women. You've got to give him credit. Not all guys are like that. Most guys want women to orbit around them like lesser moons orbiting around the sun, or small clouds that are never going to get a chance to grow into a storm. Gwendolyn, big, black and blonde, strutted around, overwhelming the small lobby, circled toward the front door, back stepped, then zeroed in on Arky and asked him to help her move her couch. He was only too eager to help.

Monday December 10 1973

I took my last ride with Arky the day before he delivered my yellow car. The limo was quiet except for the steady whisk of windshield wipers. We didn't talk about me leaving. It was too emotional. I didn't want to see Arky cry. Me? I never cry. You know that.

I heard from Detective Sergeant Ronan O'Hearn again. I don't know why he keeps bothering me. He says that Tony Amendolito is missing. He disappeared. I think he gave the hot tip to Millie Mangano. I can't prove it. It's one of those things you just know. Same thing with Stewie. He just kind of disappeared. And Henry Kagan? They haven't found who killed him. It's an open case gone cold.

Detective Sergeant Ronan O'Hearn thinks I know something about all three. Tony Amendolito. Farley Stewart. Henry Kagan. Please don't try to find a connection. There is none. I know that their deaths arrived on three separate clouds. I think the detective just wants to get into my pants. He can add that wish to his pension and maybe it will become a big payout. Let's leave it at that.

I'm seventeen and I'm leaving home. I said I'd never look back. But I don't know if that's true. Some of the dumb little things that happened to me as a kid are really important to talk about. I wouldn't want to grow up anywhere else in the world other than Yonkers.

Growing up in Yonkers makes me understand there are many ways we discriminate against one another. Race is only one way. Anything that unfairly shuts out most people and only lets a few people in—is nasty. I want to find a Fair World and a Kind World. But I know I never will. I know I will have to keep fighting. I know I don't give up easily. People who are determined and full of courage have gumption. They don't give up. I know I have gumption. Guts. Do you?

Listen to what I say cause I'm going to say it slowly so that you will hear it. I could say that I grew up with no help from nobody. Anybody. But that's not true. There were a few owls who came my way. My owls gave me protection and showed me a way out of here. I don't have to tell you who my owls are. I'm sure you can figure that out.

I don't have to say goodbye to everyone who counts as a friend. I'll be back someday. It will be as though I had never left. I can keep people in my heart. Forever.

Monday is as good a day as any to leave Yonkers. I did stop to say goodbye to Zelda. The fortune she spat out said: *Follow whatever calls you.* I will miss Zelda! Now I will have to get my fortunes from fortune cookies in a Chinese restaurant! I also went to the Owl Hole. Remember my Owl Hole? The Owl Hole is my secret hiding place below a deep stairwell that has not been used in years. It's hidden from the street by massive weeds. Bushes and hedges too. The Owl Hole—that's where I do my best thinking. It's also where I hid some of my money. I hid my money in a few other places too. Good luck trying to find it. I guess you could say that I diversified my assets.

Life is a mystery. Mysteries in real life are left unsolved. Unresolved. Not everything can be sewn up and wrapped up like a present to give away to somebody. There is no such thing as a happy ending. Life goes on like My Clouds of Meaning.

I'll be on my way now. There is a full moon tonight. Still looking for that painting. My Clouds of Meaning. Maybe someday I'll find it. I'm driving right through those dark clouds and I'm going to get to those small patches made yellow in the setting sun. I'll let you know when I get there.

Someday...Hell if I know when... I'll write new pages in between the old pages in my journal. I'll write about more than my feelings. I'll tell you what was really going on. I'll fill in the blanks. My palimpsest of extremely bad writing. Someday I might use commas. I don't know. I hate commas. Don't you?

I almost forgot to mention. Money isn't everything. The End.

-ccc

End Notes

The Characters:
Cookie Colangelo left Yonkers at seventeen and never looked back.

Donny Colangelo became a research physician specializing in infectious diseases.

Johnny Colangelo died in the 1990s. It wasn't until many years later at Johnny Colangelo's funeral that Cookie had an understanding for the depth of her father's courage. A man came to the funeral to pay his respects and to express gratitude. In the winter of 1950 on the battlefield of Korea, Johnny Colangelo had saved his life.

Kitty Colangelo became a floral designer and worked in a florist shop for ten years. She and Johnny never divorced.

Isabella María Fernanda Donovan, Izzy, graduated from Sarah Lawrence College, later married a hedge fund manager and had three children.

Toni Ferlinghetti married a New York City Cop.

Henry Kagan is a fictional character. However, on July 1, 1979 a young man named Peter Gray was killed by a hit and run driver out in front of The Playroom. The driver was never found. To this day, his murder remains unsolved.

Mabel Kerry worked at the Yonkers Carnegie Library until she retired in 1978.

Arky Lovato is a gypsy cab driver who picks up passengers from the Metro North train station at Larkin Plaza (Yonkers Station) in Yonkers.

Herman Lynch became a professional dancer at the Alvin Ailey Dance Theater.

Reenie Ruggiero became an attorney with the ACLU.

Fran Ochiogrosso retired and moved to Florida.

Louie Santamassino was an American mobster and an underboss of the Lucchese crime family, which was one of the five families that controlled organized crime in New York City. The Lucchese family conducted business activity at the Yonkers Raceway and on the Hudson River waterfront in Yonkers. Santamassino died in 1992 at the Federal Correctional Institution in Cumberland, Maryland, where he was serving a life sentence for extortion, illegal gambling, and murder.

Venues in New York City:
Elaine's was once located at 1703 Second Avenue at 88th Street in Manhattan. Owned by Elaine Kaufman from 1963 to 2011, the restaurant was a celebrity haunt serving writers, actors, sports figures, politicians, and media personalities. The restaurant was not known for its food; however, it was once considered to be an iconic symbol of old New York.

Max's Kansas City, known as one of the coolest bars in New York City during the 1970s, is where the famous routinely rubbed elbows with the not-so-famous. The bar gained celebrity status when Andy Warhol and his entourage began frequenting the club. A favorite hangout for beat poets, artists, music stars, and mega-watt celebrities, the notorious passageway to its back room had an installation of a sculpture that was made by John Chamberlain. Made from the crushed metal of a crashed car, the sculpture had sharp, jagged edges. In the back room of the club, Dan Flavin's light sculpture of a neon cross cast a bloody hue on the bar's patrons who cavorted, schmoozed and imbibed an excessive amount of drugs and alcohol at all hours of the night.

The Photograph of three men wearing tweedy jackets, standing in front of a marble plinth supporting a sculpture, was taken in San Francisco, California, October 1946. The three men are the artists Clyfford Still and Mark Rothko and the art historian and museum director Douglas MacAgy. The man described as "holding his hat in his hand" is Clyfford Still.

The Marlborough-Gerson Gallery in New York City, exhibited Clyfford Still's paintings from November 25, 1969 to January 3, 1970. A full-color catalogue accompanied the one-man show.

Clyfford Still's oil on canvas painting 1950-E (Ph-372) was painted in San Francisco in 1950. Today it is on view in Gallery 920 at the Metropolitan Museum of Art in New York City. Other works by Clyfford Still are exhibited world-wide in private collections as well as at the San Francisco Museum of Modern Art, The Museum of Fine Arts Houston, The Museum of Modern Art (MOMA), and The Art Institute of Chicago. The Clyfford Still Museum in Denver is one of the world's most significant public collections of any major artist and offers nine galleries of Clyfford Still's art.

Venues in Yonkers:
Blessed Sacrament Academy closed in 1975 and the nuns relocated to Warwick, New York in 1991. The building located on the site of the former girls' school retained its structural integrity that included its new roof. In 1996, the property was sold for use as a medical and social service center run by the Greyston Foundation for people with HIV.

Christ the King Elementary School closed in 2010 and the building is currently being leased as an annex by Yonkers Public School #16. Christ the King Church still stands.

Loew's Theater was torn down in 1974. A McDonald's and a parking lot took its place on the site where the theater once stood.

The Playroom, housed in an old bunker-style building on the site of the Dellwood Dairy, achieved its notoriety as a gay bar in the 1970s and 1980s. The bar was also the frequent target of vandalism and homophobic violence.

Untermyer Park underwent a revitalization and renovation effort beginning around 2005, restoring its architecture and gardens to its original grandeur.

The Yonkers Carnegie Library was razed by the city of Yonkers in 1982 and the library's bookmobile service was also terminated. The new Yonkers Waterfront Library opened in 2002.

About the Author

Patricia Vaccarino is originally from Yonkers, New York. After college, she traveled across the country in a battered Chevy Impala on I-40 and up the California coast on Pacific Highway 101 to "see America" and landed in Seattle, where she worked as a paralegal in antitrust law, and later went to law school. She began writing professionally and was asked by a film production company, Kaye Smith Productions (founded by Seattle businessman Lester Smith and Hollywood celebrity Danny Kaye), to do their Public Relations outreach—that was her start in P.R. She founded Xanthus Communications, a national P.R. firm, and the media company, PR for People®, where people share their news with the world. Patricia Vaccarino has written award-winning film scripts, press materials, content, books, essays and articles. Some of her essays and articles can be found on PR for People.com and on YonkersBooks.com. She has written three works of historical fiction that take place in Yonkers, and a monograph about the razing of the Yonkers Carnegie Library.

www.ingramcontent.com/pod-product-compliance
Lightning Source LLC
Chambersburg PA
CBHW050855210726
48290CB00004B/1247